Praise for Christine Carbo's *The Wild Inside*

"Carbo paints a moving picture of complex, flawed people fighting to make their way in a wilderness where little is black or white, except the smoky chiaroscuro of the sweeping Montana sky . . . an evocative debut."

—*Publishers Weekly*

"Sharp, introspective Systead is a strong series lead, and Carbo rolls out solid procedural details, pitting him against Department of the Interior bureaucrats. The grittiness of the poverty-wracked area surrounding Glacier plays against the park's dangerous beauty in this dark foray into the wilderness subgenre. Put this one in the hands of those who enjoy Paul Doiron's Mike Bowditch novels and Julia Keller's Bell Elkins series."

—*Booklist*

"Stays in your mind long after you've put the book down. I'm still thinking about it. Prepare to run the gamut of emotions with this fine treat of a story. Then, in the years ahead, be on the lookout for more from this fresh new voice in the thriller genre."

—Steve Berry, *New York Times* bestselling
author of the Cotton Malone series

"Fans of Nevada Barr will love this tense, atmospheric thriller with its majestic Glacier National Park setting. *The Wild Inside* is a stunning debut!"

—Deborah Crombie, *New York Times* bestselling
author of *To Dwell in Darkness*

"An intense and thoroughly enjoyable thrill ride. Christine Carbo's literary voice echoes with her love of nature, her knowledge of its brutality, and the wild and beautiful locale of Montana. *The Wild Inside* is a tour de force of suspense that will leave you breathlessly turning the pages late into the night."

—Linda Castillo, *New York Times* bestselling
author of *The Dead Will Tell*

"Grizzly bears, murder, mauling, and mayhem mix in Carbo's debut novel. Ted Systead's past and present intersect in an unexpected—and chilling—manner against the incongruously gorgeous backdrop of Glacier National Park."

—*Kirkus Reviews*

"The brutality and fragility of Glacier National Park's wilderness provides the perfect backdrop for this well-crafted, absorbing novel about the barbarities and kindnesses of the humans living on its edge. Christine Carbo is a writer to watch."

—Tawni O'Dell, *New York Times* bestselling author of *One of Us*

"If the key to a mystery's success is keeping the reader guessing, *The Wild Inside* is a fine example of the genre."

—*The Billings Gazette*

"As haunting and vivid as the scenery it depicts, *The Wild Inside* is a masterful portrait of the savagery of nature—both the great untamed outdoors and the human soul. Highly recommended."

—Kira Peikoff, author of *Die Again Tomorrow*

ALSO BY CHRISTINE CARBO

The Wild Inside

MORTAL FALL

A NOVEL OF SUSPENSE

CHRISTINE CARBO

ATRIA PAPERBACK
New York • London • Toronto • Sydney • New Delhi

ATRIA PAPERBACK

An Imprint of Simon & Schuster, Inc.
1230 Avenue of the Americas
New York, NY 10020

First Atria Paperback edition May 2016

ATRIA PAPERBACK and colophon are trademarks of Simon & Schuster, Inc.

For information about special discounts for bulk purchases, please contact Simon & Schuster Special Sales at 1-866-506-1949 or business@simonandschuster.com.

The Simon & Schuster Speakers Bureau can bring authors to your live event. For more information, or to book an event, contact the Simon & Schuster Speakers Bureau at 1-866-248-3049 or visit our website at www.simonspeakers.com.

Manufactured in the United States of America

10   9   8   7   6   5   4   3   2   1

Library of Congress Cataloging-in-Publication Data
  Names: Carbo, Christine, author.
  Title: Mortal fall : a novel of suspense / Christine Carbo.
  Description: First Atria Paperback edition. | New York : Atria Paperback, 2016.
    Subjects: LCSH: Police—Montana—Fiction. | Wilderness areas—Fiction. |
    Murder—Investigation—Fiction. | Glacier National Park (Mont.)—Fiction.
    | BISAC: FICTION / Suspense. | FICTION / Crime. | FICTION / Mystery &
    Detective / General. | GSAFD: Mystery fiction. | Suspense fiction.
    Classification: LCC PS3603.A726 M67 2016 | DDC 813/.6—dc23 LC record
    available at http://lccn.loc.gov/2015037955

ISBN 978-1-4767-7547-0
ISBN 978-1-4767-7548-7 (ebook)

For my husband, Jamie

I must create a system or be enslaved by another man's . . .

—WILLIAM BLAKE, *JERUSALEM*

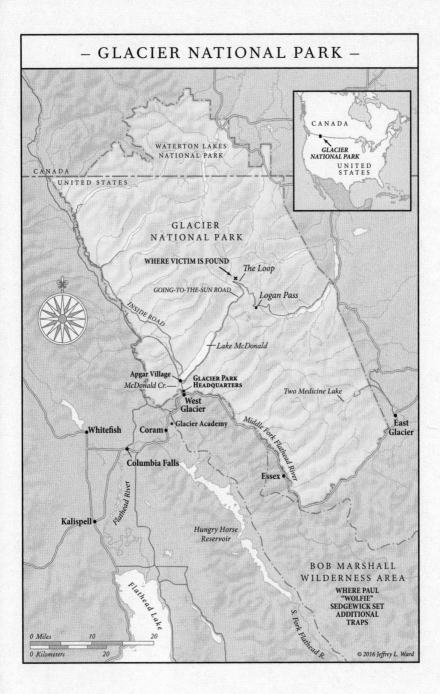

Prologue

I SLOWLY SLID ACROSS the torn seat to the open car door where my brother's friend, Todd, stood braced against the wind. My best friend, Nathan, sat next to me looking equal parts resigned and irritated. The wind nipped my face the second I stepped out. I wrapped my arms around my chest as we walked off the road, into the dried, grassy field toward the tree. We followed my brother, Adam, and Todd, and another friend of theirs, Perry.

All three were in high school. Nathan and I were four years younger—in seventh grade and still gullible at twelve years old. We'd been talked into going with them. Nathan had warned me that it was just another trick played by Adam and his buddies, but this time, I thought it was different. I had begun to believe—or maybe just *wanted* to believe—Adam was telling me the truth for a change.

Plus it was Halloween night, and I was up for something different, something other than staying home watching Dad drink too many beers while trying to convince my mom that the trick-or-treaters knocking on the door weren't coming to kill us.

The moon slid out from behind moody clouds, casting a shimmering dust of light. Adam and his friends strode toward the stately tree guarding the old cemetery like a faithful sentry. Confident and sure of themselves, their frames loomed tall in the pale moonlight while their shoes scuffed the tangled grass and weeds. The tombstones squatted to our left, dark bumps scattered haphazardly and surrounded by the overgrown meadow. I tried not to pay attention to them crouched off to the side, tried not to think of them as menacing animals watching us and getting ready to pounce. In fact, I pretended we weren't in a cemetery at all, when Todd halted about thirty feet before the tree and just stared at it, his head tilted to the side.

"Which branch do you think they hanged her from?" he asked in a loud whisper.

"That one." Adam pointed to a thick, longer arm that reached out to the side as if to point toward the headstones. Perry had told us that he learned from his history teacher that there had been a woman hanged years ago in the cemetery for being a witch.

"Probably," Perry said. "Let's go closer. Check it out. They say you can hear the tree whispering if you stand under the spot it happened, can hear it saying her name: *Lucinda, Lucinda, Lucinda.*" Perry turned and looked at us, his mouth hanging open, his eyes wide.

"You two, you go first," Adam said.

"No way," I protested. "You go." But before I knew it, Adam had my arm, and Todd and Perry had Nathan's. "Hey, stop," I screamed. My brother's fingers dug into me like steel clamps as he pulled me in front of them toward the tree. With one hard shove, I went plummeting forward, and I saw Nathan tumbling to the ground next to me. Nathan yelled too, but before we could stand, my brother and his crew darted back to the car.

"Hurry," I yelled to Nathan as we pushed ourselves up. We ran, trying to catch them, but we were too small and they were much faster. I saw them reach the Pontiac and dive in, hooting and yipping like coyotes. The chassis rocked with their shifting weight, the doors slammed, the engine sprang to life, and the headlights fanned out on the gravel road.

Nathan and I stopped and stood gasping for air when we reached the spot the car had just left. The dust from the tires still lingered, and our panting plumed urgently before us. We watched as they sped off, the exhaust streaming behind them.

Something inside me wilted. I looked at Nathan, at the sheer anger in his eyes. After all, he had warned me. I wanted to say I was sorry, but I was breathing too hard to speak, and I wasn't sure what to say anyway. To this day, I don't know what I could have said, if anything could have made a difference. But that was the last time I trusted my brother, though a part of me never quit wanting to.

. . .

Memory is a tricky devil. Twenty-two years later, I recall the headlights sweeping across the pale dry grass stooping sideways in the wind, the cluster of birch trees with golden leaves clinging to their branches, the dusty red Pontiac with torn black vinyl seats, the yellowed stuffing pushing out like infected, swollen tissue. I remember the smell of sweat and dirty tennis shoes. I also have an image of steam rising from ripples under pale moonlight. But the condensation isn't something I'm sure I actually saw. How could I? I wasn't near water. But I've always known that with that night crept something much darker—something more threatening that sneaks through my dreams and slouches just under my awareness, nudging memories forward like a black wave pushing debris ahead of itself. I've always promised myself that I would find a way to stay ahead of it, to avoid its pull and not get swept away in the undercurrent.

1

I LIKE DETAILS, EVIDENCE, and organized notes. When I possess facts, I can clear the detritus around me, think straight, and proceed cautiously. Some might argue that this response is an overreaction to a complicated upbringing, or an overzealous affection for order; and in fact, that might be true. So when my intuition niggled at me that something wasn't quite right with this particular accident, I tried to ignore it. The facts are that every summer in Glacier Park, there is at least one if not several hikers or climbers who stumble on unstable rock or lose their balance on wet, slippery boulders, sliding wildly out of control and catapulting to their demise on the jagged terrain below or into a raging stream, whisking them away.

All of us Glacier Park Police officers and rangers know that the most dire situations are frequently born from small, seemingly insignificant errors of judgment where a hiker is impatient, for example, and thinks the shortcut across an early-season snowfield is a stellar idea. So this tragedy was no different other than the fact that the Loop—the hairpin curve on the west side of Going-to-the-Sun Road—was an odd place for a hiker to go down. Although incredibly steep in places close to the pass, it was, after all, near the main road and a small buildup of natural stone formed a roadside barrier at the curving, sheer edge.

I stood with Ken Greeley, another Park Police officer, Charlie Olson, one of our seasoned rangers, and Joe Smith, chief of Park Police, on the short rock divider with Heavens Peak to our left. Nearly nine thousand feet of mass pushed to the sky and dominated the view west from the

Going-to-the-Sun Road. Scraps of clouds reached northward from the permanently snow-coated peak like silk pennons.

"Looks like a bad fall." Ken chewed a piece of gum vigorously as he peered down at the foot and leg twisted at an unnatural angle. "Any chance he hiked in from a different route and is still alive?"

"Unlikely," Joe said. "He hasn't moved since Charlie reported it. But I've got S&R on standby."

We had gotten word an hour before from Charlie. A tourist had spotted something white poking out from a dark shadow in the steep ravine, found Charlie talking to some folks near the outdoor bathroom facility, and asked him to take a look. Although difficult to make out details with the tricks shadows like to play on rocks, Charlie did agree—with the help of some binoculars—that it appeared to be a shoe, a light-colored sock, and an ankle illuminated by a bright strip of sunshine piercing the crevasse.

"Think maybe it was a suicide?" Ken asked.

Joe shrugged. He'd been particularly quiet for the past eight months since the well-known case dubbed Bear Bait, in which we'd found a man bound to a tree near McGhee Meadow in Glacier Park. The victim, Victor Lance, was killed and fed on by a grizzly, and one of Joe's family members had been involved. I'd assisted a lead investigator from the Department of the Interior on the case.

"Possibly," I offered on Joe's behalf. "Can't tell for sure, but from the looks of where he is, I don't think he actually fell from this roadside after all. There's some slippery rock." I pointed my chin to a spring seep that coated part of the slope across from us. The June sun spread across my back like the hot palm of a hand. Summer often arrives late to these parts, the fresh tang of spring sometimes hanging on until past solstice, but today seemed to mark the season's first solid lunge forward. It was going on eleven a.m., and Glacier Park vibrated with new life and promise. Here today, gone tomorrow, I thought morosely. "He might have gone off trail to take a picture or a piss and misjudged how slippery those rocks are when they're wet."

"Maybe," Joe said, then sighed and looked at me. "Monty"—his voice sounded tired and the brim of his cap shadowed his eyes—"you'll handle the investigation. And you"—he turned to Ken—"will assist. Once you're down there, I'll need you to assess the scene. Like I said, if he's still alive, we've got Rescue ready to go." Then he turned to Charlie. "You and I will secure the area and begin directing traffic. When the victim's ready to be removed," he added, "I've got a short-haul team on standby. Looks too steep and rocky to haul him up without the chopper and we'll need to close the road for a while. Tourists are going to get way backed up today."

Twenty-five minutes later, Ken and I had our anchors set and we were ready to gingerly rappel over the edge, down two hundred vertical feet into the shadowy ravine. Two other experienced rangers, Karen Fortenson and Michael Bridwell, were brought in to man the anchors and assist with the ropes from above so that the weight was transferred appropriately through the pulley system. Each full-time park ranger and all Park Police officers are trained in basic emergency medical service, including Search and Rescue and rope rescue, but some have more experience than others. I was glad to be with Ken who I knew had been on a fair share of rope rescues in the past few years.

In addition to some on-the-job training, I had been scaling mountains since high school. I joined a local hiking and rock-climbing group in Columbia Falls, my small hometown located at the mouth of the canyon leading to Glacier Park. I had seen a flyer for the group on a bulletin board at a grocery store and called because I wasn't the type to mope around at home after completing my schoolwork. Since it was just getting started and had only a few members—a few mellow twentysomethings—they welcomed me, even though I was only a teen.

I spent many weekends roaming the surrounding mountains of the Flathead Valley with the guys in the group, who asked me very few questions and basically treated me with respect, something I wasn't used to from my own father or brother. They taught me what they knew about backcountry hiking, camping, rock climbing, and rappelling. I loved the notion that I could challenge myself by moving through untamed places that forced me to handle myself and my emotions on a grander scale. And, Jesus, to simply escape! To leave the house for hours to cleanse the mind under an endless sky, to be away from where the air always seemed thick and the ceiling heavy.

With a hard hat on and the sit harness around my legs and waist, I walked backwards out and away from the cliff where Ken and others stood. I controlled the brake with my right hand and descended slowly, keeping my feet close to the cliff until I made it down into the ravine.

I removed the carabiners from my harness and watched Ken make his descent. He was a large, muscular guy with almost no neck, a shaved, shiny head, and shoulders perpetually raised toward his ears with the bulk of his muscles. I was the opposite: lean and just shy of five foot nine, thick hair with graying sideburns that contradicted that I was only thirty-four, and dark, determined eyes that looked like I trusted everyone, but rarely took no for an answer. When Ken reached the ground, we hiked over cool, shadowed rocks and through brush.

A few yards from the victim, I stopped, took off my glasses and rubbed my eyes. I could feel my own heart thumping in my chest. The surprise and shock I felt from seeing the damage inflicted upon bone and flesh from smashing into rocks, the violation of our everyday perception of the human body, was something I never could get used to. I held out my hand for Ken to halt as well, then I let out a low, soft whistle.

I put my glasses back on and took in the scene. It felt suddenly quiet and intimate, as if the breeze had quit rattling the leaves, the hawks had gone silent, and McDonald Creek below us had ceased to roar from its full flow of spring runoff. But I knew none of this had happened; it was just an effect of my shocked senses in spite of how many times I'd seen it before: five to be exact. Three climbing incidents on the popular climbing peaks at the top of the pass, one fall into McDonald Creek, and one hiking accident in which the man had slid down a snowfield and off an abrupt ledge.

Before us, blood had stained the rocks around the back of the victim's head. His skull was flattened, broken open like an egg with cerebrospinal fluid, gray brain matter, and blood drained out onto the rocky ground. His face was crushed, torn, swollen, and unrecognizable, but I could see what looked like facial hair streaked with blood and dirt. Every single limb lay twisted in awkward and unnatural angles, badly gashed and coated with dried blood. He had hit rock probably several times on the way down, using his hands instinctively to try to break the first slam. His hands and wrists were shattered up to his elbows, one thumb completely ripped off. The other arm lay hidden and abnormally cocked under his back with his shoulder joint dislocated. He looked like a badly broken Ken doll.

There was something familiar about the illogically crooked, disfigured body and at the same time, nothing at all recognizable. The man had long, dirty-blond and curly locks, also marbled with dirt and caked blood that had turned the color of rust. He had on army-green shorts and a tattered T-shirt that looked like it might have been white or yellow, but it was torn, covered in grime and body fluids and was hard to tell. One foot missed its hiking shoe, which had probably popped off on impact and been cast into some bushes even farther below.

I could hear tiny insects buzzing and zigzagging. Small blowflies had already swarmed into the mucus in his eye sockets, his mouth, and other wounds. My mouth went dry, then began to water. He smelled of death, a copper odor mixed with beef gone bad. I ignored the queasy sensation in my gut and pulled some nitrile and vinyl gloves out of my pocket, put them on, and walked to him. The instinct is to offer comforting words as if the person was still alive, to say, *Are you okay? Help is on the way*, but I shook the urge away and knelt beside him. Still grasping for the ordinary, I began to reach out with my two fingers toward his neck to check his vitals, then stopped. Checking for a pulse was as futile as trying to console him. It was obvious his neck was broken, his skull lacerated, and the life gone out of his one partially open eye, already gone opaque. The other was swollen shut. I withdrew my hand and shook my head to Ken.

Ken didn't say anything. I could hear him breathing—strong exhales through his nostrils and he had ceased smacking his gum. He was usually hard to keep quiet and was not acting like his chatty and eager self. I chalked it up to the task at hand.

I grabbed my radio and pressed Talk. "Chief, you read?"

"Yep, please report."

"Deceased. Judging by the color of the blood and his eyes, looks like he's been here at least since yesterday. Rigor mortis has set in as well and it doesn't appear to have begun to wear off. Doesn't appear to be chewed on though, so no animals have been around yet."

"Bonus," Joe said, and I could hear him sigh like he didn't want to be doing this so early into tourist season, which really fires up around the Fourth of July.

"We'll look around, take notes and photos," I said. "I'll let you know when we're getting closer to being done down here."

We signed off, and l looked up at the clear cloudless sky. "Since he's not alive," I said to Ken, "and no rain in the forecast, there's no major rush in getting him up. Let's study the area as carefully as we can."

Ken took out a tissue from his pocket and plucked his gum out with his thumb and forefinger. He briefly looked at it with disgust, then wrapped it in the tissue and placed it back in his pocket. I didn't bother to tell him he'd be better off continuing to chew it or to grab a new piece because it helped minimize the full onslaught of death's odor. I wasn't much older than Ken, but I had gone through some recent forensics schooling while he'd had very little, just the initial training program—stuff like criminal investigations, park and recreation law, criminal procedure, and penal law. I was certain Ken had only been on one or two death scenes before, and only as a bystander, although he'd been on plenty of Search and Rescue missions. Fortunately, I had recently spent hours in Georgia going over forensic analysis with a cadaver before me.

After my time with Department of Interior agent Ted Systead on Bear Bait, I'd decided I wanted to enhance my knowledge of investigative services. I'd always been a fully-trained, permanent full-time law enforcement officer since I'd been employed by the park, but since I'm a good organizer and notetaker, I'd been pulled into administrative duties with the super. And before becoming a Park Police officer, I was a game warden in eastern Montana close to the Divide.

But I hadn't been on a crime case in a long time until the Bear Bait case popped up. After it, my hunger to be involved in investigative services deepened, and I'm sure it was no coincidence that my desire to plunge into something wholly absorbing coincided with being separated from my wife, Lara. I admit I have a propensity for a bit of tunnel vision, for working feverishly on things that catch my interest. Lara would tell you that it was a problem at times—how I could tune out our lives and escape into the pull of a new task. I've been this way for as long as I can remember.

So once I caught the investigative bug, I no longer wanted any part of the administrative duties I'd been mixed up in for the past few years. I asked Joe, and he agreed to send me to a refresher course in Brunswick, Georgia, on Crime Scene Investigative Procedures, Evidence Collection and Analysis, and another on Modern Forensics.

I removed my pack and pulled out another pair of gloves for Ken, some evidence markers, and my notepad while he grabbed the camera.

"Here we go," I said, ready to put my recent training to work. "We'll see if I can do this without taking forever." I kneeled down again by the body and pressed my forefinger into the blotched and bluish-purple skin of his arm. The skin was cold, still in the shadows and, of course, the algor mortis—the death chill—well underway. The flesh stayed purple. I noted that and said to Ken, "Looks like hypostasis has spread evenly and isn't responding to pressure."

"Huh?" Ken mumbled.

"The discoloring of the skin—you know, the livor mortis."

"Yeah, right," Ken said. He looked away, to the cliffs above us. A hawk sailed by.

"Probably means he's been out here for more than ten to twelve hours," I offered. "After five or six, the lividity blotches start to merge, but the skin still goes white when pressed. After ten, give or take depending on temperature, it stays this bluish-purple color. And," I noted, "rigor mortis hasn't yet begun to wear off as it does about thirty-six hours after death. Although with the cold last night," I reconsidered, "what was it? Maybe forty-five, forty-eight degrees?"

"'Bout that," Ken agreed.

"Might've slowed both processes down quite a bit. The coroner or pathologist should be able to tell us more, depending on how far this goes." Often with accidents like these, an autopsy is done regardless—just to be thorough because with a fall, it's always harder to know if foul play occurred. Of course, the family's wishes would be respected, but we'd request an autopsy, get the ducks in a row. Better safe than sorry.

Ken, now a little green around his mouth and white in the face, scrunched up his nose and stared at me with a slightly dazed expression. "You want me to take photos of the body now or after you inspect it and take your notes?"

"Now would be good." I backed away and motioned with my gloved palm to signal *all yours*, and he snapped away. Flashes disrupted the shadows in the ravine until Ken stopped, moved the camera away from his face, swallowed hard, and wiped his forehead with the sleeve of his uniform shirt. I could still hear his breathing, heavier now. "You okay?" I said.

"Yeah, I'm good."

"You sure? Here." I held out my hand. "Why don't I take the rest of the pictures and you can scoot over there and check out that disturbed rock up there. I think he probably hit that ledge." I pointed about thirty yards above us. Glacier is known for its sedimentary rock, which is crumbly and unstable. "See it?"

Ken looked up, squinting into the sun now moving slightly farther to the west, shining directly on where I was kneeling and exposing the victim from the waist up. "Yeah, I see that. Right." He handed me the camera. "Probably a good idea."

"Check for blood, disturbed dirt, you know, scrape marks from sliding, clothing, that sort of thing, but don't touch anything. And, Ken," I said, "might want to grab another piece of gum."

He looked at me confused, and I waved him on. I didn't want to deal with him getting sick on me. Then I turned back to the victim, brought the camera to my eye, and focused on his hair and face again. I found myself tilting my head to slightly alter my perspective. Slowly, I lowered the camera from my eyes. "Ken," I said. "Mind coming back over?"

He shuffled back. "Yeah?"

"Past the swelling, past the distortion. . . . Doesn't this guy, I mean, call me nuts, but doesn't he look familiar to you?"

Ken took a step back, also tilted his head to the side and squinted, his thick, sunburned neck bunching on one side.

"The hair especially," I said. "I swear I know this man."

Ken brought his head back to straight, his beefy shoulders tensing and pulled in his chin like a turtle. "Yeah, you're right. Shit. You're right. I think, oh God, I think it's Wolfie."

"Wolfie," I repeated, under my breath. "Yes," I nodded. "Damn, that's it." I grabbed my radio to call Joe and recalled the last time I saw the man. I was with Lara, my now-estranged wife, and he was with his wife and kids—all bright smiles while eating dinner at the Pizza Hut in Whitefish. "I guess we can't be sure, but, holy shit, yeah, I think it's him."

2

_____

THE ROAR FROM the helicopter filled my ears and rattled my bones. Small green leaves, dust, and white feathery filament from the cottonwood trees flurried madly as the chopper hovered above like a parent waiting impatiently for Ken and me to complete the long-line retrieval. Bright orange ropes with carabiners and a litter—a metal basket used to place the body in—dangled above us.

We'd already wrapped the corpse in fabric and placed it in a maroon body bag. I was still in shock after realizing it was Wolfie. If it hadn't have been for his large frame and his distinct blond, wavy locks that looked like they belonged on an adolescent and not a grown man, I wouldn't have had any recognition.

Paul "Wolfie" Sedgewick was a biologist and one of the lead researchers of the Wolverine Research Team. He had been nicknamed Wolvie early on, but over the years, the _v_ had drifted to an _f_. It was easier to say Wolfie than Wolvie.

Ken and I had been on the scene for over three hours, photographing the victim from all angles, inspecting rock crumbled away by the velocity of the body crashing against it and skid marks from the sliding. I'd taken notes and we'd tweezed samples from his clothes torn off by some of the more jagged rocks above, at least the ones we could climb to. We couldn't get to some of the higher points above that he'd potentially hit on the way down, presuming we had judged the launch point accurately.

Joe had radioed down to us that they found a car in the Loop Trail

14

parking area with a license registered to Paul Sedgewick. His ID was also in the glove box.

Ken and I looked for evidence of suicide or foul play, but saw none. No note on him, no suspicious injuries that might have been from something other than the fall, like a ligature mark or a gunshot wound, but the coroner or pathologist would be able to look more closely.

I couldn't wrap my head around the idea that a man with so much experience in the back country could fall this close to the Loop, so near the main and only pass through the park. His team of wolverine researchers had skied all over Glacier Park in the dead of winter, in subzero temperatures and biting wind chill, to set the mini log-cabin traps used for baiting them. Wolverines were the least-known and most elusive animals in the Northwest and cunning and tenacious enough to run off a grizzly bear over a dead carcass with its long claws, sharp teeth, and badass attitude. Wolfie's team had trekked across large massifs, scaled monumental crags, rambled up high summits, and skied across iced-over lakes tracking the creatures and looking for their dens, hoping to find clues about their behavior and how strong their population is after decades of being trapped in the Northwest.

Ken and I divided the ravine into grids and searched for signs of the animal just in case Wolfie had tried to foolishly climb down to track one. We looked for the telltale triangular-shaped print made from the animal's five toes, which would splay out when its paws compressed into the dirt or mud, its sharp-pointed claws leading the way. We checked for scat—cylindrical pellets with fur, bones, and feathers from its scavenging. We found nothing along those lines other than Wolfie's other hiking boot nestled in some bushes lower down.

Had this burly, blond man been so consumed in his research that he'd gotten careless and simply fallen to his death? Or had he been suicidal, drinking, or on drugs? I pictured Wolfie—his long, loose locks blowing in the mountain breeze, his wide grin, and his healthy, weathered, and ruddy skin. I couldn't conceive of any of those scenarios, but it was too soon to make assumptions.

When the large metal hook from the helicopter finally reached ground, Ken and I moved Wolfie carefully onto the metal litter, hooked up the four lines to the center catch, and signaled for the chopper to lower a bit more. When the hook came into reaching distance, I grabbed it and snapped the catch from the litter onto it and signaled for the pilot to rise. I watched the basket, hanging underneath the chopper like a fly in a spider's filament, swing away. Slowly, they'd take the body to a gravel pit near McDonald Creek, an opening used for construction vehicles where the coroner waited.

I glanced up to Heavens Peak again, then up Logan Pass to the panorama surrounding it. The Crown of the Continent stood massive and indifferent, beautiful and rugged. A place where time loses its significance and history shoots up out of the ground, its presence overwhelming and demanding, making you feel useless and small. The biologist—trying to understand the near-mythical creature known for its toughness and resilience but threatened by the loss of the glacial snowfields necessary for its winter dens—was now officially done with his research. Officially done with his life, his family. The finality of it was every bit as humbling as the peaks towering above us. I thought of Lara—how our once rock-solid bond had slowly but surely crumbled—and felt a weight fall upon me like a heavy cloak.

I undid the strap under my chin and removed my hard hat to get some air. My scalp was sweaty, the tips of my close-cropped hair gathered into wet points and clinging to the back of my neck and around my ears. For some reason, I suppose in homage, I held the helmet over my chest as if I were honoring the flag. I watched the chopper fly down the line of McDonald Creek, its dark strip of water flickering in sunlight and carving through the countryside at the base of Heavens Peak. I watched it all the way until it grew very small and its roar softened to a faint growl as it went around the bend toward the gravel pit three or four miles down the road.

I put the hard hat back on and let out a groan in the silent contrast. "It's not going to be easy telling Wolfie's wife and kids."

"No," Ken agreed. "It's not."

. . .

Joe was waiting for Ken and me when we came up from the ravine. After we removed our gear, Joe gave Ken instructions to help Karen and Michael lift the anchors and put the rest of the climbing equipment away.

"I've already gone over what we think the launch point is," Joe said after waving me over. I followed him toward the Loop Trail. "But it's hard to say for sure. I want you to look at it since you had perspective from down below."

We started toward the trail that sits above the ravine where we found the body. The Loop Trail to Granite Park Chalet, one of two stone chalets in Glacier's high country, sits above a nearly four-mile steep hike through the remains of a spruce and fir forest burned by the 2003 Trapper Fire. This time of the year, it's a hot and sweaty hike until you reach higher elevation above the fire zone and reenter the forest, which eventually takes you to a wind-swept subalpine fir and spruce area where the chalet sits and the Highline Trail cuts along the Continental Divide. The Highline Trail sits under a steep rocky rim known as the Garden Wall and takes you about seven miles to the top of Logan Pass. At nine thousand feet, the top of the Garden Wall, built from primordial ocean bottom, forms the top of the rim.

There is also another eleven-mile trail to Many Glacier Campground on the east side of the Divide and a 2.2-mile trail to Swiftcurrent Lookout, a popular place to spot grizzlies or wolverines playing on snowfields in the early summer. I wondered if Wolfie was heading that way.

"We're not thinking this is the spot," Joe said when we approached the slick rocks I'd mentioned earlier while standing above the ravine with Joe, Ken, and Charlie. "No slip marks around and the trajectory isn't right."

"Yeah, definitely not right." I looked down the ravine and could easily see it wasn't the right line for the body to have launched from. The area was marked with tape, though, I presumed, to preserve the mud already covered with print marks from the soles of many tourists' boots. Since Logan Pass's higher elevations had only recently been cleared of its snowpack several weeks before, but had been plowed up to the Loop since late April, many people rode their bikes or drove to the Loop during the spring and hiked the Granite Park Chalet trail as far as they could before hitting snow. "You get some castings from some of these?" I asked anyway.

"Yes. There's quite a few so it will be hard to distinguish one clean one out of the bunch, and we have no evidence that this was foul play. Since it's Wolfie though, and very odd that a man of his experience would fall here, I did have one of Walsh's guys from the county bring the plaster kit and grab as many partials as he could."

We continued over a bridge with an early-summer crashing stream that would peter out by mid-August. I felt the cool air created by the stream wash over my face and forced down a full breath of it. A little farther up the trail, Joe stopped at a shallow outcropping of rocks where the trail bends right.

The late-afternoon sky held a new cluster of wispy clouds gathered and fraying over Heavens Peak. Something scurried in the brush beside the trail, probably a striped chipmunk. I felt myself flinch slightly and shook it off. I was beginning to feel jittery and tired at the same time from being down in the ravine for hours without food. I'd unintentionally skipped breakfast because of a phone argument with Lara.

Now standing up at the higher elevation and peering down to the area where Wolfie's body had been made me feel light-headed, like I'd just been in a car or a plane for too long with too much caffeine.

"We think this is it." Joe pointed. The area had been marked off with yellow tape, and I made sure not to step into the small outcropping.

"Find any evidence?"

"Not much of anything. Those broken shrubs there." He pointed to the side of the ridge.

"Any blood or fibers from clothes?"

"No, but we've got part of a boot print in the dirt on that edge of the rock leading onto the outcropping. It's pretty faint, but we've got a plaster. Could be any of hundreds of tourists walking by this area. We're basing it primarily on the trajectory of where the body was."

I peered down to the ledge Ken and I had climbed up to document. "Yeah, I agree. This looks like the spot." I searched the ground, noticing the large flat rocks forming a narrow upward scalloping of rock to the lip of the ridge. "It's almost concave here. He'd have to have been up on the very edge. Maybe scanning for wolverines and somehow just lost his footing, but I don't see any signs of slippage?"

"No, me neither. You find any binoculars?"

"No, but that doesn't mean they didn't pop off his neck or fly out of his hands and land in some bushes. I can go down again tomorrow and look some more."

Joe shrugged. "We'll see what the pathologist finds."

"Has the family been notified yet?"

Joe sighed heavily. "Not yet. Nobody knows who he is yet except you, Ken, and myself and I've given strict orders to Ken to not open his mouth except to chew that damn gum of his. You up for talking to the family?"

"Yes, sir, if I need to be."

"Just thought you might want to lead this—being recently out of your refresher courses and all. Give you a chance to ask the right questions. See how they feel about an autopsy."

I wasn't looking forward to the job at all. I'd only done it once before and my partner had taken care of the hard part while I simply stood by and listened. "I'll do it as soon as I get back."

Joe gave me a solemn nod, placed his hand on my shoulder and gave it a pat. Joe usually took that god-awful task and had informed more families than I can imagine of the accidental deaths of loved ones in Glacier. I knew part of his enthusiasm to send me to DC for the classes was fueled by his desire to have someone relieve him of that burden. Something left unspoken inserted itself between us—a surrendering—that what had transpired with the Bear Bait case had taken too much of a toll and he no longer had the resilience to tell anyone of any loss ever again if he could avoid it.

I walked over to the other side of the tape, knelt down, and inspected the edge of the ridge. "Doesn't really look like much foliage has been disturbed here other than a few broken shrubs. If he'd lost footing and slipped, wouldn't he have taken more of these plants with him?"

"Maybe, maybe not. These plants are green with new life, they're moist and resilient this time of the year and would spring back to their upright position in no time at all."

"A big guy like Wolfie, though? He'd at least have tried to grab onto some. Ripped them clean out. Not just broken them."

Joe shrugged and I could see he wasn't interested in being pressed at the moment. "If he didn't get a good grip, then that wouldn't have happened."

"Perhaps," I agreed. "I'm not seeing much in the way of scuffle marks, but it's always harder to tell on rock bases. You find any?"

"I didn't," Joe said.

"Yeah, well, okay, what next?"

"You visit the family and we wait for the coroner's exam results. Otherwise, at this juncture, there's no reason to call this anything but an accident."

"But you want me to look into it?" I knew any unattended death of an otherwise healthy individual needed to be investigated—that all unobserved deaths were treated as suspicious until shown they weren't, but I asked anyway just to confirm that he wanted it to be *me* doing the checking.

He nodded. "Find the last person who saw him, who spoke to him. Check credit card spending, possible extramarital affairs, unpaid bills, debt, that sort of thing. You know the drill." Joe looked me in the eye and it felt strange, as if I hadn't seen his in a long time. They looked pale and distant, slightly rimmed in raw pink. "If he committed suicide," Joe said, "something will show. If it was truly an accident, everything will be pretty much status quo."

3

KEN AND I turned off Whitefish Stage Road onto the long gravel driveway between the towns of Kalispell and Whitefish. To the side of the drive, a vibrant yellow field of blooming canola spread picture-perfect until it hit a border of deep-green trees near the Stillwater River. The Columbia Range under a sky so blue it looked artificial stood in the background and completed the country picture, making it perfectly serene.

My stomach tightened and I felt short of breath at the thought of fracturing such a scene—of looking Cathy Sedgewick in the eye and telling her that she would not be seeing her husband, and her children would not be seeing their father ever again. But I had no choice; this was my task.

"Ranch Lane should be right up here," Ken said, studying the map on his cell-phone GPS app.

I made a right where a small farmhouse with green shutters nestled among tall cottonwoods with deeply furrowed bark. A small porch sat in front with flower boxes below the large windows. Above the slanted porch roof, two windows looked out across the field from the small A-line second story.

A barking golden retriever ran toward the car. I rechecked the house number on the mailbox as I passed to make sure I had the right place and parked the Explorer in front of the garage. I sat for a moment and looked at the dog, its tail wagging eagerly.

I let out a breath as if releasing steam from a pressure cooker. It didn't feel real; the evening was too perfect for this. I glanced at Ken and he looked at me questioningly. "Ready?" I asked. Ken nodded and I forced myself to get out. "Hey, buddy," I said to the dog solemnly and gave him a pat on the head. We walked toward the front porch and a warm breeze tickled my face. I could smell steaks from a grill from their backyard.

The front door swung open and Cathy stepped out and started walking toward us calling the dog—Max—to her. I knew it was Cathy because I recalled her from the time at Pizza Hut, and I'd seen her with Wolfie a time or two at other local restaurants when I'd been out with Lara.

She smiled and waved, then pushed a strand of dark curly hair behind her ear. She wore shorts, a faded purple T-shirt, and flip-flops. The sun, still intense but lowering in the western sky, painted her skin tawny. "Monty?" she squinted at me through a questioning smile.

"Yes, hi, Cathy, good memory." I tried to smile, but I couldn't. I noticed her eyes drift to my badge, to Ken, then flicker to the NPS vehicle. I was only a distant acquaintance and would never have a reason to stop by under normal circumstances. Her smile faded, and she narrowed her gaze as if sensing something wasn't right.

"Yes, of course I remember you. What brings you out to visit us?" she asked. "Paul isn't here right now."

"Cathy, this is Officer Ken Greeley. I'm not sure if you've met, but he's also with Park Police. May I ask if the kids are home?"

Cathy nodded, her eyes growing large and scared. "Jeff's out back with a friend playing badminton and Abbey's upstairs." She pointed up. "Is everything okay? Have you seen Paul?"

I motioned to the porch and started that way slowly. I didn't want to tell her out in the driveway. Ken walked with me, and she followed. I felt bad delaying it, making her trail us like a puppy, but I wanted her by something substantial she could at least lean or sit on. Ken and I walked up the steps, but she stopped at the bottom. "What's this about?"

"Cathy." I stepped back down. "I'm afraid I have very bad news. There's been an accident."

She put her hand to her mouth and a terrible worry sprang to her eyes.

"We found a man this morning in a steep ravine below a drop-off near the Loop. He"—I shook my head—"he didn't make it."

"Wha—" Cathy looked confused. She dropped her hand to her chest, her mouth forming an O shape with the half-spoken word. She was trying to process what I'd just said. "He's hurt?" She peered down the drive as if someone would be coming up with her injured husband so she could nurse him back to health. "Where is he? I need to see him."

"No, he's not hurt. He didn't make it. He was already gone when we found him."

Confusion swiftly changed to something wild flashing across her face. "No, that's not possible. What do you mean, the Loop? What in the hell do you mean?" Her hands were on her hips now, defiant, and she glanced at the peaks of the park. They shone white with spring's remaining snow, bright and beautiful in the late afternoon sun casting across their tips. A pair of large, sleek ravens launched from a tall pine and flew overhead. Max started barking wildly, rearing off his stiff front legs as if the black birds were the problem here, as if he needed to protect his family from them. But there was no protecting them from what we were bringing.

"Cathy, please. Look at me." I waited until her eyes focused on mine and Max had stopped barking. Her eyes were wide with fear and the colors looked amplified—light brown with cinnamon flecks. "Paul has passed away," I said. "He fell a long distance off a steep ridge and the fall took the life from him."

"But, but, that can't be true. Why, why on earth would he fall—that's not even possible." She looked from me to Ken like we had just made a big blunder. "Someone's made a mistake here."

"No, no mistake. We both went down into the ravine. We both recognized him. And his car was in the Loop parking area with his registration."

She put her hand to her mouth again, her confusion slowly turning to comprehension and her eyes turning wet with tears. "No." She whispered a sound that was partly a moan. "Oh God, no. It can't be."

I dropped my gaze to the sunlight hitting the wooden porch, trying not to think about the repercussions of this—how the waves of pain were going to keep pushing outward to her children, to Paul's parents, to his siblings if he had any. How we were shattering their entire world. I could feel a sheen of sweat gathering across my forehead and between my shoulder blades. "Is there someone—a friend or family member of yours I can call to be here with you, to help you tell the children?"

Cathy wrapped her arms around her waist. "Oh God, oh God, the kids." Her breath sounded suddenly frantic and her knees began to shake. I reached for her arm and helped her down to sit on the porch step while she continued to repeat, "Oh God, oh God, the kids." Max tried to lick her face, but she pushed him away.

"There's a chaplain," I said. "He's available to help for situations like this if—"

She held up her hand for me to stop.

"Cathy," I said. "I know this is so hard, but I need to ask you some questions."

Tears continued to flood her eyes. "How did he . . . ?"

"We're not entirely sure, but we think he just"—I shrugged—"lost his footing. But I need to ask you, when was the last time you saw him?"

Before she answered, I heard the creak of the front porch door and all three of us turned.

"Mom?" a boy with thick and wavy blond hair like Wolfie's peeked out. "The steaks are burning."

Cathy nodded, tried to say something, but it came out as a choked sob.

"Mom, what's wrong?" He stepped out, tentatively walking over to us.

I went onto the porch. "I'm Monty Harris and this is Ken Greeley. We work for the National Park Service. Do you mind giving us just one more second and I promise she'll be right in. Maybe turn off the grill. You know how to do that? Officer Greeley"—I tipped my head to Ken—"he can help you."

He was tall and lanky and resembled Paul with full, round cheeks. A healthy line of sweat gathered at his hairline and his cheeks were flushed, probably from playing badminton. I figured he was around twelve or thirteen—in middle school. He looked at me funny, then nodded and backed into the house. Ken glanced at me and I nodded for him go around back and make sure all was okay with the grill. The last thing we needed was a fire.

After Ken left, I turned back to her. "I'm very sorry."

"How, how in the world could this have happened?" There was an anger mixed with impotence in her voice, and I felt the same mix of emotions reverberate through me. I wanted to answer her question, but I couldn't.

"We don't know yet. But I promise we're doing all we can to figure it out." Max now sat in front of Cathy and let out a whine.

"Where is he?"

"He's with Dr. Pettiman in Kalispell. The doctor is waiting for you if you want to speak to him, and like I said, a chaplain."

Cathy stared up at me, searching my face, as if waiting for me to come clean about the horrifying and cruel joke I was playing. She started to get up, but I put my hand out. "No, just stay." I sat down near her on the lower step, and I caught a faint whiff of coconut, perhaps her soap or lotion. The smell triggered more summer—things happy and fun. The contrast to the current reality hit me with a poignant and bitter sting.

"Cathy, when was the last time you saw him?"

"I, I saw him yesterday. In the evening. He was heading to Glacier as always to do more research. To, to pick up some wildlife footage. Said the wolverine transmitters were picking up signals near Granite Park Chalet, the Highline, and the Loop."

"Footage?"

"Yeah, I guess one of the motion cameras is posted near the Loop and he wanted to check it. Said he was going to pick the memory card up, then head over the pass and camp near Many Glacier and hike into Lake Josephine to pick up the card from one of the other cameras there too. He's staying a few nights. He's coming home on Sunday." She looked at me with hope, as if saying the words that he's coming home would make it all go away.

"Was he with someone?"

"No." She shook her head. "Not that I know of. But, but we could call the rest of the team. Kurtis Bowman or Sam would know. They both work closely with Paul."

"Sam Ward?"

"Yes, or even Pritchard. Tom Pritchard."

"The vet?" I asked. Not only did I know Pritchard from the Bear Bait Case, but I knew he sometimes helped the biologists by trekking into the backcountry and implanting the transmitters with steady veterinary hands accustomed to operating on animals.

I pulled out my pad from my pocket. "What time did Paul leave yesterday?"

"Around six or so, after working in his office all day." She motioned to the house. He wanted to wait until the pass got less busy and with the late sun, he'd have plenty of time to stop at the Loop, head over, and still have enough light to pitch his tent on the east side."

"Do you mind if I take a look at his office?"

Cathy looked at me strangely, her eyes distant. Ken came back around the house with another boy, shorter than Jeff, with darker hair. "The kids," he announced, and I understood that we couldn't keep them waiting any longer. I stood up. "Abbey came down from upstairs," he said. "I've asked both to wait out back. Figured we could give Parker here a ride home."

Jeff's buddy, Parker, looked completely confused and a little freaked out with a wide-eyed stare. Cathy stood abruptly and faced me. "I can't tell them. I don't even know if this is true. How do we know there hasn't been a mistake?"

Before I could answer, Abbey burst through the front door, older and more commanding than Jeff. Her hair wet and combed sleekly behind her ears as if she'd just taken a shower. "Mom, Mom, what's going on? Is this about Dad?"

Cathy stared at her daughter, holding the post by the steps. "Oh baby," she whimpered.

I identified myself to her. "Abbey, maybe you could go get your brother?"

"No," she said defiantly. "What's going on?"

"Your father," Cathy cried, "I'm sorry baby, but he's, he's had an accident."

"What?" she ran to her mom and Cathy caught her in her arms. "Where is he?"

"He's, I don't know. They say he's gone, sweetie, and he's not coming home anymore."

Pain registered on Abbey's face, like a child falling in a playground, and she began to wail. With her sobbing, Jeff came barging through the porch door, a sad and hopeless look in his eyes that said he'd already figured it out—that there was nothing but crushing news coming his way.

4

—

ONE OF THE things I loved most about working in the Park was
how happy everyone always looked, content and smiling. Glacier Park
could be as wild and brutal as it comes, but on many summer days,
it is pure peace and bucolic bliss replete with fresh air, dancing but-
terflies, cold mountain streams, valleys filled with a mosaic of vibrant
wild flowers, and the high peaks of the Divide kissing cobalt skies. If
you catch it on these perfect days, your blood pressure goes down and
it buoys your soul, lifts you to the sky—makes you forget that there
might be things hidden inside us all, things able to erupt if not diligently kept in check.

But today not even nature's glory could keep the darkness from entering our gates. Wolfie would not be going home from a perfect early
summer day in the Park with a sunburn and more data on the wolverine. He would not be going for another exploratory hike, another
camping trip, another barbecue with his family this day or any day
again. The reality of it was as sharp and final as a slap across the face.

I had quickly looked around Wolfie's office while Cathy huddled
with the kids on the deck and Ken and Parker waited in the car. After
I found nothing remiss, we drove Parker home, then went to Park
Headquarters. We parked outside the 1960s-looking Arizona brick
structure, like some utilitarian building out of the old Eastern Bloc.
A rectangular patch of lush green grass carpeted the area between the
parking lot and the building. Off to the side of the lot, the Rocky Mountain Maples, more like large bushes than their large illustrious eastern

28

cousins, provided foliage for several mule deer sporting their scruffy, shedding coats. The prettier imported eastern maples on the west side stood in full bloom with green leaves lazily resting on one side of the roof.

Ken looked completely spent and I could see this might have been one of the hardest things he'd done on the job yet.

"You good?" I asked, trying to be sensitive to the fact that it was his first investigation of this type.

"Yeah, just tired. That really sucked."

"Go home to your family. Get something to eat and I'll see you in the morning." I knew Ken had only been married a little over a year, but had one young boy about two years old. "We'll head up early to look for that wildlife camera."

"Sounds good." He sighed and headed to his car.

I saw an office light in Joe's window even though there was still plenty of light in the sky. The sun was low on the western horizon. It was going on eight and most employees had left, but in late June, it doesn't go fully dark until after eleven, making the days feel endless and bursting with promise. I grabbed my briefcase from the passenger seat of my Ford SUV, which I used only in the park for the most part, hit the auto locks, and went inside.

I stopped by Joe's office first. It has two old, worn leather chairs for guests, and Joe waved for me to sit. The air felt stuffy and Joe must have noticed when my hand went to part my collar because he stood, leaned over, and cranked open his window. "How'd it go?" he asked, sitting back down, his narrow readers low on his nose.

"As best it could. They weren't expecting him until Sunday." I opened my case and took out my notepad. I explained how he left on Wednesday to supposedly pick up some footage near the Loop, then drive over Logan Pass to Many Glacier to camp for the night, hike into Josephine Lake, and pick up footage there as well, do a little research, camp another three nights, then drive home on Sunday.

"Does she"—he checked a report in front of him, lifting his chin to look down through his glasses—"Cathleen, Cathleen Sedgewick want to see him?"

"Goes by Cathy. Yes, but I told her she couldn't."

"Good. I'd hate to have her go through that since he's been disfigured. But we still need an official ID. If we brought her in, there'd be a very small possibility of misidentification, right?"

"Yeah, she could be so freaked out by the face, she could definitely mis-ID him, out of strong denial. She already thinks there's been a mistake. Thinks he'll still come through the door on Sunday. But ID'ing him could theoretically be best for her in terms of eventually moving through the grieving process." I knew I sounded a little like a procedural manual on dealing with family members of victims, but I couldn't help it. I liked to deal with life's messy curveballs exactly by the book because, let's face it—this kind of stuff wasn't easy and help, however we can get it, is well appreciated.

"And I suppose Ken and I could be mistaken, but the car and his ID?"

"It's a good verification, but of course, cars can be driven by someone else."

I chewed the side of my lip. "I just can't see putting her through it," an image of the smashed face and shattered skull popped into my mind. "I'm thinking odontology and DNA." I produced a plastic baggie with Wolfie's toothbrush. "I grabbed this just in case, but hopefully dental records will do the trick instead. I'll get this to Gretchen though and see if we can't get a rush to match the DNA. Save Cathy the trauma. I'll also find out who they use for a dentist. Plus I'll find out if the west entrance routine surveillance tapes were running. It'd be good to see if he drove in alone and if it matches the time Cathy says he left the house."

Joe agreed, placed his knuckles under his chin, and stared at the toothbrush I had placed on his desk. "Odontology should do the trick, but if not, we should be able to get a rush on this. I'll make some calls. But you know, if she insists on seeing him, we have no choice. Either way, I'd like him officially ID'd as soon as possible because I'll have to release a name to the press. The accident will already be coming out in the paper in the morning."

"I think that's doable." I reconsidered the effect it might have on Cathy Sedgewick. Even though it was already Thursday evening, Wilson should have the body by the next day, and hopefully the postmortem soon to follow.

Joe leaned back into his black ergonomic chair with a high back and removed his readers. He looked frail, and I resisted the urge to ask him how he was faring, how he and Elena, his wife, were doing and if he was getting enough sleep and food these days. I knew the Lance trial had originally been set for March, but had been delayed and was set to start in two weeks. Showing for work each day was the only thing keeping him sane. "Anything out of the ordinary?"

"Not a thing, sir." I leaned forward and placed my elbows on my knees and looked at my notepad again. "Very normal reactions. Stunned, disbelieving, appropriately shocked. Nothing to suggest suicide or foul play. But the wildlife footage interests me." I looked up and tapped my pad with my pen. "I've called Bowman to ask about the cameras. I lose track of where they place those and I wasn't aware they had one set up in the Loop area, were you?"

Joe shook his head. "No, I wasn't. The biologists are always moving them around—bears, wolverines, fishers, pine martins, now they're into ducks too." He shrugged. "Ever since the wolverine guys found harlequin duckling feathers in the wolverine's dens, they had always assumed the ducks don't breed in the park since they're mainly a coastal bird. Now they're studying migration patterns, trying to understand why they come inland to McDonald Creek to breed. But Kurt, yeah, he'd know where the camera is at the Loop if there is one, and maybe it's got some footage of someone in the area that day and evening."

"That would be a gift. Let's hope it does."

"You didn't find any film on the victim?"

"I didn't. Shorts were ripped on one side with the entire pocket flap torn open. The other pocket was intact and I checked, but there was nothing in it. I'd like to take a peek at Wolfie's vehicle, search it as well. There were no keys on the body either."

"Yeah, I found them in the car. Didn't bother to lock it, so it makes sense he was just going to grab the film and take off again. After finding the ID, his cell phone and his camping gear in the backseat, I didn't search a whole lot more than that." He picked up a plastic bag with the ID and phone inside and handed it to me. "While we had the road blocked, we had it transported to our side lot here. You can look at in the morning or even right now if you'd like."

"I'll do that." I stood up and thanked Joe.

"No," Joe said. "Thank you. Tough duty telling the family like that." He closed his eyes for a moment and when he opened them, said, "Been through that too many times."

"Yes, sir, I know you have. Happy to help there." I snapped open my briefcase and placed my notepad and the plastic bag inside. And when I clicked the case shut, I felt a sudden blast of purpose. In spite of feeling completely played out from telling the victim's family, I had a job to do and it involved organization, details, research, calculations, and wit.

You'd be surprised. Families had questions; they often wanted more details than you could ever imagine. What we found—how far their loved one had slid, what hit first, did they die instantly, were they able to call out, how cold it was . . . Once the initial shock subsided, the Sedgewicks would want more. And, of course, if there was ever a reason to go to court, the facts needed to be meticulously recorded and relayed. I may not be able to fully comfort Wolfie's family, but I could get the details down right for their sake, for his sake.

When I shut my briefcase, the realization clicked in my brain that this was my purpose, this was my calling and I, Monty Harris, was the right guy for the job. I knew well enough there were things in life—emotional things—that no one could take charge of, but shepherding an investigation of a bad fall—this I could do.

5

I THANKED THE LATE sun smoldering on the peaks as I walked to Wolfie's old Subaru wagon parked in the lot by headquarters. A vehicle's interior was usually a good indicator of its driver's habits. I pulled my gloves on and opened the front door, stuck my head in and took a big whiff. This wagon was clean and did not smell of fast food, alcohol, food gone bad, cigarette smoke. . . . Not that I necessarily expected that from Wolfie. Nor was it littered with odds and ends, which I did halfway expect—maybe a bottle of sunscreen or a water bottle on the floor, but it was clean and tidy.

A polyethylene file box sat on the floor of the passenger side and a fat blue binder lay right in the middle of the passenger seat. Papers stuck out unevenly. I flipped open the title page and read: "Wolverines: A Circumpolar Species and Indicator of Global Warming." There were a few plastic dividers, one of them labeled "Wolverine Pop Assessments/GNP," another "RM Research Stn Progress," another "Clim Chg Effects." And the last, "Trap/Monitor Sites." The box contained numerous research files with tabs holding many more documents. Wolfie's small office contained even more files and books on all kinds of northwestern animals, habitats, and research.

I went to browse through the other files when I heard a car pull into the lot. I looked up to see Eugene Ford, the park's super whom I used to work closely with until the Bear Bait Case. He parked, got out of his car, and strode up, his straight-backed, tall stance not betraying his age in the least. Ford was in his mid-to-late sixties, and ran the park with an eye to the best public relations possible. I couldn't blame him. His duties as a superintendent called for vigilance about all aspects of park management. He set local park policy based on Department of the Interior, National Park Service, and regional guidance, and interpreted enough regional and national policy to make your head spin. But he loved the place, and he could be like a cranky dog clenching a bone when it came to his desire for the park to run smoothly and efficiently—zero snags. He was a stickler for clean restrooms, efficient entrance-station operations, and friendly staff. He expected his rangers to personally greet visitors. Plus he hated anything sensational or dramatic that might scare tourists because Ford liked numbers, and each year he became obsessed with achieving a higher visitation record then the previous.

"Smith filled me in," he said as he emerged from his Tahoe, which featured many of the same markings as my field Explorer, including the thick green stripe and dark brown NPS arrowhead emblem. "Said you'd be out here checking the accident victim's vehicle."

"Yeah, poor guy," I said. "Bad deal."

Ford's face was stern as usual. He leveled his gaze on me. "You wrapping this up today?"

"Probably need tomorrow too," I said. "Just to get everything recorded and investigated properly."

"What do you think happened?" Ford asked. "What's your impression?"

"Not sure." I wondered if he was testing me somehow. I knew he'd not been particularly pleased with me the past year since I told him I wanted back into the field. I had been helping him with the park inholdings and mining claims in the controversial Ceded Strip, a large swath of land that makes up the majority of the eastern half of Glacier Park that was originally part of the Blackfeet Reservation that was ceded to the federal government. The Blackfeet tribal leaders claimed they never agreed to sell the lands outright and only leased the strip for a fifty-year mining agreement that expired in 1940. I was in charge of researching and documenting to support the case that Glacier needed to stay 100 percent federally protected ad infinitum.

Ford had also relied on me to get a lot of his other busywork done that the assistant super didn't have time for because he was busy trying to secure funding for park projects. As I told him then, it was highly unusual for a fully trained law enforcement officer to be acting as his right-hand man anyway. I just got roped into it because I was good at research, and I was meticulous.

When I moved back into the field, he'd made several snide remarks to me before I left for Georgia for my courses: "Headin' on to bigger stuff, Harris?" "On from Boy to Eagle Scouting?" Since I'm on the clean-cut and fastidious side, it wasn't the first time I'd been compared to some kind of a scout. Although actually, I've never even been in scouts: not Cub, Boy, and certainly not Eagle.

And I guess with being slight, some people like to compare me to an adolescent. Aside from the premature sprinkling of gray around my temples, I have to admit that if I put on an oversized coat, I can look almost boyish. But I'm no weakling. I may be wiry, but my muscles are corded, sinewy, and strong. And I know I'm fast because I time myself frequently. Last I checked—four days before—I ran a mile in five minutes and twenty-eight seconds. I don't train for anything in particular; I just like to stay fit, especially in my line of work. "Not sure I trust first impressions, sir," I answered.

"I don't mean for you to. Just, you know, trying to get my head around it being Paul Sedgewick." Ford would not be one to use a nickname, even though I knew he was aware of the Wolfie nickname.

"I know. That's the odd thing considering his experience. Trying to figure it out. Was it really an accidental slip, a suicide, or a push?" I asked rhetorically.

"Push?" Ford jerked his chin in and cringed as if he smelled something foul. "Come on, Harris, just because you took a few courses on this stuff, I wouldn't get too ahead of yourself."

"Well, sir, you're right." I ignored his condescending tone. "There is no evidence suggesting foul play, but even though the ankles are badly broken, the lacerations seem more prominent in his head as if he hit there first. Now, does that mean he was pushed? Not sure," I answered my own question. "He could have hit leg first, then tumbled to his head for the second hit after sliding off the first ledge."

Ford listened intently, his eyes squinting in perpetual criticism. "I would highly doubt this is anything but an accident. I mean, the guy was probably tipsy or high on something and misjudged the ledge. It happens, even to backcountry experts."

"We'll know more from the autopsy report," I said.

He looked at the Subaru beside us. "This it?"

"Yeah, just checking it over."

"All right, well, listen, let's get this processed quickly. We need to get the Loop Trail open as soon as possible. I'd like to see it reopened by tomorrow morning."

"I can't do that, sir. Maybe by late afternoon."

Ford looked across the lot in the direction of my Explorer. "Like I said"—he looked back at me—"as quickly as possible. The chalet's one of the main attractions for hikers in this part of the park. It's not good business in the heart of tourist season to have such a high-volume place closed to the public. Tomorrow's Friday, which is bad enough, but I'll give you that. But I want it open by Saturday. The weekend after solstice is usually a big one."

"I understand, sir." I was beginning to feel the pressure that Systead had experienced when dealing with Ford on the Bear Bait case, only he had a personal vendetta against Ford. I got along just fine with the guy even though he had a knack for making the entire area around him hum with a watchful disapproval. Right or wrong, I understood it's the way he operated, and only the insecure let it get to them. "I'll do my best," I offered.

"Good enough." He tipped his wide-brimmed hat and sauntered off.

I turned back to the Subaru and finished searching it and found nothing of interest. Besides the Subaru manual, the glove box held

ChapStick, a tire pressure gauge, a Farmers insurance card, and topographical maps of Glacier, the Bob Marshall Wilderness, Waterton Park, the Whitefish Range, and more. Tucked into the visor was a coffee punch card for a local coffee business with kiosks in all the towns located in the Flathead Valley: Whitefish, Kalispell, Columbia Falls, and Bigfork.

The back of the wagon held a faded beige heavy-duty, but lightweight backcountry pack filled with extra clothes: some polypropylene long johns, a light raincoat, a pair of khaki shorts, and a T-shirt that read: *No, I don't want to read your blog!* A faded-green down sleeping bag was attached by straps on the top of the pack and at its base hung a small, two-man tent in a navy bag. The pack's front pocket held freeze-dried stew, oatmeal energy bars, trail mix, and some apples. A CamelBak designed to be worn on the chest was filled with water and ready to go.

I grabbed the pack and camping gear, the box, and the blue binder and placed them in my car. The vehicle and all its belongings would eventually be going back to Cathy, but for now, I wanted to take a look. I certainly knew I had the time once I returned to my place.

· · ·

When I first split with Lara over nine months ago, I temporarily moved into dorm 213 near the Community Building not far from Glacier's headquarters until she and I could figure out what the hell we were doing. Let's just say the two of us had gotten to the point where we needed some space. She had been angry with the world. And me? I'll admit I'd gotten a little stubborn, a little bullheaded.

Lara and I met when I lived in a small town named Choteau that sat close to the eastern front of the Great Divide. I was fresh out of college with a double major in criminology and psychology from Montana State University in Bozeman—the psych part of the equation an attempt to make sense of my upbringing through textbooks. I wanted nothing to do with counseling as a profession, though, and while I found much of the information useful and interesting, I certainly had no intention of wallowing in any of it.

Wardening, on the other hand, seemed like a good fit for a guy with a criminology degree, a love of the outdoors, and a hunger to instill order, so I enrolled with the Montana Fish, Wildlife and Parks warden program. I passed all the entrance exams, physicals, and psychological evaluations and promptly attended the twelve-week basic course at the Montana Law Enforcement Academy in Helena. After graduating, I did some on-the-job training in a Fish, Wildlife and Parks regional office in Great Falls and was later assigned to Region Four in Teton County.

I rented a small house in Choteau that had wall-to-wall brown carpeting, pale yellow walls, and smelled like cat piss because it was all I could find available. I furnished it with a lumpy futon on its last leg, a small entertainment center and queen-size bed I brought with me from my apartment in Bozeman to Great Falls and on to Choteau. I then quickly got to work patrolling the districts, looking for poachers, checking hunters' licenses, and, in general, trying to protect some of the most diverse flora and fauna in Montana.

I first saw Lara one glorious autumn afternoon when I'd been making a routine visit to check the licenses of the out-of-state visitors staying at a pheasant-hunting spread huddled against the dramatic eastern front. It was called the Painted Horse Ranch, and Lara had just graduated with an accounting degree from Carroll College in Helena and had moved to Choteau to do the books for it. When I walked up, she was sitting outside at a picnic table eating a sandwich and reading a magazine. She looked peaceful and radiant at the same time, her auburn locks blowing gently in the breeze. The Rocky Mountain Front towered behind her, the Teton River babbled in the background, and golden aspens glowed, their leaves quivering. When she glanced up at me, she gave me a friendly smile and a small wave and asked me if I wanted her help in finding the owners.

We didn't actually have all that much in common. She liked the outdoors, but wasn't crazy about it like me. But we were chemically attracted from the get-go. A numbers person, she was logical and reasonable, but she could be spontaneous and bubbly too. She surprised me on one of our early dates—a picnic by the Teton River—when she stripped off her clothes and went skinny-dipping. And she talked about her large family of eleven with great respect and love. That alone intrigued me—that so many siblings in the same household remained caring and warm in spite of everyone's individual complexities. We were married two and a half years later. I was twenty-six. She was twenty-five.

When we tied the knot, Lara knew I didn't want to have children and that was fine for the first seven years until it just wasn't fine anymore. Call it instinct, call it hormones, or even call it the seven-year itch—either way, she changed her mind. Just like that. I don't want to sound coldhearted; I agonized over it because I love Lara, and it's not like I don't understand the drive to bear children that can grip a woman as her life priorities change. But I have my reasons for not capitulating. When paranoid schizophrenia runs on one side of your family, I figure not having children is the responsible thing to do since it tends to be a genetic problem.

In addition to being somewhat bullheaded, I'm a good risk manager ninety-nine percent of the time. But there's that one percent when I'm too driven, too intense, to not take a few chances. Apparently even I can't escape my DNA, which consists of large doses of impulsive behavior, especially on my father's and brother's side. So, around nine thirty, when my lonely evening began to linger a little too long, the cabin's steady hum of solitude began to get a little too persistent, and thoughts of Lara kept pushing their way in, I welcomed the buzz of my phone. The biologist Kurtis Bowman called to tell me where the wildlife camera near the Loop was located. I tried to tell myself it could wait until morning, that I was tired and needed a good night's sleep, and it certainly didn't make sense to take the drive up to the Loop at such a late hour.

But dead bodies stay with you, clinging like leeches to all attempts at normalcy, and I kept seeing Wolfie's mangled features and purple skin. I got up and went over some of my notes from the day, but Ford saying that he wanted the trail reopened quickly made me antsy. Thoroughness requires time and if I left the task until morning, I might not have enough to get everything I needed done.

Eventually I couldn't resist throwing on my uniform gear belt, which I'd begun wearing since I'd been back in the field, but usually didn't wear when investigating in public outside the park. It contained my sidearm, handcuffs, Counter Assault spray for bears, pepper spray for humans (which is smaller with a different concentration), a Taser, and my impact weapon (an expandable baton), all concealed in small, nifty leather compartments with fold-over pocket flaps. I threw on a light windbreaker, grabbed my keys, and took the forty-five-minute drive up to the Loop in the ten-thirty twilight as remaining crimson embers clung to the peaks above. I wanted to get my hands on that memory card.

I reached the Loop around quarter after eleven. The parking area was mostly deserted since we had cordoned it off earlier and because traffic decreased dramatically at night. Five parked vehicles stood empty and ghostly in the dark. They most likely belonged to tourists leaving them locked while they hiked to either backcountry campgrounds near Granite Park Chalet or to the other side of the Divide to the Many Glacier area. I parked close to the Loop trailhead where Joe and I had walked earlier, killed the engine, locked my car, and grabbed my flashlight.

The night air was cool on my skin and I could hear the flowing water from McDonald Creek, but other than that, a quiet solitude permeated the area. I shone my light ahead of me and walked onto the well-maintained trail, careful not to stumble on protruding rocks, exposed tree roots, or loose shale. The sound of my scuffling boots was amplified by the still night air.

The summits of Heavens Peak and the others at the top of Logan

Pass shimmered like jagged fangs in the pale silver moonlight casting across the tips. The light from the three-quarter moon illuminated part of the cloudless sky dotted with glittering stars though it hadn't come fully into view above the tall peaks. In another hour, it would be a little brighter. But now, if I turned my light off, the trail would be pitch-dark.

Carefully, I made my way around the bend, over the footbridge, around the seep, and finally past the launch site Joe and I had examined earlier. Bowman had said to go about thirty yards past the footbridge and up around the bend to the right. The camera was mounted six or seven feet above the ground on the trunk of a tall lodge pole pine, so it would have a broader view of the landscape it was pointed toward. He said the tree would be obvious because it was the last pine on the boundary of the burn line from the Trapper Fire near a cluster of aspen trees and the only pine near them.

I stopped when I thought I'd reached thirty yards and illuminated each tree. The burned trunks left standing like spears stood high and eerie in the dark. Despite his claim that the tree would be obvious, it took me a good ten minutes checking out each pine tree in the area. Thank goodness they were all on the side of the trail away from the abrupt ledge, but the slope was still relatively steep and it was no easy task navigating the thick summer regrowth brush and the burnt, fallen logs that crisscrossed like hard bones.

Finally, my light caught a glint of metal or glass among a copse of aspen trees I had already passed. I backtracked to the lone pine. I was almost there when I heard scuffling sounds to my right that made me stop dead in my tracks. I shined the light in that direction but saw no glowing eyes. I lifted the flap over my bear spray and took it out to be safe, but all went quiet again. I briefly thought of my one-time partner, Ted Systead, whose father had been killed by a grizzly in Glacier in the eighties, then shook it off, knowing how rare such incidents were and how the forest was alive with all sorts of small furry sorts: chipmunks, skunks, weasels, ground squirrels, marmots, pine martins, lynx . . .

I certainly hoped it wasn't a mountain lion or a grizzly. There are very few creatures that aren't afraid of grizzlies, the wolverine being one of them. Even though my coworkers and I were well aware of the fact that grizzlies wanted nothing to do with us unless they needed to protect their young, it would be foolish not to fess up to the real and primordial fear one feels when traipsing through grizzly country.

Glacier has about 350 of the great bears, more than one for every five or six square miles, but it was important to consider that whatever it was—even if a bear—it was equally, if not more, afraid of me—some strange and unwanted guest trekking through its home in the peaceful, spectacular night.

I started walking toward the tree again with my light in one hand, my spray in the other, thankful the camera was within reach and required no climbing up its narrow trunk. I set the spray back in its holder, held the flashlight up with my left hand, and reached for the camera with my right. It was a motion-detection camera, a rectangular-shaped unit a little bigger than the size of a postcard mounted on a slightly larger piece of wood, which was strapped to the trunk of the pine. It had a latch that swung open to the inside of the unit where the batteries and memory card were housed. It took me some time to find the small mechanism that popped open the small latch and while I fiddled with it, I heard more of the same scuffling sounds to my right up the ridge. My pulse skyrocketed until I realized they were coming from farther away.

I found the latch on the lower right corner, slid the switch, and held the flashlight under my armpit. I used both hands to open the mechanism containing the small digital video card, but when I couldn't see it, I grabbed the flashlight again and looked more closely.

The card was gone.

6

I woke with the sun at 5:40 and waited an hour to call Joe. I needed to tell him that the video was already gone and that I planned to make another evidence-gathering trip down into the ravine to see if I could find where it may have been flung, assuming Wolfie had already grabbed the memory card from the camera before his fatal fall.

Joe said it was fine and to take Ken along again. Then I texted Bowman with the same information. I went to make coffee and realized I didn't have enough to make a strong, full-size cup, so I had a bowl of Cheerios and pulled out my notes from the day before. I spread them on the card table in the small oak-paneled kitchenette. While investigating, I had scratched the essentials in a pocket-size notebook that I could access quickly. The morning hours gave me the opportunity to write my notes and descriptions in a spiral-bound notebook.

For no particular reason, several notes stood out to me:

No real signs of foul play or struggle // Face lacerated and skull fractured—Was this consistent with a fall head first or had the body hit leg first—femurs severely fractured as well // binoculars? // Wildlife Memory Card? // ripped shorts and pockets from the rock while falling // Lip and concaved ground near launch area.

I also made a list of the things I needed to do: check Wolfie's credit cards, phone records, and get ahold of the surveillance tapes posted at the entrance gate in West Glacier, one of the few entrances that actually have surveillance cameras.

I called Ken and told him I required his help again anchoring and assisting the lines while I went back into the ravine and met him at headquarters with two cups of coffee that I'd fetched at the Glacier Café facing the entrance to West Glacier before the west entry to the park.

"Thank you very much." Ken gave me a wide grin and grabbed the to-go cup. I could tell he'd gotten over whatever shock and queasiness he was fighting yesterday because his energy was ramped up and he'd returned to his usual talkative self. "Good deal that we have another cloudless, dry day to tackle this," he added.

"Definitely a good deal," I said. "Might want to use your sunscreen."

"Nah, man, I like the mountain sun. Plus we get so little the rest of the year." Ken looked at the tan he'd accumulated on one thickly muscled arm and clicked his tongue with pride.

I wasn't about to give a lecture on high-elevation sun and the dangers of skin cancer if he didn't get that by now. "Mighty nice of you to bring this," he added, lifting the cup in a cheers gesture and took a sip.

I nodded *you're welcome* and we headed into headquarters to the equipment room and grabbed all the rappelling gear and the camera we'd used the previous day.

.   .   .

Ken sat big and burly in the passenger seat, the top of his head nearly brushing the roof of the SUV. I kept my attention on the curving narrow road while he asked me questions as we headed back up to the Loop.

"So you think he'd already grabbed the memory card, then fell?"

"Yeah, that's what makes most sense. I've got a call in to Bowman to double check that none of the other biologists have been up there in the last few days to fetch it and he just hadn't heard."

"What are the chances of finding it?"

"Something this small"—I held up the tip of my thumb—"very,

very, very—did I say *very* low, but that doesn't mean I'm not going to try. Wondering if he had binoculars too, but not counting on it." I thought of the ol' axiom repeated in my courses, *one takes the victim as one finds him*. In other words, don't try to imagine stuff that isn't there.

We drove the rest of the way with Ken telling me about the two fall incidents he'd worked since he'd joined our ranks three years ago. One on the east side of the park near Apikuni Mountain where a man fell eighty-five feet and had died, and the other near Allen Mountain where a man had survived a forty-foot fall. He gave me a blow-by-blow detail of the rescue, how the family members handled it and how they considered him a hero.

"Perfect," I said to him and meant it. It was always great to hear a survival story, and I wished we could have done the same for Wolfie. Of course, I already knew every detail about the rescue because I'd helped him complete and file most of the paperwork when it happened.

I found a parking space in the lot near the Loop, which now re-opened for tourists to stop, but the trail was still roped off to the public. We set the rappelling gear up on the opposite side of the ravine near the launch site this time, careful not to interfere with the taped area.

"How long are we keeping the trail closed?" Ken asked.

"If we don't find the card showing anything interesting or find any other reason to assume this was anything but an accident, we'll remove the caution tape and the trailhead ropes by tomorrow morning. Of course, we want to hear what the coroner ME has to say." I felt a small pit in my stomach at the thought of reopening the trail and going back to business as usual because although I had no specific reason yet to believe this was anything but an accident—other than that the victim was an experienced mountaineer—there was still something that felt entirely wrong about the whole thing. When we were done rappelling, I planned to check the victim's credit cards, cell records, and the lot. "We already have enough photos of these sites from yesterday," I added.

I stepped into the leg loops of my harness, threaded the waist belt through the buckle, and doubled the line back. I put my helmet and gloves on and rechecked the anchor and its webbing. Finally, I clipped my carabiners to the belay loop of my harness, screwed the gates to lock them, and leaned back against the rope in my dominant hand near my hip. I slowly backed over the edge and made my way down with the rope sliding smoothly through the belay device, while Ken stayed above to man the lines.

This side of the ravine felt a little trickier to navigate with rock crumbling at my every landing. When I made it near the first slanted outcropping where I figured the victim had hit, I used my brake hand to slow my speed. When I was almost halfway down the cliff, I slid the latch on the belay device for it to cease feeding rope and made very careful, small side steps as close as I could to the area without straining my ropes. I paused to look around.

Small shrubs stuck straight out from the cliff rocks and I inspected them for any sign of the camera card or any additional evidence. I didn't see anything other than slide marks, disturbed rock, and some blood verifying that the victim had hit the spot first. I had the camera on a strap around my neck making it easy to snap photos.

When I had enough pictures, I opened the belay and continued down. When my feet touched down to solid ground near the spot Ken and I had already climbed to from below, I released my harness from the ropes and began searching that area again. I looked in every bit of brush, around and under large rocks, in the large slope of scree. . . . It was like looking for a needle in a haystack.

There were no binoculars and I certainly couldn't find the miniscule digital camera disk. I searched for another half an hour as the sun began to heat the area. Sweat gathered on my chest and I took a drink of water, then climbed back up to the ropes and clipped them back to my harness and radioed up to Ken that I was ready to go back up.

• • •

When we reached the parking lot and loaded up the Explorer, I noticed a man about my height but a little stockier coming our way. As he got closer, I recognized him. It was Sam Ward whom I'd also met a time or two because he worked not far from headquarters in an RMRS extension office in Glacier Park. He had assisted Wolfie on the Wolverine project.

"Sam." I reached out to shake his hand.

"Monty, Ken," he said as a greeting. "Cathy called me last night. I promised her I'd drive up and check things out this morning. Plus . . ." He paused like he needed a second to take a breath and keep his composure. His eyes were red and his unshaven, rugged face had a look of anguish.

"I'm really sorry, Sam."

He looked at his trail runners and ground a loose pebble into the pavement with the point of one of them. "It's, it's—I don't know, it just doesn't seem real." He looked up at me, his eyes searching my face for some explanation. "Just doesn't seem possible."

"I know, I know. We're trying to make sense of it all."

He peered over to the Granite Park Chalet trailhead. "I see it's cordoned off."

"Has to be until we finish checking things out."

"But he's been lifted out of there, right? Cathy said he was . . ."

"Oh yeah, absolutely. We did that yesterday. Keeping the trail closed is just a temporary thing for now. You know, for us to thoroughly investigate the scene."

"But, but what the hell happened?" He looked at Ken and me, his eyes going back and forth between us.

"He fell, Sam. Off that ridge over there." Ken pointed to the area. "It happens. You know that."

"But here—" He held out his hand, palm up. "By the Loop for God's sake. In mild weather?"

"Perhaps that's when we're the most confident," I said. "When we're the least careful."

He lowered his brow sharply as if he wasn't buying it. "I don't know, Monty. Something just doesn't seem right with this."

"I promise, Sam. We're doing all we can to thoroughly investigate this incident."

He looked down at his shoe again, then reached in his pocket and held out his palm. In it was a small memory card and my hopes rose suddenly that he'd grabbed it. "You have the wildlife camera card?"

"Yeah, the replacement," he said.

"Not the one that's been in it since the end of May?" The biologists like to keep the cameras on the video setting. Depending on how often a moving object triggers the video, the memory card can run down in weeks.

"No, I spoke to Wolfie the day before he was leaving. He was going to grab the footage, but he said he was out of replacement cards and I told him not to worry about it because I had a package of them in the office and wanted to drive up here anyway. The plan had been for him to take the old memory card the other night so that I could replace it today. That's what I was going to say earlier, that I promised Cathy I'd look around and that I also needed to replace the card. I just didn't realize that you'd have it roped off, but it makes sense."

"So, that . . ." I lifted my chin to point at Sam's open palm, the small card still lying in the center like a dead bug. "It's just blank."

"Yeah, it's just blank. And I promised . . ." His face suddenly grew even more sad and drooping. "Wolfie was my friend and my research teammate. I know he would want me to get this in that camera if there were wolverines around to capture. Kurtis told me you said he'd already gotten the card, so the camera is empty now. Wolfie said he was getting signals up here. Can I cross the rope and go in and replace it? For him?" his eyes pleaded.

"I understand, but I can't let anyone cross right now. You can give it to me and I'll go back and put it in or you can wait until tomorrow. We should have the trail reopened by tomorrow."

"Okay," he said. "Yeah, I'll come back tomorrow. It's the least I can do."

"And, Sam—" I went and opened the driver's side door of the Explorer and grabbed my notepad. "You mind if I get your number?"

He gave it to me and I jotted it down. "You said you spoke to Wolfie the day before he was planning to come up here?"

"That's right. In the evening. We met for a beer."

"He seem normal to you?"

"Completely," Sam said.

"Not down or depressed or burdened by any particular worries?"

Sam chuckled. "Wolfie? God no. Other than the fact that he hadn't seen a wolverine in the wild for a while, he was his usual self."

"It seriously bugged him when he hadn't seen one live in a while?"

"No, no, nothing like that. I was just using that as an example of how normal he was with his one-track mind to locate them. Not just him, our whole team feels that way." He shrugged. "I know we all sound nuts, but every day in wolverine world is like a powerful drug. It's an addiction. I don't expect anyone other than those of us who do the research to understand."

But I did understand. I had caught the power of the truth-seeking drug myself. Amid the sad and burdensome world of death and destruction, the quest for what really happened, for the big *T* can consume you. I felt it creeping up on me when Cathy was asking me for answers, and I had felt it full force on Bear Bait. I could imagine the quest to understand the fierce and relentless wolverine was just as catching—that amid the world of dwindling glaciers and increased rate of climate change was a potent urgency to unravel some of the secrets of one of the most mysterious species in the contiguous states and what it requires to survive.

"I mean," Sam continued, "he was telling jokes and was excited to see if the cameras had caught any footage. Told me all about how Jeff's baseball season was going—that they'd just had a tournament in Sandpoint. He was so proud of Jeff." Pain filled his eyes at the thought of the boy. "It's just—" He shook his head. "It's just so unreal." He swallowed hard and I could see his Adam's apple jerk up, then down. "So unfair. So incredibly unfair."

I looked around, but didn't say anything. He was right, there was nothing fair out here at all in these mountains. But there was nothing *unfair* in them either. Glacier Park spans about sixty miles along the Montana Rockies and every inch of its jutting contours and colorful rock layers hollers stories of a landscape that is billions of years old. The mountains towered above us daily, and you either survived them or you didn't. Wolfie would have known that better than anyone.

7

KEN AND I drove back down to headquarters, my third trip down
this curving narrow roadway that I knew by heart. This time of the
year, the line of cars moves slowly with tourists taking it all in. Plus
there's no cell service in this part of the park, a blessing for visitors—a
chance to wean themselves from the rat race. For us, we had the use
of the radios, but it was easier to work from a phone at headquarters.
I was slightly frustrated but ready to get to the busywork of checking
Wolfie's credit cards, phone records, and to get ahold of the surveillance tapes posted at the entrance gate in West Glacier.

I thought of the adage that if a murder has been committed, it
must be solved within the first forty-eight after it's occurred or forget
it. What they reminded me in DC was that forty-eight hours within the
commission of the crime is not exactly true. It's partially true, but not
completely true. It's more a question of people forgetting how things
went down past two days' time, in *any* situation, not just crime.

In this case, I had no witnesses that I knew of anyway. Joe and I
had asked the media to press for anyone witnessing the fall or anything
strange around the Loop the previous day to come forward with information regarding the incident. But more frustrating to me was not
knowing if we were even dealing with a crime. My instincts whispered
to me that we were, but so far the lack of evidence suggesting foul play
said we weren't.

I had already placed a few calls in the morning over coffee and
had some faxes waiting for me in the incident room Systead and I had

51

used in the last case. A government pea-green counter traversed one wall of the room with a printer and fax machine smelling of toner and paper dust on one side and an old coffeepot next to the sink on the opposite. A long conference table with metal chairs hogged the center of the room and a gunmetal file cabinet hid in the corner with a wilting ficus on top. I smelled a slight antiseptic tang mixed with the familiar old and dusty scents of the building.

We'd moved the printer/fax machine into the room at that time and everyone got used to using it where the sink and coffeemaker was, so we kept it there. I felt strange but energized at the same time to be utilizing the room again for something other than a staff meeting. "I'll need you to check the phone records while I hit the credit card statements," I said to Ken.

"Gotcha," he said. "What exactly am I looking for?"

I leaned my hip against the counter and thought about that for a minute. I turned my head and set my gaze out the window at a plump robin picking at worms in the lush lawn and wondered whether I had the right guy helping me, then decided I was being unfair. Ken's day did not usually involve investigative work. It normally consisted of ticketing speeding tourists, responding to petty thefts at a campsite, attending to disorderly conduct reports, keeping people out of dangerous situations, helping someone get into their rental cars after accidentally locking the keys inside. . . . In fact, that's what *my* day consisted of now that I was out in the field more.

"Just look for numbers that are out of the ordinary," I said. "If they're not his wife's or kids', see who they belong to."

"Okay if I grab something to eat first?" Ken looked at me wide-eyed, his hand on his stomach. "I'm starved."

"Sure." I smiled. "Grab a bite, but if I'm not here when you return, after I finish with the statements, I've gone to talk to Dr. Pritchard, Wolfie's research vet."

• • •

There was zero pointing to anything remiss in the Sedgewick family statements. They were good, responsible people who paid their bills on time with the exception of a late payment to an Old Navy credit card that Cathy paid soon after the first notice of delinquency had arrived. Jeffrey's baseball club and Abbey's dance studio fees were put on the Visa card. Gasoline purchases were as well and once in a while, groceries. There were some car maintenance fees: thirty-dollar oil changes and $575 to a Subaru dealership repair shop.

When I didn't find anything interesting on the statements, I placed a call to Cathy and asked if she could come to headquarters later for a few more questions. I figured a less personal environment might be conducive for her to talk. Then I called Dr. Pritchard, whose practice was halfway between Columbia Falls and Whitefish on Highway 40. It was coming up on his lunch hour, so we arranged to meet at a local pub in downtown Whitefish. It was a popular place to go because they had great sandwiches and a wide selection of microbrews on tap.

I found parking on the main drag going through the town, which was tough to do in the summer with all the tourists visiting. I could remember a time in the nineties when you'd rarely find more than ten cars downtown on any given weekday, even in the heart of summer or ski season. Now, people from all over the United States and especially Canada swarmed the place. Many had second homes in the area and others were just visiting the mountains and all the Flathead Valley had to offer in the summer: boating, golfing, mountain biking, fishing, rafting. . . . I stepped out of the car and walked the busy sidewalk until I reached the bar.

Whitefish was prospering, but it was conflicted about its growth, trying not to seem too contrived and Aspen-like with the influx of wealth, and at the same time, trying to keep from bulging into a basic, midsize sprawl with typical billboards and chain stores that would destroy the very quaintness that lured tourists in the first place. Right now, it was chaos, with roads under construction and the building of banks, office buildings, and new restaurants on several of its corners.

I looked up and saw the ski hill. Barely even ten minutes and you could be up in the Whitefish Range enjoying the wilderness. I felt an intimate connection to the wilderness surrounding me and thought of how lucky I was to have my job in the park, in spite of the recent tragedy.

After Lara and I remarried, she no longer wanted to live in Choteau and wanted to return closer to her family, west of the Divide. She had grown up in Hamilton, a town south of Missoula in the Bitterroot Valley, so she began applying for accounting jobs around northwest Montana. Eventually, she was offered a full-time position for the hospital in Kalispell in the Flathead Valley, not too far from my hometown of Columbia Falls.

I put in for a transfer to Region One, which included the Flathead Valley and encompassed Kalispell, Whitefish, Bigfork, and Columbia Falls. I didn't really care for returning specifically to my hometown, but Lara wanted to accept the position in Kalispell, and I wanted to make her happy. And I had to admit: I did love the Flathead Valley.

Then I heard the park was expanding its force, taking new hires and immediately, the Park Police position beckoned me. The salary was about the same as the warden job—nothing to brag about—but one could do a lot worse than having an office in Glacier National Park.

My best and most memorable days were spent hiking and climbing in Glacier with the group I joined in high school. The sheer geological scale of the continent's crown jewel brought humbling perspectives and made my adolescent worries seem trivial. Its beauty basically stunned me, and I knew I could easily make Glacier my place of work. I applied, did the extra training, and was a shoo-in with my wardening background.

Now, looking at the Whitefish Range, where I'd also spent ample time as a teen with my climbing group, the sun spread a soothing warmth across my face and I almost took an extra few seconds just to continue standing there, but then a woman with a stroller came upon me suddenly and I had to step into the shadow of the bar's awning to get out of the way. I opened the door and slid into the darkness. I could smell beer and french fries and garlic from the kitchen—maybe pickles. Most of the tables were already taken and I saw a hand go up out of the corner of my eye and noticed it was Pritchard waving to me from the bar. I shuffled over and shook his hand.

Dr. Pritchard looked like he belonged in a *GQ* magazine: tall with relaxed movements, russet skin, fine features, tousled dark hair, and just the right amount of stubble on his chin and weathering around thoughtful eyes. Rumor had it that plenty of women not really all that interested in keeping a pet got one anyway just to have the chance to go in for an appointment to witness his ridiculous good looks and soothing manner first hand.

"Tables were all taken," he said. "Hope you don't mind the bar."

"Fine by me," I said and took a seat.

"The pastrami is really good here," he offered. "I already ordered. If I don't get back to the clinic on time, I get really behind."

"I appreciate you meeting me. I know you're busy."

"You caught me on a good day. Usually, I don't get a chance like this to break away. There's always some emergency, but luckily, my partner's in today."

The bartender asked me what I'd like and I ordered an iced tea and took Pritchard's recommendation and ordered the pastrami. Pritchard introduced the bartender, calling him Will. He was about my height, maybe a little taller, with a full head of dark, Brillo-like hair.

"So." Pritchard looked at me when Will walked away, a sadness filling his eyes. "I just can't believe it."

"I know. It's really strange and sad. I'm sorry for the loss. I know you worked with Wolfie quite a bit."

He nodded. "Thanks. Not as much as Sam did, but yeah." He smiled faintly. "We spent some wild and good times in the park tracking those hardy little creatures."

"When was the last time you saw him?"

He thought for a moment, his face pensive, his eyes heavy-lidded. "A few weeks ago. But he left me a message the other evening on my phone. Said he and Ward were meeting for a beer—actually here—and wanted to know if I wanted to join them. I couldn't, though. I was in surgery late that day."

"You call him back?"

"Yeah, left a message later that night on my way home from the clinic thanking him and hoping to catch him another time."

"And which evening was that?"

"That would have been on Tuesday."

"And a few weeks ago?"

"I went with him to a trap he'd set up the South Fork. A wolverine had taken the bait and he needed me to implant a transmitter."

"The South Fork? Outside the park?"

"Yeah." Pritchard sat back and let his shoulders sink into the back of the barstool. "It's a long story, and you probably already know about it, but lately the park's been less, shall we say, enthusiastic about wolverine research."

I actually didn't know that. "Less enthusiastic?"

"Yeah, Bowman's sick about it, but apparently he's been getting orders from Rick Phrimmer to start phasing out the project. I guess they're getting flak from Washington—that it's costing too much and it's getting harder and harder to get available grant funds."

I sat listening. Phrimmer was Glacier Park's assistant superintendent. He worked with Ford doing mainly administrative duties to support park management and secure new funding for park projects. I didn't know the wolverine studies were lacking funding, but none of what he said was surprising. I'd done enough work for Ford involving DC's politics. And all park employees knew that when Glacier was established in 1910, it housed about a hundred fifty glaciers. Now, our warming climate had reduced the number to twenty-five and they were shrinking about four times faster than they were just fifty years before. The last one is expected to disappear in less than a few decades. And as far as I was concerned, that wasn't something to shrug about. Glaciers cooled air masses and without them, we had an earlier onset of spring and higher soil temperatures on the slopes. Its run-off fed streams important to just about the entire ecosystem.

"I didn't know. I thought they were going strong," Pritchard added. "Could be anything from the fact that Phrimmer has always had a thing against Wolfie to something larger, like the fact that the wolverine is an indicator species and like the polar bear, wolverines—at least to those talking about it—have kind of become a poster child for climate change issues. You know, with their survival so closely tied to the state of snowfields and cooler temperatures."

I knew that the wolverines relied on carrion preserved and refrigerated in the ice until it melted in the spring. Then they feasted on it through spring and early summer. Will brought my iced tea and I took a sip.

"So Wolfie figured if he was eventually going to get shut out of the park, he'd better start setting box traps elsewhere. I believe he'd gotten permission from the station to set them into the Hungry Horse and Bob Marshall Wilderness regions. So far, with Sam's help, they've put them along a twenty-five-mile range along the South Fork."

"So wow, Wolfie was really increasing his research efforts," I said. "At least while he was still working the park."

"Yeah, well, not necessarily for long." Pritchard frowned. "Like I said, Wolfie and I went to one of the traps where he'd gotten a signal that the trap had sprung." He shook his head. "And when we got there to anesthetize the animal and implant the receiver, we found the trap rigged with another steel-jawed trap that was obviously put there to kill the animal. It had gotten a healthy female about two or three years old."

"You know who set it?"

"Local trappers. Wolfie said it wasn't the first time. That it had happened twice before. He was sick about it and said he'd fold the studies before he'd help the local trappers kill more of them."

"Just trying to score extra pelts?"

Pritchard took a sip of his water. "Maybe some of them, but Wolfie thought the whole area was so fired up by some local rumors that our work was just going to be used to throw up state restrictions against trapping or snowmobiling or even mining. You name it. There's a lot of fear around these parts. I'm sure you know with your job. Basically, Wolfie and the rest of us were coming to terms with the idea that once the glacier studies were over, the chances of being able to study an intact population in an undisturbed setting—unhunted, unlogged, unmined—ever again were unlikely."

I nodded. A waitress with short, bobbed hair came over and set Pritchard's sandwich before him and he thanked her.

"Had Wolfie begun removing the South Fork traps?"

Pritchard nodded. "He had, but I'm not sure how many are left. Ward might know. Wolfie hated to give in like that, but he couldn't bear basically helping the locals kill them. You have to understand that a lot of the wolverines around the park had come to trust our type of traps. They knew they never got hurt and often got a free meal from us. Without our specially constructed log traps, the trappers didn't stand a very good chance of capturing them. The wolverines were too smart to go into steel jaws after bait unless it was cleverly disguised."

I remembered hearing from Bowman how fierce a wolverine in the mini log-cabin traps could be. Researchers basically had to rig a long pole with the needle attached on the end in order to poke them with the sedative. "What will happen to the studies now?"

Pritchard lifted a shoulder. "I'd like to think we can continue. That Ward will take the reins, but I don't know. I mean, I just help with the implants. The first time they tried to implant the GPS chip into a young wolverine they'd caught, he ended up dying because it was subzero temps and the pup's body temperature dipped too low because they gave a little too much tranquilizer, a mixture of diazepam and midazolam." Pritchard sighed. "Like I said, Wolfie was upset, he swore he'd never do an implant again without the help of an experienced vet. I use ketamine and Domitor. It seems to work well. Anyway, I do what I can," he said humbly. "But I have a family and a practice. Sometimes he has to use Doc Kaufland if I'm not available."

I jotted Kaufland's name down and looked at my notes. "You mentioned Phrimmer earlier? That he had a thing against Wolfie?"

"Oh yeah, that. Well." Pritchard half-smiled. "Small town, right. But, apparently Phrimmer's wife, Kate, you know her?"

"Sure, I've met her several times, here and there, but mostly when she came to headquarters to visit Rick." I thought of the petite redhead, no more than five feet two. Freckled and feisty. I remembered seeing her all dolled up at some holiday party back in December. I went alone. Most coworkers knew Lara and I had split, but she hadn't and she had asked me why she didn't come. She looked sincerely upset that things were in such a state for us.

"Well, then, do you know she used to date Wolfie years ago?"

"I didn't know that," I said.

"Yeah, I mean, who knows?" Pritchard rolled his eyes. "I don't gossip much, but Wolfie said it himself, he was kind of laughing about it, but I don't know, I sensed a seriousness there."

"Laughing about what?"

"That he didn't know if it was DC that really wanted the research to end, or whether Rick was simply sabotaging things, still carrying a grudge after all these years because he used to date Kate before he met Cathy, and apparently Kate always felt like Wolfie was the one that got away. Supposedly drives Phrimmer nuts." Pritchard had barely taken two bites from his sandwich when his phone buzzed. He looked at it and bit his lower lip. "I'm sorry," he said, then excused himself—said that he needed to take it because it was the office.

When he hung up, he apologized but had to get going—his partner was elbow high in some other emergency and the dog he'd operated on in the morning that was doing fine when he'd left was now exhibiting labored breathing. He then asked Will to bring him a to-go box and tried to leave a twenty on the bar. I handed it back, insisting I wanted to pay for lunch. I handed him my card and told him to call me if anything else that might be pertinent to wrapping up the investigation came to mind.

Before he walked off, he tilted his head and squinted at me. "You really believe this was an accident?"

"I can't say just yet."

"Hmm," he said. "Know how many really dangerous slopes we've attempted trying to track those animals? Crampons, ice axes, ropes . . . You name it, just praying the slope would hold. We weren't idiots, but we did tempt fate more than a time or two. It just doesn't make sense."

"I know," I said. "It's like a trucker who's covered millions of miles getting in an accident a block from his own home."

"I guess that's one way to see it." He shook my hand, thanked me for lunch, and left.

. . .

When my pastrami came, I ate it while writing a few more notes until my phone buzzed. I saw it was Lara and hit Decline to ignore the call and shoved it back in my pocket. I didn't want to talk to her at the moment, and I had a pretty good idea why she was calling anyway. We had already had words about it the day before. All her relatives were coming into town for a few days for a reunion at our house on the Flathead River. It was complicated, but she hadn't yet told anyone in her family about our breakup. She said she was embarrassed—that she wasn't ready for her parents to know until we were sure we were going through with the divorce.

Lara and I began thinking about the reunion a year before we even split. We had wanted to have it that summer, but several of her brothers couldn't make it because of other trips they'd planned, so we put it off for the following one, having no idea we'd be separated. Not long after Lara put the emails out about the reunion, she began talking about getting pregnant, and we began to argue all the time.

"I thought you were sure," I had told her the morning before when she began to say she was having second thoughts about going through with a divorce.

"Yes, but, I don't know," she had said. "Maybe I should, I don't know, reconsider."

"Reconsider? Lara, it's been ten months since we split up, and every time we get close to giving it another go, you freak out and say you're not ready and not sure you can. Well, in the meantime, while you've not been ready, have you ever thought that maybe I'd be moving on?"

She had started to cry, at first softly and quietly until she spoke and her voice sounded choked and strained. I've never dealt with weeping females very well.

Early on, I felt that my connection to her and her family was a lifeline to normality. I liked being a part of a network of relatively sane people always smiling and happy, always talking about church and family outings, always seeming to be there for one another and knowing the consistent domestic and religious rituals. When around them, I sensed there was a system that worked, unlike the fragmented home I came from. One knew their place, knew they belonged and were safe.

It seemed like a second chance to have the happy household I'd missed out on. But I was wrong. Very little alters what you've been born into. Her family, which seemed fascinating and comforting at first, eventually began to bug me, began to seem naïve and judgmental, and even righteous. They'd act as if they had no problems and that their religion not only guarded them from all sin, but placed them above the muddy transgressions that plagued other people.

I became ashamed of my upbringing and was reluctant for Lara's family members to meet any of mine. In fact, when we married, Lara and I fought over the fact that I didn't even want my parents or brother to come. To make her happy, though, we invited them. My dad and Adam came, drank way too much, while my mom stayed home. She couldn't make it because she was in the throes of a bad spell. Now, ironically, here Lara was in the system I initially found comfort in— not feeling safe enough to tell them the truth about our separation, which was her idea in the first place.

"Look, look." I was silent for a moment, then she sighed. "Just don't worry about it, Monty, okay? I'll deal with it."

"Deal with what? Have you forgotten that this was *your* idea?"

"Deal with my family, I meant."

"We can talk about your family later. Okay? But you know what I think—that you should tell them. It's crazy not to tell them."

She didn't answer and while I stayed on the phone listening to her silence and the chickadees' long, casual morning whistles outside, I got the call from Joe Smith and told her I needed to get going. We'd been down this road so many times, and I knew nothing was going to get accomplished by lingering on the phone.

I finished eating and waited for Will to swing by to pay the bill. When he brought it over, I said, "Do you work here in the evenings?"

"Sure do, this is my only day shift of the week. I work nights Monday through Thursday."

"You know a couple a' locals named Paul Sedgewick—known as Wolfie—and Sam Ward?"

"I think so—know of them, not personally." He grabbed the bill with my credit card on top. "Is that the guy that . . . ? In Glacier?"

I nodded.

"I heard about that. Crazy." He shook his head. "Just falling like that." The waitress with the dark, bobbed hair working the floor stomped up and handed Will a ticket of drinks to make. He looked at it and wrinkled his nose. "A *slippery nipple*? Now?"

"That's what the lady wants." The waitress smiled.

"She just turn twenty-one or something?"

The waitress splayed both palms up and shrugged. "It's Friday," she said.

"What's happening to the Wild West?" Will rolled his eyes, then ran my credit card and set it and the receipt back down for me to sign.

"Yeah, so you were working the other night when he and Sam stopped in for a beer?"

"I was."

"Notice anything unusual?" I handed him the signed slip.

"Unusual?" he looked confused. His face was flushed and a sheen of sweat shone on the back of his neck and I could tell he worked hard during these busy months.

"Yeah, like was he angry or worried or anything?"

Will shrugged. "Honestly, I couldn't tell ya. I mean, they both seemed normal to me, but I was busy, so it's not like I spend much time people watching. And I didn't really know them. Just seen 'em in here a few times is all." He grabbed a bottle of butterscotch schnapps to start making the slippery nipple, his brow furrowed in concentration. "Monica," he called. "She want Irish cream or Baileys with this?"

I thanked him and left. He had work to do, and so did I.

8

I WAS BACK AT headquarters. Ken had finished checking the phone records and saw nothing unusual there either. Most of the calls were to Cathy, texts to the kids, calls to Sam and Pritchard. Bowman also called and told me what I already knew—that no other biologists aware of the camera stations in the park had picked up the memory card at the Loop site.

I called Dr. Pettiman and rechecked with him as well that there was no disk in the victim's clothes and he said he had not sent the body to Missoula yet, but would in a few hours. Right as I hung up, Brenda, the receptionist at headquarters, knocked on the incident room door to tell me that Wolfie's wife was here to see me. I straightened out my shirt and pants, and tucked the wolverine files away in a cabinet under the counter so she wouldn't have to be pained by seeing her husband's research.

She came in and I was struck by how her face looked so different than the day before—grief having zapped the joy from her eyes. They looked bruised with dark circles and were rimmed in red. Her cheeks looked as if they'd been slapped, but I knew nobody had slapped her; they were just mottled and swollen from crying. I stood up and motioned for her to sit.

"Thank you." She took a seat.

"You're welcome." She sat before me and looked around at the bare walls.

"How are you faring?" I sat across from her and leaned on my elbows.

"As best I can." She pursed her lips and looked at me intensely.

"And the kids?"

She shrugged and tears sprang to her eyes momentarily, then she fiercely swiped the back of her hand across her eyes, working to keep it together.

"So, as I told you on the phone"—I cleared my throat—"I simply would like to ask you a few more questions."

She said nothing, just stared at me and for a moment—other than two lines ironed deeply into creases between her brows—I thought she looked like a sad, but angry, child. She held her lips in a thin, stretched line and they'd gone nearly white.

"Let's start from the beginning if you don't mind." I rechecked the things I'd already asked her: the last time she'd seen him, when he left the house, what his plans were, his mood. When all of that stayed consistent with what she'd told me the evening before, I added, "Do you have any reason at all to think that Paul has been depressed or down about anything lately?"

"See," she said, more anger spilling into her eyes. "That's just it." Cathy stood up and put her hands on my desk. "People are saying he committed suicide or that he was on drugs, but I'm here to tell you that he would never commit suicide and my husband did not do drugs. Let me repeat: he did *not* do drugs."

I held up my hand. "I completely believe you, Cathy. I'm only asking for the sake of the investigation. We need to be thorough and check out all possibilities. But you need to know it's early in the game and when the autopsy is performed, a toxicology screening will occur and the issue of drugs can easily be cleared up."

"Like I said. You won't *find* anything. He did not do drugs." She began pacing by her chair, little short steps back and forth. "Then"— her eyes began to pool with tears, but she swiped them quickly away— "and this whole suicide issue . . ."

I couldn't tell if she was pausing before saying more or asking me a question. "Well," I answered, "that's a little harder to understand, but if there was no reason for a grown man—no depression or other signs pointing in that direction—then it's not like we're just going to assume he went that route."

"Good. Because I can tell you he didn't do that."

"He had no medical history with depression or anything else that you know of?"

"No, nothing."

"No heart disease or something that would have hit him out of the blue?"

"No. None. He had to get a full checkup for our insurance company just three months ago. Everything was good."

"What about the wolverine stuff? I mean, was he upset about the park or what was going on in the South Fork with the trappers?"

"Yeah, of course he was upset about that, but not abnormally. I mean, *hello*, he's a biologist. It goes with the territory." She threw a hand outward as if motioning to the mountains outside us, surrounding us. "He loves those animals, but he's not crazy. He knows what it entails to study any wild species. And he's done it all—fishers, lynx, wolves, grizzlies, pine martins. He's seen plenty of destruction and yeah, it bothered him, but not like what you're suggesting."

"I'm not suggesting anything. I'm just trying to gather the evidence."

"And you better, because look, I don't mean to be out of line here, but, yeah, well, I'm upset." She stopped pacing and faced me, her hands on her hips. "In fact, I'm angry. Paul was a professional and that's how my kids should remember him. I don't want them exposed to all this crazy talk." Again, she threw her hand out and circled it frantically around. "And worse, I was a stay-at-home mom. I had to be because Paul's job took him away a lot. Yeah, I do some meaningless, low-paying part-time work at a used bookstore when they're at school now, but before that, I was home with my kids. It was our plan from the get-go. Paul and I talked about it and we took out a good-size life insurance policy in case something like, like"—she took a deep breath—"well, happened to him while at work. It's not a secret or something to feel guilty about."

"Of course not," I said.

"It's responsible. But I never—" She began to tear up again and suddenly sank back into the chair, the wire frame squeaking. "We never, we never thought anything would really happen." She stared into some foreign space, her eyes pained and momentarily distant. "But the kids and I"—she refocused on me and her gaze held mine intensely—"we need that money. If your investigation claims this is suicide"—she looked at me with real fear—"I don't know what we'll do."

"So far, there is no evidence suggesting he took his own life. We can assume it's much more likely an accident."

"But see, that doesn't seem right either." And suddenly, she burst into a full sob. She cupped her face into her hands, her shoulders hunched and shaking.

I got up quietly, went down the hall and grabbed a box of tissues from the bathroom. When I reentered, she had gained a bit of composure and pulled several tissues from the box.

"I'm sorry, I just . . ." Her shoulders were still shaking.

"Cathy, please, no apologies. I know this is very tough."

"It's just that none of this makes sense. Like I said, Paul was a professional. Do you know how well Paul knew the park? He lived and breathed it. There's no part of it he hasn't trekked, on- and off-trail tracking those animals and others. How could he possibly have just"— she held both palms up, tissues threaded through the fingers of one— "just have slipped?"

"I know," I said. I felt like a broken record. I was repeating the same conversation I had with both Ward and Pritchard. Apparently, anyone who knew Wolfie couldn't make sense of an accidental fall. "We are asking those very same questions. Trust me, all of us here in the park, police, rangers, administrators know what kind of ground these researchers cover. We are taking this very seriously. That's why I wanted to talk to you today. I mean, do you have any reason to think it was deliberate?"

"I just don't know. No, I mean—*no*," she repeated. "Everyone loved my husband. He was just"—another fresh and sharp sob rose in her throat—"a nice guy. I know he didn't commit suicide, but I could never, ever think anyone would want him gone. I'm just very confused and I don't know what to tell the kids." She put her forehead in her hand. "It's so sudden and strange."

"I know it is. The autopsy will help considerably."

"And if it doesn't?"

"We'll cross that bridge when we get to it, but for what it's worth I promise you that I will do everything I can to understand what really happened here. What about alcohol? Could he have been drinking?"

"No. I told you. He was a professional. This is what I'm talking about. People are coming up with crazy ideas like this out of the blue. What? That he stumbled out on that trail to go grab the memory card? I mean, yeah, he liked a beer or two like anybody else, but he never got out-of-control drunk and I highly doubt he stopped for a beer before heading out to the park that evening anyway. I kissed him good-bye from our house around five."

I jotted a few notes and looked back up at her. "And again," I said. "The autopsy should help with that too." I wish I had more to offer her than the hopes of what a doctor may or may not find, and I wished it was already completed. Presuming this was either suicide or an accident, it didn't take the same precedence with the coroner that an actual crime would. "Like I said, I will do all I can to figure this out."

She nodded and glanced down at her soggy tissue.

I felt a hollowness settle in my chest as I stood to walk her out. When we got to the exit and I held the door for her, I said, "Are you okay to drive?"

She nodded.

"Are you sure?"

"Yes." She went to push her hair behind her ear, then stopped and looked at her hand as if it was a foreign appendage. I wondered what she was thinking, that there was no point in straightening her hair under such circumstances, with her love now gone forever. She had probably performed this habitual move millions of times in her life without thinking, and suddenly, in the throes of shock, it seemed foreign to her. I thought of how grief did such strange things to people, and briefly, a shoved-down image of my long-lost friend Nathan Faraway bloomed in my mind. Nathan disappeared on a menacing Halloween evening in my seventh grade year, and no one was ever able to determine whether he died or ran away. His parents were never the same again. Cathy clutched the strap of her purse instead. "You promise?" she whispered and I felt the ache in my chest radiate further out.

"Yes," I said. "I promise."

"I'm holding you to it," she said. "I'm sorry, Monty, but I have to hold you to this one. The kids and I—we're relying on you to get this right."

9

THE WALLS OF the Glacier Café in West Glacier were naturally lined with photographs of the park, mostly mountain goats, grizzlies, and big horn sheep. Country music played in the background—some Toby Keith song, which meant TJ was cooking and I'd order the chili. When his wife and co-owner, Carol, cooked, the stew was best.

"Sit wherever you'd like, Monty," Carol said, gliding past me with numerous plates precariously balanced on a large tray. She had her frizzy, dishwater-blond hair tucked behind her ear.

I found my usual spot in the corner and after I ordered, I took out my notes but couldn't focus. I drank black coffee, fiddled with my spoon, and studied the faces of all the dining tourists. I couldn't help but weigh the comparative joy in each.

Most were well sunned and smiling contentedly from a glorious day in the park. A few looked strained and pale—a middle-aged couple dressed like they'd been in an airport all day, both in khakis. I could tell they'd just arrived, hadn't had time to unwind yet, and they hardly spoke. A day in the park would work wonders; tomorrow their eyes would tell a different story.

Another woman at the table next to the khaki couple, younger—late twenties maybe, bounced a rosy-cheeked baby sucking on a pacifier on her thigh. Her husband looked content as he spread a map on the side of the table, trying to plan their next day of adventure.

I thought back to Nathan Faraway's parents again. I remembered them stricken and pale, Mrs. Faraway clutching Nathan's dad's arm as

70

if she couldn't stand without holding on. The next day was Saturday. I knew we would reopen the trail and it bugged the hell out of me. Cathy's face kept pushing into my mind, and like a junkie with a one-track mind, I wanted to study that ridge where he fell again for any clue that would put this puzzle together for me. Somehow, for no good reason other than the sorrow I felt spreading in my chest and the curiosity climbing higher in my mind, I couldn't shake the feeling that Wolfie's fate was somehow interwoven with mine, and I felt even more deeply compelled to discover the truth of the incident.

I thought about getting my hands on the crash-test dummy from the Kalispell police force. We called it Jed for reasons unknown to me, but we'd used it once before years back to study a fall pattern of a man from Mount Reynolds who was secured to go on trial against a local and corrupt group of money-laundering bank managers. Officials were suspicious about his death, but could never prove he'd been pushed even with the simulations of Jed.

But without the autopsy report and nothing suggesting foul play, I was not going to be able to convince Ford to let me keep the trail closed while I experimented with a borrowed dummy on a heavily visited tourist trail. I could just see him shaking his head about my recent training and how it was costing the government more than it was good for.

I couldn't stand the thought of not taking one more peek, though. I ate my chili, paid the bill, put away my notes, and grabbed my phone and called Ken. When he answered, I said, "You up for an early drive to the Loop in the morning?"

When he agreed, I said, "Good. We've got one more rappelling trip to perform before we open the trail."

. . .

When I pulled up to my wood-planked dorm with government-green trim Lara was waiting in the driveway in her silver-beige Honda. Dapples of evening sun filtered through the trees and created soft swaying patches of light on her car. When she saw me, she stepped out. "I'd have called, but I knew you'd just silence your phone and let it go to voice-mail." She wore capri jeans, a pink T-shirt, and flip-flops. Sunglasses, no longer needed in the fading light, tucked her short, dark wavy hair back and a few short tendrils of soft, babylike strands fell before her ears. I hadn't seen her in several weeks. A part of me was annoyed to see her while another part of me instantly softened, weakening as always when she showed her pretty face.

I walked over, resisted giving her a hug, and waited for her to say more.

"Aren't you even going to say 'hi'?"

"Hi," I said. "I've been busy the past two days."

"Yeah. I read someone fell."

"Joe's having me take care of it all. So"—I flicked my keys and glanced at the green door of my dorm—"why did you come?"

"I wanted to see you. You're still my husband, you know."

"Lara." I sighed. "We've talked about this. It just makes it harder. Either we're ending this or not. But neither one of us can go on like this—*I* can't—in limbo like this." After Lara had insisted I move out because she needed space to think and to be alone since I wouldn't agree to start a family, it was gut-wrenching for both of us, but a huge relief. We'd been fighting over everything, and tension hung in the air, sticky and palpable, with every activity we tried, every conversation we attempted, and each mundane task we did in each other's company. Just going to Home Depot together became a challenge when she'd inevitably comment on the couple in the next aisle with the tod-dlers and how happy they looked. The issue was always in the room with us.

After a few months apart, the tension slowly went away and was less permeating, but the bitterness stayed. I felt betrayed—that she'd changed the landscape of our marriage when she knew how I felt be-fore even getting married and that she'd actually want to move out. I had tried to compromise, suggesting a puppy. Big mistake. Then I even suggested adoption, but she refused, saying that there were no guarantees with the mental health of an adopted baby either, so we might as well just have our own.

And she felt betrayed by me that I simply wouldn't budge—that I must not have loved her enough if I wasn't willing to have a child with her. But the bottom line was that we still cared for each other.

"I know. I know. But our conversation ended so abruptly and I, I don't know." She tilted her head down. "I miss you."

I held up my hand for her to stop. I didn't want her to be angry, but I didn't want her to be sweet either. I wanted neutral. Unemotional was good. She glanced at the door and I didn't say anything. If I let her in, I knew where it would lead. The last time she'd gotten all homesick for me, we'd ended up on the couch with her crying and my arms around her until one thing led to the next and we ended up in the bedroom.

"What?" she asked. "I miss you. Is that a crime?"

"No. No, it's not." I could hear the chickadees singsonging their three languid evening notes from the pine forest to my side, *Cheeeeeese Burger*. That's what Ken said they were saying, but Mr. Fit was always thinking about food. "Why don't you save us all some stress and tell your family that we've split up? I don't want to come to your reunion and put on a fake show."

"You don't have to put on a show." Lara leaned one hip into the side of her car and crossed her arms, a move I'd seen her do a thousand times throughout the course of our relationship—it was her stubbornness displayed in one familiar stance. "All you have to do is be yourself, Monty. All I'm asking is that we don't ruin everyone's good time by dropping this on them at the last minute, especially my parents when they've been planning and looking forward to this for a long time—a chance to have the entire family all together at once. It means so much to them."

I narrowed my brow, studying her. Suddenly I felt very tired. I raked my fingers through my hair. "Look, Lara, I have a lot of work to do."

Her crossed arms stiffened more and she shifted to the other hip, her mouth instantly pouty—another thing I'd seen many times over. "So that's it? End of discussion just because you're tired?"

"I don't want to do this."

"*Do* this? What? Talk about our lives?"

"We've talked this to death already. You could have told your family months ago, and it wouldn't have been last minute and it wouldn't have been so disappointing to your parents. And as far as us, which, if you ask me, is the bigger, more important topic right now, well, there's nothing more to say. You've had a decision to make, and eventually your indecision becomes your decision."

Her mouth hung open in surprise. "Are you telling me that it's over for you?"

"I didn't say that. All I said is that I'm too tired to go over what we've already gone over a million times." I could feel my pulse speed up. Why did I let her do this to me? Make me feel guilty, then do all I could to get back in her good graces. Why couldn't I just say, *Yeah, that's right; it's over. I'm tired of this drama*? But I wasn't sure it was over for me. Even though we'd been apart for the better part of a year, I still missed her, and undeniably, we still had chemistry. A part of me considered her my lifeline to normalcy—an anchor to routine and stability, a pathway to a happy family. Lately though, I could feel that ache of being apart from her receding as the months dragged on. I could also feel my anger growing with time. On multiple levels, I felt betrayed.

She looked strained and glanced toward the woods, the fir trees creating shadows and breathing cool air. I could hear chipmunks, squirrels, and magpies scurrying around in the distance and the chickadees still sang, now even busier. I jangled my keys and looked toward my door again and her gaze followed. "Look, babe, I know you're tired. Why don't I come in and make you some dinner. I've got some groceries in my car." She motioned to the back seat. "Pasta? You have olive oil, don't you?"

I stared at her without saying a word and sighed. She turned, opened her door, and grabbed a bag of groceries.

.   .   .

We had it ready in twenty minutes. Fresh butternut ravioli with a little olive oil and Parmesan cheese. I made the salad. The entire time we ate I kept telling myself I was not going to let her stay the night.

"Are you eating well?"

I shrugged. "Yeah, good enough."

"You sure? Looks like you've dropped a few."

I shrugged. "Not sure."

"Well, I need to fatten you up a bit before—"

"Before the reunion." I shook my head in disappointment.

"No, well yes, that's what I was going to say, but I didn't mean it that way."

I put my fork down, pushed my chair back, and walked to the fridge.

"Monty," she pleaded. "I'm sorry. I didn't mean it that way."

"What way did you mean it?"

"Just that, that . . ."

"Um hmm." I nodded. "That's what I thought. You're, you're just too much," I said softly.

"Please, just sit down." She held her hand up. "I won't mention it again, I promise."

My cell phone rang as she finished her sentence. She dropped her hand back to the table. I looked at the ID and didn't recognize the number. "Go ahead and answer it," she said.

"Monty, this is Ward. Sam Ward."

"Sam," I said, moving to a kitchen cabinet and resting against it, eager to hear why Wolfie's wolverine-study partner was calling. "What's up?"

"First, Pritchard mentioned to you about those sabotaged traps in the South Fork, right?"

"Yeah, he did. You know something more about that?"

"No, nothing more. It's something else, probably nothing, but I just was over visiting Cathy and the kids, and Cathy said something that made me think I should share it with you."

"What's that?" It flashed across my mind that Sam was a close enough friend to be a comfort to Cathy. Against my intuition, I briefly considered whether there was something more between them. I knew how the quest for truth could be a demanding mistress. If Wolfie was that obsessed with his research, it was certainly possible that his wife might confide a little too much in the family friend. I looked at Lara sitting at the table. Her body rounded forward and slumped in sadness. She pushed her food around her plate with agitation, and in that instance, in the collapse of her frame, I knew that I was way off about Cathy Sedgewick. I was just jealous. Cathy's love for Wolfie was palpable and real, and just because Lara and I had ripped a hole in our marriage and let our stability leak away didn't mean I had the right to make ridiculous assumptions.

"Well, it hadn't occurred to me before but Cathy was saying how Wolfie would never commit suicide, not like that kid last summer."

"Kid last summer?"

"Yeah, I don't know if you ever heard about it, but we had hired a guy to help us out with setting some traps out the spring before and when we started running low on our budget the following fall, we had to let him go. Sweet guy. Kind of quiet, but a hiking machine. He'd go anywhere we asked through all kinds of weather. Anyway, after we let him go, he was found about two months later, before Christmas, in his apartment. He had OD'd."

"I remember reading that in the paper, but I had no idea you guys had hired him."

"After it happened, we all felt really bad and Wolfie especially felt awful. He wondered if our letting him go and not having a job had anything to do with his depression."

"His name?"

"Brad. Brad DeMarcus. He was actually the brother of Will, who's the bartender at the Snow Ghost Bar and Grill in Whitefish."

"Oh really?" I thought of the bartender's joking about the silly drink and the Wild West.

"Yeah. Anyway, not sure it means anything at all, but thought I should mention it."

"Thank you," I said. "Every piece of information helps. I'll look into it."

Lara was looking at me with wide eyes, her head resting on her hand. She had quit fiddling with her food and she didn't look particularly irritated anymore, so I'm not sure why I felt my anger prickle. "You have to go?" she asked.

I stared back for a moment. I didn't have to go anywhere. What Sam had shared was interesting, but nothing urgent. But slowly, I felt myself nod. "Yeah," I said. "I'm sorry."

Lara looked at her wineglass, took another sip, then stood and began clearing the table.

"It's okay. I can get that later."

"No." She held up her hand. "I'll get it now. I can let myself out. You can just go if you need to."

I went to her and placed my hand on her shoulder. "I'll call you tomorrow."

She bit her lower lip as if she was holding back words and nodded.

"Okay then," I said, grabbing my keys and leaving through the kitchen door. I had a knot in my stomach that I'd just walked away from her like that, leaving her alone in the place I'd made my own—where I wasn't married to her—to clean the dinner we'd made together, not to mention that it was the first time I had ever lied to my wife.

10

ANOTHER SPECTACULAR DAY took shape before Ken and me, and I tried not to dwell on my dissembling with Lara the night before and her pouty face when I left—how I'd gone to the office and looked through Wolfie's files for any information on Brad DeMarcus, rewatched the surveillance tape capturing Wolfie driving into the park around seven p.m., exactly as Cathy said he would be, then drove by my dorm an hour and a half later to make sure she was gone before going in. When I got ready for bed, I could smell the faint, lingering remains of her flowery perfume in the small bathroom. I tried not to feel guilty about leaving her like that, and finally, after a long period of tossing and turning, I fell to sleep.

Now, by quarter to eight in the morning on Saturday, the sun was drying the dew and the Loop was already busy with cars passing by to head to the visitor center at the top of the pass. Some stopped to use the restroom and take photos of the view, and one car with two twentysomething women—one blond- and one dark-haired—hopped out and strode up to Ken and me in short jogging shorts and well-toned, tanned legs. The one with a long, dark ponytail looping out of the hole at the base of her cap asked if the trail to Granite Chalet was open.

"Not from this end yet, but it is from the top." I pointed up the mountains where Going-to-the-Sun snaked its way narrowly to the visitor center. "From there, you can take the Highline Trail to the chalet. It's a few miles longer but much more pleasant since it traverses below the Garden Wall and isn't such a big vertical rise as it is from here." I knew it was two thousand feet worth of elevation change going up from this point.

"We don't want to hike it that way. We *want* the vertical rise, the hike up. You know, for the workout." She looked at me incredulously. "It's too easy to go in from the top."

"Well, it *is* seven miles," I offered. "From here, it's only three point eight. Plus you still have to hike back which is uphill and would make it fourteen round-trip."

"Like she said," the blonde chimed in, tilting her head to her friend, "we *want* the elevation change."

In the past few years, we were seeing more and more of the younger generation interested in what kind of a workout they could achieve rather than the enjoyment they could gather from the unsullied scenery. Mountain bikes were not allowed on most Glacier trails because they rutted them out and alarmed wildlife and hikers. Some trails permitted horses and alpacas. Lately, more were jogging the trails— getting their workouts in—and we'd received complaints from elderly hikers and nature enthusiasts feeling startled on narrow, dangerous trails by runners suddenly approaching from behind, obnoxiously yelling, *On your right*, as if it was a ski hill and the hikers in front should nimbly and quickly hop to the side of the narrow ledges so the joggers didn't have to interrupt their workout pace.

"It will most probably be open by this afternoon." I smiled. "You're more than welcome to wait."

The dark-haired one let out an exasperated sigh and sauntered off complaining to her friend. "Maybe they can catch a Pilates class when they're done with their hike." I rolled my eyes at Ken. "I'm sure they'll get their glutes worked today one way or the other."

"I'm sure they will." Ken chuckled as we grabbed the gear from the back of the car. "And nice glutes they are."

I smiled, shut and locked the back of the SUV, and we made our way toward the trail. "Another trip into this ravine," I said to him once we got beyond the roped off area and made it to the launch spot. "Bored yet?"

"Nah." Ken had his gum again and vigorously worked it.

"Good, I just want to make sure we're not missing anything."

He shrugged his indifference. "Whatever suits you. Can't imagine you're going to find anything more than you did the other day, though."

"Yeah, I know." I shoved my hat in my pocket and placed the hard hat on when we reached the spot. "It's just that I had this idea that if I go down the other side of the first contact spot, down a different line, I might find the memory card."

"Like I said, whatever you think," Ken said as he searched for a sturdy tree to set the first anchor. "It's this or directing traffic on the other side of the pass where there's been a frequent-flyer black bear. Or," he added, "issuing traffic violations and I can't tell you how many times I heard "You can't give me a ticket; you're just a ranger" last week. I don't even bother saying anymore that I'm Park Police."

I chuckled. I'd heard it my fair share as well and the fact of the matter was that some rangers were trained in law enforcement and perfectly enabled to give tickets for violations in the park, just as we were.

"I like this better," Ken added. "No fumes."

"There ya go," I said.

"But I don't really need any extra trouble from Smith or even Ford for not getting the trail open." Ken had knelt down to secure a line around the sturdy trunk of a pine and stopped what he was doing to look up at me. "They don't have the kind of faith in me that they do you."

"What?" I said.

"He trusts you," Ken said.

"Who?"

"Smith. He's got a lot of confidence in you. You don't see it?"

I shrugged. "I guess so. I think he just has confidence in all his people—including you—and good thing, 'cause I think he's worn out and he needs us to take the reins here, and I'm more than happy to help."

"I can see that." Ken looked at the line and tugged on it a few times. "All set from this end."

"You won't get in any trouble," I assured him. "This is my call and we'll have this trail open in no time." I set the backup anchor around a second pine nearby, then stepped into my harness and secured the rest of my gear and headed down for the third time, this time farther north of the victim's launch area. When I reached the area a little lower from the sloped ledge with the slide marks and blood spatter, I stopped to look and took more pictures from the new angle. Another day and night of sunshine and summer breezes had faded the spatter even more.

Then I shimmied over so I was even slightly farther north of the ledge. I hung shy of a drop-off that concaved inward. I was careful to go no further. I knew I didn't want to free-rappel—to lose contact with the wall—since it's more dangerous and I was already off my descent line where the lines were most secure. There were several outcroppings on this side, so I rested my feet on a small one and scanned the area looking for the disk, looking for anything. I peered around to see if it had flung against the cliff, bounced down, and nestled onto some small rock projection.

For a moment, I took in the view. With my ass hanging in the air in a seated position in the rope's webbing of my harness, I peered out at the colossal sky, the mountains indifferent and braced against it. That really brought it full circle for me. Even as Wolfie tumbled to his demise, those mountains didn't flinch. I was viewing the pristine sweep of the Great Divide, specifically the Livingston Range marching northward into Canada. The stubborn, unforgiving whisper from the vast carved rock faces felt more intimately dangerous than ever before, their soft murmurs humming and vibrating, engulfing me. Usually it didn't affect me, but today it was making me edgy and making the thin hairs on the back of my neck stand up.

People were often shocked and captivated by the news of grizzly or other animal attacks. Such freak occurrences made them feel unsafe in the wild. But these folks didn't fully consider the uncomplicated fact that something as simple as falling in Glacier was much more frightening because it was much more likely to happen, like a car accident could take your life in a split second way before a serial killer was ever going to take it.

A speck of dust on the cliff's edge, my existence felt intensely connected to the fabric of it all, but still a mere glitch; my rappelling ropes seemed inadequate and unsafe. I knew finding the disk was a hope in hell. Suddenly I considered myself extremely unwise and perhaps irresponsible for wasting Ken's and my time, not to mention keeping a good number of tourists, including those women, from hiking the Loop Trail to Granite Chalet and affecting the chalet's business as well.

"Yeah, yeah," I said out loud to it all, my voice faintly bouncing off the rock cliff. "I'm foolish enough all right, looking for something so small out here." I set the camera down against my chest and was just about to shimmy back over to my descent line, when from down below, from the different vantage point, I caught a glimpse of something shiny about seventy-five feet below me. I squinted at it and brought the camera with its telephoto lens back to my eye, but could only make out a shiny pinpoint of light. For all I knew, it was a piece of broken glass from someone having dropped a bottle while hiking up above.

A little voice inside my head echoed Ford's sentiments: *Enough already, Monty. Just because you took a couple refresher courses doesn't mean there's a crime. Go back up and open the damn trail.* I grabbed the radio from my belt. "Ken, you read?"

"I'm here."

I paused, the radio at my mouth.

"Ten four. I hear you," he reiterated.

But why not, I thought. It was going to bug hell out of me if I didn't. No one was ever going to accuse me of being sloppy, and I had made a promise. "I crossed the line over the nose," I told him, "and I see something shiny down below from this side. I'm going to head back over straight below the anchors and go back down and walk over to check it out. It's farther north of where we searched yesterday, like I said, around the nose."

"Ten four," Ken said. "Your wish is my command."

"Thank you." Carefully, I made my way back to my original descent line and lowered myself to the ground. I removed the roped carabiners from my harness and began picking my way through the talus and around the front of the cliff to the other side of it to where I spotted the shiny object.

It took me some time to get to the spot, but once I arrived, something inside me recoiled. It was like I was looking at a puzzle at first, then as I put things into perspective, noted the rocks, the brush, and the surrounding dirt, the dark stains, I realized what it was.

I was viewing part of an arm and its hand.

A large hawk let loose a brash caw from above, startling me into the stark present. An acrid taste formed at the back of my throat, and I swallowed hard. Flesh was still on it from the elbow down and a sports watch remained clasped around the wrist. I wiped the sweat on my forehead and squinted at the dismembered limb. Slowly, I made my way closer and noticed several yards away and covered in dirt, other parts of the body—part of a torso with some bare ribs exposed, a head, and part of a dirty and ripped denim-clad leg.

I felt dizzy as I grabbed the radio. "Ken," I said. "Looks like we're not going to be opening the trail this afternoon after all."

11

Two hours later, we had a team of people working the top again, including Joe, Karen, and Michael who had joined Ken. Also, Gretchen Larson, the lead crime scene examiner who worked for Flathead County was called in. Luckily, she wasn't afraid of much and insisted on rappelling down with a backpack full of forensic gear. Ken helped her down and I walked her to the spot where we both spent another few hours examining the second body we'd found in three days below the Loop trail. "You keep agreeing to come down these steep areas, and they'll have no use for me anymore."

"I don't intend to make a habit of it," she said.

Since the west side of Glacier Park was contained in Flathead County, the county held concurrent jurisdiction with the feds and could be used for law enforcement matters. I knew I could use the extra expertise on this one since it had been out in the elements longer and had been fed on by some type of carnivore. I liked Gretchen and I was happy for the help, not to mention that she was easy on the eyes with baby blues and honey-colored shoulder-length hair pulled back and tied at the nape of her neck. She made me feel like I was in some TV crime show where the crime scene investigators were all ridiculously beautiful and perfectly dressed. I was pretty certain it didn't go that way in very many counties around the country. Gretchen wasn't fashionably dressed and maybe not quite the right type for one of those shows, but she was cute. I was pretty sure she got quite a bit of male attention on and off duty, but she was the type to buy her own round anyway. She could put anyone not treating her as she saw fit in their place with a cutting glance or a few brief words.

"Possibly a lion or a lynx," I said to her. "I found some tracks around the area that look like cat—four round toe prints widely spread, no claw points suggesting retractable claws, and the leading edge of the heel pad has three lobes." I stopped a good twenty feet from the remains. "Probably too large for bobcat. My guess is lion, although it's unusual for cats to feed on something already dead. They like their prey alive unless it's a young one that's hungry and been pushed out of territory, and these prints look on the smaller size."

"I see," she said. Gretchen was from Norway and from what I'd heard, she'd come to the United States for college about ten years earlier and ended up staying, but she still spoke with a slight accent, adding a bit of unintentional sexy to the cute. "No bear prints?"

"I'm not seeing any so far."

"This is as good a place as any." She looked around at the rocks, removed her pack, and set it on a large flat boulder. "Any chance this lion or whatever it was is coming back for trouble?"

I tapped the capsaicin on my belt. "Since there's flesh left," I offered in an attempt to make her feel safe while she worked, "it's likely whatever got it is temporarily storing it and coming back for more. But we're large enough to scare whatever it was away, or at least keep it to the sidelines, unless it's a griz, and like I said, I don't see any evidence of that. But I'm here with plenty of spray."

Gretchen pushed her dark-rimmed glasses higher on the bridge of her nose and stared at me for a moment, as if she was considering whether to mock me or just continue giving me a look. "Thank goodness you're here," she said with sarcasm. Her *th* sounded like a *t—tank goodness*—then mumbled, "because gee, I've never worked cases out in the woods before." She reached into a front pocket of her pack and slid out a bottle of capsaicin bear spray and placed it on a rock.

I looked away. "I didn't mean it that way," I offered. "I just, you know, wanted you to know you could focus without keeping one eye over your shoulder." I was definitely out of practice with women, and it didn't really matter. I knew there would never be any others, even while separated from Lara. It wasn't my style to cross those kinds of lines—to do things I'd later regret or feel guilty about.

She laughed, but didn't reply. I couldn't help but smile, even out among the macabre and wild aspects of it all—the stench of rotting flesh, flies and insects buzzing frantically, hawks cawing, several picas throwing out their squeaky warnings, the roar of McDonald Creek rising and echoing off the carved canyon walls. I was still a sucker for pretty women, and I certainly hadn't made any promises to myself to not notice when someone was attractive.

She removed the rest of the items from her pack one by one and I noted much of her cache was similar to mine: her evidence log, storage bags, mask, evidence markers. I'd been sent to Georgia was because, in the park, although we needed to treat each death with extreme care, there was no need to bring a crime scene specialist into dangerous, steep areas to work a scene that was most likely an accident. This time, however, it was just getting too strange with two bodies in the same vicinity.

She pulled out biohazard coveralls and shimmied them over her hips and onto her shoulders and zipped them up. I was impressed that she bothered with them this far out with scattered remains. "Hey," she said reading my mind. "A crime's a crime, and what are the chances they were both accidents?"

"Not sure," I said. I pulled out my water bottle and took a gulp. I could feel the heat from the rocky ground intensifying and rising up. "It's strange all right, but I'm wondering if maybe this guy went down first and Sedgewick, the man we pulled yesterday, was only tracking his wolverines, knowing they were in the area, but not knowing why. Maybe a wolverine was going to feed on some of the leftovers down here." I knew wolverines were the ultimate scavengers, their jaws strong and capable of mincing bone.

Gretchen held up her palm. "No need to figure out a story for me.

I'm only here for the facts. Story comes later." She put up her mask and headed to the lone arm and wrist with the shiny watch face.

•   •   •

I stood a few feet off to the side and gave Gretchen space to work while I studied the scene, trying to envision what the hell had happened that would produce two bodies in the same area. She called out to me several times, filling me in as she worked. "I think you're right. Looks like a mountain lion," she said. "Although considerably eaten, victim fell first. Remaining bones are severely broken and consistent with a long fall. The neck and skull are not punctured by teeth, just crushed by rocks."

"I was wondering about that," I said. "If this victim had taken a different route in from lower down by McDonald Creek or he'd fallen, just like Sedgewick."

"He definitely fell," she said. "By the looks of what's left of his cranium, he hit headfirst."

"I thought the same thing when I first looked it over, but the animal covered him with quite a bit of dirt. If you're okay here, I'm going to look around," I told her. "I want to follow the drag marks and find the spot he fell."

"Good with me," she said. "But if you hear me screaming, best come runnin'," she winked at me.

"You can count on it," I gave her a half smile.

It didn't take long to find the spot since there was a blood trail and skid marks that the body left from the animal dragging it from its original landing spot over the slope to the rocky, brushy area where I found the arm. The landing area was literally just around the nose of the cliff from where we found Wolfie.

I took copious photos from as many angles as possible of it all: the drag marks, the lion prints, the blood spatter at the original spot. There was a lot of blood, so I assumed this person only hit once. After I finished studying the area, I went back to Gretchen, and she came over

to me, wiping her forehead with her sleeve. "I've got the remains secured in the body bag. Looks like there's so little left of this guy, I don't
think it's worth taking him out by air. And since he's been moved by the
lion—I think we can literally transport what's left of him in our packs."

I nodded. "I'll radio Smith and let him know. Any chance of ID'ing
him?"

"The watch might help, but I'm more hopeful about that arm you
spotted first. There's part of a tattoo left, and we're very lucky it hasn't
been eaten yet."

"Prints?"

"Possibly, the hand is still intact on that arm, but the elements and
decomposition have dissolved the ridges. You find where he hit?"

"I did." I pointed my chin up the talus slope. "Since it was around
the nose of that cliff, it wasn't one of the areas in the grid that Ken and I
searched the day before, so we missed it entirely." It was below the area
that I had been careful not to free-rappel into since it cut inward. "But
from up above," I told her, "the launch spot for the victim would not
have been far at all from Paul Sedgewick's spot."

"It's curious all right. When we get these remains to the lab, we
should be able to figure out more about the time of death, see how it
lines up with the other victim. Is he"—she lifted her brow—"with Pettiman in Kalispell or Wilson in Missoula?"

"Pettiman at first," I said. "But he's being transferred to Missoula.
I'm guessing this one should go to Missoula too?"

"I need to take a quick look at the landing spot and then I think we
should get it up and refrigerated as soon as possible."

I radioed Joe and told him our plan. After she got enough photos
of the area he was dragged from, together we headed back to the rappelling lines carrying the remains of another human being lost to the
wild. I thought of the man's flesh being torn by the menacing jaw of
a stealth lion, helping to build his or her sleek muscles. "One way or
another," I said, "I guess we all eventually get reprocessed."

She looked at me and shook her head. "I don't think I'll respond to that one."

I sighed. "Best not to. But what you can do for me is use whatever clout you have with Doc Wilson to expedite the autopsy."

She tilted her head and smiled. "That I can do."

12

Two victims in the same area." Joe scratched the back of his neck.

Joe, Ken, and I were sitting in the incident room. "Yeah, strange," Ken agreed.

"Coroner called me fifteen minutes ago," I said. "He just got him on his way to Missoula. Looks like this one's been out there for several days and that's what Gretchen thought as well. At this point, he's unidentified. I've contacted missing persons and so far nothing. The coroner thinks once he gets him to Missoula, Wilson might be able to get an ID from the tattoo on the arm. Just might take a little time."

"And there was no car in the lot?" Joe asked.

"Not that we know of. We've considered the possibility that he parked on the east side and hiked over, so I've got Schaeffer checking the lots over there." Marina Schaeffer was Park Police also and stationed on the east side in St. Mary. A twelve-mile-steep trek over the Divide could get you on the west side, but it would be a full day of strenuous hiking. "It's also possible he took a shuttle up, hitchhiked, or got a ride up from a friend."

"Your thoughts on the two falls in the same area?" Joe scratched his chin.

"I don't know. It seems highly unlikely it could be a coincidence unless they both fell at the same time, maybe fighting or something, but since the guy I found today has been out there longer, it rules that out."

"Serial killer?" Ken offered.

Joe and I looked at each other. "Doesn't feel right," I said. "Serial killers like to hurt their victims. I'm not saying it's not possible. It's just that a push would be too simple, over too quickly unless there was abuse taking place first and we're not seeing signs of that, at least not on Sedgewick. But maybe we need more analysis on him."

"What about one homicide, one accident?" Joe asked.

"I thought about that. First guy is pushed and Wolfie picks up a wolverine signal heading to the area and he, well, he falls. And that might feel right if it was anyone but a field biologist. It just doesn't make sense given his experience in the wilderness."

Joe nodded. "Yeah, I know."

"Either way," I insisted, "I'd like Wolfie's body transferred from Pettiman to Wilson as soon as possible for further analysis."

. . .

The next morning was a Sunday, and there was nothing to do in the meantime but focus on Wolfie. With Wolfie, it was a process of elimination: was it suicide? Was it an accident? Was it homicide? There was no reason to believe it was a suicide, possibly an accident, but with a second body in the same area, my suspicion meter went way up. I pulled out Wolfie's files and looked through them, hoping to find something to point me in some direction or to link Wolfie to anything questionable.

There was file after file filled with notes on wolverine sightings, maps of where they'd been, drainages they'd been up, valleys they'd denned in, ridges and peaks they'd muscled up. There were specific classifications on the different animals, most of them titled M1, M2, M3, and up for males, and F1, F2, and F3 for females. There were personal notes in a separate folder, just scribbles of observations, mostly about his awe of the wolverine:

I see a major self-respect, a self-reliance and a dignity in the tenacity of the creature, the way it fearlessly scales precipices and wants to rip us apart for interfering with their routines to try to implant our transmitters. Gotta love these little bastards! They do not go gentle. But, they are playful too. Saw three playing hide-and-seek on a snow-field above Avalanche Lake, hiding, peeking, chasing, somersaulting and sliding—all for fun because they would climb back up and do it several times in a row.

He would also comment on the grizzlies he'd come across and how when he'd see one, he could practically feel its air of unfettered power descend upon him and make him feel very small and humble.

Sadness overwhelmed me to think the love, awe, and respect emanating from Wolfie so effusively was suddenly vanquished. I sensed some deep understanding in him of the natural world he engaged with more than I'd seen in our own tribe of rangers and Park Police—some part of Wolfie's soul, perhaps, that identified with the wild animals and their quest to keep moving and to remain ungoverned.

Then I thought of his family, of Cathy and the kids, and how they deserved more and how I'd fleetingly considered Sam Ward might have something more going on with her. A twinge of guilt shot through me again. The Sedgewicks seemed graced with the ability to have a loving, connected family. Suddenly, I felt that strong need welling again, an urgent necessity to somehow help them and to try to make things right in whatever small ways were possible. And layered beneath that urge, from someplace dark and tangled, I sensed that such an urge stemmed from the knowledge that I would never be able to revel in a normal, warm family myself. Judging by my separation after eight years of what I considered a good marriage, ultimately, a happy home life eluded me.

I moved on and opened another file. I read about the population of the wolverine. How the estimate for Glacier was between thirty and thirty-five, and how in Montana as a whole, there were maybe somewhere between a hundred and a hundred fifty and that there might be a handful in the Tetons, in Idaho, and in Washington in the North Cascades, a fragmented number at best. There were genealogy charts linking offspring to the parents and notes on which wolverines had died, some accidentally by violent avalanches, some at the jaws of other predators, possibly even other wolverines, and far too many by human hands.

At the end of the file, an undated personal note written by Wolfie read: *Call from DOI—high ranking official—pressure about report.* Then I saw a smaller, index-card-size note tucked between some pages. It read: *South Fork—Rowdy? Outlaw's.*

I grabbed Ken and when he asked where we were going, I replied, "Down the Line." I was referring to the canyon between the Flathead Valley and Glacier Park, which was known for gimmicky tourist spots as well as a tough population of often-lower-income and unemployed folks.

"Where?"

"The Outlaw's Nest in Hungry Horse."

"You jones'ing for a beer?"

"No, I want to talk to the manager of the bar, Melissa Tafford. I'm hoping she knows a local who goes by Rowdy."

"Rowdy?"

"Yeah, you heard of him?"

Ken shook his head. "Not sure I want to."

. . .

We drove through the town of Hungry Horse, past the dilapidated larger-than-life cutout sign of a white horse, past the huckleberry ice cream stands selling huck pies and ice cream made from huckleberries frozen from the summer before, since the berries weren't ripe until July at the earliest. We passed the east side turnoff to the Hungry Horse dam clogging and creating the large reservoir up the South Fork drainage and parked at the Outlaw's Nest. Only a few cars sat in the lot since it was a Sunday. As we entered, the scent of bleach from either the late-night or early-morning cleaning detergents hit me. I figured they must need some heavy-duty supplies to get up all the spilt liquor from the night before.

"I see you have a different sidekick." Melissa lifted her chin toward Ken when we approached her at the bar. "What happened to the other one?" She was referring to Systead on the Bear Bait case. We had pressed Melissa several times for information on her meth-dealing boyfriend during the investigation.

"Went back to Denver."

She shrugged, a good-riddance look on her face. "Well, whatever brings you here, don't bother asking, 'cause I can't help you. Stimpy and I broke up months ago."

"I see." I refrained from commenting that—for her sake—it was probably for the best. "Well, this has nothing to do with him. Just need a little help."

She set two mugs under some taps and pulled the handles, the golden liquid filling each. When they were full, she tipped the foam, then added a little more. She looked better than she had the previous fall, her face softer and less angled. Maybe she'd stopped using if she and Stimpy were done. She grabbed a mug in each hand and walked over to a table with two middle-aged guys in jeans and T-shirts. While we waited for her to return, I read a poster that had been taped to the wall to our side describing a local band, the Woodtics, who would be performing in the Outlaw's Nest on Thursday, the thirtieth.

"I'm looking for a guy named Rowdy," I said when she returned. "Know him?"

She shrugged.

"I guess that means you do."

"Didn't say that."

"Didn't say no either."

"Yeah, I know of him. Everyone around here does. He's been around these parts longer than the mountains." She flicked her hand in the air. "What do you want with him? He doesn't bother anyone."

"Not entirely sure," I said. "Just trying to figure out why a guy who fell in the park might have had business with him."

"That guy that fell? The wolverine research guy?"

"Yeah, why would he have business with your Rowdy?"

"I have no idea." She looked around as if she wanted to make sure no one could hear her, wiped the counter with a dirty-looking rag, and pursed her lips.

"Nothing? No idea at all?"

She bit her top lip and shook her head.

I stayed quiet and studied her, watching as she wiped the counter before her, then tossed the rag over the side of the sink. I've found patience works best in situations like these. Ken took a seat at the bar and made himself comfortable.

Finally, she said, "All right"—she pointed in my face, one eye narrowed—"not because I like you, but because if I *had* to like one of you, I'd like you better than that Systead jerk."

"I appreciate the compliment." I smiled.

"But you didn't hear any of this from me." She looked around carefully again.

I held up my hand as if under oath.

"All I can tell you is that a few weeks ago, a group of guys got together in here and they were all riled up because that wolverine guy had made some comment in the local news that wolverines might need more protection in the backcountry. And you know, we're sick of being told what we can and can't do with our land. More protection for some stupid animal nobody cares about anyway means less hunting, snowmobiling, ATV'ing," She tilted her head to the side, her eyes hard and set.

"Which guys were in the group?"

"Can't say. Can't really remember."

I knew she was lying, but I knew I couldn't push her if I wanted any more information about Rowdy. "Rowdy was with this group?"

She nodded. "Yeah, they bought him whiskey and wanted his advice about something because he used to be a game warden. They had some questions about trapping or something. About filing complaints."

There were a total of about seventy-five game warden personnel for Fish, Wildlife and Parks, and I since used to be one of them, I was well aware that most of us knew or had at least heard of each other no matter which region we worked.

But Rowdy? I'd never heard of a Rowdy before. "What's his last name?" I asked Melissa.

"No clue. Don't make a habit of learning everyone's names in here."

"He go by another first name?"

"Probably. Sounds like a nickname to me, but I wouldn't know any other."

"So they wanted to file a complaint?"

"Not sure. Or deal with a complaint made against them or something. But more than anything, they just wanted to talk, you know, to try to be organized."

"Organized?"

"Yeah, have some kind of a strategy for how to protect the land around here from people like you who work for the state and the feds. Can't say I blame 'em." She picked up the dirty rag again. "Now, if you don't mind, I gotta clean that table." She motioned to one that had been sitting with empty beer bottles since we'd come in.

I nodded and thanked her for her time, and Ken and I left her to her quiet Sunday in the gloom of her dingy bar.

13

GRETCHEN CAME THROUGH. Wilson had both autopsies finished by the next morning, and I left at six a.m. to get to the Forensics Science Division of the Montana Department of Justice's State Crime Lab for a nine a.m. viewing.

Wilson greeted me in powder-blue scrubs and galoshes and took me back to the autopsy suite. He knew that I had worked with Systead on the last case from the park and sighed. "The body's been badly eaten. Just like last fall. And, as you know, animals are hard on bodies. Often, all the fleshy meat is gone and parts get torn off, carried away, buried, or covered with dirt, leaves, and twigs. I'm surprised you found it," he said as I followed him down the hall.

"It was a stroke of luck."

"Well, when you really think about it, how often do you come across a deer carcass?"

"Almost never, unless it's road kill."

"Exactly." He grabbed a face mask and handed it to me. "So, with as many deer as there are around here and with as many predators of deer, you'd think you'd come across one more often, but you don't, right?"

"Right." He wasn't telling me anything I wasn't familiar with.

"Well," he added, "trying to find human remains in the woods is just as difficult."

I thought of Nathan Faraway again, and a memory of the officer talking to my parents in our small house in Columbia Falls, essentially conveying the same sentiment, flashed in my mind. As we entered the suite, the smell of disinfectant blended with the stench of the remains in the refrigerated air, and I tried to shake the feeling that the specter of Nathan seemed to be following me quite a bit lately.

Before us, two bodies lay on the dissecting tables under long-armed lights that looked like the kind seen in a dentist's suite. One was Paul Sedgewick, or Wolfie, the already severely torn skin peeled away from his crushed skull. His crooked body lay opened from groin to shoulders to reveal broken ribs, fat, and muscle. The other was in a feeble state of disarray on the dissecting table: bones and scant, rotting flesh that appeared blackened from the enzymes in the bacteria eating away at the leftover flesh. I figured Victor Lance from Bear Bait must have looked similar to this the previous fall—a smattering of pieces put back together, definitely like something's leftover meal. I felt only a little queasy, and was once again grateful we'd done numerous stints in my recent classes in the autopsy units.

"We'll start with the victim you found first." He gestured to Wolfie. "Entomology will clarify even more, but I can say for sure that he has been out there less time than the second one you found. This one died less than forty-eight hours before you found him at the bottom of the ravine. His manner of death is consistent with trauma from the fall. We got lucky with him that no third parties or animals got on him. Paul Sedgewick. I think you've ID'd him correctly. Odontology verified that the dental records are a match."

"Good to know," I said.

"His growth plates are fully fused, so I had known he was over twenty-five before we got the confirmation."

"Yeah, born in 1969."

"And time of death?"

"Definitely within thirty-six hours of when he was last seen. In this case, I'd say he'd been out there at least twelve to seventeen hours. I've based that on the stage of rigor in the large muscle groups of the lower extremities and stages of lividity. And of course, I've taken recorded temperatures from the area for Wednesday night into consideration."

"His wife last saw him around six p.m. on Wednesday."

Wilson gave a quick nod in agreement. "That fits. The earliest would have been 6, 6:30. I'm thinking between 6:30 and 11:30 p.m. on Wednesday."

"We've got a toxicology screen taking place and other than that, it's your basic fall. Judging by the state of his skull, you were probably correct in assuming he hit head first."

"Is it possible the head was hit on a second or third hit and not the first?"

"I'm taking an educated guess that his head hit first, his ankles on a later one due to the severity of the crushed skull, but you can never say for sure with a fall like this."

"Any signs of foul play?

"Not that I can determine, but it's very difficult to conclude something like that on a specimen that is in this kind of shape. This one," Wilson pointed to the other meager pile of remains on the second table. "Even worse shape. Male also. From the pelvis and the size and shape of the forehead on the skull." He pointed to the narrow pelvis first, then the skull. "He was the first to die for sure. Ribs tell me he's over twenty-five as well, but most of his ribs have been destroyed by a mountain lion."

"Lion for sure?"

"The puncture wounds in the flesh that's left on the arm and between the ribs indicate it's a feline larger than lynx or bobcat. I know it's strange. I've only seen it once before—a lion feeding on a dead carcass. Usually, they like their prey alive. They're stalkers, hunters. This one must have been young and hungry."

I fidgeted. Again Nathan's small, round face flashed in my mind and an anger at my brother—a fury I hadn't felt so strongly since I was young—surged through me like a drug and made me feel flustered and light-headed. To think that Nathan might have been stalked that night by the stealthiest hunter of the woods—a lion with sharp vision and graceful, undetected moves, an animal capable of leaping great distances—because of Adam's cruel trick made me shudder. I shook off the image of Nathan's slight frame being crunched in a mountain lion's steely jaws and chalked it up to the fact that I was still a little nauseous standing before these corpses with the smell of decay and disinfectant permeating my senses.

Wilson gave me an *Are-you-okay look*, tucking his chin in. I could tell he was used to this scenario and made a habit of checking to see if anyone was going to faint on his table.

I gave a small nod to signal I was fine.

"Again, entomology will clarify the gestation and that should narrow the time of death to at least the correct day or two." Wilson pointed to one intact rib. "This is the fourth rib, and we usually can get close to the age by looking at the third, fourth, and fifth ribs through the amount of pitting and the condition of the edges. With this fourth one"—he motioned his finger along the rib's edge—"I see just enough pitting to suggest he's past his twenties, possibly into his early forties, but probably not late forties or over. I'm guessing he's in his midthirties to early forties. I see no arthritis at all in the joints that are left, which also suggests he's either around or under forty."

"DNA?" I asked.

"Yes, we were able to get some from the eye sockets. Hopefully it's not contaminated from the lion. It's possible he's in CODIS." He was referring to the Combined DNA Index System, the FBI's program of support for criminal justice DNA databases. "But I wouldn't get your hopes up because we've soaked the hand with the fingers—the one with the watch still on it—in glycerin and been able to get some pretty accurate prints, but there's no matchup with anything on WIN AFIS."

WIN was a consortium of state and local law enforcement agencies that used a shared network and Automated Fingerprint Identification

System so law enforcement services could search criminal and civil fingerprint records of member agencies. So far, Alaska, Montana, Oregon, Washington, Idaho, Nevada, Utah, and Wyoming used the WIN AFIS service bureau containing millions of print records and a growing number of palm prints and other record types.

"And he's not in the system?"

"Nope. So, as I said, chances of being in CODIS are slim too." If there had been no prints supplied for WIN, then he'd never been arrested and the chances of DNA samples were slim, unless a sample had been collected from some other crime.

"What about the watch or the tattoo?"

"Ah, yes. I was saving the best for last. So, this tattoo here—we couldn't have got any luckier, unless, of course, he was in the system and we already had a match. But without that, the tattoo is a very, very good lead. A bison and an arrow . . ."

"Yeah, almost looks Native American."

"Yes, it does, but it's not. Or, I should say, he's not. He's definitely Caucasian. The tattoo is done in a very simple, minimalistic form with only one color of ink. I've given it to our chemist to check out the pigment to see how much carbon it contains. I think with a little luck"—he lifted his head to me—"we should be able to track down the artist. Judging by the look of it, I'm guessing he's local. Plus there's always broadcasting the tattoo and watch over the media and seeing if it sounds familiar to anyone. The watch is nothing special and won't tell us anything. Your basic Fossil, could even be ordered from Amazon. There is a serial number if you want to track it."

"Yeah," I agreed. "That could help. Will you be able to get a good tox screen?"

"We should. We've got enough fluids," Wilson said.

14

AFTER RETURNING TO Glacier, I told Ken about the call from Sam Ward regarding Will DeMarcus's brother working for Wolfie. We decided to head to the Snow Ghost in Whitefish for a visit, but it was the lunch hour and when we went in, another bartender told us that Will wasn't working. We got his address from the restaurant manager who looked up his paperwork and drove to an area by the railroad district in Whitefish, where Will was renting an apartment in an affordable housing complex, one of only two in the town. The weather was starting to change with bruised, gray clouds forming over the mountains and the temperature dropping rapidly from the midseventies to the low sixties. Green trees vibrantly lined the streets, their leaves quaking and shimmering like opal chimes in the cold, strong breezes pushing in.

"This bartender? You think he has something to do with all of this?"

"Not sure. Just checking all tips. I've met this guy before when I talked to Pritchard the other day. He didn't say anything about his brother working for Wolfie, and I find that omission strange, but maybe he just didn't know about it."

Ken looked out to a row of recently built condos housing private residences and various businesses, the town's attempt to gentrify the area by the railways of the Burlington Northern Santa Fe. A little farther north, I found a spot near the housing complex to parallel-park.

I put on the hand brake even though the street was flat because you never can be too careful.

"So, Mr. Detective." Ken opened his door. "Do you have *any* ideas at all about what happened out there?"

"I don't," I admitted, ignoring the *Mr. Detective* teasing as I got out of the car and locked the doors. "All I can do is follow whichever leads come our way. The thing that's bugging me is that one had a car"—I pointed to ours—"and one didn't. It would suggest they're unrelated."

"Hmmm." Ken humored me. "Just coincidental then?"

"Seems unlikely, but stranger things have probably occurred," I said as we walked over to the apartment complex. "In this line of work, we kind of stick with the adage that there are no coincidences."

"Hmmm," Ken said again.

I smiled, glad to have him along even though he wasn't offering much. We climbed to the second floor of the two-story complex. Will lived in the third one on the right. We stopped in front of a paint-chipped brown door and I knocked.

"Who is it?" the voice barked from inside.

"Mr. DeMarcus?"

"Yeah?"

"Park Police Monty Harris." I glanced at Ken and whispered, "Not as friendly as I thought."

Ken shrugged.

"We'd like to talk with you a bit," I said.

He opened the door wearing jeans and no shirt. His hair was crumpled, and he wiped his eyes. He must have been sleeping, which explained his grumpiness. "Oh, yeah, I remember you. From lunch the other day."

"That's right. Can Officer Greeley and I come in?"

"Sure. I worked the late shift last night. Just trying to catch some shut-eye. Can you tell me why?"

"We'd like to ask you a few questions."

"I already told you I don't know anything about that guy you were asking me about."

"Not only about that."

Ken glanced at me and then eyed Will DeMarcus. Will was about the same size as Ken, pale-skinned and muscular in the arms, but a soft paunch beginning to form around his waist. Will opened the door farther and stepped aside to let us in, motioning grandly with his hand for us to enter.

Will's living room was small and cluttered, opening to a balcony that looked out to the ski runs of the Whitefish Mountain Resort. The ski hill used to be called Big Mountain until, rumor had it, online booking options increased, and Big Sky Ski Resort in the Bozeman area started popping up instead of Big Mountain, so the ski area's management decided to change its name. The locals would forever call it Big Mountain.

Ken walked over to the window and peered out. "Nice view," he said, flicking his gum forward on his lower teeth. The room smelled like smoke. A dirty ashtray and some Bud bottles sat on the coffee table along with an open and empty pizza box.

"Thanks, yeah, it was an unintentional perk. I didn't rent it for the view. I had a buddy who was living here and when he left, I took it over. Hard to find good rentals in this town for the right price."

I motioned to a beige chair by the couch. "Okay if we sit?"

"Yeah, sure." Will moved some clothes off the side of the couch and Ken took a seat while I took the chair. Will sat next to Ken.

"So I hate to bring this up, but we're here to ask you about your brother."

"My brother?" Will squinted.

"Yeah, I'm sorry for your loss, but I've been informed that he used to work for Paul Sedgewick—the guy who lost his life in the park a few days ago."

"*Wolfie* was the guy my brother was working for? The guy who died?"

"Yes, weren't you aware that your brother worked for him?"

Will shook his head, grabbed a box of Camels, and fished out a cigarette and tapped it on the side of the pack. "Okay if I smoke?"

I personally hated cigarette smoke and, thankfully, working in the park required very little of my time in its presence, but I said, "Sure, no problem."

"Anyone?" He held up the pack and moved it between Ken and me. We both declined.

"I knew he worked a short stint in the park in the spring," Will said as he put the cigarette to his lips. "But I didn't know exactly for who and doing what. My brother and I weren't that close. He was kind of a recluse. Liked to keep to himself a lot. I called him one day last summer and he said he was working up there, helping some guy with some research or something, but he didn't say what kind, and that made sense to me because I figured that most seasonal workers for the park came from all over the nation for just the summer months. I figured he had to be working for someone local doing something in the park, and not the Park Service itself."

"And you didn't know Wolfie—Sedgewick—was a biologist doing some research in the Park?"

Will shook his head as he lit his cigarette, drawing in a few times to get a strong glow at its tip. "I think I knew he was some kind of a scientist, but not sure what kind and no, I didn't know that he was doing anything in the park workwise." He furrowed his brow and studied me, "But"—he sighed—"my brother committed suicide. There was no foul play or anything. What in the world would he have had to do with this? Are you concerned there was some kind of foul play with my brother?"

"No, nothing like that and not necessarily Sedgewick either," I said. "We just have to look at all angles, for insurance purposes, for the family, and all that. You can understand."

"Yeah, sure," he said. "But what does that have to do with me or my brother?"

"Just that your brother used to work for him. Again, just checking all angles. Wondered if you knew something we didn't." Suddenly, it began to rain and all three of us looked to the windows where heavy drops flew sideways, popping against the glass.

"I knew our June had been too nice so far," Will said, but his face looked suddenly sad and tired.

"June moisture keeps the August forest fires at bay," Ken offered.

I looked down at my notes. "Your brother," I said. "How did he take his life?"

Will looked at the floor for a moment and rubbed the back of his neck in a fatigued gesture. "He OD'd on Vicodin. Respiratory failure."

"Did he have drug issues?"

Will shook his head. "He had depression issues."

"I'm sorry to hear that." I, if anyone, understood what it was like to have a family member with such issues. "Who found him?" I asked.

"His landlady. After a few days when she didn't see him coming or going, but saw his car out front hadn't moved the entire time." DeMarcus crushed his cigarette out in the dirty ashtray and looked at me, his face serious and sad. "It took us off guard. It's been hard, especially for my mom."

"I can imagine," I said. Hearing the rain tap against the glass, I felt a pang of empathy and melancholy for him.

"Is there anything else? Because I really need to get some sleep this afternoon or I won't be worth shit at work tonight."

"Just to dot the i's and cross the t's," I said. "Have you been up in the park for any reason in the last week or past few days?"

Will smiled and half-squinted as if to say, *Is this for real*, then shook his head. "No, no, I have not. I've been working a lot lately. Feel free to ask my manager."

I closed my notebook, thanked him for his time, and Ken and I headed into the pouring rain, letting it splatter our jackets as we ran down the street to the car.

15

W E'VE GOT AN ID on the body," Gretchen said as she came into the incident room. She was wearing her hair loose on her shoulders and not tied back as it usually was when she was on duty. She had on khaki cargo pants and an *I Heart Montana* T-shirt with a report in one hand and a dripping raincoat in the other.

I reached out as she handed me the report.

"The tattoo turned out to be helpful after all. We were able to locate the artist who uses the ink, and he remembered the tattoo, even took photos of it for future design selection for his own records. Said the guy's name was Phillips—even had his name and address on file with the photo. Once we had a name to go on, odontology clarified it. We checked and found he lived alone and worked in his office only part-time, which is why he never hit missing persons."

"Entomology clarified TOD also. The hatch of the bluebottle blow-fly larvae looks to be about five to seven days underway before we got to the body on the twenty-fifth. They took into consideration the day, evening and night temperatures for that week using forty-five to fifty degrees at night and midseventies during the days."

I took the report out of the manila folder and skimmed it. Phillips, Mark. Forty-year-old male with a Whitefish address. "Mark Phillips," I whispered.

"Yeah, Mark Preston Phillips."

"Huh. I think I knew him." It occurred to me how strange the un-dergrowth of our lives was, how roots, weeds, and shrubbery tangled themselves and looped around in peculiar, and sometimes grotesque, ways.

"You *knew* him too?" Gretchen said. Rain still steadily fell and everything outside my window was a lush, deep green. Gretchen's skin looked clear and dewy in the natural light. I stared at her, perhaps a moment too long. I was not only taking in the complete view of her fair skin and vivid blue eyes, I was also remembering Mark Phillips. The attractive, vibrant person before me contrasted with the old, faded image—like sepia in my mind—of the man I'd found eviscerated on the side of the mountain. She fidgeted, waiting for my answer.

"I, uh, yeah," I said, rubbing the back of my neck. "Some time ago."

Mark Phillips. The name burned a hole in my mind. I had not heard it in years and with it came a link like an anchor to things dark, things under the surface that I'd long ago gotten a grip on and stopped thinking about. Now, all of a sudden, like a mean wave from the past, it was pushing, dirty and murky into the present through nothing but chance, coincidence . . . I hated to think, fate.

Something in my face must have shown strain. "Something bad happen with him?" She tilted her head to the side, her blond hair fanning across her shoulder.

"Nah," I said, and it was true. Nothing bad had happened with Phillips. It was what happened *before* Phillips—what happened to send my brother to the place Phillips worked at. "Just trying to remember. I knew him years ago. Must have been in his early twenties at the time. He was a counselor at Glacier Academy." I threw my head in the direction of where the academy still resided about seven or eight miles down the road. "My brother used to go there his last year of high school and our family would visit him on Sundays. I remember seeing him around."

"What's he do now or what *did* he do I should say? Does he still work there?"

"I have no clue. I haven't thought about the place in years."

"It's still running, right?"

"Yeah," I said. "Last I heard, it was." I made a mental note that I should check into it. It was at least twenty years ago that I'd remembered Mark working there, but perhaps he continued to work at the place for many more.

I could picture him now. For a counselor, he seemed wild and reckless, and slightly complicated. All the kids there were supposedly troubled in one way or another, and I really had no idea what kind of snags their lives might have had. In my mind, they still seemed unburdened, sane, and well ordered in comparison to mine and my brother's, riddled with all its complications.

My mother, dealing with her severe bouts of paranoia and depression, stayed in a lot, while my father, a functioning alcoholic and prone to his own bouts of moodiness, held the fort down, eventually running one of the largest construction companies in the valley at the onset of its boom in the early and midnineties and going through a six-pack or more every night after work.

This left large pockets of time for my much larger and older brother to—shall we say, take me under his wing. Although "wing" is much too delicate a description for my brother. Wing implies feathery softness and gentle nurturing. My brother's definition of care was accusing me of being a candy-ass and showing me that bucking up and taking the pain was the law of the land—that bullying was acceptable and, in fact, a man's way—a sort of survival of the fittest.

Eventually, my brother got himself into all sorts of trouble, drinking and doing drugs until my father, suddenly rolling in some dough from his booming construction business, sent him to the Glacier Academy, a therapeutic school for troubled teens mainly used by wealthy families from other parts of the United States who could afford to send their kids somewhere in the hopes that counselors, teachers, and the unforgiving Wild West would set them straight. Tough love at a premium price.

Glacier Academy squatted in the canyon, past Coram, close to the park. My dad and I (usually my mom was too down or ill to go) would get in the car and head there on family day on Sundays. Despite my complaints—that I'd rather go hiking instead—my father would insist I go with him and would give me a choice: either go there with him or stay with Mom in the house with the shades drawn. I decided it was better to get out of the house.

When we'd arrive, we were shown into the campus lodge made out of dark coffee-colored stained logs and a green metal roof. It had a large great room that was used as a cafeteria and all the boys and girls shuffled in to greet their family members with long faces.

I remember having spaghetti and garlic bread, which I ate heartily. Adam wouldn't say much and would barely touch his food, as he was still sulking and angry at my dad for admitting him and furious at me for too many things to count. After dinner, there was a session for just the parents and the children and one of the counselors usually suggested I go outside and enjoy the scenery.

I met Serena then. She was a little older—about thirteen at the time—and she was there for the same reason: her older brother was enrolled. She showed me around, and we went into the woods where she'd found an old tree stand for hunting deer, and we climbed it and sat talking about school. She went to the middle school in Kalispell, in the center of the Flathead Valley, and I was in the middle school in Columbia Falls, near the mouth of the canyon where Glacier Academy sat. For the good part of a year, every Sunday on family day, I met her there and we'd spend an hour or two exploring the woods, playing soccer or badminton on the campus lawn, hanging out by a nearby creek and talking about other kids. She was my first real kiss.

"You know if he has family around locally?" Gretchen's voice brought me back.

"I don't, but I guess I'll be finding that out. What brings you out here?" I asked. "You look like you have the day off."

"Yeah, I'm off, but couldn't stand not nosing in. You know, the case is interesting."

"You don't have a family to go hang with?"

She shook her head. "If this turns into more than two accidents, are you calling Systead or another Series Eighteen-Eleven in?"

"That would be up to Joe, but I'm hoping it's not necessary." I doubted it would go to that level until we had more details, and that's exactly what I planned to get. Right now, I was adrift in a vast sea of unknowns.

· · ·

After Gretchen left, I passed the break room where Ken was microwaving a burrito, grabbing some coffee, and chatting and laughing like a frat boy with two rangers, one of them Michael Bridwell who had helped secure the Loop area when we found Wolfie. I smiled and said hello as I passed and knocked on Smith's door.

He called me in and I laid out what Gretchen had found from Wilson. I told him that I had remembered our new victim, even though I'd never met him, and that he'd worked at Glacier Academy when I was a kid.

Smith listened closely, then placed his chin in his hand, and said, "Are there other family members?"

"Yes, his mother is in Coeur d'Alene, Idaho. The father used to be in Missoula, but is no longer at the address we found. They're divorced. And apparently he has an ex-wife—a Lisa Nash—and a son in Cleveland, Ohio."

"Okay, start with the parents first."

I sat there for a second, because what I was thinking was that my brother had gotten into a bar fight a little over a year ago with Mark Phillips, and I never really knew why. I only knew about it because a local Kalispell cop told me about it. Trust me, it can be a very small town when it comes to gossip and other news around the entire Flathead Valley. Neither was taken in to the station; the cop just broke it up. But for a second as I put away my notepad, I had this image like a movie clip suddenly playing in my head of my large, scowling brother pushing Mark Phillips off the Loop Trail in some revenge-fueled fury.

But my brother wouldn't be caught dead in Glacier Park, and I tend to have an active imagination. What good is a detective without the ability to imagine things? The trick is to not let your imagination run wild. The brawl was inconsequential, so I decided not to mention it to Smith. I went back to the incident room where I found the phone numbers for Randall Phillips in Missoula and Marlene Phillips—she'd kept her ex's last name—in Coeur d'Alene, Idaho.

16

THE PHONE CALLS went as well as could be expected. I have to say I was selfishly relieved to not have to deliver the news in person and Ken was even more relieved than I, but it wasn't exactly pretty over the phone either. I've always known that delivering the news of the death of a loved one was definitely the worst part of being an investigator, but now, with the burden fully on me, I realized that it would never get an ounce easier to do this dreadful task no matter the amount of practice.

I had asked an officer from Marlene Phillips's jurisdiction to stand outside the residence to help take down contact information, confirm that it wasn't a prank, and set her up with a local chaplain. I could have had him take care of the whole miserable task, but I wanted to speak to her myself in case there was any clue to be gleaned.

Luckily, poor Marlene Phillips had her boyfriend home with her so she wasn't alone. When she began to sob and could no longer talk, he picked up the phone and I was able to give him more details and directed him to the officer outside. He gave me Mark's son's phone number (a teen named Devlan who lived with his mother in Ohio) and told me Mark's ex-wife worked as a wealth advisor for a financial institution in a suburb of Cleveland where her family lived.

Mark's father, Randall, was harder to track down. He wasn't at home and neither Marlene nor her boyfriend knew where he worked, or if he worked. Last she heard, he'd left for the Bakken Oil Fields to find employment. She gave me his cell phone number, but it was no longer in service.

I was able to track his Social Security through the IRS to recent wages coming from Moore Electric and to get a different cell phone number from the company. I sat for a moment before calling him, imagining the Bakken Oil fields in North Dakota. Since the drilling had begun, there had been a striking rise in crime in the makeshift communities full of hungry-for-wages men: drug-related crimes, gambling, brutal rapes and murders, prostitution. We kept a close watch on it since some of the crime had been spilling into the eastern part of Montana and many of the workers used Highway 2, which runs right through East and West Glacier, to either get home to their families and loved ones in the Flathead Valley or to simply get away from the crazy conditions in the fields.

I picked up the landline, called his cell, and got his voicemail. I left my name and number and politely asked him to call me when he had a chance.

· · ·

Mark's ex-wife, Lisa Nash, had already got the news from her boy's grandmother. When I spoke to her, she agreed that it would be good for Devlan to talk to me, to hear it officially. When I spoke to Devlan, he got quiet, then after a long pause, sighed, and said, "They've told me, but I can't believe it. How . . . how did it happen?"

I told him about the Loop and he said he was familiar with it because he grew up in Kalispell, in the township of Evergreen to be exact, with his mother mostly. His parents were divorced when he was five and they moved to Ohio when he was ten. He hadn't spoken to his dad in over three weeks, since sometime in late May when his dad called to wish him a happy birthday.

"What did your dad do?" I asked.

"He's a cartographer. Works for the state, the county, or whoever else contracts for his services." Devlan didn't catch his use of the present tense, and I didn't expect him to. Sometimes it took time for reality to sink in, especially when the news had come by phone and not in person. There were no physical images, no somber looks from the official delivering the news, to lock the reality into place. The other end of the line suddenly got very quiet, and I asked Devlan if he was okay. I could hear him breathing.

"Yeah, I guess," he mumbled. I could tell he didn't feel up to any more talking, so I asked if he could put his mother back on, which he did without another word.

Lisa got back on and I apologized for how difficult it was. She said she understood and asked how she could help.

"Did he have a significant other?" I asked.

"My ex has"—she paused, sighed and lowered her voice, probably so Devlan couldn't hear—"*had* trouble with relationships. He's had several since we've split. Some lasted for three years, some as long as five, but he always seemed to blow them in the end. I don't know exactly why. Let's just say Mark had trouble being there for people when you needed him the most. He had an addictive personality. He never could do anything just a little—it always had to be all or nothing. He was an odd mix of health and utter destruction."

"How so?"

"He loved to hike, bike, eat right, meditate, you name it, and on the side, he gambled, drank, took drugs—"

"Drugs?"

"Yeah, pills mostly. I don't even really know what exactly. I just remember seeing some heavy-duty stuff around at times—like Oxycontin and Dilaudid. There were always sleeping pills around as well. I guess he had trouble sleeping. Basically, he could be the nicest, most helpful and caring guy around and at other times, the most selfish, meanest, and ridiculing person you could know."

I wrote notes and encouraged her to keep talking, but she paused as if it suddenly occurred to her that she was revealing personal qualities about her son's father to me and that she was somehow betraying her son by doing so. When I could tell she wasn't going to offer anything more, I asked, "Did Mark know or ever mention a Paul Sedgewick, also known as Wolfie?"

"Not that I know of."

"Do you know the name of his last girlfriend?"

"It was Bev." Her voice sounded smaller now. Small and afraid for her now-fatherless child, even though they lived a long way from him. Perhaps the fact that she'd moved her son far from his father would take on a different light. Maybe she was suddenly regretting the lost time he not only experienced with him alive and well, but would now never make up. "Beverly Lynde," she added.

"And one more question"—I paused, and she didn't say anything—"did your ex-husband ever mention working at a place called Glacier Academy?"

"Of course," she said. "That was years ago, but that was where he worked before I met him at the community college in cartography school. He had quit because he wanted to go back to school. Said he was tired of working with manipulative, messed-up teens who were going nowhere fast. Funny"—she huffed, a sound like a horse makes—"in retrospect, how I came to . . ." Her voice drifted off.

"How you came to?" I prodded.

"Oh, I don't know. . . . I shouldn't say, but, well, how I came to know Mark as the manipulative one."

I thanked her, told her again how sorry I was for Devlan, and reminded her of resources for teens dealing with grief in public schools and in the communities.

17

THE NEXT DAY the papers announced that another body had mysteriously turned up in the same area as the body of Paul Sedgewick, but we had not yet released his identification.

Cathy Sedgewick called me and I told her what I knew—that the death could be a coincidence, but it definitely raised our suspicion level to the point where we were considering the possibility that the two incidents were related. And if so, it meant that neither one was an accident since the time of death on the bodies indicated there couldn't have been a struggle in which they both fell at the same time to their demise. I reminded her, though—mainly to manage expectations—that the second body did not rule out a freak coincidence of two accidents occurring around the same time and in the same vicinity. Stranger things had happened. *Night of the Grizzlies*, a well-known book among Glacier Park visitors, explored how two unrelated females were attacked on the same night in two separate parts of the park. The very fact that it happened on the same night had captured people's imaginations for years.

Still, my suspicion meter was staying high as Ken and I headed to Mark Phillips's residence. He lived on Colombia Avenue in Whitefish in an old white house in need of a new coat of paint with two bedrooms, a small living room, a tiny office, and a medium-size kitchen all on one floor.

We began in the garage where Mark's truck was safe and sound: a Toyota Tundra. Inside lay some stray empty and crushed cans of soda on the floor beneath the passenger seat, a bottle of sunscreen on the front seat, and his registration, insurance card, car manual, and some maps in the glove box. "Interesting," I said to Ken. "That his car is here. Means he got a ride from someone into the park."

Inside Phillips's house, which opened directly into the living room, I paused and recalled what my Investigative Procedures instructor in DC had said about searching houses. They supposedly were much easier to handle than outdoor scenes since they were naturally contained. Peter Mack, the teacher—a short, balding guy with a gray mustache— stressed the process: *Divide the house into a grid, handle each room slowly, methodically and one by one.*

"Okay," I said to Ken. "Let's divide it up. You take the north side— the two bedrooms and bathroom. I'll take the south—the kitchen, living room, and office."

The living room sat quiet and plain with basic furnishings: a dull beige, past-its-prime sofa, an old trunk used as a coffee table, a big-screen TV hanging on the wall that looked pricier than all the furniture in the room combined. Wires snaked from the cable box and the DVD player up the wall to the backside of the flat screen. A small plate with leftover crumbs and a dirty glass perched in the corner of the trunk while some of last week's newspapers hogged the majority of its surface. Very few mementos stood on the built-in shelves on the side of the room: just two silver candlesticks empty of candles, and a picture of Phillips and a small boy who I presumed was Devlan when he was younger.

I knew exactly where in the park it was taken because I recognized the boardwalk leading up to Hidden Lake from the top of Logan Pass. Two early-summer scruffy mountain goats stood in the background and Phillips, with short, wavy dark hair, a prominent nose, and a crooked, half smile kneeled down to get closer to his son's height for the picture. Devlan looked maybe six or seven, big grin, with thick unruly hair flopping over his ears. I took the photo with me.

Yes, I vaguely remembered what Mark Phillips looked like and could see him in my mind standing on the wooden deck at Glacier Academy, barking orders at one of the students who was sweeping the deck for him. *Do as tell you or I'll . . .* Of course, I'm not sure what he actually said, but that's what was ringing in my ears for no particular reason.

Several bestsellers like *Lonesome Dove, The Da Vinci Code, The Girl with the Dragon Tattoo* (not the whole series), *Shutter Island, Carrie, Misery,* and Michener's *Alaska* and *The Covenant* stood on the shelves, but mostly gave way to nonfiction: *Glacier Park's Best Hiking, Hiking in the Rocky Mountains, Northwest Montana Hikes,* and some books on random topics: astronomy, the cosmos, evolution, eating right, afterlife experiments, Buddhism, and Hinduism.

"Okay, so you read a little, but you mostly like to learn something when you do," I whispered to myself. "And you like to hike."

In the kitchen, the cabinets were full of cereal boxes—one completely empty, but still on the shelf, a box of reduced-sugar instant oatmeal, peanut butter, cans of soup and black beans, refried beans, and green beans. Stray Cheerios and Special K flakes scattered across the shelves, unlined with paper to protect them the way Lara always did when we moved into a place. Sticky-looking stains and more bits of food lay on the counters and when I opened the fridge, a foul smell sprang forth, telling me he'd been away long enough for something to be going bad.

But even without the milk and meat going bad, he seemed sloppy, maybe lazy in certain ways—except for the hiking—and something inside me instinctively prickled, telling me I wouldn't have liked Mark Phillips if I had ever gotten to know him.

His bookshelves were nothing like Wolfie's, crowded and showing a deep thirst for knowledge. I didn't begrudge his curiosity, but there was something about the smattering of these that seemed like a façade, as if Phillips wanted to dabble in some ideas, but didn't want to dive too deeply into any one subject. Of course, this was pure speculation and probably more than a little judgmental on my part. "Why are you not liking this guy, Monty?" I whispered out loud to the empty room again. I wondered if it was simply because he represented Glacier Academy, the place that was supposed to have been Adam's salvation. But things are never that easy. Plus the fact that he and my brother had been in a fight grated on me. There was no reason I should care about that. My brother and I hadn't spoken in over four years.

Maybe he simply reminded me of Adam.

Ill-tempered, volatile, and quick to express his not-so-kind beliefs, Adam and I made no music together. We were opposites, not only in build and stature, but in pretty much everything: dress, demeanor, tidiness, thoroughness, religion, and if our politics happened to line up, it was for all the wrong reasons. Basically, all those years ago, I was a snitch, and Adam never forgave me.

About a year after the Nathan Faraway incident, Adam began getting into more and more trouble, getting into fights after school, drinking, and taking speed. I told on him, and when my dad found out that it wasn't just pot and booze, that it was speed and some stronger stuff too (I overhead one of his friends say heroin, but I was never sure), he'd sent Adam to Glacier Academy, relying on the school to help solve Adam's problems—to come to the rescue when his wife couldn't and he had a job to go to each day.

And when my mom died four years ago in a car accident, Adam and I managed to get into it. He had accused my dad of not caring, of not keeping the car keys well hidden. In an attempt to ward off an all-out fight between Adam and my dad at the small reception at our house following the funeral, I'd simply pointed out the obvious: regardless of what occurred, it was a difficult situation—trying to facilitate the leading of a seminormal life . . . letting her drive a car to have some independence, versus trying to keep her safe.

The fact that I was sticking up for Dad sent Adam through the roof, and Adam's way of dealing with his anger was always to pounce, especially when it came to me. Some of Dad's friends pulled Adam off. Right then and there, utterly embarrassed before the few friends my parents had, I made a promise to myself that if I could avoid it, I'd never talk to the guy again.

I left Phillips's kitchen and went into the office, where it was even more haphazard, littered with bills, torn envelopes, and papers. Crumpled sweatshirts and a pile of jackets that he hadn't bothered to hang in the coat closet slumped over the desk chair. I had already checked the mailbox. Mark Phillips had quit bringing in his mail five or six days before. I wrote this in my notebook.

On the wall hung a large, framed beautiful topo map of Glacier, with the east side of the Divide in a calming salmon color and the west side in pale green. Other warm tones of yellows, oranges, and burgundies were woven into the terrain to denote the changes in elevation. It was a meticulous work of art and, recalling what Devlan said, I was certain Mark had made this map. The attention to detail and the beauty of it was completely incongruous with the disorder of his house, and I thought of what Mark's ex-wife, Lisa, said: *all or nothing*.

I opened the top drawer of the desk to see more papers in disarray, pens and pencils, a plastic calculator saying *Compliments of Forever-Clean Carpets*. I lifted up some of the papers and saw his mortgage payment book. He had yet to make June's payment, but had made May's. The second drawer contained paper clips, a plastic water bottle, some old plastic key chains, boxes of matches from various nonlocal bars, a stack of folded topo maps of Glacier, the Bob Marshal Wilderness, the Mission Mountains, and the Swan Range. An old tube of some kind of hydrocortisone cream lay in the corner and in the very back, behind the stack of maps, sat a shoe box.

I pulled it out and lifted the top to find more odds and ends: a poem written on old, yellow-tinged paper about love being deep like a river. It was signed with the name Diane—perhaps a girlfriend from years back—in faint cursive at the bottom. I turned the paper over and saw a sketch drawn lightly of a young woman with long hair standing behind a man seated in a chair. Her hand rested on his shoulders, but her fingers were close to his collarbones so you couldn't tell if she was lovingly resting them or closing them around his neck. A cartoon bubble coming from the man said, "Honey, that's too tight."... I neatly folded the paper and carefully put it in my pocket.

As far as I knew, Mark Phillips lived alone and the place showed it. A box of more books, these on cartography, sat on the floor next to his desk collecting dust, several old cameras in leather cases sat next to the box of books, and a plaque a little bigger than the size of a hardback from a cartography association was propped against the wall next to the cameras, supposedly waiting to get hung on the wall. I wrote the name of the cartography association from the plaque in my notebook, tucked it back in my shirt pocket, and walked out to find Ken in one of the bedrooms, looking in the closet.

"Anything interesting?"

He shrugged. "Not really, a few old, very dated suits, and some regular pants and button-up shirts. Some flannel. I don't get the feeling the guy cared all that much how he looked."

"No, not himself or his house." I glanced around the room, sterile and unadorned with art or knickknacks that might warm it, but still cluttered. More clothes lay strewn across the floor and some ratty T-shirts and jeans draped over a single chair in the corner by the only window in the room. Some blue used towels lay near the chair as if he'd showered and just dropped them by his pile of clothes when he dressed. A laptop sat by his bed and was plugged into an outlet. I unplugged it and tucked it under my arm.

The bathroom was not very clean, old toothpaste, hair, and soap scum everywhere. Ken said the other room was used for working out as I stepped around the corner and peeked in. It was empty of furniture and just held some free weights, a bench press, a CD player and speakers, and a lone crocus plant. Nothing much to consider except that the plant was not in good shape, and Mark Phillips was not taking good care of it.

On the floor, off to the side of a small mudroom leading to the back yard where the garage sat, were several sets of the same-size man's boots in all types: work, snow, and hiking boots and some pretty beaten-up trail runners. On the wall, several coats and two hiking packs hung on hooks. One pack had capsaicin spray still attached to the waist strap. I pulled both of them down and gave them to Ken to carry since my hands were full.

· · ·

On our way out into the chilly day, I paused on Mark Phillips's porch with the guy's laptop tucked under my arm, the poem and note folded in my pocket, and the picture of Mark and his son. Ken had the two packs and the capsaicin bear spray. The temperature had dropped even further and it felt close to midforties. Snow in June was not unheard of, and the gunmetal sky goaded me. The air smelled of grass, fir needles from a nearby spruce, and the sharp tang of offending sleet or snow at the start of summer.

The gloom echoed the weight of the case, not only that now there were two deaths to investigate, but that I had an odd sensation that it was somehow nudging up against old memories. One particular memory flashed in my mind: my brother standing on the porch steps of our childhood home on Fifth Avenue in Columbia Falls, angry and worked up, yelling, "You pussy, don't you know it's been me who's taken care of you all these years? And this is how you repay me?"

I had stood in the doorway in my favorite Seahawks jersey thinking my mother was still asleep and wouldn't do anything anyway even if she was awake. My dad was at work and wouldn't be home for hours, and when he did come home, he'd have already downed a few beers and would go straight for the fridge for more. I figured Adam would rush at me to hit me, and I was prepared to bolt to my room and lock myself in, but instead, he turned his angry, flushed face away and stomped off across the lawn, calling me a fucking wimp. I watched him leave, not sure whether to feel guilty or relieved.

18

I HAD MY REASONS for feeling fairly confident my brother was capable of pushing someone off a cliff when I sat before Smith in his office the previous day. You have to understand Adam. And to understand Adam, you have to understand what happened to Nathan Faraway.

Nathan, Nathan Faraway. I guess we all have defining moments in our childhood, some more dramatic than others, and some so profound that they alter your path, send you reeling in a different direction or spinning in one place forever. Nathan Faraway was my childhood friend through elementary and middle school. We were both on the small side with dark hair, and people used to think we were brothers. He was the friend who made my boring school days better, the one who made me laugh by making stupid faces, but who had a higher IQ than most of the other kids in my class. But because he was brainy, the kids liked to pick on him. Tease him about getting one-hundreds in math and science.

The night my brother insisted Nathan and I go along with his and his buddies' plans was the night that would tilt the world for me because it was the night the worst happened. I thought the worst was my family—that life couldn't go down from there. But it did.

My recollection of the events often came in a menagerie of disjointed scenes and senses, like a spotlight moving on a stage illuminating one scene, then another. That particular fall night, my brother had come to me the day before and woken me up. I remember feeling cold and noticing the frost on the outside of the window and his breath smelling of nicotine and beer. "Monty, Jesus, wake up. I'm talking to you."

"What?" I rubbed my eyes.

"The boys and I," he whispered, a hissing voice in the dark. "We've been talking. We need your help."

"My help?"

"Yeah, yours and Nathan's."

I squinted at him in the dark.

"Perry. You know Perry?"

I nodded.

"He really, *really* likes Nathan's sister."

I held up my hand. "Stop, Adam. This is just another prank." My insides instantly felt shaky. Any trick played by my brother involving *the boys* was never an innocent or remotely enjoyable experience. Since I was small, his pranks involved things like debagging, Indian burns that made my arm red and chafed, titty twisters that went on too long and hard, leaving me sore and bruised, to more elaborate schemes.

One time, he'd invited some lonely kid to come hang out with him and his buddies after school and told him to meet by a 7-Eleven a few blocks away. I know this because I overheard my brother hatching the plan the night before with his friend Todd. I convinced Nathan to walk to the store after school and saw the guy standing outside by a post waiting, his shoulders lifted to his ears in the cold, his hands buried in his pockets, his breath pluming before him like wishes in the air. He was much older—in tenth grade. We were only in sixth, but after painfully watching him stand there for a bit, we went over as if I thought I could save him. I told him Adam wasn't coming. When he didn't say anything, I asked if he wanted to come hang out with Nathan and me instead. He still didn't answer, just lowered his head in embarrassment, and left. In retrospect, it would have been mortifying for him to come hang out with two sixth-graders.

No, his coming to *me* for help was not very believable at first.

"I swear. No trick. I promise. It's just for Perry, for Halloween. He really likes her and just wants to spend some time with her."

"Molly?" I thought of Molly, her long brown hair, her curvy body, her fruity smelling bubble gum. Sometimes she watched TV with Nathan and me and she smelled like sweet apples and vanilla. "Nathan's sister?"

"Yeah, but we need your, and Nathan's help."

"I've already got plans for tomorrow. Nathan and I are doing something."

"Bullshit, you're just being a candy-ass. What? You two going to go trick-or-treating like little boys?" Adam knew good and well trick-or-treating wasn't something in our history because Mom always seemed to be off her meds whenever Halloween rolled around and never could get it together to help us create outfits when we were little. When she felt pressured by us to do so, she got nervous and weird, telling us that Halloween was a time for bad people to come out, a time when evil people would do harm to us. She'd sit at the window and stare through a part in the curtain looking for those ill-meaning people until she got more and more nervous, took her imipramine or Haldol, then float to some softer, fuzzier place.

By the time I was old enough to scrape some half-assed outfit together by myself, like the time I borrowed my dad's overcoat and went as a gangster, I felt too awkward to enjoy going door-to-door and having adults look at me suspiciously, as if I might kick their pumpkins in since I was an awkward preteen and not cute like the little kids.

"Look," Adam said. "Just hear me out."

I sat in bed and listened while he made his case: Molly had told Perry that she couldn't go with him because her parents wanted her to hang with her brother while they went to a Halloween party across town. She wasn't sure yet what Nathan had in mind to do for Halloween, but whatever it was, she was bound to go along and make sure he stayed out of trouble, even though she admitted that he was way too old to have her looking after him. Her parents—Adam said she had told Perry—were just nervous since it was Halloween. "So all you need to do is come hang out with us and then she'll come too. It's that simple." Adam smiled at me.

"I'll think about it," I said slowly. "But I'm not promising anything."

"That's fine." Adam held up his hand innocently, but his eyes said *if you don't do what I say . . .* "All right. You think about it."

I wish I'd never even heard the idea.

19

I SPENT A GOOD part of the afternoon at headquarters finding pieces of information on Mark Phillips, both by reading online and by making phone calls to his colleagues. The dates on his mail confirmed that he'd been missing about five or six days, as had the usage of his cell phone. There were only small bits here and there online about maps he'd worked on. Several were topos of Glacier Park and some of both the Bob Marshall and Scapegoat Wilderness areas.

I looked up the organization named on the plaque, Montana Association of Geographic Information Professionals, and double-checked that it was, indeed, Flathead County he was contracted under: Flathead County Geographic Information Systems, known as the GIS office.

Since Ken and I had found the Toyota in Phillips's garage, I wondered whether he might have a second vehicle that he'd been driving into or near the park the day he died, so I checked his car registration and found that he had the truck in the garage but no other vehicle was registered in his name. Then I checked with his company to make sure they hadn't issued him one. They hadn't.

I had also gotten the West Glacier entrance surveillance tapes for the last weeks and had asked Ken to go through them to look for Sedgewick's Subaru, Phillips's truck, or any other signs of either victim entering or leaving the park. Unfortunately, not all entrances have surveillance, and anyone accessing the park through the North Fork could easily go undetected.

I grabbed my notebook, and Ken and I headed out to visit Beverly

Lynde, Mark Phillips's former significant other. Ken loosened his collar and cracked the window just enough to let in some air but keep out the rain. We were lucky it hadn't snowed and wasn't any colder, but it was a biting, raw rain, nonetheless, and it chilled me to the bone. Early summer is like this in Northwest Montana: a series of false starts, like tricks played on us all: at times nice balmy weather—eighty degrees—then, a thirty-degree temperature drop to sometimes below freezing, even in late June. If we were lucky, it was only rain sending us huddling into raincoats instead of snow to our down jackets.

"You warm?"

"No, just need a little air," he said.

"You okay?"

"Yeah, I'm fine."

"You hate this work?"

"No, I didn't say that. It's fine."

"You wish you were in the park, writing tickets?"

"Not necessarily. I was just thinking about these guys, you know."

I perked up. I knew Ken was loquacious and I had been wondering why he hadn't said as much as usual in the past few days. I just figured he was perhaps feeling a little out of his league doing investigative work. "What about them?"

"I don't know. Just so weird—two of them."

"That just sink in or something?"

Ken shrugged. "No, it's been bothering me since we visited Wolfie's wife. I guess it's harder for you to understand. I mean, you don't have kids."

"No, I don't. I guess I can imagine, though. I did have parents."

"Yeah, well, of course. It's just, well, hard to swallow how fragile we all are." He looked down at one arm and I wondered if he was measuring in his mind all the effort to build his muscles, what it meant in the scheme of a physical world—a body—that could be demolished in the blink of an eye.

We parked and walked up the drive to a small half-wood, half-stucco house in Columbia Falls off Nucleus Avenue, near the Flathead River. The gardens were well maintained and the lawn nicely cut. Ken stood back while I rang the doorbell.

"Who is it?" The voice from inside sounded high-pitched.

"Park Police Officer Monty Harris. Looking for Beverly Lynde."

A second later the door opened and a slender, short-haired brunette woman with doe eyes looked curiously at us. I guessed she was in her late twenties or early thirties. She wore jeans, sandals, and a floppy pale-blue sweater, and her toenails were painted pale green. I couldn't help but wonder if her feet were cold.

"Beverly Lynde?"

"No," she said. "She's not here. She's at work. Can I help you?"

"You are?"

She gave a tentative smile and tilted her head shyly to the side. "Marisa. I rent a room from Bev. She owns the place."

"I see. Where does Ms. Lynde work?"

Marisa pushed her hair behind her ear. "In the park."

"The park? Glacier?"

"Yeah, she drives one of the park tourist shuttles. Has every summer for the past few years. You've never seen her?" She looked at my badge.

"No, I guess I haven't. She's there now?"

"Far as I know. Said she works till seven tonight."

I thanked Marisa and we drove back to the park, this time past headquarters in West Glacier, through the west entrance pay gates and a few miles down the road to the new Apgar Transit Center where the free bus and shuttle services ran. The Transit Center was built in 2007 and instituted the shuttle service to accommodate park visitors so they could access most destinations along Going-to-the-Sun Road while reconstruction occurred, an attempt to minimize traffic, parking, and exhaust problems. Hikers and sightseers alike quickly took to the system. We asked the ranger behind the main desk to see the shuttle schedule for Beverly Lynde.

"She's got number eight." The woman checking the logbook looked up at me through wire-rimmed glasses similar to mine. She wore the green ranger uniform—army-green pants and a lighter green, almost beige, short-sleeve button-up. "She should be in for a break in about forty-five minutes. Then she has to go back out at the four-thirty run to the Logan Pass visitor center and back. I can call you at your office when she gets here if you'd like, or you can wait."

Ken seemed happier now after seeing the roommate, Marisa, whom he commented was cute, asked me if I'd noticed her big breasts and wondered if I thought they were real or, as he put it, store-bought. When I said I wasn't entirely sure, but that I thought they were real, he said he was hungry, so we grabbed some soup at the West Glacier Café. When we came back, we only waited five minutes for Beverly to show, and we watched her pull into the large lot in the white vehicle with GOING TO THE SUN ROAD SHUTTLE written across its side and overlapping a graphic design of large peaks. GLACIER NATIONAL PARK stood under those words.

She stepped out, and locked it up. She was tall, maybe five foot nine or ten, with a thick braid of reddish-blond hair over one shoulder. She wore a cap, khakis, and a white T-shirt, the shuttle driver's uniform, and threw on a raincoat as she walked toward us. She angled her head slightly to the side as if tilting it a certain way would make the slanted rain miss her.

I walked toward her and held out my hand and introduced myself and Ken. "I hate to interrupt your break, but do you mind if Officer Greeley and I have a quick word with you. We just have a few questions."

She looked at us both, her hazel eyes clear and large. "Sure. Have I done something wrong? Is there a report against my driving?"

"No, no." I held up my hand. "Nothing at all like that. This is about a man you apparently used to date, Mark Phillips?"

"Mark? We broke up over a year ago."

I held out my hand to motion to the deck with an overhang to the side of the building. "Here, let's get out of this."

She followed us over, and I motioned for her to sit on one of the wooden benches reused from native trees in the cleared area. "That's okay," she said and leaned against the wood railing instead. "Been sitting a lot already." I stood against it too, and Ken sat on one of the large rock platforms surrounding a massive log pillar supporting the roof over the deck.

"So what's this about?"

"Working up here, I'm sure you've heard about the two bodies we've found below the Loop."

She nodded, her brow furrowed. "Horrible deal. I had several trips delayed because of those incidents."

"I'm sorry to inform you that one of them was Mark."

"Mark?" she put her hand to her mouth.

"I'm afraid so."

She stared at me, stunned, dropping her hand to her sternum, her mouth open in shock.

"Do you know if he was currently involved with anyone else?"

She shook her head slowly. "I don't." She swallowed hard. "I heard things here and there. That he had a date or two. Oh my God, Mark? Really? Are you positive?"

"Yes, we're certain."

She put her head down, cupping her face in her hands, then looked up, pursed her lips and shook it off. "What happened?"

"We're not sure. Right now, all we can assume is that we had two accidents in the same place."

"That's what I've heard, but holy shit. That's insane."

"You can say that again," Ken chirped up.

"Ms. Lynde, when was the last time you saw Mark?"

"It's been a while. Last fall, before the service closed for the winter. He took my shuttle up for a hike. He hiked a lot. That's how we met. Before they built this place." She motioned to the building and new parking area. "The old shuttle system we ran out of Lake McDonald Lodge. I was waitressing there back then. He used to come in for oatmeal and coffee before catching a seven a.m. shuttle to wherever he planned on trekking for the day. He did it every weekend."

"Did he continue that ritual after you broke up?"

"I think he did. Like I said, just last September he was headed up for a hike—that was a few months after we ended things."

"So you have no idea what was going on in his life for the past few weeks here?"

"None. But"—she sighed—"I do know his habits. We dated for over six years."

"What happened?"

She sighed even louder and blew out a large breath. "Mark was a complicated guy. Never happy. I'm pretty sure he was an addict. Always running from himself, could never sit still unless he was making a map or working on something."

"What was he using?"

"Hell, I don't know. Some painkiller. I have no idea where he'd get them from, but I'd seen them around. He saw some doctor for back pain he claimed to have, but it didn't seem to interrupt his lifestyle. I guess he had a bulging disk. Said hiking helped it. Drank a lot of alcohol as well and probably mixed the two. He liked to gamble and was always broke because of it. Loved to exercise like crazy too, not just by hiking. He went to the gym a lot. Superfit. But, you know, I figured he was addicted to adrenaline too." She glanced at Ken's muscles and looked away. "I'm not saying everyone fit is addicted to adrenaline or anything," she added, I presumed for Ken's sake.

"As far as I know," I said looking at Ken, "the only thing this guy is addicted to is Juicy Fruit."

Ken chuckled and Beverly looked confused, even though Ken was clearly working a piece as we spoke.

"Anyway, my point is that you can simply just be an addict about a lot of things and don't necessarily need just one drug of choice."

"I'm sure that's true." I thought of my dad and Adam too. "So is that why you broke up?"

"Yeah, among other things." She glanced at the flagpole off to the side of the building, droplets of water clinging to it. "He could really be mean at times. I figured it was all part of his addictive nature. The edginess. And I was lonely with him. He didn't seem to love or be at peace with himself, so how could I expect him to love me?"

"Sounds complicated," I said as if I'd never had a hand in that particular game with complicated people, Adam in particular. Probably my father. Maybe Lara too, and I just hadn't fully recognized it until the past several years.

"He could be a great guy too, really charmed me in the beginning—superbright and enjoyable to talk to, but somewhere along the line, he just kept more and more to himself as if the closer we got, the more he pushed me away. I was always catching him in stupid little lies that I swear he told only out of habit. I wanted to get some couples counseling, but"—she threw her hand up in the air—"I don't know why I'm babbling on like this. Bottom line is that addicts don't change. They sacrifice anything and anyone around them to keep their vices."

"Well, if hiking was a vice, it sure was a healthy one, but it looks like it got the best of him," Ken said.

Beverly bit her top lip and she looked like she was holding back tears. She looked at her van, then said, "I should probably go inside before I have to go back on the road."

"Just one more question: Do you know anyone who might have wanted to hurt Mark?"

"Mark could piss a few people off, for sure. God only knows if he pissed off someone in Chicago. That's where he called to place his bets. Some guy named Lucky." She shook her head and laughed. "Sounds like a bad movie, doesn't it?" A tear sprang to the corner of her eyes and she wiped it with the butt of her hand. "See, that's the shit I needed to get away from."

I thought of Mark Phillips's ex, Lisa, and her son, Devlan, moving all the way to Ohio. "Know a last name?"

"No. I just know the name Lucky."

"Where did Mark work out?"

"That big community one in Whitefish."

"Anything else you can think of?"

She looked at Ken, then me and shrugged. "Like I said, I think he had a few people along the way who didn't like him much. It didn't take a lot to set him off, and I pulled him off a few fights here and there when we'd been out having a good time in the bars over the years. I'd heard rumors that when he was younger, he was quite the bully. One guy called him that in the bar after we dated for about a year and when I asked him why, he didn't have much to say. Just shrugged his shoulders and said the guy was an asshole and a troublemaker, but I always got the feeling there might have been more to the story. Plus I found a Dear John letter from an old girlfriend among some of his old pictures one time and when I asked him about it, he got really angry at me for looking through his things."

"Do you remember her name?"

"It was signed Diane, She must have meant something to him to have kept it. I mean, the letter was dated in the early nineties, maybe '92 or '93. I can't remember exactly, but he had to have been only in his early twenties at the time."

"Did it mention anything in particular?"

"Just the usual young love thing—that she thought he was the one, that it would be the real deal with him, but that he had let her down. That she couldn't date someone capable of the things she knew he was capable of. That's what I'd asked him about and that's when he got so mad and turned it around on me—that I was in the wrong for looking at his personal things. And I suppose I was. But secrecy begets secrecy."

"Yeah," I agreed. "It does. You still have that letter?"

"Oh no, he took all his stuff when he moved out. It's probably at his house though, unless he finally got rid of it."

"Would Mark have taken a shuttle up this year?"

"Possibly." She squinted to think about it. "Most of the old drivers know him, but some of the newer ones might not."

I thanked Beverly for her help after finding out where Mark's cartography office was in Whitefish and left her in whatever sadness would fall upon her as she took in the death of her ex-lover.

20

THAT EVENING, I sat in my dorm apartment and took a break from scouring Phillips's phone records. He had very few incoming or outgoing calls, mostly to coworkers and to several friends around town that we had already checked out. As far as I could see, he had no current relationship going and no particular hiking buddies.

I was sitting in the old small couch that came with the place and gazed at the system-provided pictures flashing across on my laptop screen saver—scenes of lush rainforests, bronzed deserts, and African savannas. The drizzle had ceased for the evening and in the typical coyness of the park's spirit, sunlight dipped low enough to break under the clouds and spray the lush foliage with coppery light as if to say, *See it's still stunning here even on the rainy ones*. The upper branches of a tall birch outside cast yellowish shifting shadows on the wall beside me and I thought of what Beverly Lynde said about Mark Phillips's personality. Then I considered his house again. It was not as neat as my place, but I had to admit, it was obvious I lived alone too. I had very few personal touches even though my orderliness showed with my dishes clean and put away, my bed made, throw blankets neatly folded, and my counters tidy.

Then I thought about Adam. Last I heard, he was living in Coram in a run-down log cabin he'd helped a friend build years ago and doing odds and ends around town for people in the canyon: construction, maintenance on buildings, grounds-keeping for some local hotels, mechanical work on some cars. . . . I had no desire to visit him, but was beginning to wonder what he and Mark Phillips fought about so violently that the police became involved. I didn't know what I could ever do for Adam, what he expected from me, if anything, and what compensation he needed from me for—as he would claim—"ruining his life."

The room felt quiet and peaceful and in my solitary stillness—and because I'm a positive person—I tried to remember the good things about Adam before things turned bad for him, before my dad sent him to the wilderness academy. I had a vague image of a child pulling at my mom's skirt and trying to ask questions as she shooed him away while frustratingly trying to feed me as I sat in a high chair. I was probably conjuring it up because I couldn't imagine my memories going that far back. The image was wispy like a feathery cloud, ready to float away at the slightest interruption, and I strained to hold it in my mind but couldn't. Instead, my thoughts once again drifted to that Halloween night.

It was appropriately windy and moody with creaking trees dropping their golden leaves under shadowy clouds. The night sky held a pale-purple glow from the three-quarter moon, lighting the bruised clouds creeping across the western horizon. I remember thinking that Nathan had a point as he yelled at me, spittle flying from his mouth, "Crap, Monty. Why can't you ever stand up to him?" He kicked his foot across some dried, dead weeds. "Can't you tell by now he was just going to play some trick on us like always?"

My brother and his friends had just left us in a cemetery north of town—just driven off after cajoling us out of the car.

"I do stick up to him," I said in a meager defense.

"*Stand*, not stick," he said, disgusted. "And, no, you don't."

"Stand," I corrected myself. "But I . . . I swear, I didn't know. I thought it was about Molly. That's all."

'Well, great." He shook his head angrily. "Fucking loser. That's what your brother calls you. I think he's right."

"Don't say that. You're a fucking loser."

He stared back at me, his face twisted in anger. I could feel it heaving from him in waves like the fierce wind pushing through the dying leaves and bending the branches. And it wasn't just anger; there was something else. Perhaps fear. "I trusted you," he said, and I realized it was disappointment I was seeing in his expression, not just worry.

"I know, Nate. Really, I'm sorry, but I thought they wanted our help this time."

"You should've known." Nathan turned, mumbling and swearing under his breath, and marched off into the woods. He crossed a fallen log and went into the darkness of the trees, which swallowed him almost instantly.

It was complicated. My acquiescence to my brother's proposals and demands wasn't just borne from stupidity or blind faith. There were a whole host of emotions that played out inside of me: the need to fit in, the hope for my brother's approval, the raw fear of rejection . . . of abandonment.

"I really did," I yelled. "I thought they'd be nice for a change," I called out and started to follow him. I stepped on the same log he'd gone over, but my foot caught a soft, rotted-out piece and came crashing down into a dip in the ground. My heel jammed backward under the log, and I had to take a second to pry it out, leaning forward like a track racer at his starting line with my fingers splayed in the wet leaves.

By the time I stood back up, I couldn't see him. I called to the trees, the patches of darkness from the tall pines swallowing the surrounding landscape, and the clouds shrouding the pale moonlight casting like a film of silvery dust.

I called several more times, "Aw, come on, Nate. I'm sorry. Come on, wait for me. It's creepy out here. And freezing. We should stick together."

But Nathan didn't answer, and I kept walking into and through the woods, searching for him in the murky shadows, through the trees, listening for his footsteps but only hearing the groan of the angry wind and the sound of creaking branches. I went farther and farther for I don't know how long until, cold and exhausted, I saw the lights of a neighborhood and eventually found my way home.

I never saw Nathan Faraway again.

. . .

Afterward, it was the not knowing that cut Adam and me more deeply, and I can't imagine what it did to Nathan's family.

Adam had sworn up and down that it was only supposed to scare us—only to be a trick—that they slowly wove through the cemetery, out to the highway to stop at the 7-Eleven three-quarters of a mile down the road for some Snickers and Mountain Dews and then returned to fetch us, the radio blaring. They had no idea we'd take off into the woods for home.

I stared at Adam from the doorway to his bedroom. His eyes burned big and round as if they'd never relax again, his mouth stunned and half open. Then, suddenly his brow plunged into a deep furrow, and he broke into a full sob. I'd never seen him cry before, and I was certain he'd been taught some kind of lesson—his bullying backfiring like a pistol. Teachers said bullies were insecure deep down, and it wasn't until I saw Adam break down and later drinking too much and getting into more drugs that I was convinced it was true.

I was full of hope that they'd find Nathan, but I had a sinking feeling in my gut, some instinctive blade—sharp and dangerous as a scythe—slicing into me that things were only going to get worse. Each day that passed without finding Nathan was laced with blackness, and slowly shock gave way to grief. Later, the police's words to my dad rang in my ears: "We've searched every corner of those woods and every house in the neighborhood, and we've also looked for large animal tracks—bear and mountain lion. Sometimes we never find what we're looking for in the woods. Animals have a way of clearing things completely." I knew then, deep in my bones, things were never going to be the same again, not for the Faraways, for me or my brother. And as I realized that my brother *had* received some type of lesson that night, I wondered more fiercely what had come Nathan Faraway's way.

21

THE NEXT MORNING I got up, showered, shaved, and put my contact lenses in. Usually I wore my eyeglasses because they were easier and more comfortable, but sometimes I used my contacts if I knew I'd be outdoors so I could just wear my nonprescription sunglasses. And sometimes I simply liked to change it up. I was well aware that I could appear a little too serious, too studious. I didn't care most of the time. But once in a while, for the sake of how approachable I was in an investigation, it didn't seem like such a bad thing to pay attention to.

I headed straight for Glacier Academy for no great reason other than because of my conversation with Phillips's girlfriend, Beverly, and what she said about Mark being a bully. Plus the fact that the date on the letter from Diane that Beverly mentioned would have been around the time Phillips worked at the Academy also snagged my attention. It sort of fit perfectly into my vague memory of him on the porch yelling at some kid to sweep it, "*or I'll* . . ."

The rains had passed through and were replaced by blazing sunshine. Northwest Montana is usually dry, but an unusual humidity pressed in as I drove through a conifer forest, up a long hill, and turned right to the big log building. It looked like some money had been pumped into the place since I'd seen it years ago, the window framing sparkling white against the cinnamon-colored logs. Additional buildings had been built off to the sides and the landscaping looked more professional compared to the rough lawn and encroaching weeds from years before. The grass was cropped evenly and several flower gardens were carved into their own enclaves amid the lawn. Orderly, I thought. It looked proper compared to before, like an orphan taken in and cleaned up.

Off to my left was a clearing with a volleyball net and a bigger glade past it with goal boxes on each end of the old makeshift soccer field, now completely level, freshly fertilized and appropriately lined.

I parked, locked the car, and sighed. "Probably just pissing in the wind here," I mumbled to myself, thinking it could be a shameful waste of my time when I was already five days into the investigation, but my curiosity about the place had been piqued. I considered that there might be some important connections to Mark—that perhaps he'd stayed in touch. I also understood that information gathered from all directions would most likely provide context. The more avenues I went down, the more terrain I could confidently rule out. I would go down as many as needed to make sense of things.

I found the main office easily on the entry-level floor below the side deck and went in. The smell of the logs hit me. It had a certain bittersweet tug.

"Oh, hi, sorry." A woman at a desk on her computer smiled at me. She had a cup of coffee in one hand, was staring at the screen, and had startled when I entered. "I wasn't expecting anyone. Good morning."

"Morning." I smiled. "I'm Monty Harris."

"I'm Penny." She stood up and set her coffee down. She was wearing a white cardigan over a pink top, had slightly graying hair and glasses. "What can I help you with?"

"I'm a police officer for Glacier Park and I just had a few questions for you if you don't mind."

Penny's eyes opened large. "Oh," she said shyly. "Okay, what for?"

"Well, for starters, can you tell me who owns this place now?"

"The Bremers own it. They bought it about fifteen years ago from some organization that, I think, disenfranchised. Before that, I'm not sure."

"Are the Bremers around?"

"Dr. Bremer is. Gets in early every morning to prepare his therapy plans."

"Did you work here when it was owned by the last people?"

She shook her head. "I've only been here for about three years."

"Do you know why they sold it?"

"Just that they were moving to a different area. I believe Portland or somewhere closer to the coast. And"—she pursed her lips like she knew a secret—"heard there were a few lawsuits here and there, but I don't know. That was some time ago."

"What were the suits about?"

She shrugged. "I don't really know. Did you want to see Dr. Bremer?"

"I don't have an appointment, but if he has a moment, that would be great."

. . .

Dr. Bremer wore his wavy, graying hair to his shoulders and was deeply tanned, as if he was much younger and lived the life of a surfer. But when he walked, he moved a little crookedly and with a slight limp like he'd played too hard. He came toward me, studying me with his slightly narrowed eyes after Penny introduced us, then smiled and shook my hand and told me to call him Pete.

"What can I do for you, Officer Harris?" He motioned for me to sit and I did so before his oak desk.

I wasn't quite sure what angle to lead into it with, so I decided to hit it head-on. "I'm investigating the death of a man who used to work here."

"*Here*? At our school?"

"Yes, but it's been years. Perhaps before you bought it."

"Oh, so how can I help then?"

"First, I was wondering if you had any records on any of the employees that were here under the previous ownership?"

"I'm afraid just a few. I think the Leefeldts cleared most of those out when they left, but I can double-check files in storage for you. Who, may I ask, are you looking for?"

"A guy named Mark Phillips. Worked here in the early nineties." I wrote the Leefeldts' name down in my notebook.

"Doesn't sound familiar to me. He might have left before I bought the place. I can have a look around, but unless he stayed on through the transition, it's unlikely we would have an employment file on him. Not that many employees from the previous ownership stayed on. Our chef and a few others long gone now."

I nodded. "Why's that?"

Peter Bremer looked out the window. There was a tapping coming from outside. "Damn woodpecker. Excuse me for a sec." He went to the door and poked his head out. "Penny, that woodpecker is at it on one of the beams again. Can you please have Mitch scare him off?" He closed the door and came and sat back down. "Sorry about that. They do a lot of damage, you know."

"Try a decoy owl," I offered. "Doesn't always work because eventually they figure it out, but it might distract him in the beginning, just long enough so he finds some other wood."

"I'll do that." He smiled, crow's-feet fanning out from the corners of his eyes, and pointed his pen at me. "So, where were we?"

I felt like I was buzzing, like I had a humming motor inside me broadcasting my eagerness to ask questions. "I was wondering why not many employees stayed when you bought the place."

"Mostly, it was our decision: my wife's and mine and the other two therapists who were part of our team. There were some lawsuits associated with the last place and we didn't want to bring any of that—shall we say, energy—into our new model for running things."

"Model?"

"I don't know how much you know about these types of schools, but there are different frameworks for running programs, sometimes no system at all and just a free-for-all. There are no federal laws, like there are in public education. Anyone can hang a shingle and use whatever behavior modification programs they choose for these troubled teens. Often the people running them are more interested in the money than in the well-being and maturation of the children sent to them. Families pay anywhere from forty to sixty a year for their child to get"—he hung quotation marks in the air with two fingers hooking on each side—"*straightened out.*"

"So there's no federal oversight?" I felt silly for not knowing such a thing given the fact that my own brother attended such a school. I'd put very little thought into it as it was a decision made by my father and that was that. In retrospect, it hadn't really helped Adam all that much and now I wondered how much my father paid to have him attend, not because the money mattered, but because it seemed an injustice that no real benefit seemed to come from it. Adam was still an angry, miserable alcoholic with little maturity or ambition.

"None. So the states can oversee the facilities but state regulators often hesitate to step in because the programs exist in such an ill-defined area of the law, many of them running under religious affiliations that can avoid government oversight, which, of course, includes the state. Anyway, our team tries to make this place"—he gestured with one hand to his surroundings—"different. We really have good outcomes here because we really do *treat* our young adults, not just discipline and punish them. We've worked very hard over the past seven years to make this a state-of-the-art facility with a high success rate."

"So were the suits against the last place because their model was based more on discipline and less on treatment?" I thought of Adam again and his sulky, angry face, and wasn't sure I wanted the answer, but I still felt the hum inside me, revving, wanting answers.

"I'm not sure of all the details, but that's the idea I got. There were allegations of mistreatment and abuse by some of the adolescents and their families. They filed suits. The Leefeldts . . . they weren't the owners; they just managed the place. The actual owners were a corporate entity called Global Schools. Apparently"—he cringed—"one of their schools paid four million even without the company admitting liability some years after a seventeen-year-old girl hanged herself in a bathroom stall at one of their facilities in Utah. Since then, the place closed, and after that, other suits came rolling in.

"Global Schools divested ownership of them. A number of them closed and some of them survived like ours, but many of them continued to use the disciplinary template of Global, which in my humble opinion is quite ineffective." He sighed, then proudly lifted his chin. "I have an MD in psychiatry, and I fully believe there can be no effective treatment without a well-thought-out and careful multipronged approach of counseling, education, academics, physical exercise, and duties that lead to individual successes. Fostering maturity through confidence is key."

"Sounds difficult," I said. I could still hear the tapping coming from outside, like a persistent dare.

"It's a challenge, but worthwhile." He smiled and seemed truly sincere. I thought of my mother and her lack of proper care: various doctors all prescribing different medicines with none of them taking the time to talk to each other to get the protocol straight."

"Can I ask what type of disciplinary procedures were in place here before you took over?"

"That I couldn't say. I'd just be speculating, but if you were really interested, I suppose those suits are public record. I did hear one story from a cook that stayed on with us that one student was required to carry buckets of water for hours and hours as a disciplinary measure for cutting herself; whether that is gossip, I can't confirm. Again, I just want to stress that these facilities can be highly effective if done with proper therapeutic supervision and care, and this one is." He narrowed one eye at me. "You're not here to generate old, bad press for us, are you? I mean, we had enough of that when we started and we've worked hard to make this place what it is today."

"No, doctor. Absolutely not. Just trying to understand the poor fellow we found at the bottom of a cliff, that's all," I said, trying to decide if I liked Peter Bremer. I usually do with a guy who likes to get the job done, but I wasn't quite sure about him. "Last question, Dr. Bremer."

"Please, Pete."

"Pete," I called him. "The chef you mentioned—does he still work here?"

"Yes, he does."

"Do you mind if I ask him if he remembers Mark Phillips?"

"Go right ahead. His name is Nick Ferron. Penny will know when he comes in again for his shift."

He paused. "And I have a question for you: Does this have something to do with the guy found below the Loop? The man I read about in the paper?"

"Possibly." Since it hadn't been released yet that the second man we found was Mark Phillips, I didn't want to say much more. I flipped my notebook closed and stood up. "I'll check with Penny on the way out." The tapping continued as Dr. Bremer walked me to his door. "Better get that owl," I said as I left his office.

. . .

Some amount of adrenaline had surged through me while talking to Dr. Bremer and had me amped up. I told myself to be careful, that I was not, most definitely *not*, getting paid to look into Adam's young adult life. I figured I better watch my motives and use of time, but I was feeling a strange sort of revving hunger after talking to the doctor, and I wasn't sure if it was coming from the fact that I was now not only a policeman, but I was an *investigator*. And, let's get this straight: I was really liking detective work. I thought of that woodpecker determinedly tapping away. I could relate.

I stepped outside. The air smelled of spruce and fir needles and the sharp tang of recently passed rainstorms. For five and a half years, I was a game warden, four of them spent manning game stops to check that hunters had the appropriate tags matching the game in their vehicles, patrolling the field, testifying in court, and listening to poachers' excuses and flat-out lies for why the female pheasant was shot, why the grizzly was *accidentally* killed, why the lynx was taken without a permit. Then, as Park Police, I was often still in the field of lies and dishonesty: some poor excuse for why someone was speeding, stole something from another camper, or was camping without a permit. Or worse—having to put myself in the middle of a married couple fighting at their campsite under the brilliant stars or trying to negotiate with neighboring campers jumping into petty rows over parking spaces.

All of that involved common sense, a keen eye, and wits, but with detective work, it was a different kind of game of gotcha involving a finely tuned intuition and lots of research. A comment from Wolfie's notes flashed in my mind, *that wolverines seem to come into this world wired with mega amounts of attitude.* There were several accounts describing their ferocity against even the most formidable foes, such as hungry grizzlies at feeding time. I couldn't help feeling that same surge of power within me—that even though I felt far away from answers, I was equipped to conquer this case with the combination of my wits and my skills. I was pretty certain that was what was making me feel electric. This was no simple case of issuing a speeding ticket.

However, I was no idiot. My thorough nature compelled me to pay attention to a yellow flashing warning light in the corner of my peripheral instinctual vision signaling to me that I could be getting matters confused—that I was somehow crossing the desire to understand some element of my past—hence all the thoughts of Adam and Nathan breathing down my neck lately—with the investigation at hand.

Wolfie, I thought. Think of Wolfie. That's where the case began. I pulled out my phone and listened to my messages. Cathy Sedgewick left a message wondering what progress I'd made on the case, and Lara wanted me to ring her back. I called Ken to see if he'd had any hits on a man named Rowdy because I wanted to ask him about the wolverine traps. I also wanted to speak to Nick Ferron, the Glacier Academy cook, who would be coming in at three in the afternoon to prepare for the school's five p.m. dinner. As for Cathy and Lara, I'd put those calls off for the time being.

22

So it's the traps you're wondering about?" The man, Rowdy, said to me in the Huckleberry Stop Café in Hungry Horse. Ken hadn't found anything about Rowdy—who he was or his whereabouts—so I went back to Melissa's at the Outlaw's Nest and she told me to try the café because he apparently hung out there a lot.

"Yes," I said. "The ones the biologist set out up the South Fork, near the reservoir and toward Spotted Bear Campground."

He stared at me, his face wrinkled and leathery and his hair turning white as cotton above his ears, around his temples and on his scraggly beard. I figured he was around sixty. The rest of his lighter brown hair fell in an uncombed mess, parting in various greasy gullies to reveal his scalp. I thought of the times my dad had asked me to help my mother brush her long, brown hair when she was too depressed— too lacking of energy—to do something as simple as that. I pushed the thought away. "Why do you want to know?"

"I'm investigating some suspicious falls in the park."

"So I've heard," he said, smiling and chuckling.

"Do you think that's funny?"

"Not funny." He shrugged. "I just smile when I'm sad."

"I see," I said.

"So, you're a cop?" Rowdy pulled out a small flask and added a good amount of what looked like whiskey to his afternoon milk shake which he had explained to me was strawberry because the huckleberries weren't out yet and wouldn't be for two or three more weeks. "Need a splash for your coffee?"

I ignored his offer. "I'm a police officer for the Department of the Interior. I work in Glacier Park."

"Woo hoo," he said sarcastically. "*Big*-time crime."

The exhilaration I'd felt earlier was quickly evaporating. "I hear you wish you were a game warden," I threw his way, trying to find some higher ground, then took a sip of my coffee.

"Me? Nah, are you kidding? Game warden? Who'd you get that from?"

"Don't tell me you don't know that's what you're referred to 'round here? But, yeah, I know you've never been one, at least not in Montana."

He quit smiling and for a split second, his face contorted into a sad frown, then he forced a grin again and stared at me with his head cocked to one side.

"So, what's the story? Why do they call you a warden if you're not one?"

"I guess 'cause I know law," he said, "and I know a thing or two about trapping laws. I've given advice to some folks around here on some legal matters involving poaching charges and whatnot." He waved his hand in the air.

"Legal advice?"

Again, a flicker of sadness flashed across his face before he plastered another grin onto his face. "I used to be an attorney," he said matter-of-factly.

"Attorney?" I wasn't sure whether to believe him or not.

"I went to law school at the University of Montana in the early seventies, and I practiced in Columbia Falls for a number of years, but in the long run, things, well, things just didn't quite work out the way I'd planned."

I sat silently, taking in what he was saying. He wore a dirty white T-shirt and baggy cargo pants stuffed into untied boots. He was wiry and bony with no belly at all and a jagged scar traced from his collarbone to somewhere under his shirt, toward his right shoulder.

"What?" he pressed. "You don't look like you believe me?"

"I believe you," I said. "So why didn't things work out the way you planned?"

"Just didn't." He took another sip of his whiskey-spiked shake, and I had a feeling that booze had some role to play in his plans going awry. I suspected drugs too, possibly meth, given its copious supply in the canyon and Rowdy's jaw looking too sharp and slightly caved in, one of the effects of meth use. If I knew his real name, I was certain I could find him in the system. But in general, he looked like a guy with many secrets. His eyes reminded me of what I could recall of my brother's: almond-shaped and flashing with a life's worth of harm, sadness, and a sprinkle of satisfaction derived from all the mischief created in the process.

"But as you can see, I'm a happy man now." He rapped his fingers on the table and fidgeted in his seat. "I live a simple life doing odds and ends."

I thought of Adam. "What kind of odds and ends?"

He lifted the shoulder his scar ran toward. "Painting houses, fence repair, lots of stuff." He smiled again. "I've repaired some steel-jawed traps for folks too."

"Hence the legal advice," I said.

"Yep. Just warning folks about what to be careful of and helpin' 'em out when things get red tape-ish, that's all. No harm in that, is there?"

"No, no harm in that," I agreed. "Did you know Wolfie, also known as Paul Sedgewick?"

"Not personally. Just heard about him. The locals around here weren't too enamored of him. Said he wanted to pave the future for further restrictions on land use—hunting, fishing, snowmobiling, ATV'ing and the likes—by getting the wolverine listed as an endangered species."

"You believe that?"

He took another sip of his shake, smacked his lips, and wiped his mustache with a napkin. The smell of bacon permeated the café. "I don't think he was pushing for restrictions anytime soon. I think he was gathering data, and if he could get the wolverine listed, he would've been thrilled. I'd seen that guy you're talking about in the woods trying to track his critters, with his radio equipment and such. Seemed harmless to me and like he was a decent guy. Obviously loved his work, but I'm no dummy.

"I know biology studies can have a huge impact on land protection, and I can see how that might not be in the best interest of some of the locals 'round here. Because believe it or not, they want jobs. It's not just about hunting, fishing, and snowmobiling; that just gets the attention of more people. Logging, mining, natural gas extraction are harder subjects to talk about these days, but we all know how the grizzly bear has been used as a tool to shut down development along the spine of the Divide."

I narrowed my eyes at him, studying him. His appearance was completely at odds with his intelligence. "Did you meet with Sedgewick at the Outlaw's?"

"No."

"Did Sedgewick want to meet?"

"I have no idea, but maybe. Yeah, I heard he was asking around for me. Wanted to know where I hang out and stuff."

"Why would he be doing that?"

Rowdy shrugged. "Maybe 'cause I know folks around here. Same reason you're talking to me."

"Why did you meet with that group of trappers in Melissa's place a few weeks ago?"

"Ah, you've been doing your homework, but what may I ask does my social life have anything to do at all with your accidents in the park?"

"That's a good question," I said, "and I'll tell you: Guy like Wolfie turns up dead in a place that is highly unlikely that he'd turn up dead, and I find out that he's been setting federally sanctioned wolverine traps up the South Fork and getting sabotaged in the process. So I'm hoping folks like yourself will level with me."

"And if folks like us don't?" he said in singsong.

"Well, then I start needing to use other legal tactics to get some information."

Rowdy smiled again. "That supposed to scare me?"

"No, but like I said, I'd appreciate your cooperation. If you can't manage that then I'll have to go snooping around in other places, maybe other areas of your life and your buddies' lives. Plus I have some connections around here. It's not like I don't get help from the local force, the county, the whole crew of game wardens to boot, and trust me, it's not fun when the cops start to make a project of you and your personal life in a small town like this."

Rowdy quit smiling. "Sounds like you're threatening me. If this is your way of getting me to cooperate, you're not too wise." He stared at me with a flat gaze as if to say he was done talking.

It wasn't my style to play tough guy, and I was probably going about it all wrong, but the adrenaline I'd felt earlier was still in me and this guy was effectively pushing my buttons. I could feel my fingers tingling and my face heat up. I had the urge to take brusque action even though I knew I was much more adept at getting information out of someone by means other than pissing them off.

Basically, though, something about his attitude was getting to me. If it's true that he'd been an attorney—and I'd find that out soon enough—his fall from professionalism struck some unpleasant chord with me. I don't like waste or sloppiness. My thoroughness and tidiness had, to a large extent, been borne out of survival—to prevent my mom from going into a paranoid stint. (*That blanket wasn't unfolded on that chair two hours ago. My God, someone's been in our house . . .*) Making the best of things, and doing the things you do to the best of your ability has always been my standard. But this man before me exuded an I-don't-give-a-shit attitude. I could see the intelligence in his dark eyes, deeply incongruous with his tattered, deteriorating, and cocky presence. "Do you know who'd been messing with Sedgewick's traps?" I said calmly.

"No, so just as well I didn't meet with him."

"All right." I stood up, still irritated, and dug out a five from my wallet and threw it on the table to more than cover my cup of coffee. Then I threw my card on the table. "You change your mind about helping me out, just give that number a call."

"Ain't got a phone," he said.

I could tell the use of *ain't* was forced. "For an attorney, I'd think you'd know better than to use *ain't*. But I guess meth tends to mess with one's language skills." I walked away, past the blue vinyl booths and formica tables; by the curious eyes of the locals and tourists eating their late breakfasts and early lunches; by all the curios near the cash register—the key chains with hundreds of different names alphabetized, the T-shirts, hats, stuffed animals of fuzzy black bears and snow-white mountain goats with small, shiny black horns made of pleather; past the postcards of big horn sheep, grizzlies, elk; and almost to the glass-door exit when Rowdy called out, "Hey. Officer Harris. That right, Harris?"

I looked over my shoulder, down the line of booths to see him wave me over. I walked back and stood by the table, figuring my mentioning of meth must have struck some chord.

"Sit." He waved his hand to the vinyl bench that I'd just been seated in.

I sat back down and felt the seat was still warm.

"The guys I met with," he said. "They wanted to know what kind of trouble they could get in from messing with traps sanctioned by the US forest service."

"What did you tell them?"

"The truth. That it depends on the animal. If it's federally protected, they'd be dealing with the feds breathing down their necks. And if the traps were sanctioned by the forest service, it was either funded by the state or funded by a grant from the federal government. As you know, the state would bring on a game warden to investigate and the feds, well, you know, they've got their own agents."

"So one of the guys must have had a run-in with Sedgewick if he was worried."

Rowdy stared at me and drummed his fingers again on the table, weighing whether to give me anything more. He bit the side of his lower lip, then said, "Couldn't say on that one."

"I'll need you to write down your proper name and the names of all the guys you met with in Melissa's bar." I slid my pen and a piece of paper I tore from my notepad his way and gave him my best level gaze to say I meant it.

• • •

I picked up a turkey sandwich on the way back to the office at a little sub shop closer to Glacier, unwrapped it at my desk, and before I took a bite, Lara called.

"Hi, Monty," she said. "Are you busy after work today?"

"I'm pretty much busy around the clock at this point. What do you need?"

"The old gas grill in the backyard—I need to move it to my car. I'm getting rid of it."

"Why?" I could hear the squawk of a crow outside my window and the sound grated and sent a twinge down my spine. I could picture Lara in our backyard inspecting the grill—our first gas grill—that my father gave us for a wedding gift.

"It's rusty and it doesn't light when I hit the switch. I always have to use a match. And with my family coming to town, it'd be nice to have something that works."

My irritation rose higher. We hadn't even fully decided on a divorce and here she was getting rid of our shit. The crow continued to screech again from outside my window and Lara tried to make light of it. "You get a new pet?"

I chuckled in spite of my irritation. "Look, Lara. I don't want to sell that. It works perfectly fine."

"Then you come get it and you use it. And speaking of pets, it wouldn't hurt for you to stop in and give Ellis a snuggle. He misses you." Ellis was our cat, sleek and all black with cool, yellowish-green eyes. Lara had gotten him the first year we'd moved to the Flathead Valley.

"Fine then. I will, but when I have time, and I just don't happen to have time this week." I said good-bye, irritated and angry for no good reason.

I stood up and stretched, rubbed the back of my neck, sat back down at my desk, and got to work, pushing away lingering thoughts of Lara. I felt of two minds about the relationship. On the one hand, it already felt ruined by the wedge she'd placed between us by wanting the separation in the first place. On the other, I still felt connected to her. We had a decade of history. We spent time building a life, constructing what I thought was a stable relationship. For me, I wasn't sure I could just throw it away because she was changing the game.

I turned my focus back to Phillips, and scoured his financial history, realizing that he put very little on credit cards and used mostly cash. I found the Toyota registered in his name. He made decent money as a cartographer, had very few expenses, but didn't have a lot in savings or investments, which sort of went with the idea that he liked to gamble as his ex, Beverly, had suggested.

I took out my notepad and started to scribble furiously, mapping the many avenues I needed to explore, from searching for Rowdy's real name (because in spite of asking him to write it down, he didn't, and when I pressed him, he clammed up even further) to speaking to the Region One game warden who covers the canyon and the Bob Marshall Wilderness Area to see if Wolfie reported the tampered traps, and much, much more. My list was ballooning.

I called Ken into my office. My jaw felt tight. I was anxious and excited for all the ground we needed to cover. I made some coffee while I explained to Ken that I wanted him to check the health club in Whitefish for the last time Mark Phillips had worked out and to check the shuttle services for sightings of Phillips. I gave him a photocopied picture of the one I took from Phillips's house of him and his son up by the boardwalk near the visitor center at the top of the pass. "You up for it?" I asked Ken.

"Sure," he said. He looked bright-eyed and energetic.

"Okay, good. But, you'll need to be really careful. Write everything down, okay?"

Ken smiled, flicking his white shred of gum forward with his tongue, then back again. "I've got it, Harris. Really, I've got it. Other people can be thorough too."

I nodded. "Okay, okay. Go then, and let me know as soon as you get any information."

"Will do," he said, saluting me lightheartedly and snapping his gum on the way out.

I lowered myself into my chair in front of my computer. I could hear muffled voices from down the hall, the crow still intermittently cawing, and the sound of coffee dripping into the carafe. The heavy and sharp smell of the black liquid began to permeate the room.

I know I can be a sucker, but basically I'm not the kind of guy who doesn't help out when someone asks, especially Lara. I was feeling bad about being so childish with her, even though I knew better than to let my emotions go there. The grill really was on its last leg, and she had good reason to want a new one, especially with her family coming to town. I knew she was having the reunion on Saturday catered, but I was sure several of her siblings would be staying longer and would probably come to the house for dinner. I wondered what excuses she'd have for why I wouldn't be there. Work, I figured.

But just like with Ken, my quest for thoroughness sometimes extended to judiciousness and practicality, and I believed in using things to their last leg. I don't like waste, and I saw no basis for buying something new if something old was still working. But, I reasoned, I *could* be overbearing.

I picked up my phone and texted: *I can swing by after work.*

23

I DROVE BACK TO Glacier Academy at three p.m., the time Penny told me that Nick Ferron would be in to start prepping for dinner. When I pulled up, a group of kids—all shapes and sizes and varying ages—were out in a clearing playing volleyball. An instructor wearing gym shorts and a whistle around her neck stood watching them and yelling praises: *That's it, Bodey. All right. Way to go, Spencer. Good get!*

I parked and went in and asked Penny where I could find the kitchen. She said Nick was expecting me and walked me out of her office, up some stairs to the upper level of the large lodge, and to the wing opposite the main office.

In the kitchen, Nick Ferron had his head down and was cutting red and yellow peppers. He was wearing a white, well-worn chef's apron and a purple bandanna around his head in a do-rag style. He looked up when Penny introduced me, his eyes curious to have a visitor. He wiped his hands on his apron and held one out to shake.

I asked him if I could talk with him since he'd worked here the longest. "Yeah, I guess so," he said. Penny left and he motioned to a small table in the corner, walked over to it, and removed some manila folders and stacked them on a shelf holding dozens of cookbooks off to the side. We both took a seat. "Would you like something to drink? Tea, coffee?"

"Maybe a glass of water."

"Sure." He grabbed a cup and filled it with tap water. "Ice?"

"No, thanks," I said.

"Water's good here. From a well—fresh and cold."

"Thank you." I took the glass. "Look, Mr. Ferron, I know you're busy, so I'll try not to take too much of your time. Do you remember a man who used to work here named Mark Phillips?"

He nodded. "Sure, I remember him. Only knew him for about a year. He was here sometime before I was hired."

"When were you hired?" I asked.

He scratched the side of his face, screwing up his mouth to think. "I believe I started in '95. Yeah." He nodded slowly. "Yeah, 1995, because that was the year I finished cooking school down in Hamilton and then moved up here. I saw this position advertised and got it right away. I only planned on it for a year or two before moving onto something bigger, something high-end—you know—some fancy restaurant. But this paid fairly well and they were eager to keep me once they tasted my cooking, and I was in no hurry to go. I kind of enjoyed feeding the kids, you know, like I was doing something more meaningful than only cooking for people's pleasures for a night out. Now, holy shit." He chuckled. "Who would have thought I'd be here going on so many years now?"

"That's a long time, all right. You must enjoy it."

"I do." He shrugged. "Has its ups and downs, but I run the whole shebang. Nobody tells me what to do, nobody's breathing down my neck, and nobody's pissed off at me for not pleasing some uptight customer in some hoity-toity restaurant. Sometimes I miss the high-end stuff, and with kids, you can't get too sophisticated, but a few times a year, the parents come and I get to be really creative then. Plus, to this day, it feels like I'm contributing to the kids' mental health through the physical sustenance of their bodies. These kids—they're not growing up on crap fast food, not while I'm doing the cooking." He placed his palm flat on his chest and smiled with pride.

"And Phillips?" I asked. "He was here in '96?"

"Yeah, but only for like a year or so. I'm not positive, but I think he left in '96, the year after I got here."

I did the math in my head. Adam fell apart the year following the Nathan Faraway incident. Adam would have been at the academy five years before Nick Ferron arrived. I briefly pictured Adam pushing away his spaghetti, refusing to eat it, his cheeks puffed out with anger. But Phillips would have been here then because I remembered him. "So Phillips was here from at least '90 until '95?"

"I suppose. I couldn't tell ya when he started, but I know he left in '96 because it was after the whole Miranda thing."

"Miranda?"

"Yeah, you don't know about that?"

"No," I said. "What happened with Miranda?"

Ferron thoughtfully traced a finger along an irregularity in the wood. "Apparently not that many people really know about it. They did a good job of keeping it out of the papers and such since she was a minor. I don't think the family wanted it to go public. Plus the lawsuit was filed against Global, which was headquartered in another state."

"What happened?"

He bit his lip and studied me for a moment. I couldn't tell if he was making me wait, setting up a little suspense for some self-satisfying reason, or if he was thinking it through—deciding exactly what to share with me. After so long, he must have felt a certain loyalty to the place, as if the school was family, and family secrets weren't to be blabbed about in any carefree fashion. "Miranda hung herself," he said at last. "In the bathroom stall about five months after I started here. Bless the poor girl."

I felt my pulse instantly race and set down my cup of water. Bremer had told me it had happened in Utah, and I figured I would remember something like that from the local papers, but I realized I would have been readying myself for college around the time and probably not paying attention to every bit of local, breaking news. "A student hanged herself here? At this academy?" I pointed to the honey-colored oak floor as if it symbolized the entire academy.

"Afraid so." Ferron sighed. "It was awful, all right. Took me a long time to get over it, to feel okay about this place again even though I didn't know Miranda well or anything. But I'm sure that's why Phillips left and then when the Bremers bought it, they pretty much changed the whole staff up. For the best, if you asked me."

"Do you know what happened?"

"Not really—just rumors. I was new and an outsider, having just begun working, so not that many people talked to me. But from what I remember, she was pretty disturbed and"—he shook his head with a look of disappointment on his face, as if he was saddened by the behavior of one of his own children—"this was a different place back then."

Again, I noticed my pulse picking up and my palms suddenly going moist. *Back then* meant back when Adam attended.

"Some of the disciplinary measures being used didn't really help her at all," Phillips added. "If that isn't an understatement," he huffed. "I heard one of the counselors made her carry water for several days straight because she'd been finding thin, sharp rocks—shale I think—and sanding 'em down farther on large rocks so she could cut herself since no one's allowed to have razors and whatnot. So they gave her a large bucket and made her haul water back and forth from the creek"—he pointed out the window—"to an area near the garden for a really long time. Even after the garden had been watered enough, they made her continue to just dump buckets full in the woods off to the side. And water, shit, it gets heavy in a big bucket."

I flipped through my notes. "Dr. Bremer mentioned the water hauling, but didn't mention a suicide. He said the hanging was in Utah . . ."

"Oh yeah." Nick stood up and walked over to his veggies. "You mind?" He glanced at the clock. "Dinner will be late if I don't get to work."

"No, of course not, chop away."

"So yeah." Ferron pulled out a large heart of elephant garlic from a supersized stainless fridge and expertly began slicing like he was on one of the Food Network shows that Lara loved to watch. "That's right. There was another in Utah. Very similar to this one. People said it was a copycat. That word had gotten around to other schools owned by Global and some of the kids had gotten wind of what Miranda had done and, well, someone followed suit. Crazy, huh?"

I nodded. I felt a little sick in my stomach for reasons I couldn't quite pinpoint. I also wondered why Bremer would mention the Utah incident but not Glacier Academy. "So the Bremers? They bought this"—I checked my notes—"in 1996, not long after the incident?"

"Yeah." He scraped the finely chopped garlic into a stainless pot that already contained an assortment of beans and turned his attention to the peppers. "And thank goodness for that. These folks really care about the kids here, and they have a very high success rate. None of that brutal disciplinary stuff. All counseling, communication, and accountability."

"That's good. Why do you think he would mention the Utah incident but not the one here? Surely he knew of it."

"Oh yeah." Nick lifted a shoulder. "Probably isn't interested in drudging up bad, old memories of this place. He's worked hard to change the image."

"And were there other incidents that you knew about when Global owned it?"

"I just heard things here and there." He held up his spoon and stared at it for a moment, lost in some recollection, then looked back at me seriously.

"Like what?"

"I think other boys were sometimes locked in some form of solitary confinement."

I stood quietly, waiting for him to continue.

"Before the Bremers remodeled the place, there used to be a small shack over by the creek that the counselors would lock the kids who'd violated rules into. Crazy shit. As if this was some prison we were running.

"Tell you what"—he jammed the spoon back in the pot—"if that shit would've continued, I don't think I would have worked here for very long. Again, I'm grateful the Bremers bought the place."

"And you think Phillips was involved in the mistreatment of the students?"

"Not sure." Ferron dumped some finely sliced peppers into the pot. "I remember seeing one of the counselors, I thought it was him, but I'm not positive, go into the shed a few times with kids and not come out for a good hour or more. When I questioned Mr. Leefeldt about it, he said it was just a disciplinary counseling session, but I'd heard some yelling and"—he sighed—"I don't know, the whole thing didn't feel right to me. Like I said, I was already thinking I'd be leaving by the end of the year, but then the Bremers came in and bought the place, offered me a raise and such."

"Did you ever talk to any of the kids who had been locked in the shed?"

"Not really, but I overheard them over dinner. One kid said that Phillips and a guy named Ryle—can't remember his last name—held him on the floor for a really long time, twisting his limbs into painful positions until he quit yelling and resisting. Again, when I brought it up with the owners, they just said that the school had a ninety-eight percent satisfaction rate and to trust the process. He said these kids are tricky, very manipulative, and chances are that they were making it up and exaggerating. And trust me, they sure can be manipulative. That's the reason many of them are here. A lot of them make stuff up so they can cause drama or be sent home, or worse, just because it's ingrained in them to lie and be dishonest for no particular reason at all. It's mostly attention-seeking." A sad look suddenly washed across his face. "I don't know," he said. "I was so new, I had no idea what to make of it all at the time. Poor Miranda. She was a sweet girl as far as I could tell. There was no reason to abuse her like that for cutting herself. They didn't get it."

"Get what?" I asked.

"That she was already punishing herself. That's what cutting is: punishment, healing, re-punishing, healing. . . . Punishing her even more probably tipped her over the edge. It really makes me sick when I think of it."

"Yeah, I can see that it would," I said, fully meaning it.

"You talking about that ghost?" A young kid with dark, shiny short hair stood in the doorway, startling us both.

"Gee whiz, Connor." Nick turned to the door. "Ever hear of knocking?"

"Oh, sorry about that." He shrugged and seemed sincere.

"You here for your kitchen shift?" Nick asked him.

"Yup, that okay?"

"Yeah, it's good."

The teen came in, went to the sink and began washing his hands. I was impressed he did so without being told. I thought of what Dr. Bremer said about fostering maturity through confidence.

"Ghost?" I said to Ferron after he introduced me to Connor and put him to work measuring out large quantities of rice.

"Oh yeah." He tsk'd. "Even though Bremer'd like to keep it quiet, the word's kind of taken hold 'round here over the years among the kids." He turned to Connor. "What have you heard?"

"Me?" Connor looked surprised to be asked. "About that Miranda girl?"

"Yeah."

"Just that Sam said he saw her a few months ago on his way to the bathroom, really creepy. Still has the old rope she found in the woods dangling around her neck, all frayed from where they cut it to get her down. Bleeding cuts all over her arms." He rubbed his palm up one of his arms and made a dramatic shiver.

"Hmm," Ferron said. "You see?" he turned to me. "Like some Sleepy Hollow or Harry Potter scene. What're you going to do?" He rolled his eyes. "Teens like ghost stories, especially when they're derived from real events."

"I suppose," I said, flipping my notebook shut and standing up. I half-expected to feel dizzy and was thankful when my legs felt sure and strong. This place had literally been a nightmare when Adam was here. "Thank you very much, Mr. Ferron." I shook his hand. "You've been very helpful."

. . .

On my way back to headquarters, I stopped at a convenience store to get some gas and called Shane Albertson from the parking lot. Shane was the game warden assigned to Region One's Middle and South Fork districts. I knew him personally from my days with FWP. I asked him if he knew anything about the tampering of wolverine traps up the South Fork drainage and Hungry Horse Reservoir area.

"I'd heard some rumors about it but nothing official," Shane said. Shane had the deep voice of someone tall and megashouldered with sharp features but was really a medium-height, stocky guy with a baby face.

"Sedgewick never reported it to you or to Fish and Game?"

"Nope, if he had, I would've been on it. Where there's tampering going on, there's usually other weird shit going on too."

"Do you know of anyone in the past involved in wolverine poaching?"

"I haven't seen or heard of it in a while. Lots of black bear and grizzly poaching going on lately. Just made an arrest with some couple who had taken a minimum of fourteen black bears illegally and killed at least three grizzlies last month."

"I heard about that. Congratulations on breaking that one," I offered.

"Yeah, thanks. I worked it for some time. It was a good bust. They were total lowlifes."

"So what were the rumors you heard?"

"'Bout that Sedgewick guy?"

"Yeah."

"I just heard from someone in Hungry Horse one day that there'd been an altercation between the wolverine researcher and a guy named Martin Dorian—someone I like to keep my eye on. We've fined him numerous times in the past for poaching elk on the off-season. There's some other things about him and his clan that I'm looking into. I was surprised that he would have anything to do with wolverines, but I know he has a temper and would throw a fist at pretty much anyone who crossed him the wrong way."

Martin Dorian was one of the men on Rowdy's list. I put a star by his name and jotted "altercation" in the margin. "What kind of other things?"

"Well, I don't have enough evidence yet, but I've got a source that says he and his boys have been stockpiling weapons and some illegal explosives as well. They're definitely part of a neo-Nazi group and are members of a social network hate group called Whitesquad. It's like a dating site for supremacists."

"Lovely," I said. I had heard about the site and knew that the members had issues with many different groups of people, complaining about crimes committed by blacks against whites, about the influx of Latin Americans, about gays and feminists living unholy lives, and about Jewish people, who they feel are controlling our government. "You hear any specifics about the disagreement with Sedgewick?"

"Not really. Just that they got into it over at the Outlaw's in Hungry Horse. I don't think it got physical. Just some yelling and name-calling. I have no idea what about, but I could do some checking around for you."

"That's okay," I said. I didn't want anyone scaring these guys before I had a chance to look into matters, and I figured some Glacier Park Police guy outside their area of interest was a lot less threatening to them than a game warden, at least at this point. "Hold off on that for now. I'll let you know if I need you. Just keep me posted if you hear of anything on the wolverine front, will ya?"

"Definitely, I will," Shane said.

After hanging up, I called US Fish and Wildlife Services and the national office of Rocky Mountain Research Station, with the USDA, in Fort Collins, Colorado, to ask if one of their grantee partner-program managers, specifically Paul Sedgewick or Sam Ward from the Glacier Park wolverine study, had made a complaint to them about the tampering of traps made from federal grant money. They had no complaints on record either.

Then I called the county and ordered a printout of all and any criminal activity associated with any names with the nickname Rowdy attached to them as well as anything on Martin Dorian. All I found on Dorian was a DUI five years before. Rowdy, a Mr. Louis Rowland, was busted for possession of cocaine in the early nineties and suspected of, but not charged, with possessing methamphetamines in 2007. He did pass his bar examination in 1988, and later filed Chapter 11 in 2001.

24

ON MY WAY into Glacier, I decided to stop and speak to Sam Ward, Wolfie's coworker and friend of the family. I thought again about how I had briefly suspected him of cozying up to Cathy, letting the idea trickle back in for no good reason other than I felt it was my duty to keep considering all possibilities whether they went against my intuition or not.

I found him in the small extension office set up, in part, by RMRS, one of the funding partners—among others—for the wolverine project. It was only around the corner from headquarters and not far from my own dorm. He brought me into his tiny office and I took a seat among stacks of files against the wall.

"How's it going, Monty?" Sam sat down and looked at me, his eyes big and brimming with hope as if I might have brought Wolfie back from the dead or at the very least, had all the answers for why such a thing had occurred.

"I've got a lot of irons in a lot of fires," I admitted, trying to make it sound like a good thing and not a complicated mess.

"And?"

"Well, I wanted to ask you if Sedgewick had said anything to you about the traps in the South Fork. If he knew who was sabotaging them?"

"Oh." Sam held up a finger. "Oh my God. Yes. I never even thought of that. But, yes, of course you'd investigate that. Why didn't I think of that." He bonked his head with the palm of his hand in a "I should've had a V-8" motion. "Yeah, he had some ideas. Some guy named Dorian and his crew."

"I've got that figured out. What I don't understand is why Wolfie or even you—your office—didn't report the tampering to the state or even your federal office?"

Sam looked at me, his head tilted, and bit his lower lip, considering my question.

"I mean, the traps were the property of the US government, were they not?"

"Yes and no. But mostly yes. We're certainly funded by RMRS and other grants, but we also get private donations and funding through the park for the work in the park. But, yes, we thought long and hard about whether to report it."

"Why? Wasn't it a no-brainer?"

"Again, yes and no. On the one hand, it felt like our duty to report it. On the other, you can see how alerting the state wardens or worse, the feds, and having them looking into it would inflame an already tense situation in the area."

"But why would you care?"

"You know the locals have their own way of dealing with things sometimes. Plus Wolfie didn't want the US Forest Service sticking their noses into the situation either."

"Because?" I canted forward, listening with my arms resting on my knees.

"Because in the past, some administrations have not been so kind about our research. Believe it or not, we got a call from the secretary of the interior—Steven Garcia. He had the nerve to tell us that we needed to put some very careful thought into what we put into our reports about the wolverines and their habitat. Look, I know you work for the park, but I don't know how much you know about RMRS." Sam leaned into his desk toward me. "As a branch of the US Forest Service, we're the leading force in midsize forest carnivore studies, but generally, wildlife research is not high on the Forest Service's list. Priorities lie with foresters and engineers focusing on timber harvesting and road building. With RMRS, we were designed to remain independent of political pressures. It was supposed to be a beautiful thing." He nodded. "So when conservationists started pressuring federal agencies to figure out the wolverine, we became passionate about our assignment because wolverines are one of the rarest and least known carnivores in the American West, you know, because of their low numbers and inaccessible habitat. They're very difficult to study, like studying phantoms, but one of the coolest animals you'll ever see if you begin to understand them.

"Up until the past decade, just a few field studies have been done. Compared to other carnivores like grizzly bears and wolves, we know so little about gulo gulo. Uh, that's the Latin name for wolverine, but you know that, right? Means glutton."

I nodded that I did. Most who worked more than seasonally in the park knew that. Wolverines were also sometimes referred to as skunk bears since they belonged to the mustelid family, which people originally thought skunks also belonged to, but later discovered through DNA analysis that they didn't. Weasels, otters, badgers, ferrets, mink, martens, and the like belonged to the mustelids. Hang around the park enough and you begin to learn these things whether you're into biology or not.

"But Wolfie and I," Sam continued. "We've been hell-bent, obsessed you could say, on changing this because the more we know about them, the better we'll be at making decisions on how to sustain them into the future. And it's not just them; it's the whole ecosystem—all living systems. If the areas we do protect aren't big enough and interconnected, then we aren't really protecting them. They're just islands unto themselves. Like Glacier. With only islands, the species interbreeds, becomes weaker. They need access to other animals in other protected areas that are connected to stay strong as a species. We've seen it with the grizzlies. Their numbers may look better in Glacier, but as they continue to interbreed, the species weakens. Just like people if they are forced to interbreed."

"And what does this have to do with not informing the feds about the tampering of the traps?"

"Adding to our urgency is the current rate of climate change and some administrations—in fact, almost all of them these days—find it conducive to conceal or conveniently ignore relevant research, and this wouldn't be the first time the DOI has meddled into designation of imperiled species and habitats. Several years ago, a senior appointee resigned under pressure after some investigators discovered that he'd altered scientific evidence and basically removed species and habitats from the endangered species list."

"I remember that," I said.

"So it turns out, even though RMRS is supposed to be a unit unto itself, it can't be. Not entirely, because funding still comes from the Forest Service, which walks a very fine line to appease Congress. It just simply can't come across as championing any particular species. Wolfie"—Sam frowned—"well, he didn't want anyone knowing he might need extra resources on our studies, especially investigative law enforcement, since funding is dwindling as it is, as well as possible stonewalling from our own administration."

I nodded that I understood and remembered the note I found in Wolfie's reports about receiving a call from a high-ranking official. "It seems that Wolfie and this Dorian got into a fight in Hungry Horse, outside the Outlaw's. Did he mention it to you?"

Sam shook his head. "No, he didn't. But I would have thought he would have."

"Why do you think he didn't?"

Sam shrugged, then looked down. "We didn't always have time to discuss everything."

"Sam, were you and Wolfie getting along before he fell?"

"Yes, of course. Why?"

"Just seems like something he would have shared with you."

"Like I said, we didn't share everything. *Most* things about our work, but not every detail."

"Okay then." I looked at him seriously and he looked back at me. There seemed to be something perceptible hanging in the air, a tension I could sense, but perhaps it was just Sam's grief and the burden of the project now falling entirely on his shoulders.

"Wolfie got most of the traps out of the South Fork when he saw how many wolverines were getting killed in them." He sighed loudly as if my waiting had made him surrender a pent-up breath he'd been holding. "The South Fork was his idea. He didn't run it through the proper channels. I refused to be a part of the studies in that region and continued with the Glacier end of things. He may have not told me because of that. I approved of the studies there. I just didn't entirely approve of foregoing the correct channels because once a biologist quits playing by administrative rules, it can be the kiss of death to their credibility. But that needs to stay between us, okay? Cathy and the kids." He frowned. "They've been through enough here. They don't need to think Wolfie was doing anything wrong. And he wasn't really. There are no laws saying he can't run a study up that drainage. Ultimately, it's volunteer work on his part, but like I said, he just didn't run it by RMRS in the same way we have with other studies."

"Because he didn't want the politics?"

"Precisely."

"But that research," I said, "having not gone through the proper channels, would have no credibility. So what good would come of it?"

"Exactly." Sam nodded sadly. "No good in terms of documentation, papers, and ultimately where land legislation is concerned. The only good was that Wolfie himself would understand the animal more. And for Wolfie, that's what the quest had become—an intense mission. He was beginning to quit caring what others thought. He just wanted to understand the animal, whether the research could be used or not. And who's to say that if he understood something from the South Fork area, that that information couldn't be slid into the legitimate Glacier studies? It's all closely connected, and the same wolverines from Glacier cover the South Fork."

"But that's not good science—to use studies from a different area and pretend they apply to another."

"No, no, it's not. So now you understand where our disagreement came from."

"So"—I lightly tapped my pen on my notepad—"avoiding the politics from your own agencies, that's the reason you didn't report the tampering?"

"Yes, along with the other stuff I told you. Again, he wasn't doing anything illegal, just not exactly as the organization would have expected."

I took it all in for a moment. Sam's face sagged and he looked deflated. Eventually, I thanked him for his help and told him that if he remembered or heard of anything else relating to the South Fork situation or Wolfie's death to please call me. Then after I got in my car, I pulled out my notebook again and put a star by Sam's name with a note saying, "*maybe he and Wolfie not getting along as well as we all think. Claims to not know of altercation with Dorian.*"

25

GRETCHEN CALLED ME twenty minutes after I left Sam Ward's office to tell me that the lab results were in. I was heading into town to help Lara with the grill when she called. She was somewhere noisy— a café or coffee shop—because I could hear bustling and many high-pitched voices in the background.

"Wilson faxed me the results on both victims," she said. "Said he got the lab to rush 'em in spite of being backed up for about four weeks."

"Awesome," I said. "I'll have to call him to thank him."

"Or maybe just send him some milk and cookies," she said jokingly. Most of us who'd met Wilson knew that he looked more like a young college student than an accomplished, highly acclaimed forensic pathologist with his faux hawk and untied sneakers. "But I'm sure he'd appreciate either." Her voice sounded distant and muffled.

"Where are you?" I asked. "I can barely hear you."

"Just got out of the office and was supposed to meet a friend in Whitefish at the Snow Ghost, but he just texted and said he can't make it. Got stuck at work. Anyway, I guess it's happy hour here, but I can go outside. I haven't ordered anything."

I could hear her mobile jostling a bit as she walked and suddenly it got much quieter, but instead of saying, "That's better," I said: "If your friend's not making it, I'll just come meet you and you can fill me in on the results."

"Are you close?"

"Yeah, I'm heading into town anyway." I thought of Lara. I had not given her a time for when I'd be over to help her.

"Tell you what. Let's meet across the street at that hotel bar instead. Too loud in here."

"Wherever you want," I said.

. . .

"So the tox screen was negative on Sedgewick." Gretchen pushed her fair hair behind her ears with both hands, dipping her head forward as she did so. "No drugs, no alcohol, no medications. He was covered in his own blood and the trace of outdoor elements, as expected: dirt, rock fragments, black cottonwood seeds, pollen—all the usual suspects for someone who's fallen, and all consistent with Glacier's soil and rock composition. Phillips was covered in trace too, exactly the same. There is no evidence that these bodies expired before the falls and were later dumped at these sites."

"No, I never thought they were. Too much blood and Wilson confirmed it."

"And, the footprints you got near that seep don't help at all. Most of them are so blurry and smeared from overlapping that they're of no use."

"Yeah, I wasn't expecting much from those either. But is there nothing? No clothing fibers that don't match their own?"

"I'm getting to that." Gretchen took a sip of draft beer she'd ordered before I arrived. We were sitting at a small table near the wall opposite the bar. Pictures from the early 1900s of old railcars filled with timber and loggers with wide smiles lined the wall. Back then, in the early 1900s, Whitefish was initially called Stumptown because to make room for the town, a huge number of trees were cut down, leaving so many stumps behind that they created traffic and construction problems. Thankfully, the name never stuck and the town's name switched to that of a nearby lake, a few years later. "There were some fibers on

Sedgewick that did not match what he was wearing, but nothing distinctive. There were some hairs on him that match his wife, several that match his son, and some that are canine, from the golden they have."

"So the fiber—anything worth searching?"

"Again, just some type of cotton blend. Probably from one of the kids' clothes or the laundry room."

"Damn." I frowned.

"And," she said, "toxicology was negative for Phillips too. A small amount of alcohol was in his system, nowhere near sufficient to cause impairment, and certainly not death. There was no way to study his stomach contents, as you know."

"Yeah." I pictured Phillips's meager remains on the table and felt lucky we got any toxicology report on him at all. "So, alcohol. Are you sure?"

"I'm sure." Gretchen gave me a level gaze, her eyes intense and intelligent. "Wilson used the vitreous fluid of the eye, which gave him the approximate BAC one to two hours before his death. It's interesting that he was up at the Loop—out hiking."

"That would suggest he had drank either before starting his hike or while on his hike, which would seem like an odd thing to do." I was thinking specifically about how he didn't have a car and wondered if maybe he had had a flask with him. "So first guy to drop has alcohol in him, but not the second. I'll be damned, maybe I've been wrong. Maybe these two really aren't related cases. Maybe the first guy was tipsy enough to trip."

"I'm not sure if this means anything, but"—Gretchen gave me a half smile, like she was saving the best part for last—and I sat up taller in my seat. She held up her hand. "Don't get too excited. It's not that great. It's just that along with the dirt and dust, there is a very small trace of a soap residue, a commercial or industrial type with lye—sodium hydroxide—which we found on Phillips's intact hand, under his nails. It suggests he washed his hands sometime before the hike or walk at the Loop. I can get you the exact makeup of it, but it does not match the soap he has in his home, which is an organic soap. It's definitely the type you might find in a convenience store or gas station bathroom, some fast-food joints—that type of soap."

"Okay, that's something. Not sure what, but something." These two cases were beginning to make my head spin. I had a strong inkling that they were somehow related, but I had no hard evidence to prove it, other than the fact that they had occurred in the same area. "Any sign of struggle at all? DNA under fingernails?"

"No, but these bodies as you know, weren't in the best condition. But both Wilson and I find it interesting that there is nothing under the nails of significance. Somebody slipping close to the trail would be grabbing for anything possible for purchase. There should be sediment and broken nails at the very least."

I nodded. "Yeah, the absence suggests a clean break away from the edge—a suicidal jump or a push. Plus"—I recalled Wolfie's launch area—"it was lipped and concave where we figure Sedgewick went off. Hard to slip off from."

"So it's not a lot to go on, but it's something. Don't advertise this, but from a CSI's perspective, pushing someone off a cliff is probably the cleanest way to get away with murder."

"Yeah, I wish we could have at least gotten some DNA or something to go on, but thanks for trying," I said to her, and I must have looked disappointed because she reached out and touched my wrist—just lightly and only for a split second, but it surprised me and sent a zing of electricity through me.

"You'll find something one way or another—something either to link them or extricate them."

"Hopefully soon," I said, the beer making me feel more relaxed. "So this guy who let you down tonight—boyfriend?"

"Let me down?" She laughed. "I hadn't thought of it that way. But, no, not a boyfriend really. We've had a few dates. Nothing serious, but he's nice."

I held up my hand. "Not really my business, is it?"

"It's okay. I don't mind. What about you? You divorced yet?"

The question was so simple, but most people in my circles never asked because either they didn't want to make me feel bad or they figured it was too personal. But to hear it so rationally and plainly made me realize how pathetic it was: Lara and I married, but split for the better part of a year. Not together, but not divorced. Me, Mr. Get-'er-done, finding it acceptable to hang on month after month in limbo all because Lara continuously vacillated between wanting out and missing me. Suddenly, I felt ridiculous. "No," I 'fessed up. "I'm not."

"How long have you been separated?" She asked, no hint of anything. She inquired just like an interested coworker might.

I didn't answer right away, as if I gave her that information something in the air around us would shift and make this easy, casual acquaintanceship even less accessible. She looked at me thoughtfully, her mouth in a soft curve, and I realized I was being foolish and reading way too much into something very simple.

"The better part of a year," I finally admitted. "But enough of that," I said and looked down at my phone because it vibrated. A text from Lara came in: *Where are you?*

I excused myself and texted her back: *I'll call in a bit.* "Would you like another?" I looked back to Gretchen.

"Sure." She smiled. "Why not? We can talk about this case some more. I'm pretty decent at this sort of thing."

"What happened to, 'I'm only here for the facts'?"

"Oh, that was while working. I'm not working now, so I can go into theorizing mode."

I slid the phone back in my pocket and got up to go get us another round.

• • •

After that second beer with Gretchen, I walked her to her car and thanked her for meeting with me. When I got to my Explorer, I called Lara back.

"Where have you been?" she asked.

"Working," I grunted, irritated that she felt she had the right to check on my whereabouts at this point, but I knew that I wasn't being fair either. I had texted her earlier that I would come over when I was done for the day.

"I thought you were coming over?"

"Sorry, but I got busy. This case has a lot of unknowns, and I've got a lot of work to do."

"Can you come over now?"

I thought about it without answering right away. The car was warm from the evening sun, and I turned the key so I could roll the windows down.

"Monty?" she asked. "Are you there?"

"Yeah, I'm here." I was kicking myself for texting that I'd go see her. All I really wanted to do was to go home and continue chipping away on the case. But I had promised, and I'm a man of my word. "Okay," I said. "I'll be there in ten."

26

THE LILAC TREES were still in full bloom and draping over the side fence when I pulled up to the house Lara and I had lived together in since we moved to Kalispell from Choteau six years before. I could tell she had recently mowed the lawn and the scent of freshly cut grass and sweet lilacs enveloped me when I stepped out. To the left of the house stretched a large field that we had to buy a riding lawn mower and large quantities of buffalo grass seed to tame. It was where she planned to have the big reunion with white tents, music, and caterers. The field ran down to the Flathead River and although waterside property, we got the place for a steal because we bought at the right time and the house was run-down and in need of a new roof, furnace, and all sorts of other repairs that we spent a lot of time doing after we first moved in. I missed the place, in many ways—it was home.

Lara came out onto the landing when I shut my car door. The sun had dipped low in the western sky, but the evening was still aglow with light and her face took on a golden warmth. I thought of the other evening when the light had held the same quality and I told Cathy Sedgewick that her husband wasn't returning. The days would be getting shorter now with summer solstice behind us, but it was staying light past ten still. Lara was wearing a cream-colored T-shirt, blue shorts, and sandals. Her legs were the color of honey in the sunlight. "Hi, you made it," she said.

"I just need help moving it into my car."

We walked around back and I took in the smaller rectangular

patch of lawn directly behind the house and hemmed in with a white fence. The apple tree stood near the back, the main reason Lara had fallen in love with the place when we were house hunting. There had been days when we couldn't keep up with the number of apples fallen to the ground, pitted with wormholes. Lilac bushes lined the side of the house and were at least twice the size as when we first moved in.

I shouldn't have come here, I thought. The sweet flowers and grass smells were blending together and triggering something wistful inside me. I suddenly recalled us having a playful tousle on a chilly fall day, pushing each other into piles of leaves we'd spent the whole day raking, and later paring apples to run through the vegetable juicer we'd bought.

"See." She was standing next to the old grill, her hand on one hip. "It's seen better days."

I nodded, agreeing with her and went over and closed the lid, unhooked the gas line, and grabbed the side of it. She grabbed the other and we carefully walked it over to the gate, set it down to open the latch, and continued to the car.

After getting it situated, Lara said, "Come inside to visit Ellis."

I followed her to the back again and in through the kitchen screen door. Ellis sat perched on the kitchen windowsill and meowed demandingly several times in a row when he saw me.

"Aw," Lara said. "He's missed you."

I felt something achy sift through me, picked Ellis up, and rubbed behind his ears. He began to purr.

"Do you want something to drink?" Lara asked.

"No, I'm good. Thanks anyway," I said, awkwardly standing in the kitchen as if it had never been my own home. "I need to get going."

"Those accidents still?"

I nodded. "With two of them, there's just a lot more work." I put Ellis down and he rubbed against my leg.

"But you'll still be coming to the reunion, right?"

"I can't think about that right now. But we'll talk."

She looked at me and bit her lower lip. I could tell she was holding back from saying more.

"Soon," I repeated. "Soon." I had my hand on the screen door and was opening it.

Lara tilted her head and looked at me with a mixture of sadness and confusion as I said good-bye, slipped out the screen door, and softly shut it behind me.

•   •   •

That night—the moment before sleep where you're in a cocoon of problem solving and dreaming, my mind gnawing on the case, casting and reaching to the corners of my mind for answers while simultaneously sliding to images of Lara with her chestnut hair tucked behind her ears and her large eyes the color of espresso. While she watched me pet Ellis, who was distorted and had a much longer, sleeker body—like a wolverine—I slid into a dream of Gretchen. She stood before me in my office with her soft mouth and fair skin, a drop of moisture slowly sliding down her cheek. I couldn't tell if it was a raindrop or a tear and I felt determined to find out. I was asking her if she was sad or if she'd come in from the rain. I had my notebook because I wanted to get the answer down correctly, and I didn't want to miss anything. Gretchen just smiled and didn't answer. I could sense, like the smell of lilac permeating the air, that I was overlooking something about someone—Gretchen or Lara—or maybe the case, but I didn't know what.

I woke with a start at six a.m. to the sound of a train barreling through West Glacier. Outside I could hear the birds and ground squirrels clamoring with their morning routines. I got up, showered, shaved, dressed, and went to the office. Ken had some news. He'd found a man who drove a shuttle on the eighteenth of June who—after looking at Phillips's picture—said he recalled driving him from the Loop to the Logan Pass visitor center at the top of Going-to-the-Sun Road.

"From the Loop?" I asked. "You double-checked?"

"Yes, the Loop, not from Lake McDonald or from the Transit Center. From the Loop." Ken angled his head, his eyes wide, as if to say, *You gonna trust my work or not?* And before I gave him an answer, Joe came in with a cup of coffee in his hand, a vacant look in his eyes and deep, pronged worry lines between his eyebrows. I wanted to ask him how things were with his daughter, but decided not to in front of Ken.

"How are you boys this morning?" Joe asked.

We updated him on what we'd discovered so far, but I left out the part about visiting Glacier Academy, because I felt like I was admitting to sloppy investigation techniques if he knew I was tracking down stories of troubled teens who'd hanged themselves fifteen years before. I did tell him that Phillips used to work for the academy, and I figured that was enough for the time being.

"So," I said. "If it's true that Phillips caught a ride from the Loop to the top, then he must have hiked the Highline Trail to the chalet and hiked back out to the Loop. And if so, he still needed to get from the Loop to somewhere if he didn't have a car."

"Maybe he met someone at the chalet to hike the rest of the way with and had a ride from the Loop down with them?"

"Maybe," I said. "His truck was safe and sound in his garage. He had to have gotten a ride from someone." In the park, there were many spectacular trips that were best done if you could start in one place and finish in another, rather than hiking in and back on the same trail.

"And if you can find that someone," Joe said. "You might get a lot of answers to this."

"Problem is"—I nodded out the window in the direction of the Loop—"we don't have an exact date to go around asking about. I've put in a request for all the surveillance footage from the entrance gates—west and east sides, but that still doesn't cover all the exits. I wish we had a more specific time of death for Phillips."

"But you do for Sedgewick?"

"Yes," I said as I slid my notebook back into my pocket. "We do, and I eventually intend to see if Martin Dorian has an alibi for the evening of June twenty-second from six p.m. to around midnight."

. . .

Nick Ferron, the chef, looked surprised to see me again so soon. He closed the large stainless steel refrigerator door when I walked in and set several large Tupperware containers on the long, spotless counter. "You keep a clean kitchen." I smiled.

"Absolutely. I wouldn't have it any other way."

I thought that if I were a chef, I'd run a tidy one too.

"What brings you back?" Nick asked.

"Just something that has stirred my curiosity about Mark Phillips."

"What's that?" Nick motioned for me to sit and I declined.

"I won't take much of your time. I'm just wondering if back when you started this job if you knew of a young woman named Diane?"

"A student?"

"Student, coworker, girlfriend of Phillips maybe?"

"Hmmm." Nick tucked his lips together, thinking. "I think, but I'm not completely positive, but I think there used to be a gal working then that he may have dated, but I don't remember her name. Tall, pretty; long, straight hair. Yeah." He nodded slowly as it came to him. "I think she and Phillips had something going on there, at least for a while. I have no idea for how long."

"But you don't know her name?"

"I'm afraid . . ." He paused, tilting his head to the side. I could see him trying to tap into old memories, then he shook his head, "No, I just don't remember. But if it comes to me, I'll call you."

"You have any idea how to reach the previous owners?"

"I have no idea what became of them."

27

It was a flimsy excuse and perhaps unprofessional of me, but I called Gretchen and not Ken to see if she'd go with me to the Outlaw's Nest. It was just a hunch and I wasn't sure anything would come of it, but I remembered the flyer that said the Woodtics were playing on Thursday evening and I figured Martin Dorian and his boys might be there since it seemed to be their hangout of choice. I decided I'd look less suspicious digging around for information with a female date than with an overmuscled, no-neck Park Police officer. Plus I didn't want to take Ken away from his family during the evening.

Gretchen said she needed to work at least until four thirty, but could arrive around five thirty, so we agreed to meet at a little restaurant in Columbia Falls on Nucleus Avenue before heading to the Outlaw's Nest.

I went home early and changed out of my uniform, showered, and put on some jeans and a decent button-up and waited for her by the small bar in the restaurant. She came in wearing khaki capris and a rusty red shirt that made the ends of her hair radiant, the color of creamed honey on the tops of her shoulders. She smiled casually, and I instantly felt glad to see her. I figured that meant I ought to watch myself, and I quickly reminded myself that I was only looking for a friend, someone with a sharp mind who understood the field of crime.

A wood-paneled entrance led to a small room lined with oil paintings of the park: Lake McDonald on a stormy day; Two Medicine Lake and Sinopah Mountain rising behind it, bathed in a copper sunset; St.

Mary Lake with its small island in the middle of its turquoise waters. The bar opened up into the restaurant, which was also lined with wilderness pictures. "Haven't had enough of the park, huh?" she said.

"Never." I smiled. "Although, yeah, I have to admit it would be nice to see something different in the art department, maybe something abstract for a change. The bar or a table?" I motioned to the small room.

"The bar's fine," she said, and we both grabbed a stool. A flatscreen TV hung off to our side and the bartender, a young guy no more than twenty-five, set a couple cocktail napkins before us and asked us what we'd like. Gretchen asked for a glass of white wine and I ordered an IPA. "So," she said after taking a sip, getting down to business. "What's going on?"

I filled her in on Wolfie's situation, that he'd been setting traps and they'd been tampered with by some guys I thought might be at the Outlaw's Nest for the band.

"And you think you'll learn something?" she looked at me skeptically.

"Yeah, I know it's a long shot, but you never know."

"What exactly are you looking to find?"

"I'm not really sure. I just know that these guys were up to no good with Wolfie. Sam Ward, as well as some guy named Rowdy from Hungry Horse, claim that some of the locals were fired up that the study would lead to restrictions on land use and were sabotaging his project by rigging his box traps with steel jaws." I pulled out a photo that Shane from Fish and Game had emailed me earlier of Martin Dorian and showed it to her. "I just want a good peek at these guys, especially him." I pointed to the photo. "I know Wolfie had an altercation with this one—guy named Dorian—and the rest have had meetings before to discuss Wolfie's research. Seems they feel he was threatening their land usage rights."

Gretchen bit her lower lip. "So this Dorian could be a suspect?"

"I don't have much on him but an old DUI and some state poaching fines, but I'm definitely interested in finding out more about him."

"And does he have anything to do with Mark Phillips?" The sunlight coming through the street windows shone brightly and every time a car drove by and created a flicker, the light danced in her eyes. She handed me back the picture.

"No, absolutely nothing. And so far, there's nothing about Wolfie that has anything to do with Phillips. At this point, I'm following several different threads on each victim. And as you told me, Wilson has found nothing linking the two. No similar fibers, no—"

"Looks like we timed this just right." Gretchen lifted her face to the TV where a brunette with long, perfectly straight and shiny hair and a button nose announced that the second of the two men found below the Loop in Glacier National Park had been identified. I was expecting it because Joe had told me he'd be releasing the name.

"In a strange set of circumstances, the second man that was found dead on Saturday of this previous weekend below the infamous Loop in Glacier National Park has been identified as Mark Phillips, a local cartographer," she announced.

There was another couple at the bar near the end and both murmured something, then looked back to the screen.

"Phillips had not been reported missing as he lived alone, but authorities believe he had been out in the elements since sometime last week. Police have neither confirmed nor denied that the death is suspicious, although this is the second body found in the exact same area within two days of one another. Park Police are appealing to anyone with information about these victims to come forward."

A tip-line number scrolled across the bottom of the screen for a moment, then cut to a long-faced male reporter with a high forehead and receding hairline. He stood on the short stone barrier by the hairpin curve of the Loop, squinting in the sun and announced: "This is the Loop, where below me the first body was seen last Thursday by a tourist who spotted the body below. The first victim, a Paul Sedgewick, was a well-known biologist spearheading a wolverine project for the Rocky Mountain Research Station and Glacier Park under the federal government. The scientific community is devastated at the tragic death of one of their top researchers in the Rocky Mountain area. The second man, Mark Phillips, is an accomplished cartographer who will also be missed by another community of experts in the field of global mapping."

The screen cut again, this time to Joe Smith outside headquarters not far from my office window, being interviewed by the same reporter. Joe was wearing his Park Police uniform, and the badge on his chest was catching the sun and glinting distractingly on the screen. He spoke calmly and slowly, explaining that Park Police was investigating all avenues relating to both deaths and in the meantime, his deepest sympathy (and he said he spoke on behalf of the entire department and Glacier Park) went to the families of the victims.

Gretchen lifted her brow to me. "That the coverage you were expecting?"

"Pretty much."

"So, tell me," she said. "What's the real reason I'm meeting you here?"

"What makes you think I didn't give you the real reason." I felt a slight heat rise to my face.

"You need a front? A date? Why couldn't you just go by yourself if you thought it would look funny to go with Ken?"

"I never said I couldn't."

"Hmmm." She took a sip of her wine.

"Figured it would be more fun with you. So if it doesn't suit you, why didn't you just say no?"

"I never said it doesn't suit me." She lifted her glass to toast mine. "I just like to know what I'm getting into."

. . .

The parking lot of the Outlaw's Nest was already packed. Gretchen and I found a space on the outer edge of the lot under a flimsy street lamp propped on a skinny pole. Gretchen said she wanted to drive, and I didn't protest, figuring she felt better having her own wheels. She had followed me to my dorm to drop mine off, and we took hers from there. After she slid the keys out of the ignition, I looked at her and suddenly felt a little ridiculous for bringing her along to something I had no real strategy for.

"You okay?" she asked.

"Yeah, yeah, I'm fine, but you know I have no real plan in mind, right."

She laughed. "I wasn't expecting any Navy seals action or anything."

"Good then. We're on the same page." I looked over to the bar. Glowing neon signs for Budweiser and Coors beckoned—or cautioned—from the windows. I could hear the Woodtics pounding away on some unidentifiable tune—a deep throb of bass, heavy and muffled—through the old, semidilapidated wood walls with brown peeling paint. The building backed up into thick pinewoods with a tin roof tilting off one side to make a carport covering a bunch of weeds.

"I'm not sure what page you're on, but I'm just planning on going in, listening to a little music regardless of how bad it might be. Let me see that picture again." She held out her hand. I dug it out and gave it to her, and she studied it for a minute. Then she handed it back, opened the door, and swung her legs out of her car.

"Like, I said: on the same page," I offered. "We just go in and see what's up."

As we walked across the lot, a couple laughing and clinging to each other tumbled out the front door, the music getting crisper and reaching a fuller spectrum, shrill and cutting. I could now hear the lead guitar and drums. "I guess they're from around here," I said to Gretchen, referring to the band.

"I figured." She smiled. "You know—name like the Woodtics."

I laughed. "Maybe they'll surprise us."

"Maybe." She opened the door and we stepped in.

Inside the crowd was loud and full of energy. We made our way through it and found a small opening to the side of the bar near the wall with a jukebox. I could see Melissa working hard. She had two others helping her: a tall, thin younger guy with wavy hair that looked like he could be her brother and another overdyed, brassy blonde around the same age as Melissa, maybe late twenties.

"You good here?" I asked Gretchen. "I'll see if I can squeeze in and grab some beers."

Gretchen nodded that she was fine and pulled me closer to talk in my ear against the noise. "I'll scan the crowd for your guy," she said making my ear tickle from the vibration of her voice.

I nodded and nudged my way to the bar and waited to catch Melissa's attention. When she saw me, she shook her head in disappointment, then came over after grabbing a few beers for some guys next to me. "And—let me guess—you're here for the music?" she said sarcastically.

"That and a couple of beers."

"What can I getcha?"

"Buds, please." I held up two fingers. Melissa grabbed them and I looked around. The Woodtics were playing at the other end of the room and some people were already dancing in front of the band even though the place didn't have a dance floor. Young, middle-aged, and elderly alike danced loose-limbed and smiling, unselfconscious and clearly at home in this decrepit but safe haven—at least to its usual patrons—that Melissa and the owners of the Outlaw's Nest had created. I felt a certain disdain and envy simultaneously for the ease of their comfort in the place, for the way they fit in like pieces of a puzzle that effortlessly belonged together. All the booths along the edges of the room were filled and the tables too. I threw some cash on the bar to pay for the beers and tossed another twenty down. "Which one's Dorian and his crew?"

She picked up the twenty, shoved it in her pocket, and said: "You're the cop. You figure it out."

I walked back over and handed the beer to Gretchen. The band was cranking up to a chaotic and messy finale of the Red Hot Chili Peppers' "Tell Me Baby," so I just toasted Gretchen's bottle and waited for the crescendo to fall. They were using too much bass and I could feel the beat pounding up my spine and through my sternum.

"I think they're over there." She pointed with the neck of her bottle after the Woodtics struck their final, battering chord.

I looked over and saw Dorian, his hair longer than in the picture and slicked back behind his ears. He had also grown a thin Fu Man-chu that went low enough to trail down his budding double chin. He had his arm around a big-busted redhead with permed hair and tons of freckles, and his hand dangled over her shoulder and down low enough to cup her good-size right breast. Three other men sat with them. They were all smiling and laughing and numerous empty draft mugs crowded their table. "Yep," I said. "That's him. And guessing the others on are with him too." I thought to myself: Joel Rieger, Pat Sea-men, and Darryl DeWitt.

The band had now moved onto Pure Prairie League's "Amie" and Gretchen and I watched until the tide of the crowd shifted slightly and a spot opened up at the bar. We squeezed in and Gretchen took the stool. I stood by her, leaning on the thick wooden slab with my eye on Dorian's table. The discussion seemed to have changed to something more serious, the smiles and laughter transforming to severe expres-sions and angled gestures. Then one of the guys from across the table from Dorian pointed to the bar and Dorian shoved the guy next to him in the ribs until he scooted out and stomped up to Melissa. He pushed some other guys standing by the bar out of the way and yelled at her to come over. He was leaning over the counter, trying to point in her face and holding his hands open to the ceiling when he wasn't pointing, as if he wanted an explanation but wasn't going to settle down to listen to one anyway.

She said something back, her hands on her hips, her face angry. I wished I was closer and could hear what they were quarrelling about when suddenly—perhaps intentionally, perhaps not—Melissa's eyes slid over to look at me, dark and angry. Dorian caught it and fol-lowed her gaze, but before his stare fell on us, she had looked away. He scanned the crowd some more until his glare settled on us. His mouth slowly spread into a sly grin, his eyes flat. "You've got to be fuckin' kidding me," he said. Now I could hear him since he faced us, his voice booming our way. "*That's* him?" he regarded Melissa, then turned back to us. "*That* guy? He's the one sniffin' around here?"

He snatched a mug of beer off the counter that belonged to some other person and came over, taking a gulp as he bashed through a group of people near us. I moved slightly away from Gretchen and stood still, watching him approach.

When he reached me, he looked me up and down. He was a good head taller than me. He was wearing blue jeans and a T-shirt that showed a wolf in a crosshairs. *Smoke A Pack A Day*, his chest said. He started chuckling again, then turned to Gretchen and took her in, his gaze grazing over every part of her.

"You got something to say to me?" I asked.

He turned back to me and pulled his chin in as if my words alone had struck some nerve of disgust. "You the one pokin' around in our business, askin' about that wolverine dude that had no business around these parts in the first place?"

"Yup." I nodded, taking a sip of my beer. I wanted to seem casual and unfazed by him, but I have to admit I was a little worried. These men from the Line had their own code of ethics, sometimes including law and order, sometimes not, often depending on how much alcohol and drugs were in their system. And at times, no chemical mood-altering was necessary, and they would definitely consider my slightness as an invite to exert their power. "That's me all right."

He started laughing again, forced and false. "This pip-squeak?" he turned to Gretchen. "You with him? Belle of the ball like you—with him?"

Gretchen sat still, glaring at him, giving him nothing.

"I asked you a question. You deaf?" he said loud and sharp to her.

"Hey, if you've got a problem with me," I said. "No need to yell at her."

"Ooooh, okay. Yeah, right, right." He held up one palm, reached over Gretchen with his other arm to set the mug of beer on the bar and purposely tilted it, sloshing it down her shoulder.

I grabbed his arm and pushed him away from her, deeply regretting that I'd asked her here. I said, "Let her be. You want to talk to me, we can talk."

Suddenly, a rage flashed across his eyes and he shoved me with both hands into the wall we were near, taking two guys behind me out. I could feel a searing pain across the middle of my back. "Don't you touch me. Who the fuck you think you are coming here? Just 'cause you have some piddly job in Glacier Park doesn't give you the right to act like you got something over us."

I stood up away from the wall he'd sent me into and stared at him, holding my hands up in a surrender position. "I didn't come here to fight with you."

"Obviously not. You'd sure as hell lose if you did."

I shrugged and that seemed to piss him off all over again, the same rage flooding his eyes. He lifted his fist and threw a punch.

Let's just say that being on the smaller side and growing up with an older brother capable of his own fits of rage has taught me how to dodge a few. I ducked to the side, darting out of his way, his punch flying to the wall and making him almost lose his balance. I could hear the crowd yelling and screaming. When he regained, he was twice as furious and came at me swinging again, only this time, when I went to dart out of the way, I couldn't budge. Two of the guys Dorian had been sitting with had grabbed me, one on each side.

Melissa came around the bar screaming, the guy who looked like her brother following. Gretchen yelled something out of the corner of my eye as they locked me into place. The crowd had turned from the band to us and was yelling, or cheering. Then Dorian's fist came crunching straight into my right eye socket. My head snapped back and hit the wall. I saw flecks of silver and fuzz. Then black.

When I came to a second later, I was still propped up against the wall by Dorian's sidekicks. I lifted my head, which felt wobbly on my neck, and tried to see straight and saw multiple Dorians lift their arms for another whack. I braced myself, turning my head to the side, but no hit came. When I looked forward, my vision adjusting, I focused on Dorian's thin, long nose and pudgy chin. Time slowed, even the shouting seemed elongated and it seemed as if his chubby chin didn't belong on him or didn't match his thin nose. Or maybe it was the other way around . . . his shark eyes and thin, pointy nose didn't match his pudgy chins. I almost had the urge to reach out and yank on his Fu Manchu to see if I could pick the correct one out of the three I was seeing until I remembered that he'd just punched me.

I tried to wedge myself loose from whoever was holding me, but I was dizzy and couldn't budge. Gretchen said something, calling my name, and Melissa screamed at Dorian—something about "not on my watch." Then it dawned on me that Dorian wasn't looking at her, wasn't listening to her at all. He had dropped his fist and was looking at someone else who was talking. I shook my head like a dog to shake it off, because I figured I was seeing things or had gone unconscious again and was dreaming.

The man arguing with Dorian was my brother, Adam, and as I mentioned, I hadn't seen Adam in four years.

"Look, I could give a shit," Adam was saying. "But, yeah, I know this guy from way back. He's no threat. Just let him go."

"Just like that? Just because you say so?"

"That's right." Adam nodded, his gaze as flat and hard as Dorian's, if not more rigid.

Dorian looked back at him, then to me, and spit at my feet. "Let him go," he said to the two on each side of me. "For now." Dorian's guys dropped their grips and I jerked away and looked at Adam. Something wet—either sweat or blood—trickled past my eye and down the side of my face. I resisted the temptation to reach for the wall to steady myself. I felt Gretchen take my arm.

Adam stood there looking at me, assessing me like a king of his mountain or some clever chief holding all the secrets of his tribe. His hair was short and spiked, and he still towered above me at six foot three.

"Thanks, but I really don't need your help," I said.

"Apparently you do," he said smugly.

"No," I shook my head. "What's a punch or two? A gang of guys against one. You know I can take that if it makes them feel like they've got some balls," I said loud and clear for Dorian and his goons' benefit. Then I looked at Dorian. "You may not like the law, but you may not want to forget it."

Dorian started to come toward me again and Adam held up his hand. Dorian stopped.

I looked at Gretchen, her face flushed from the heat and perhaps anger, and tilted my head to the door. We started to walk and Adam grabbed my arm and leaned into my ear. "See you at the family reunion."

I looked at him. He gave me a Cheshire cat grin and walked away. Gretchen followed me out and let me in the passenger side, where I sat back and rested the back of my head against the seat. When she got in, she said, "Who the hell was that?"

I looked down at my fingers with which I'd touched my eyes. Two were smeared with blood. "I'm sorry about this." I looked at her.

"Don't worry about it. I've forgotten how tough it can get up here. But who was—"

I held up my bloodied hand to stop her from repeating it. "Just some guy."

Gretchen looked at me puzzled, then said, "Okay, who do we call then?"

My head was still spinning, but I tried to think it through: call for assistance and make the arrest for assaulting an officer now or let it go. Investigate Dorian some more and take my chances that if I came across more information implicating him, that we would be able to detain him and interrogate him later. "That asshole is never going to be helpful," I said.

"So?" Gretchen said.

"So yeah, we call the county for backup, arrest him. Take him in, scare him, and maybe then, if I'm lucky, he talks. Maybe he tells me where he was on June twenty-second, and maybe in the long run, Shane Albertson gets another poacher."

28

GRETCHEN TURNED THE car around to face the bar entrance and we sat and waited for backup, watching patrons enter and leave. Because the park shares part of its jurisdiction with Flathead County, we've always worked together on law enforcement matters. For example, Gretchen works for the county, but she is the examiner for the part of the park contained in Flathead County.

It's the same for us when we need backup or a place to hold someone. We often use the county and local police facilities as well, including County Jail and Columbia Falls' Police Department's temporary lockups and interrogation rooms. I personally called Sheriff Walsh to see if, after the arrest for the assault, they'd allow me to question Dorian since he was still a person of interest in my investigation. Park Police was on good terms and had a solid relationship with the sheriff. I explained the case and told him that I was assaulted while on the quest for more information. He agreed to let me question him on matters that didn't involve the assault if all went smoothly with the arrest.

It was still plenty light out, and I didn't move a muscle when I saw Adam saunter out, look around, and spot us sitting across the parking lot in Gretchen's Honda. He didn't acknowledge us, just walked to his truck and left. I figured Dorian and his gang would follow soon, but they didn't and when the county guys I'd called arrived, we filled them in and they went in after him. I had also called Ken to meet us at the county jail so that he could be in the room with me when I questioned Dorian.

There were four of them, and they went in with the whole nine yards—Kevlar vests, weapons, including a pump-action riot gun in case the crowd got out of hand.

A deputy named Luke Brander was in charge and he informed me that two deputies covered the back entrance of the bar, letting the two others know when they were in position. They then went in the front, nice and calm, adrenaline pumping, but serious and trying not to scare the crowd.

It went better than I expected. Brander filled me in that the smug, cocky bastard wasn't even watching the door. He had his broad back to them at the bar, and they simply walked right up, tapped him on the shoulder, and when he turned, he jumped off his stool and tried to go for his gun tucked into his pants, but they already had their two barrels pointing straight at his Fu Manchu. They turned him to face the bar, cuffed his wrists behind his back, and walked him out with the crowd completely silent.

He came out swearing the whole way, and when he spotted me over by the county vehicles, he began yelling louder, telling us all that we'd be sorry—that we'd regret this. When I said, "That another threat?" he yelled, "Fuck you, man."

Melissa watched nervously with wide eyes from the entrance of the bar as they protected his head and put him in the car. The band had quit playing during the arrest, but I could hear them fire the bass back up as Luke got Dorian situated in the county vehicle. Even Dorian's clan would most likely go back to drinking and having fun. Just another night *up the Line* and in the canyon.

Gretchen and I followed the county sheriff's vehicle back to Kalispell where an interview room waited for us. Walsh had already let the night person on duty at the county jail know that we'd need one. We drove in silence, cutting through the canyon and not saying a word. I tried to wrap my head around what had just occurred and attempted to construct a game plan for the interrogation ahead as I stared out the window at the steep hills surrounding us and the darkening greenish-blue waters of the Flathead River snaking through them.

I wanted Ken's assistance while questioning Dorian because he was big, intimidating if you didn't know his true nature, and he knew the details of the case. We didn't have a hope in hell of getting Dorian's cooperation, but at least he was on law enforcement's turf now. So far, Dorian had been a person of interest on the level of reasonable suspicion, but not a suspect. As much as I disliked Dorian, I forced myself to not get too excited and to stick to the standard rule: motive, method, opportunity. There was possibly a motive for Dorian to kill Sedgewick, but we needed to know if he had an alibi for June 22 and if he was near the Loop on that evening. All we could do was hope for some answers.

Ken picked up the pace of his gum chewing as I briefed him in the small observation room adjacent to where we held Dorian. Ken, Gretchen, Brander, and I watched him scowl through the two-way.

"Just as well we got him tonight," I said. "Going to his residence to question him probably would have been a nightmare."

"Because of weapons?"

"I found out from the game warden, Shane Albertson, that he's definitely been stockpiling them." I bounced my pen against my thumb and looked at Ken, who had been home with his wife and his little boy, Chase, when I called him.

"You think we can get him to talk? He looks pretty pissed."

"Not sure. He already thought he had the upper hand or else he wouldn't have gone after me like that, and we didn't have enough to detain him as a suspect anyway. He'd have never come in voluntarily."

"Hell no," Brander added. "Not that guy."

"And if we'd showed up on his doorstep for a knock-and-talk, there's no way he'd have even opened the door. This is it and even now, we're lucky if he'll talk, but at least this way, he's on the county's turf facing jail time. We might be able to get something from him."

The stockpiling, in itself, was no crime unless he had a felony, which he didn't—only a DUI. Or was collecting weapons for the purposes of carrying out a felony. "A guy like Dorian with AK-47s, SK-3s, and other high-capacity assault rifles," I said. "He hates the government with a vengeance. Ten to one he thinks it will all be a one-world order takeover soon and that any government employee is the right-hand of the devil."

Ken stared at me, then looked back through the two-way. Dorian didn't move a muscle. He sat with his chin lifted toward us, no fidgeting, no nervousness that he at least cared to demonstrate.

"He's not saying anything you don't know, right?" Gretchen asked Ken.

"Nah." Ken leaned against the sidewall and put his hands in his pockets. "I just haven't thought about that type of wing nut in a while. Look at him." Ken motioned to Dorian. "He's not even fazed."

"You better start thinking about *that* type because it's thick around here, and it's right against your Glacier border even though your average tourist would never even know it," she said.

"I know the craziness," Ken added. "That some grand prophecy exists that says the government will become the beast."

"That's right, and any fire, tidal wave, or hurricane in any part of the world is further evidence of the fulfillment of such prophecy," I added.

"Or any researcher studying wolverines . . . ," Gretchen said.

I pointed my pen at her to emphasize that she might just have a point.

"Okay," Ken said. "So what's the plan?"

I considered the situation. If my suspicions were correct, he wouldn't want us within ten miles of his residence poking around without him there. "If he knows we know he's stockpiling, and we dangle some kind of bargain before him, we might get something."

29

I'm NOT GOING to lie. I was nervous. There was no way to know what to expect with a man like him—a guy filled to the brim with hatred and his own private Idaho. When Ken and I went in, he looked tired, but still angry, still in control. I knew the key to an effective interrogation was to get as much as possible from him before he asked for an attorney. I also understood that most criminals with experience clammed up and usually asked for one right away. Dorian was hard all right, but he didn't have a record, so I figured he could go either way.

"So, Mr. Dorian," I said after Ken and I got him a cup of coffee that I'd brought in for him without even asking if he wanted one or not. It's good to be polite, I figured, even if the guy had punched me in the face and I wanted nothing more than to throw the hot coffee right onto his. But being polite and in control is what made me feel like *I* had the upper hand. With the good help of my brother, I'd learned over the years that staying still, not flying off the handle, when others are angry or going hog wild is what works, even if they get even angrier that you're not going along for their crazy ride. "Good to see you again. You were very specific this evening about not wanting me snooping around your turf, well." I pointed to my eye. "You certainly made your point, so I think it's much better in here. Huh?" In Melissa's bar, he might be the toughest cat around, the hero of his own western with his illegally concealed weapon and his bad ass give-the-finger-to-the-law attitude, but in between these four walls and beneath a blinking video light on a gazing camera in the corner, he was reduced to just another criminal.

Dorian glared at me for a moment, then said. "Why the fuck am I here?"

"Why do you think? By the way, I should say for the cameras"—I pointed to it mounted high in the corner of the room—"it's 8:53 p.m. on July first. This is Officer Ken Greeley, and I'm—"

"I haven't done a goddamned thing." His voice was low and throaty, just as I remembered from the bar. I ignored the pain spreading through my upper back and focused on the fact that he sat rigidly, maybe stressed after all, and that the table he leaned on was bolted down.

"I wouldn't exactly say that. First"—I gave Ken a quick glance—"you've assaulted a police officer." I touched the corner of my eye and winced. "Damn, it smarts when I smile," I said to Ken.

"I'll bet it does. That's a good one there. Gonna turn all sorts of color shades in the upcoming days," Ken said.

"And, second, you assaulted said officer while he was simply trying to investigate a crime that took place on federal land." I flipped a page in my notes that I jotted down in Gretchen's car while waiting for backup, and quoted him: " 'You the one pokin' around in our business? Askin' about that wolverine dude who had no business around here in the first place?' " I looked at him. "Now, I'm not sure if you know this or not, but I work for the federal government, which means you've just assaulted a federal officer and that translates to a federal crime. Plus obstructing a federal investigation is a felony as well, and just so you know, I had every right to be asking questions about a federal case— call it poking around or what have you."

Dorian held my gaze for a moment, his eyes flat, just as I expected. When I became a game warden, this was one of the first things I'd realized about law enforcement, that it required a lot of near comical posturing, the use of the who's-got-the-bigger-dick stare. But I was willing to continue to play the game if it helped me solve my first case as an investigator for Park Police. I'd solved plenty of cases in the poaching arena while game-wardening for the state, but as I mentioned earlier, this mission felt different to me. This guy might be mean and tough, but he was stupid to get arrested.

"Third." I held up his Glock in a plastic bag. "Carrying a concealed weapon without a permit is illegal, even in Montana. But with all the guns you own, I'm sure you know Montana gun laws quite well, and I don't need to fill you in on those." I sat back in my chair and folded my arms across my chest as if I had all the time and patience in the world.

Dorian's eyes narrowed, then he said, "I ain't helping you with shit. Asshole cops—just as guilty as the dirtiest criminal out there. I want an attorney."

"Okay then," I stood and faced Ken. "You up for a bite?"

"Me? I'm always up for food."

"Let's go then. We'll get one of the hands to let Mr. Dorian here make a call to his attorney—perhaps Mr. Rowland, although I don't believe he's practicing law anymore. Might need someone a little more, shall we say—current—than Mr. Rowdy, I mean Rowland"—I turned to Dorian—"if you're going to avoid a few counts of felony. 'Cause you get a felony on your record, well, that changes the game entirely. I hate to inform you—although I know you're not a man who puts much stock in the law—that it's perfectly legal in Montana to stockpile weapons, unless, of course, you've got a felony on your record. That right, Ken?"

"That's the way I know the law," Ken said.

"Of course, cops are always cutting deals. Getting felonies down to misdemeanors if someone can help them out in some more important matter. Anyway, we can discuss it more after you speak to your attorney. In the meantime"—I said to Ken—"Mr. Dorian here can consider his situation."

Dorian mumbled something as we walked toward the door, but I couldn't make it out. "What's that?" I turned back to him.

"What do you want?" Dorian said louder, clear and angry.

"Just some information about Paul Sedgewick." I walked back over and pulled the chair back out and straddled it, propping my forearms on the back of the chair. "For starters, I need to know if and how you knew him. He also went by the nickname Wolfie."

Dorian took a sip of his coffee, wiped his mouth with his sleeve, and said, "I knew your dead guy. Is that all you want to know?"

"And when did you see him last?"

Dorian shrugged. "Couldn't tell ya. Can't remember."

"Well, I suggest you try real hard to recall that information. Let's try a different angle. Sometimes that helps refresh the memory." I smiled. "What did you talk about the last time you saw Sedgewick?"

Dorian kept his eyes on me. "He was snooping around where he didn't belong. Just like you, only worse—doing research in an area he had no business in."

"Why, you own that land he was on? Your property?"

Dorian shrugged.

"I take it that's a no. And let me remind you that you assaulted me. So if you think his snoopin' around was worse than my pokin' around, then I wonder what you felt needed to happen to him."

"What happened to him has nothing to do with me."

"Okay, well, that leads me to my next question. What were you doing on the evening of June twenty-second?"

Dorian stroked his Fu Manchu, his gaze adjusting slightly to the side, to the distance—as if beyond the walls of the interrogation room, then he looked back to me. "I was with someone."

"Who?"

"Melissa."

"What's her last name?"

"You know her."

"What's her last name?"

"Tafford."

"Thought you had a different girlfriend?"

"I didn't say Melissa was my girlfriend. I was just with her that night."

"Just the two of you?"

Dorian nodded.

"And where were you?"

"At her place."

"When did you go over there? Didn't she have to work?"

"Not that night. Her brother and Val were working. We got a burger, then went to her place. It was early evening."

"And where were you before that?"

"At another bar."

"Where?"

"In Columbia Falls."

"Can anyone vouch for that?"

"Yeah, Tammy can."

"Who's Tammy? Oh wait, let me guess—the one you had your arm around tonight at Melissa's?"

"Tammy and I hung out that afternoon. Had a few, but she had to go, so I went and hung out at Melissa's and, like I said, we got a burger after she got off work."

"What's Tammy's last name?"

"None of your business."

Suddenly it made sense why he had walked up to Melissa in a rage and was yelling at her. He felt betrayed that she'd given me anything, yet he was confident and entitled enough to sit in her bar with his hand draped over another woman's breast. "If you want us to clear your alibi," I said slowly, directly, "we will need her last name. If you refuse to give it, then we'll assume you don't have an alibi and then we're looking at possible charges much, much more serious than assault. Not that assault isn't serious enough, but murder . . ." I clucked my tongue.

Dorian set his jaw into a clench and glared at me. I could feel the hate emanating off him like heat from hot coals. I knew he wouldn't give me her last name, not because there was any good reason not to. He just couldn't fathom letting me win. I stared back and he refused to look away, refused to say her name.

"We have information that says you and Sedgewick got into it at one point." I switched gears.

He shook his head with disdain.

"Okay, yeah, that's a little vague. Let me rephrase that: you and Paul Sedgewick had some words outside the Outlaw's, and we simply want to know what that was about."

"You know what it was about, from Melissa." He sneered and I could tell he was still not happy with her, and she'd hear more about it as soon as he got out. Whatever relief I felt on her behalf for extracting herself from Stimpy vanished when I considered she was stupid enough to hook up with this goon.

"No, she didn't tell me anything," I lied. "But we have other witnesses that say you and Sedgewick got into it."

"I didn't get into shit with him."

I half-frowned like an amused and patient mother who knows her kid is lying. "Like I said, we have witnesses."

"Just Melissa. Lying bitch. Can't trust her."

"Can't trust her? Didn't you just say she was your alibi and here you're telling me I can't trust her?"

He gave me a piercing look that said I'm going to kill you the next opportunity I get.

"There are others." I clasped my hands together before me and set my chin on my woven knuckles. "You know Shane Albertson, right? Game warden covering the South Fork region?"

The mention of the warden's name got his attention. His gaze snapped back to me and a sharpness—another layer of hate, like blue fire—came into his eyes, which I didn't think was possible. "Fuck him. He doesn't know crap. All hearsay. Just another piece of shit working for the government."

I pulled out some photos from the crime scene and flipped through them, letting him glimpse the vague, grotesque images of Sedgewick, but not letting him focus on any of them for long. I wanted him to know this was serious. His reaction stayed the same, his eyes narrowed in hate, and his upper lip curled in repugnance. "Just thought you might know why Sedgewick would have come to the bar that day. Doesn't seem like a typical hangout for a guy like him, you know, a wildlife researcher."

"You think I care what a typical hangout is for a guy like him?"

"Apparently you care if he's doing some wolverine research in your neck of the woods."

He didn't answer, just looked away and crossed his arms, his eyes going to some distant place, a withdrawal into himself that said he trusted no one and had decided it was best to completely ignore the law, to ignore me, even to ignore the hate he was feeling. His face calmed slightly, and the room grew still. Then his gaze shifted casually and I saw his eyes settle on my chest where I had my ID clipped to my shirt pocket. At first, his eyes were blank, unobserving and withdrawn, then he squinted as something dawned on him. The corners of his mouth slowly curled into a smile and he allowed himself a big grin. "So, you cousins or brothers?

"Who?"

"You and Adam."

"It's a common name."

"Yeah, I'll bet." He started to laugh. "Now, it makes sense. I didn't think I was going to enjoy this little talk, but now, well, now I'm thinking this might be fun."

"What's fun, Dorian?" I felt my control over the interrogation begin to wither. I saw Ken sit taller out of the corner of my eye.

"This." He opened his palms out to the sides and let out an exaggerated sigh like he had just taken in a big dose of fresh air. He even acknowledged Ken—smiling at him—for the first time. "Your boy Adam," he finally said. "Might want to check with him if it's connections to Sedgewick you're after."

"And why's that?"

"Because your brother's the one who's helpin' that poaching ring out for a little extra cash, and they're the ones not wanting the feds anywhere near the land your researcher was on."

"What poaching ring?"

"Like I said. Best have a little chat with your bro. And while you're at it, make sure you clear my alibi with Melissa."

"Even if I do, you'll still be appearing before the magistrate in a day or two, unless of course, you give me information that's a little more helpful. I need more than some vague reference to some poaching ring."

"I gave you information," Dorian said. "Really not my fault that you happen to be related to the guy." He laughed again as I stood up.

"You're going to have to do better than that," I said, reminding him of his arrest, cautioning him again and going through his rights. Dorian didn't look at me once. I put my pen back in my pocket and went to the door. "We're far from done with you," I said as Ken stood up and followed me out.

"Don't you need his last name?" I heard Dorian yell as the door shut behind us, his laugh echoing through the halls. "Harris," he yelled louder. "Harris. But of course I don't need to tell you that."

. . .

In the observation room, Ken and I stood for a moment and watched Dorian as he sat motionless and composed in his chair, a satisfied glare frozen on his face and his hands on the table. It was earlier than I expected, going on eleven and I had to remind myself that we'd gotten to the bar in the early evening by six thirty and had made the arrest only an hour later. Gretchen had left to grab some coffee, and Brander was in the evidence room labeling Dorian's things and making sure the paperwork was all in place. I would have a report to write as well before I left, so I turned to Ken and said, "Thanks for coming. I'll take care of the rest."

"But aren't we going in again?"

"There's no point. He's done. Look at him, full of piss, vinegar, and satisfaction. He's too full of himself to understand the trouble he's in even after we explained it to him. Some guys strap on bombs in the name of their crazy beliefs. He'd never do that—too much of a coward—but he wouldn't bat an eye at some jail time."

Ken stared through the glass. Dorian reached up and smoothed his Fu Manchu slowly and rhythmically.

"I'm actually surprised we got as much as we did from the guy though."

"So"—Ken bit his lip, then looked at me and tossed it out—"what's this about your brother?"

"You heard him. Apparently he thinks my brother, Adam, is involved in a poaching ring."

"You know anything about that?"

"Not a thing," I said flatly. "I don't have much contact with my brother. We parted ways years ago. I'll ask Albertson about it in the morning."

"How did he put it together?"

"You were in there. He saw my badge."

Ken eyed me suspiciously, waiting for more of the story, but I didn't tell him about my brother being in the bar, even though Ken must have figured that there was more to it. He continued to look at me, part surprise, part concern—perhaps part disappointment—that I wasn't giving him more. "You think he's just dickin' you around?" he finally said in the quiet room.

"Good chance he is," I said. "Look, why don't you go home to your family and we'll look into this stuff in the morning. I'll need you to check on his alibi first thing."

More disappointment flashed across Ken's face to be dismissed. He was amped up and not ready to leave, maybe wanted to go in again, but I knew we were done for now with Dorian. Besides, Ken had given me mixed messages about this line of work. "*I guess it's harder for you to understand. I mean, you don't have kids*," he had said to me.

"The only thing that might possibly faze him is a few days in a holding cell with lots of time to think about what life will be like without all his *lee-tle friends*."

Ken smiled at my Tony Montana imitation and gave in. "I'll see you in the morning, then. Better get some ice on that eye of yours. It's not looking too good."

I felt the ache of the night in every part of me, especially my upper back where I'd hit the wall. The pain was quickly and violently spreading to my muscles and bones like shrapnel. Since Gretchen worked for the county, Deputy Brander had let her watch with him from the two-way as we talked to Dorian before leaving for coffee, but she had moved to the sitting room after returning with a few cups and one of those instant ice packs she'd grabbed from a convenience store. She had patiently waited for me to finish my paperwork and come out, and some part of me felt relieved. When I saw her, I attempted a smile, but winced instead.

"I figured I better wait for you after you sent Ken home," she said. "You forget you don't have wheels?"

"I guess I did," I said. "But you didn't need to wait. Brander could have given me a lift."

"It's no problem. Let's get some ice on that." She placed a hand on my shoulder and we walked out to her car and she drove me home. It surprised me that there was still a slight glow outside, like when you exit a movie theater and expect it to be dark. The sun had dipped well below the western horizon, but still sprayed the sky above the mountains a singed tangerine color. I figured that in spite of the recent rain, there were fires starting somewhere, maybe Idaho or Washington, for the typical pink sunset to turn so amber. The vibrant, yet unnatural and eerie glow felt as if it were predicting a very uncertain journey. I also had the strange sensation that the sky pitied me somehow. Gretchen insisted on helping me in, even though I told her I was fine. I only agreed because I sensed it was her way of processing what had just occurred, but I really wanted to be alone.

Even after questioning Dorian, Adam's face was still in my mind. Seeing him had rattled me and I could feel a shakiness somewhere in the center of my chest. I hadn't seen the guy in four years and when I finally did, he's showing up like he's in some Clint Eastwood movie saving my ass in a ridiculous, honky-tonk bar situation up the Line and mentioning Lara's family reunion? I couldn't wrap my head around it, and worse, lurking dark and murky like fish in deep water, were thoughts of what the hell Adam was involved with to have that kind of power over the likes of Martin Dorian. And now, I had Dorian telling me that Adam was involved in some poaching ring.

Gretchen made me sit and asked if I had any rubbing alcohol, which, of course, I did and she grabbed it from the bathroom above the sink along with a cloth. She wiped the blood off the side of my eye even though I told her I could do it myself. I felt strange getting such close attention from her. She was the first woman since Lara to get this personal and face-to-face in a decade, and her energy, her perfume surrounded me and made me feel dizzy. I had been punched in the eye and my head bashed against a wall, which also wasn't helping me feel grounded.

"So we did get some action after all," she said.

"Not exactly special ops caliber." I chuckled.

"Yeah, well, like you said, what's a fight when you've got three against one?"

"Story of my life. I looked at the rag she was holding, a few streaks of pinkish red on it. "Look," I added. "I meant what I said in the car. I'm really sorry about bringing you tonight. I should have thought it could have gotten crazy like that. These guys just don't like anybody poking around in their business. They've got too much to lose."

"What exactly do you think they have to lose?"

"I'm not positive, but Albertson with FWP thinks he might be part of a militia group, stockpiling weapons. He's on that hate-group site called Whitesquad. I'm pretty sure the guy I got his name from is using meth, so I wouldn't be surprised if there was some connection there as well. And now we can add some kind of poaching to the mix."

"Is poaching that serious?"

"It may not seem like it to the average person, but I used to be a game warden and I can tell you—it's a different breed that can serial-kill animals. Poachers see them as objects existing for their own pleasure, their own games. They love the stalk, the more illegal, the better, because it raises the thrill. They enjoy the slaughter, often leaving the animal's body to rot, maybe taking the antlers at best. Sometimes, depending on the animal, they take the pelt. Some cases involve huge rings for commercial trade. Guys like Dorian, my brother, they know this land in and out, and they can help people who pay large prices to illegally kill elk, moose, wolves, grizzlies . . . and I mean, opportunities to take in thousands and thousands of dollars. There is a market for the elusive wolverine pelt too."

"Sounds like Africa."

"Yeah, there's more of it going on than most people know about."

"But why then would Dorian be stupid enough to mess with the law? Seems like it would just invite trouble."

"Exactly, but these guys think differently. Force, fear . . . It's the way they operate. It's how they know to deal with things. The canyon is a world they feel is unto itself, apart from the norms, I suppose because jobs are hard to come by. It makes them feel like they can get away with more than you or I would ever consider." I knew I was being partially unfair and a little dramatic. Of course, not everyone in the canyon acted this way, and I was being critical having partaken in the Bear Bait case that involved the making and dispensing of methamphetamines. And sitting with a throbbing head wasn't helping. "Plus they hate the government, they hate the police, and they hate being told what they can and can't do, thinking anything can be solved with enough firearms. They have a sense of entitlement that is beyond arrogant and that invites stupidity."

"Which makes you think about what happened to Wolfie."

"Yeah, sure it does, but I don't have anything substantial but some hearsay suggesting he and Dorian had some words. Probably similar to the ones he just had with me. Threatening him to stay out of *his* woods."

"Hmm," she said. "Complicated. Now I know why I like the crime scene. I don't have to solve it, just determine what's there and what's not. And, I certainly don't have to deal with morons like Dorian." She narrowed her eyes as she studied my eye, then set the rag down on the coffee table before us. "I don't know. You might need a stitch or two."

"I'll be fine. I've got some of those butterfly bandages around."

"Oh good. In the medicine cabinet?" She stood up, and immediately the loss of her proximity was perceptible. "I'll get 'em."

"Do you mind grabbing some Advil while you're there?"

She came back and handed me the bottle of anti-inflammatories and grabbed a glass of water from the kitchen. She sat back next to me and placed a bandage on the skin between the corner of my right eyebrow and my eye. Then she took her forefinger and traced it over another scar I had right above my right eyebrow. "What happened here?"

"Let's just say this isn't the first punch I've taken in my life." I sighed. "Look, the guy in there who called Dorian off," I said. "He's my brother."

"Yeah," Gretchen drew it out. "I figured based on Dorian's smugness there at the end of the interrogation. So *that's* why he came to the rescue."

"Not really. He's been a bully my whole life. Coming to the rescue isn't exactly how things go with him. He's usually the one *creating* the situation that needs rescuing."

Gretchen didn't say anything. Just waited for me to say more.

"I haven't seen Adam in years. It's a long story."

"So you didn't know he was going to be there?"

"I had *no* idea he'd be there or that he hung out with those assholes. I didn't even know he was in the bar. Where did he come from?"

"Not sure. I think he'd just walked in unless he'd been at a different table or in the men's room or something. It was really crowded. You could have missed him easily."

I agreed. I thought about telling her more, about Adam's fight with

Phillips that I'd heard about the previous year and about his days at the academy, but something stopped me, perhaps the image of Adam and Mark Phillips crazily going at each other in the same irrational way Dorian had come at me. Suddenly, I felt tired and didn't want to talk about him anymore.

"He's quite a bit taller than you," she said.

"You like to be direct, don't you?" I laughed. "Yeah, he got my father's height. I, unfortunately, got my mom's. She was only five three. Thank goodness I surpassed that."

"What are you going to do about Dorian?" she asked me.

"Not sure, but I think I'll question him again after he's had a chance to simmer in jail for a bit, thinking about his weapons, and in the meantime, I'll continue to do what I know how to do."

"What's that?"

"Investigate him and his clan."

•   •   •

Gretchen made some tea and we sat on the couch facing each other and talked about her. I found myself relaxing in her company. She had come to the United States eleven years before when she was eighteen to study economics at a small university in Tacoma, Washington. Money had been available from the Norwegian government for students wanting to pursue business—a push from all the Scandinavian countries to educate their young in the markets of the world.

"But," she said, "I was bored with econ and marketing and I took a beginning forensics class on the side because I'd always been curious about it."

"Why's that?" I asked, genuinely curious.

She shrugged, and for a split second before looking down at her hands, it seemed to me that something sad or lonely swam into her eyes. "When I was young someone in my neighborhood was murdered. I remember riding my bike down the road and watching the police work. I asked my mom a bunch of questions about it, but she said we shouldn't talk about it. That just made me all the more curious. Anyway"—she threw her hair over her shoulder—"I ended up meeting a guy the summer after my last year of undergraduate studies and we got married. In part, we knew we were being hasty and marrying so we didn't have to face breaking up. We also knew that I could then stay in the U.S., work and save up for graduate school."

"Couldn't you have gone home and taken forensics in Oslo?"

"I could have, but I didn't want to." She flicked her hand away from her. That look, like she was holding something back under her non-chalant expression, flashed again. "I left a complicated family life," she said. "I didn't have a burning desire to go back to it. Plus I like America, I mean, don't get me wrong, I love Norway, but I liked America and I figured if I stayed in Seattle, got my degree, I would have options: Jim and I could stay or we could move to Norway."

"And obviously you stayed."

She smiled. "Jim was from this area, so we came out here. We gave it a try and the county was increasing their law enforcement program to include a forensics team. So here I am. I like it. There are parts of it that remind me of home: all the lakes and the endless woods full of pine, birch, hemlock, black hawthorns. Believe it or not, there are places in Norway equally remote. And sometimes the mentality is the same. There is the white supremacy, the fundamentalist attitudes, the sexism . . ."

"And what happened to you and Jim?"

"We didn't make it. We tried for three years, but in the end, we knew we should never have gotten married. It was fairly amicable."

I smiled. I felt a dull throbbing pain through my post-bar-fight numbness and Advil consumption, and thought of Lara and the distance we'd inserted between us. I wondered if we could bridge the chasm and if not and we divorced, could we remain friends. I guess you could call us amicable, but I could sense it was hanging on only by a thread, and there was something about that notion, something about the thought of letting go of my connection to her and her family that frightened me.

Gretchen and I continued to talk until I began to doze off on the couch. I was vaguely aware of her getting up and slipping out the front door sometime after midnight.

30

W‌ITH A BLAZING headache, a sore neck, and a swollen eye that was soon to turn bruised and ugly, I spent the day chasing information on both victims, Martin Dorian, my brother, and poaching rings in the area. I called Shane Albertson and filled him in on the situation with Dorian, just to keep him apprised and to see if he had any additional information on him. I asked him if he knew who Dorian's girl, Tammy, was, but he said he didn't. I would need to talk to Adam soon, but I needed more information before approaching him.

While Ken went to find Melissa to check on Dorian's alibi, I went to see Dr. Raymond Kaufland, the other vet who sometimes went with Wolfie to implant the transmitters into the wolverines and found more of the same—that Wolfie was a passionate, determined professional researcher. Kaufland had gone with him numerous times to trap sites in the park to perform implants and had attended one in the South Fork region. Thankfully, he had told me, that one was not rigged and he was able to successfully make the implant. He knew nothing of Martin Dorian and no other names, just that Wolfie had mentioned he'd had some troubles with the local trappers.

I, of course, also chased any information I could on Mark Phillips. I spoke to fellow cartographers in his office, workers at the health club he attended (not that Ken didn't do a good job at the club; I just wanted more), and even waiters and waitresses at some of his favorite restaurants that Beverly Lynde had told us about.

Eventually, I found myself on the phone calling the previous owners of Glacier Academy. They now lived in Acadia, California, after moving from the Flathead Valley to Oregon, and were trying their hand at running a tree farm in the area instead of a residential treatment center. Mr. Leefeldt came to the phone in good spirits until I told him who I was, where I was calling from, and that my call related to some individuals he used to employ at the academy he and his wife used to run outside Glacier Park. He got very quiet and when I repeated his name several times to ask him if he was still on the line, he said: "I don't need to answer any more questions about that place. Understand? I've already been through it all."

Again, I felt a prick of guilt ping through me at the thought of Adam attending during that time. "Look, Mr. Leefeldt," I assured him. "This has nothing to do with the lawsuits from years back. I'm simply inquiring about several employees who worked for you then because one of them has died in Glacier and it's a matter of course to investigate all falls in our park."

"Who died?"

"A man named Mark Phillips."

Leefeldt fell quiet again. I could hear a female voice in the background. "Not now," he said to that person, his voice falling away from the receiver. "So what does that have to do with the academy?"

"Like I said—it's a matter of routine investigation and I'm just trying to locate some people that Mr. Phillips hung out with back then."

"I have no idea who Phillips *hung out* with back then and as far as I'm concerned, if he fell in the park, serves him right. If it weren't for him, probably wouldn't have gotten into all that nonsense in the first place."

"Nonsense?"

"Forget it. Like I said, my wife and I, we're done talking about that chapter."

"Mr. Leefeldt," I said firmly. "I'm just wondering if you know a woman named Diane who used to work for you? I simply need her last name."

He didn't respond.

"Mr. Leefeldt," I said again. "Are you still there?"

"Yeah," he mumbled. "I'm still here. Hold on." He must have covered the phone with his hand because a muffled sound took over, and the voices on the other end sounded like they were under water. I waited, turning my Glacier Park coffee mug round and round. Finally, he returned: "Rieger. Diane Rieger. That's what my wife says her name was. Now, please leave us alone."

"Wait," I said. "Just one more thing. You said that if it wasn't for Phillips, you wouldn't have gotten into such nonsense. What did Phillips do?"

"Never mind. Like I said. We're over it." He hung up the phone.

•   •   •

Lara unexpectedly showed up at my office. I'd had trouble sleeping the night before thinking about how I was going to approach her about Adam. She knocked softly on the door and came in smiling while Ken and I were going over Dorian's alibis. Ken had found Melissa at her bar around eleven when she showed up for work and confirmed that Dorian was with her the majority of the evening on the twenty-second. Ken was also able to get Tammy's last name from Melissa easily—DeWitt. Tammy DeWitt.

"One of the guys with Dorian at the bar was DeWitt. Darryl DeWitt." I pulled out my notepad and double-checked. "Must be her brother or a cousin," I said just as Lara walked in. She greeted Ken first without even looking at me, and asked about his little boy, Chase.

"Oh, you know," Ken said, "he's getting into everything and keeping Val and me on our toes."

"I can imagine." Lara smiled. She was wearing dress pants and a colorful blouse, and I figured she'd probably been at work most of the morning. Over the years, Lara had worked her way up to managing the entire accounting department for the hospital, the largest employer in the Flathead Valley.

"So what brings you here?" I tapped my pen on the desk, and she turned to me and took in my face.

"Monty, oh my God, what happened to your eye?"

"Hazards of the job," I said.

"What? Someone assaulted you?"

"Pretty much." I stood up. "I'll fill you in some other time."

Ken lifted his shoulders to his ears to say, don't ask me. He apparently knew better than to get in the middle of a separated couple.

"So what's up?" I asked again to change the subject.

"I just wanted to go over some things with you." Her face was serious now, still examining my eye. "Have you put some ice on it?"

"I have. And taken lots of Advil."

She nodded, then continued. "I just wanted to make sure we're all lined up for"—she bit her lower lip—"you know, all set for the party."

I nodded slowly, then looked at Ken, who was watching us both. I set my pen down. "I'll walk you to your car and we can talk. I need some fresh air anyway."

"I've been to Costco several times. I have all the coolers and I was able to get a good deal on a new grill there too." She rattled off the details as we walked down the hall to the exit. "As you know, the party starts at three, and I know there's going to be at least fifty to sixty people. We've hired a caterer to do all the food and have a band and everything else lined up. Are you going to be able to make it?"

I didn't answer as we stepped outside. The air felt hot and slightly oppressive—unusual for Glacier. "I'd love it if you could come early, say around two, so we're both there when everyone starts arriving. And that eye of yours, well, it'll be a good conversation piece, I'm sure. Maybe a little concealer would help." She winced.

I was still holding my pen as we stepped outside. I slid it into my pocket and pictured Lara's huge family. With all her brothers and sisters now married with numerous children, it had become bigger than I could fathom. She had aunts and uncles, mostly from Butte, Montana, who were all probably driving in Saturday morning. And some were flying in the night before from various places—one of her brothers' family from San Francisco, another from Tucson, and a sister's gang from Santa Fe.

"It's supposed to be nice, clear skies, upper eighties to low nineties. I've already got two large white tents that we've rented set up, so we'll have shade. And if we get any late-afternoon rain, a place to go. We'll probably need to take them down the next morning, okay?" She looked up at the sky, slightly hazy from distant fires. "I wish it was a little clearer, but it is what it is. I hear there are fires in Idaho."

"Washington," I said. I had read the paper when I first got to work.

"Oh, well, whatever. So did you hear what I asked you? Are you going to be able to make it at two?"

I paused, turning to face her. "Why did you tell Adam about the reunion?"

"What?" she looked from the sky to me. "*What?*"

"You know the kind of terms he and I are on and here you're trying to get me to come and put up false pretenses in front of your family and you invite him? What makes you think that helps your efforts, Lara?"

"Monty, get real. I didn't, *wouldn't* invite Adam to the reunion. Why on earth would I do that?"

"I don't know, but why *on earth* would he even know about it?"

She looked at me, I could practically see her eyes flickering with thoughts, possible rationales. "Look, it was nothing. An accident. I ran into him and I was nervous and frazzled, trying to do a million things for this party and it slipped out. You know I talk too much when I get nervous."

Lara barely even knew Adam, mainly because I kept it that way. She met him only twice when we dated when I brought her to meet my mom and dad at the house. Adam had been like an annoying fly, showing up both times and I figured one of my parents must have mentioned to him that we were stopping in. He was pleasant to her, though, and I had a hard time getting her to square the brother I'd told her about with the pleasant one greeting her with a wide smile and offering her coffee, tea, or some other drink.

It wasn't until she saw him tackle me at the funeral reception that she admitted being shocked by his behavior. I told her how he had always been unstable and unpredictable, but coming from a family that would never act in such a way, she had made excuses for him, had said that it was only the pressure of losing my mom that had made him snap. I didn't argue with her, but continued to keep the promise to myself to stay good and clear from my brother.

I stared at her, not moving, my arms still by my sides. She did talk when she got nervous, and she'd do the same now if I waited it out.

She pressed her lips together tightly and crossed her arms in front of her. "That's all, Monty. It was a mistake. It just came out over a bunch of groceries."

"That's all?" My pulse was beginning to pound. Something about Adam and Lara having Lord-knows-what discussions about our separation made my blood boil.

She shrugged. "Yeah, well, I mean, he's your brother. It's not like I can just ignore him. I've never stooped to that, Monty. What's the big deal anyway?"

"What the big deal? Are you serious, Lara? So after years of marriage to me, you don't know whether that's a big deal or not that my brother thinks he's invited?"

"Well, it shouldn't be. Not in a normal family. But I told you, he's not coming to the reunion."

"*Normal* family? *Normal*? Normal is not going to your family's reunion and pretending you're still happily married to your husband."

"Look, he's not coming," she said again.

"He said he was."

"Well, he must have misunderstood, or he's messing with you. Like I said, I just mentioned it to him. Ran into him at Costco and that's that."

"Look, Lara. I don't want to come to this reunion. I know it's important to you, but I'm really busy here and I—"

"Oh, Monty, please don't say that. Please don't. You can't back out, not now. You said you'd do it."

"No." I was shaking my head, "I never said that." One year ago, I would have done anything she asked just to keep the peace, to keep it together. But recently, I'd been getting tired of being strung along with no sense of what she really wanted from me at this point, except acquiescing to the one thing I didn't feel I could do—having a child. I refused to put a child through the kind of things my mother went through. But I felt for Lara. I really did. I understood her pain. She was bitten by the bug to start a family, and I felt horrible denying her the right to give children the very thing she grew up with—brothers, sisters, pets, laughter . . . and more importantly, stable parents.

"But you never said you weren't coming either. Please, Monty." She put her hand on my chest. "I'm sorry about Adam. Really, it was a mistake mentioning the party. I don't know what I was thinking. I wish we could just be happy again."

"Well, we're not, and it's not realistic to think we can be. Not after all this." I looked at her pointedly. I'm sure there was accusation in my eyes, and hurt, and I could see guilt and tears welling in hers.

"Please, Monty. I can't dump this on my family at the last minute like this. It will destroy my parents to find out that we're split."

I took her hand off my chest and placed it by her side, then turned to go back in.

"Monty, where are you going?"

"Back to work, Lara. Back to work."

•   •   •

With my heart thumping, I grabbed my notebook from my desk and my keys and drove to Lake McDonald to get out of the office. The sun shone hot on the water and the haze over the peaks gave them a surreal quality, as if they had been painted on a canvas. I got out of the car and sat on a picnic table, stretching my legs over to the side.

My pulse quickly slowed to normal. I sat motionless, regarding the still water and the tourists mulling around. A family picnicked farther down the beach. An older boy skipped pebbles across the glassy water, and several younger children played, splashing in the lake and yelping gleefully.

Farther down the shoreline, a family of ducks dipped in and out of the shade. I thought of my brother and felt a wave of self-pity come over me. All these years later and he was still messing with me. I felt foolish for taking pity upon him while looking into the past events at Glacier Academy. I hadn't seen him in four years and suddenly I find he's been poking around Lara's and my separation like a mountain lion sniffing out a weakness and going in for the attack, helping to put the fatal bite into our marriage.

I could hear something small scuffle under a rock, probably a chipmunk coming out for some morsel a tourist had dropped then darting back under. I touched the corner of my eye, swollen and tender. Was it always going to be like this—Adam lurking in the shadows of my life even when I'd made direct efforts to stay out of his? Still, he knew how to press my buttons and that was no one's mistake but mine. I knew Adam had chipped away at me until he created a weak spot, a frailty in me, years ago, and he still wanted to play on that. But I wasn't going to let him.

"No," I said out loud, surprising myself. A passing couple looked at me. Embarrassed, I opened my notepad and made like I was busy. No, I was not going to let him affect Lara and me. My issues with Adam should not be taken out on her. I could imagine him running into her at the store, her arms full of grocery bags, in a hurry. Adam towering over her and grinning, making her nervous. Of course, she'd say, *How are you? I'm fine, just getting ready for a big family reunion.*

A lot had happened in just months to make us unravel, and absurdly, presently, and against all logic, I was feeling like it had something to do with him. I knew better, though. Sure, we had our share of troubles before the separation. I could become too focused and ignore the relationship too much when working. She could be selfish and inconsiderate, sometimes absentminded. . . . But we loved each other, and we were both aware of each other's flaws. Our real problems didn't begin until she decided she wanted to start a family, and I couldn't find it in me to compromise and had let her down. *That*, I told myself, had absolutely nothing to with Adam.

I didn't come from a normal family, but so what? It was Adam who cast a pall in the center of my being when I was a kid. It was Adam who was toxic, who unwittingly destroyed the Faraways and made me feel like something would forever be off-kilter, something that excluded me from the right to a healthy, loving wife and children.

No, this wasn't Lara's fault. It was silly that she didn't want to tell her family about us, but they were oddly traditional and had strict ideas about marriage and divorce. I could see her not wanting to broach the subject until the festivities were finished and everyone went home to their lives, a good time had by all. And I had no desire to leave her in the lurch for something we had planned together an entire year before so everyone in her huge family could make it work with their schedules.

I pulled out my phone and rang her. She answered on the first ring, her voice small and somber. "Lara?"

"Monty, I'm sorry."

"I know. I'm sorry too." I recalled how her hand felt slight and smooth when I took it off my chest and placed it by her side. I thought of a wounded bird and suddenly felt very protective of her, and I didn't usually feel that way. It was one of the things Lara had liked about me when we dated—that I wasn't particularly shielding and overbearing like her own father could be. Her father was a big, lovable man, but the type of dad who gave his daughters huge bear hugs and referred to them as his baby girls that needed to be sheltered and taken care of at all times. "I'll be there at two," I offered.

"Thank you," she said.

"But . . ." I exhaled loudly and looked up at the large, prominent sky turned hazy—obscure and fuzzy like our relationship had become. "When this is over, we make a decision: move on with our lives, either together or apart, okay?"

"Okay," she said. "We'll do that."

31

W HEN I GOT back to the office, Ken and I discussed how we could get ahold of records from Glacier Academy. The additional surveillance footage from the West Glacier entrance station finally arrived, so Ken got busy with the tedious job of watching car after car line up outside the gates, drive slowly to the station, pay, and enter the park. He was looking for Mark Phillips's car, any other signs of him or anyone else suspicious on the days of June 16 through 19, when we suspected Phillips went missing.

Then we went to find Tammy DeWitt. She lived in a very small wooden A-frame house in Coram, which is in the canyon north of Hungry Horse closer to the park. The house had a metal roof sloping down on each side, and a chain-link fence surrounded a dry and patchy yard with overgrown weeds to the side and a small porch in front. On the way in, I noticed several PRIVATE PROPERTY, NO TRESPASSING, NO HUNTING WITHOUT PERMISSION signs posted on some of the pines.

When we pulled up, three mutts of three different sizes came running—a Chihuahua-size yapper, a pit-bullish-looking tan one, and a scruffy long-haired collarless one. The woman I remembered from the bar stepped out of her screen door onto her small, rotting porch and shielded her face from the sun so she could see who was driving up.

I coasted to a stop, killed the engine, and checked out the three mutts gathering around my door, jumping and barking. None were snarling or baring teeth, so I slowly stepped out, while Tammy stood and watched without lifting a finger to come grab the ones wearing the collars or at least to call them back away from the car. "Easy boys, easy," I said, and let them sniff my hand.

When I got some tails wagging, Ken stepped out and we walked toward Tammy with the three of them staying close by, the small one continuously yapping and jumping up on my ankles. I touched the brim of my cap and gave a small nod to Tammy and introduced myself and Ken.

"I recognize you," Tammy said without inviting us up. "And I got nothing to say to you."

We walked up onto the deck anyway. I could smell turpentine and sun-heated wood. I said, "Are you Tammy DeWitt?"

She nodded that she was.

"Aren't you interested in how long your boy'll be in jail?" One of the dogs sat next to my feet, panting hot air on my leg.

She pushed her bottom lip out and placed a hand on her very round hip. She was wearing tight cutoff jeans with some shiny, silver beading across the pockets, and a tank top that showed fleshy, freckled arms, her big chest, and an extra ring of fat right above her waistline. She had blond streaks painted into her red, frizzy hair which made it look more like a color job gone wrong than anything hip or attractive. A tattoo of a rose climbed her ankle and another of a vine peeked out from the low V of her top. "How long?" she asked.

"Few days longer, at the least, until his arraignment in Missoula. So he is your boyfriend?"

"I didn't say that, now did I?" The dogs left the hot deck and went to find some shade off to the side, which looked like a good idea to me, but Tammy seemed fine standing in her flip-flops, sweating and glaring at me. She didn't look like she was going to budge.

"Whether he is or not, I need to ask you a question or two. It won't take long." I could feel the sun heating up my shirt and biting the back of my shoulders.

"And if I don't answer 'em?"

"Then you could ensure that Dorian stays in longer."

She pulled her hair up and began fanning the back of her neck with her hand. "Make it quick then."

"You want to go in where it's cooler?" I asked as I pulled out my notepad.

"No," she said abruptly, and I wondered what she may have had to hide inside. There was also a small, run-down Winnebago trailer off to the side of her property with its windows boarded up that looked suspicious. I couldn't help but wonder if there might be some crystal meth getting cooked or a stash of illegal weapons inside.

"That's fine." I leaned against the railing. Ken stood next to me, his hands by his sides. Tammy checked him out and licked her bottom lip, then pushed her boobs out a little farther and fluffed up her fuzzy hair. "You live here alone?"

"Yes," she said.

"So, Tammy," I said. "Do you recall what you were doing on the afternoon of June 20?" This was not the day I cared about, but I wanted to see if she was going to automatically say she was with Dorian to cover for him.

"I was out of town. I have family on the east side and I was visiting them."

"Okay, what about on the afternoon of June twenty-first?"

"I was driving home that day. I got home late because I didn't leave my parents until later in the day. I remember because it was the solstice."

"Okay then, what about the next day, the twenty-second?" This was the day we were sure Wolfie had died.

A raven flew over and cawed and she looked up at it, her bottom lip still pouty. "Damn birds," she grumbled. "I hate those things." Her face had a sheen of sweat and I was just about to ask her again when she said, "Oh, I was at the Outlaw's Nest in the afternoon?"

"By yourself?'

"No, I was with Dorian. I remember because he wanted to get some lunch and a drink after I got back from my trip."

"And how long would you say you were with him?"

"From about noon until three or four, but then we left."

"Why did you leave?"

"I don't know. We'd been there awhile and we wanted to go."

"And where did you go?'

"He brought me home. I wanted to go somewhere else, have some more fun, maybe go dancing later, but he said he had a headache. Didn't feel like going out, so he brought me here around four thirty or so."

I wrote it all down in my notepad while Tammy asked Ken if he was from around "these parts" and continued to lick her lips. I had a feeling that what she told us would square up with what Dorian claimed, even though I was disappointed to not catch him in a lie. I decided against telling her about Dorian heading to Melissa's. There was no leverage I could see gained from doing that, so I thanked her for her cooperation and left, the dogs not bothering to get up to see us off.

32

Lara was in full-on director mode when I arrived at the reunion. She was giving orders to the caterers, requesting for tables to be rearranged and checking with the hired bartender to make sure he had the correct reds and whites and all the booze her family liked on hand. When she saw me, she came over and said, "Oh good, you're here, and on time. Thank you." She gave me a kiss on my nonbruised cheek.

Her three sisters were there arranging flowers on the tables, her mother and father were standing in the shade of one of the tents, and two of her brothers and their wives were over at the bar helping themselves to drinks. Bright sunlight bounced off the white tents, and I could already feel sweat gathering on the back of my neck. The wind had changed because it was no longer hazy, but crystal clear with the peaks of Glacier standing proud to our north. To the southwest, huge cumulus clouds stacked higher and higher above the smaller mountains.

I regarded the mountains of Glacier, thinking how I'd like nothing more than to be in them, away from false pretenses and fake smiles. I could be spending my precious time working on the cases, and the reunion itself was a sacrifice on more than one level.

"Come say hi to Mom and Dad." Lara started toward her parents and I followed. "And please don't look so serious." She leaned in and whispered to me: "Smile."

Lara's mom, Doreen, came up and embraced me and Lara's dad, Walt, gave me a big, manly shake and a tough pat on the shoulder. "Hey, Monty," he said. "Good Lord, what happened to your eye?"

"Just something stupid from work." I brought my hand to it.

"Hmm, well, good to see you. You taking good care of my baby girl?"

I gave a fake laugh and didn't answer. I considered the question rhetorical since he always asked it, but this time, without his intention, it carried an edge. After going through similar motions with the rest of her siblings and their spouses, Lara made sure I met two new additions to the family—a two-month-old boy, her youngest sister's first baby, and a sixth-month-old girl, her brother's third child. I smiled at them both, saying how precious they were, while Lara's mom and oldest sister watched me like hawks. Finally, Lara's oldest sister, Teresa, said, "So, when are you two going to start your own family?" She was looking at me—the question all for me, not Lara, and I could tell Lara had at least let her in on our dilemma.

I just smiled again at the little ones, ignoring her question. "I hope we don't get rained on." I lifted my chin in the direction of the cumulonimbus heaping higher in the west.

"I hope it moves the other direction," Lara said, then settled her eyes on the driveway where a gang of her nieces and nephews were setting off fireworks. "The kids"—Lara tutted— "they shouldn't be so close to the road with those. They should go down by the river."

· · ·

More and more family members and friends of the families arrived until the back yard was crowded with guests. Clumps of adults gathered under the tents for shade, holding plates of hors d'oeuvres— various cheeses, chorizo-stuffed mushrooms, shrimp and pineapple skewers—and glasses of wine or other liquor. Occasionally they looked to the west at the storm clouds moving in closer and toward the road when they'd hear loud pops from the fireworks.

After several hours, I needed a break, so I stepped out from under the tent and went over to the side of the house away from the field where Lara's new grill sat—sparkling, clean, and unused. Something about its modern newness bothered me, and I considered that perhaps that's what Lara needed—a bright and shiny new start with someone uncomplicated, someone who desired to give her the children she now wanted. Someone who didn't come from a family with so many demons.

Our wind chime to the side of the porch softly sang and the warm, sweet smell of lilac hit me. I took a big whiff, and suddenly I heard a strong buzz and a whir and almost had to duck as a hummingbird dove above me toward the feeder Lara religiously filled with sugar water every summer. I watched it fight off another rufous peacefully sucking nectar. They could be tough, I thought—such small, delicate birds. They could be threatening.

I heard another pop from the kids and thought of Lara saying they should go down by the river, away from the road. The river was shallow by our property and completely safe and I agreed, they should go down by its banks, away from the main road. Once again, unable to resist the temptation to take care of something she'd pointed out, I went down the drive to the pack of kids.

Several older boys huddled over a stash of fireworks and about six other younger kids stood watching. Two girls were doing cartwheels and handstands off to the side. Four of the older boys were commanding the situation, two of them Lara's sister Patti's boys and the other two cousins from Lara's brothers. It was hard to keep them straight as the family got bigger, but I was proud of myself that I remembered their names. I walked up, put on an unintimidating smile, and waved the boys over to me. One of the girls—a strawberry blonde, around eight with freckles who was named Summer (the one doing handstands), saw me wave to them and followed the boys over to hear what I had to say.

"You kids should take this down by the river." I pointed with my thumb like I was hitchhiking. "If a car drives by and one pops into the road, it could scare the driver."

The oldest, Patrick, looked at me wide-eyed, a well-practiced innocence. He had a stash of Roman candles, the ends of three or four hanging out of one pocket and some bottle rockets in the other, the fuse ends sticking out. The other boy, Liam, was carrying a bagful. From the shapes, I figured he had smoke bombs, more Romans, bottle rockets, and some sparklers. "We're not setting them into the road at all."

"Good. Then you won't mind moving your operation to the other end of the field, closer to the river."

"But it's all weedy over there, and we asked an adult if it was okay, and he said it was."

I looked toward the river. Knapweed and leafy spurge pierced skyward in the area past our field, but beyond that it opened up to a border of trees where the ground was healthy with deep roots and the weeds kept their distance. "Closer to the cottonwoods." I motioned. "There's honeysuckle down there."

They looked at me, absorbing what I was saying, some of them staring innocently, some of them defiantly. "Okay then?"

A few of them nodded, and I turned to go when the cartwheeler came over and asked Summer what was going on. Summer answered: "We need to take it down to the river even though Uncle Adam said it was fine that we light 'em here."

I stopped and turned to Summer. "What did you say?" I asked her.

"What?" she looked surprised that I addressed her. "Just that we got permission to light 'em here."

"From who?"

"From one of the guys here."

"Your uncle?"

"Yeah." She shrugged, used to a huge family where it wouldn't faze any of the kids to call anyone an aunt, uncle, or cousin because they were used to loads of distant relatives and godmothers and fathers who weren't related, but seemed as if they were. "I mean, I don't really know him, but you know."

"What was his name?"

"He said Uncle Adam." She looked to the huge green field, where the white tents stood bright and regal as if we were having a wedding reception. "He went into the party."

I turned, squinting into the sun, scanning the crowd. "Thanks," I said to her. "Make sure you guys take this toward the river, okay?"

"Okay," several of them said loudly back.

I walked up the drive, toward the crowd looking for my brother. A soft prestorm breeze was picking up rustling the tall cottonwoods, their silver leaves vibrating and creating the effect of a flickering silent film. The band played an old James Taylor song in the background—"I've seen fire and I've seen rain." I scanned the crowds, trying to imagine who the hell he'd be talking to and why he'd come. Lara stood with a group of people I didn't recognize along with her parents. Everyone was laughing, faces rosy from alcohol and heat, and the hem of Lara's yellow sundress ruffled in the warm wind, the fabric curving up higher around her hips.

I was scanning the crowd when someone tapped me on the shoulder. I flinched and said, "shit." Adam was holding out a cold plastic glass of beer from the keg for me, but I didn't grab it.

"Sorry. Didn't mean to scare you." He pushed the beer closer to me, but I still didn't take it. "You don't want it?" he asked.

"Why are you here?"

He shrugged, gulped the beer intended for me down in one long chug and shoved his full plastic cup into the emptied one. "Thought I'd come see the festivities."

"Adam. Why are you here?" I was halfway expecting him to throw a big belch my way, but it didn't come.

"Figured it was a good place to come see you," he said. "You know, more likely to be polite and civilized around all these Catholic folk." He smiled, showing his teeth.

"See me about what?"

"Oh, well gosh, where in the world *would* we start?" he clucked his tongue. "There's so much, right? Your separation, you coming to the Outlaw's the other night. By the way, who was the pretty little blonde you were with?"

I glared at him, shifted my feet to a wider stance. The fact that he knew about our separation stabbed me and I could feel my anger rise not only at him, but at Lara. Even though I'd gotten used to the heat, I could feel it getting hot again, my scalp prickling from a fresh layer of sweat.

"Look, I'm not here for trouble, Monty."

"Uh huh," I said with a note of sarcasm that I'm not sure he caught.

"Really. I'm not. You seen Dad lately?"

I shook my head. "Have you?"

Adam took another swig of beer. "He's not doing so well. You might want to stop in for a visit."

"What's going on with him?"

"He fell. Hurt his back."

"Drunk again?"

"Probably."

"That's his problem."

"Suit yourself."

"Look, Adam, I'd appreciate it if you would kindly leave. You know you really don't belong here and who are you fooling, acting like you're here on Dad's behalf?"

Adam lifted his chin and looked down the line of his face at me. "Yeah, I'd tend to agree with that. Okay, you win. I'll get to the point."

"What point?"

"I need to borrow some money."

I laughed. "Seriously?" I said and watched his face get stone-still, anger sliding into his eyes.

"Yeah, I am. I figure you owe me."

"*Owe* you?" I said.

"That's right. You owe me." Adam rubbed his lips together, tucking them under until they made a thin line, looked at his scuffed boots, then back at me. His lids looked heavy, but underneath his eyes were piercing, gatorlike. "You still don't get it, do you?" His voice got soft and quiet, the opposite of the sharp stab from his eyes. I felt the buzz of the party around us, but separate, like Adam and I had fallen away from it and were transported to our own stillness, our own dangerous cocoon among the field of green. Chatter and bubbly laughter in the distance fell away.

"What's there to get? What? You need money for drugs?"

"No." He rubbed the back of his neck with his free hand. "It's for business purposes."

I squinted at him, cocking my head to the side as if to say, *Are you for real?*

I heard the scuff of footsteps on the drive and when I looked, I saw it was Lara, her eyes large and a sliver of panic layered into them. "Adam, we weren't expecting you," she said politely, a slant in her brow, as she came closer.

"That's an understatement," I added.

Adam didn't take his eyes off of me, didn't bother to address Lara. "I also came to tell you that you don't want to mess with Dorian."

"Why's that?"

"Look, Monty. For your own good. Stay away from those guys."

"What's your relationship to them? You owe them money?"

"No." A shadow of a smile fell on Adam's lips, and for a second, I saw a flash of something sad, something frail. "Look, Monty, I just need a few grand. You can spare that."

"Why in the hell do you think you have the right to come asking me for money?"

"You owe me," he said again, this time flat and calm.

"For what? For pulling that asshole off me?"

"That and other things."

"Whatever." I turned my gaze to the road, not wanting to look into his green, intense eyes filled with demons and other emotions I couldn't begin to pinpoint. I wanted to ask about his fight with Phillips the year before, but held back. This wasn't the right place and with Lara by our sides, the reunion pressed in on me again. I no longer felt separate, and a painful need to keep things copacetic needled in. "I need to talk to you. Yeah, I do." I pointed at him. "But now's not the time. Right now, you need to leave."

Adam shook his head. "You know Dad allotted each of us the same amount."

"Adam, I don't know what you're talking about, but it's not a discussion for this day, here, right now." I spread my arms out to the sides like wings.

"Bullshit. There is no good time. Which makes this the perfect time. Dad allotted the same amount for education and mine got used up at that shithole because of you. You're the one who got to go to college. I could have gone if it weren't for you."

"College?" I laughed hard and overly dramatic. I could see his jaw set and a vein in his neck twitch. He was getting pissed, but I didn't care because I was too. The thought of Adam going to college was absurd. Images of him high and obnoxious, at times unable to walk up the stairs to his bedroom, pressed into my mind. Lara put her hand on my arm and was saying something softly—an attempt to keep everything calm and quiet—but I wasn't paying any attention to her and neither was Adam. I sensed others gathering around us—Lara's sister and her mother and another woman I didn't recognize. "I'm sorry." I held up my palm and bowed my head in a theatrical tilt. "The word 'college' coming from you? Those were all your choices, not mine. How rosy retrospection can be, huh?"

Adam glared at me, then looked at his beer. He guzzled it down too, his throat muscles—glistening with sweat—shifting sharply with each gulp. He finished the glass, wiped his mouth, gave me one last good and long look, and walked off without saying another word.

I turned to Lara, my laughter and smile gone, with no false pretenses and an insatiable, biting anger rising in my chest, threatening to break free like a wild animal. It made my breathing quicken and my shoulders go tense.

"I didn't invite him, Monty, I swear," Lara whispered, but I was sure her sister and mother heard her.

"Invite who?" Doreen asked. "Who was that?"

Lara didn't dare answer. I took them in—the three of them, their eyes similar in shape and dark color. Doreen's gray hair and wrinkles looked pronounced and severe and Lara's expression took on a manic quality as the sunlight shifted from regular summer bright to an electric copper and purplish gleam as the storm clouds humped over us. I turned away from them and watched Adam as he disappeared from view around the back of some parked cars at the end of the drive, the breeze now turning to forceful shoves.

"Lara?" her mother said again. "Who was that?"

Lara looked between me and her mother. Thunder cracked closer than expected and Lara startled.

Again, Doreen asked: "Who was that, honey?"

"That was," she said, "that was just . . ."

"That was my brother," I said to Doreen coldly.

"Your brother? Well, we'd love to meet him, Monty. It's about time. Why is he leaving? He's more than welcome to stay."

I felt Lara grab my bicep, but I pulled away, my face flushing. "I'm going home," I said and began heading to my car.

"Home?" I heard Doreen say behind me. "But this is your home? Lara, honey, what's going on? What's he mean he's going home?"

Lara ran after me, trailing me to my car, which I had purposely parked off to the side in a different area from the others in case I needed to leave for work.

"Monty, please, please, stop. I swear, I didn't invite him."

I turned to her, my jaw clenched. "I'm sure you didn't. I'm fairly certain he's a big enough ass to come all on his own."

"So why are you leaving?"

"Because I've had enough. Because I find it strange that my estranged brother knows we're separated."

Lara stood still, her face frozen, her mouth opening and closing like a fish, but no words coming.

"How did he know, Lara?" I felt accusatory and childish—and it was not my style to be that way—but my brother had gotten under my skin. *Owed* him? If anything, I had saved his life, that's what I'd done. They were his choices, not mine.

"Monty, it's not a big deal."

"It is a big deal. You have no idea how toxic he can be; how he gets off on stirring the pot."

"He's not that bad. He's grown up. You can't hold someone's teenage mistakes against them forever."

"Obviously, he still seems to be making them, so I guess they're not just teenage mistakes, and you never answered my question: How did he know?"

She stared at me, a deer in headlights.

I shook my head and turned to my car, but Lara grabbed my arm again. "Wait. Wait. I was out with Jana. That's all. We were out for some drinks in town and he was there. He bought me a beer—to be polite. That's all, and I had too much to drink and we got to talking. He *is* your brother."

Lightning flashed again and a bruised and dark layer of clouds pressed over our field. The Columbia Range to the east glowed purple, and I could feel the electricity in the air as the wind rippled the thick fabric on the sides of the tents. Lara's hair whipped out to all sides, her eyes pleading and wild. She looked outlandish and otherworldly. "Better get your guests inside where it's safe." I motioned to the party. "Looks like there's a big one coming."

"But, Monty . . ."

I peeled her fingers off my arm, hopped in my car, and drove away.

33

I WENT OVER MY limit at the The Stray Bullet Bar just off the highway a few miles from Lara's house.

Let me explain. I'd set a drinking limit for myself in college one night when I got so drunk, I couldn't remember the events of the night before and woke up in a strange house full of sticky liquid, vomit and other groggy students. I hated that feeling of not being in control, of blacking out, and I took an oath to myself that I would not become my father. From then on, two drinks was my limit.

Randal Harris was a *functioning* alcoholic—a daily, in-control drinker for the most part, but was also capable of drunken sprees—coming home knocking into the hallway walls and lurching across the kitchen into the table that splintered beneath his weight, the sugar cup and glasses flying across the room, crashing, breaking. Fine white granules sprayed across the floor. My heroes were Spiderman, Superman, and, of course, my dad, until he threw up across the hallway carpet; and with Mom already asleep, Adam made me clean it as he helped Dad to the couch where he'd stay until morning. The smell of alcohol and bile rose into my young nostrils, made me gag, and forever altered my view of my dad. And when you lose faith in your dad—your hero—you lose faith in all heroes. I picked up the shards of glass and ceramic from the sugar bowl and swept up the sugar. I think I cut my finger. Nothing novel, really, except perhaps that was the moment I realized I needed to be brave, that I needed to toe the line for myself in this world.

I've only gone over my two-drink limit four times since my oath to myself: one evening with Ted Systead out of excitement to be on a murder case and some immature need to show him I could "hang" with the best of 'em; the night after my mom's funeral after Adam pummeled me; the day I moved out of Lara's and my house; and the day it hit the news that some kids had stumbled across a skull in the woods north of Columbia Heights that authorities had identified as belonging to an unidentified human child.

My eye was throbbing now. I was still angry at Lara, and I was completely on edge from seeing Adam at the reunion. And now I could add guilt to the mix for leaving Lara with a nasty thunderstorm to deal with and a mom who was going to keep asking her why I had said I was going home when in her mind, I already *was* home. I could practically hear a roar between my ears as if I had a bad case of tinnitus.

The bar was big, the walls painted brown with a couple of posters of skiers and snowboarders doing flips from rock outcroppings hanging on the walls. In one corner a large big-screen television hung with ESPN on, the sound muted, men's tennis—Wimbledon. Old songs from the eighties and nineties played in the background. I had planned on only the one, but when the bartender, a friendly guy with pale-blue eyes, big round ears that stuck out, a graying beard, and a hearty laugh asked me if I wanted another, I found myself saying yes, that I might as well because I sure as hell didn't want to go out into the storm I could hear pushing against the walls of the bar. The thunder and lightning raged furiously around us, mimicking my own emotions. We even lost electricity for about a half hour. Then I took another drink, and when the whiskey slid down my throat like a comforting friend, I took another after that, only giving my limit the briefest consideration.

"I knew"—I pointed at the bartender—"that when she said she ran into him at Costco it was bullshit."

"Ran into who?" he had asked me, rhythmically rubbing the spots from the dishwasher off his mugs, as if he did it all day long to calm himself whether the glasses needed it or not.

"My brother," I said. "As if *he'd* have a membership to Costco, for Christ's sake."

Hours later, when I stumbled slightly on my way to the men's room while I sang along to "I Can't Get No Satisfaction," I knew I was tipsy. When I got back to my barstool, the bartender, who I'd learned was named Doug, said, "You ain't driving this way," and pushed a glass of water in front of me. "Cops are out in force for the Fourth."

"I won't drive." I shook my head. "I'll get a ride." I pulled out my cell phone and called Ken.

"What are you saying? That you're drunk?" Ken asked after I'd mentioned I needed a favor.

"Not drunk, just, well"—I considered—"careful. One too many, you know. So can you give me a lift?"

"I'm sorry, I'm home with Chase while Val is out with some friends. He's asleep. I guess I could wake him, but—" he sounded nervous. "She'd kill me if she knew I drug him out."

"No, no, no," I slurred into the phone, and in some parallel consciousness, in some overseeing mind, I saw my dad and my brother in me and hated myself even more for drinking as much as I had that I had to call someone for a ride. "Don't get her angry."

"Look," Ken said. "Why don't I call Bridwell. I'll bet he can come and get you."

"No," I said again. Somehow through the blur, I knew that the last thing I wanted was for all the other officers to know that Mr. Control, Mr. Thorough, *Mr. Detective,* as Ken had mocked me earlier, had gone and gotten too drunk to drive. "Bartender's already got a taxi for me. Yeah. On the way. Just forget it, Ken." I waved my hand in front of myself. "Just forget it, 'kay?"

"Okay, you sure? It's going to cost a pretty penny to get a ride from there to Glacier."

"M'sure," I said and hung up.

"Want some more water?" the bartender asked me.

I nodded.

"You know, don't you? There aren't any taxis around. The last company that serviced the airport just went under 'bout two months ago."

"Yeah," I said. "I know." I looked at my cell phone. There was a text from Lara and through double vision, I could see it asked where I was. I deleted it. Then I thought of Gretchen. I felt I could trust her. I scrolled through my contacts and found her name and hit Call before I even fully thought it through. When she answered, I asked her to come get me.

• • •

In twenty minutes, Gretchen was there, looking at me with big, blue eyes and a confused and worried frown. "At your service," she said sarcastically, then added sincerely, "You okay?"

"I'm fine. Just had one too many and I'm smart enough not to get in the car and drive."

"Okay then. I'll chalk that up as a wise move. Come on, let's get you home."

"Thank you," I said, and when she grabbed my arm, I gladly leaned into her and smelled the flowery shampoo scent of her hair. When we stepped out, I could see most of the evening had passed, the sun beginning to shoulder the horizon. "Damn." I waved to the evening. "How'd it get so late?"

"Apparently drinking the hours away," she said. "That's how."

I got into her silver Honda, and set my head back. "I really, really appreciate this," I said when she slid in and closed her door.

"Yeah, well, as far as I'm concerned, this means you owe me again. What brought you"—she motioned to the bar—"here in the first place?"

"A 'reunion gone bad.' I don't wanna talk about it."

"Okay then." She pulled onto the highway and I looked out the window, at the passing stores, signs, and fields. I rolled mine down to get some fresh air. The storm had passed through, leaving the ozone smell of fresh rain and earth. A buttery light skimmed the mountains and a herd of deer fed in the field we passed, their bodies tan blobs in the distant green fields. A little farther on, a black dog loped up the side of the highway, his tongue hanging out the side. "Hope he knows where home is," I said.

"I hope so too," Gretchen replied. "The thunder always freaks a few of 'em out, sends them running like they're being hunted."

"I can't say I blame 'm." I thought of how I'd run—how I deserted Lara at the party. With my anger dulled by the whiskey, a twinge of guilt struck somewhere behind my heart, panging through my chest. I'd always had Lara's back and would never leave her in the lurch like that before. "We should stop," I said. "Check his collar."

"I think he's heading in the right direction." She looked in her rearview mirror. "He's turning down Walsh Road now like he knows his way home, which is where you need to be heading too." Gretchen glanced at me then set her eyes back to the road.

"You've really gone beyond to help me twice now. How come?"

"I don't know." She didn't say anything for a moment, just kept her eyes on the road. "Maybe because I'm bored."

I didn't say anything.

"Or maybe I feel like you're just trying to do the right thing. I mean, *really* trying to do what's right, not just because it's your job. I guess I don't come across that level of passion and commitment in all that many people."

I stared at her for a moment. I wasn't quite sure what to say, so I simply thanked her.

We drove the rest of the way in silence, through Columbia Falls and into the mouth of the canyon, where the setting sun spread a fiery glow over the deep-green water of the Flathead River moving in languid ripples. Several people fished from the banks, casting their lines from drifting rowboats as dusk swelled around them. We pushed through Hungry Horse, Coram, and into West Glacier, where odd-shaped masses of clouds left over from the storm gathered around the dark silhouette of Apgar Mountain standing like a sentry before the entrance to the park. I childishly imagined clouds forming sinister shapes like daggers, hooks, chains, teeth, claws, dismantled corpses, bloodstains. . . . I thought of the jackals outside all the houses that frigid Halloween night I walked home without Nathan.

Suddenly, something low to the ground darted across the road in front of us, Gretchen's headlights illuminating its bushy tail. She pushed on the brake, and by the time we slowed, it was gone.

"Fox," I said. A flash in the night, I thought.

"Yeah, definitely a fox. Cute little thing." She glanced at me. "You're more alert than I thought you'd be."

"I guess." I looked back out my window. The domain of wild animals wove all around the park, around the Flathead Valley and I thought of the wolverine, ominous and defiant against the world, and Wolfie, one of their strongest defenders against the humans who loved to subdue and conquer that which they couldn't understand.

I thought of Adam and how a twisted soul like his would always want to insert havoc into others' lives like a coiled and quivering rattlesnake waiting to strike, if for no other reason than to make his own chaos seem normal. Something one of my professors uttered in one of my psychology classes popped into my mind—that children from troubled homes learn to read people's emotions with acuity because they're always trying to determine when things might go sideways. I know I was always overanalyzing, but I considered Adam. I never figured him for the type to bother reading anyone, but now I wondered if he had more figured out about Lara and me than I ever imagined.

We drove under the trestle, through the gates of the park, over the bridge crossing the Middle Fork River, and to my dorm—back to my little haven in Glacier, as if the park itself was a type of medieval fortress that carried special powers and spells that could inoculate me from my past, from Adam, and from my childhood memories.

All the way home, I had watched the landscape blur outside my window. Trees, fields and buildings mixing into a pale swirl of motion that made me dizzy. I was feeling guilty and incompetent, the two emotions I hated the most. Now that I was sobering up, I could add embarrassment to that list.

When Gretchen pulled up and stopped in front of my dorm, I thanked her.

"It's not a problem," she said. "You did the right thing by calling."

I leaned over, placed a hand on her shoulder, and gave her a kiss on the cheek.

She smiled.

"Want to come in?" I asked, my fingers—thick and heavy feeling—still lingering and woven in the ends of her hair.

She shook her head. "You go in, get some sleep, and take a few Tylenol in the morning."

I nodded, gently removed my hand. "Will do."

"And if you need a ride to your car, it's got to be early because I work tomorrow at nine."

"Thanks, Gretchen. I owe you. Again."

34

I WOKE UP IN the clothes I had worn to the reunion, stood in the shower until the hot water began to turn lukewarm, and despite my usual routine, made myself some scrambled eggs and toast for breakfast because I knew I should get something substantial in my system. I had a headache and felt a little fuzzy, but I wanted to get back to work even though it was the Fourth of July. I thought of Gretchen as I brushed my teeth and rinsed with mouthwash. The night wasn't as big a blur as I thought it might be, and I clearly remembered how she had said to call in the morning for a ride to my car.

There was a message on my phone from Lara, from around nine p.m., asking where I was. I deleted it and called Gretchen around quarter to seven. She picked me up by seven thirty and drove me to my car and headed off for her day. I considered asking her what she had planned for the holiday, but I decided not to. It seemed to me that I had gone too far already and had no right to know how she planned to spend her time. I thanked her profusely and said that I owed her. "Damn right, you do," she said right back.

I got another cup of coffee at Starbucks and drove straight to Diane Rieger's—now Diane Hanson's—house. She was one of Mark Phillips's ex-girlfriends and had written the poem I found in his office. I needed to talk to Adam too, but not until I did all my homework, so I headed to Kalispell first. I found Diane's house on the east side surrounded by big maple trees green and busy with birds and squirrels and knocked on her door around eight forty-five. I wanted to catch her in case she and her family had plans for the day and were leaving early.

She answered, completely dressed in what looked like green nurse's scrubs, which squared up with the information I had found: that she worked for the valley's main hospital, the same place Lara worked.

Unlike Beverly Lynde, she was petite, even smaller than Lara—no more than five foot two or three, and I realized that she could not be the one Nick Ferron was thinking about. She wore clogs and had dark Snow White hair pulled back into a bun at the nape of her neck. Her skin was pale and spotless, her eyes the color of her pale-green uniform. Her smile revealed dimples, like parentheses on each side of her mouth, as if everything she was going to say was going to encase beautiful secrets. Yes, she was the type to write a poem, I thought. And she seemed lovely enough for any guy, including Mark, to hold onto a poem written by her, even if it was juvenile and sappy.

When I asked if she was going to work, she said she was and that hospitals don't stop just because it's a holiday. "The Fourth is actually a hugely busy day for us. Lots of stupidity going on." She smiled. I agreed and said it was the same in my line of work. Then her smile faded, and I told her the reason for my visit as she stood in her doorway. With over a decade having passed since she was with Mark, she looked confused at first. But once she understood, shock registered on her face and said she could spare a few minutes. She invited me in and offered me coffee. I told her I'd already had a bunch and was good.

She introduced me to her children, a boy and a girl sitting slack-mouthed and mesmerized by cartoons, and told me she'd have to leave a few minutes early to get them to the day care at the hospital. Then she brought me out back to her porch nestled in a small rectangular-shaped, well-mowed backyard with a small koi pond made out of stone. It was fitted with a skimmer and filtration system and looked as if it had a heater attached for the cold weather. "You keep those around all winter?"

"Try to," she said. "It's my husband's hobby. Sometimes the raccoons get in and eat them, but these've made it through this winter."

"Nice," I said.

"Thank you. We like it." We sat down at her outdoor table after she took off the cushions and placed them on a rock wall by the patio to dry because she said they were still wet from the rainstorm the night before. She said she couldn't take them out of the rain because she was at work and her husband was out of town for his railroad shift. I reassured her that I didn't mind sitting on the chair's iron mesh without the cushion.

"So, Mr. Harris," she said. "How did you even know that I used to date Mark Phillips?" She looked at me confused.

"I found this in his home." I pulled out her poem, tucked in a plastic baggie, and she reached out and took it, her fingers petite like Lara's. She inspected it through the plastic. "In his office among other memorabilia," I added. "And from there, I discovered that you two worked together at Glacier Academy and that's how I found your maiden name."

"Oh my God. How embarrassing." She put her hand to her lips, looking surprised. "This is a blast from the past." Then her dark, delicate eyebrows slanted down pensively. "And how in the world does this old poem help now, all these years later?"

"I'm not sure it does," I said. "It's a long shot that you can even help, but I'm just looking for a clearer picture of Mark Phillips. Anything might help. You can start by telling me how long you dated."

"Oh gosh, not that long. Maybe just six or seven months, but we were young and you know how those relationships feel overcharged and important even if they were fleeting. Back then, it felt like it lasted a lifetime."

I nodded, thinking of Serena—how we'd found our own haven together on Sundays when my brother was busy with duties doled out to him by the academy, most likely by Mark Phillips.

"Were you a counselor too?"

"Yes, I was. For a little over two years. I dated Mark the second year I was there."

"And did you think the place was run well?"

"Well, no, not particularly. There were lawsuits eventually. Why? What does Glacier Academy have to do with Mark's fall?"

"Perhaps nothing. Like I said, just trying to understand history, especially after finding your poem. Again, not that it means anything in particular, just one more person who knew him."

"But we're talking years ago." She held her palm to the sky to suggest none of this made sense, and part of me felt disingenuous and sheepish for bothering her, knowing my brother had been there around the same time, and I had no intention of telling her about that.

"I'm just being thorough, Mrs. Hanson. Did you keep in touch with Mark over the years?"

"No, no, not at all." She motioned with her chin to the poem. "I have no idea why he'd keep that silly thing all those years. Look, Mark and I fell for each other, but it was short-lived."

"Why was that?"

One shoulder twitched up, and I could sense an irritation rising, perhaps reentering old territory she'd worked hard to put behind. "Because, like I said, we were young, and, well, maybe I wasn't such a great judge of character back then."

"Why do you say that?"

"I don't know. That place." She threw her hand in the air. "It was just messed up. Everything started great. I was so excited to have a job helping troubled kids, to make a mark on the world, to do something heroic and useful, you know, like Greenpeace, without going to the edges of the world, but . . ." She blew out a puff of air. "I was just a kid too. I must have thought of myself as so much older and wiser, but I wasn't. None of us were, especially Mark, and the owners—they just weren't organized. I think they meant well, but they just didn't know what they were doing and having young adults like us in charge, well, that was just a disaster waiting to happen.

"I remember"—she shook her head in part disgust, part amusement—"the first time we had to go through the kids' things. You know, when they check in, they're supposed to surrender all their belongings so we can make sure there are no sharp objects, no stashes of drugs, that kind of thing. Mark, a guy named Steven, and I were in this little room with about three suitcases and backpacks and stuff from three different kids checking in, but we had no system in place. We had their stuff spread all over the room, checking underwear, bras, pants' pockets, and on and on—clothes strewn all over the floor—until we got giggly and confused and couldn't remember who owned what. It took us forever to try to get it all back in the correct suitcases." She laughed, the parentheses widening, framing her mouth as she recalled the disorder and shook her head. "It was crazy. We were just so, so young ourselves." She sounded wistful, like a part of her was lost forever and she wasn't sure how she felt about that. She tilted her head and looked reflectively across the lawn at a small sandbox in the corner with tractors and other toys embedded in it like an abandoned worksite.

But I had locked onto one particular word she had used when she began. "Why *especially* Mark?"

"Oh, I don't know. He acted so sure of himself, more confident than the rest of us, like he knew what he was doing and what those kids needed, but . . ." She caught her breath. "He was the lead counselor and he, he just shouldn't have . . ."

"Shouldn't have what?"

"Shouldn't have treated those kids the way he did."

I could feel my shoulders tense, picturing Adam and the other kids with Mark as their counselor. "How did he treat them?"

She shook her head in nearly imperceptible oscillations. "I don't know, just wrong. I guess he thought all that tough discipline stuff was the way to help these kids—a lot of them were really nasty and mean, and us so young—you know, practically needing therapy ourselves, and here we were with all this power bestowed upon us. He, well, I don't know, he was too harsh."

"How so?" I asked softly, but a squirrel in a plum tree began protesting, chip-chipping fiercely at a cat that had jumped up on the white wooden fence between her yard and the neighbor's.

"What's that?" she asked, my voice having been drowned out by the squirrel's objections.

"How was he too harsh?"

"He just . . . he did some cruel things." She frowned and looked down and picked a stray piece of lint off her pant leg. The twinkle of amusement and reflection from her earlier story had faded, a shadow moving over her eyes like dark clouds across the sun.

"Like making them carry buckets of water for hours and putting them in solitary confinement?" I asked, maybe a little too pointedly.

"Yeah." She clasped her hands together. "That kind of stuff, but again . . ." She looked at me. "Why does this ugly history have to be brought up? Does it really have anything to do with today?"

"It could," I said. "It very well could. If Mark was treating people that poorly, there might have been someone out for revenge."

"After all these years? That would be crazy."

I shrugged. "Again, Mrs. Hanson, I'm just being thorough. Sometimes in my business, you have to follow every path. Do you remember something in particular that Mark did that would make someone carry a grudge?"

"There were a lot of incidents. That poor girl, Miranda, hanging herself." Diane closed her eyes, and when she opened them, I nodded that I knew about the Miranda incident. "That was after I had gone. Thank God I wasn't there to witness that. And"—she continued, her voice lowering as if to share a secret—"before that, there was another boy, a big, strong guy, but Mark couldn't stand him—probably because he acted tough and he was competition to Mark on some level because, like I said, I think Mark was really immature and insecure himself. He disguised it well and acted all in control, but he could be really inappropriate, really mean and cunning. Mark made life especially hard for that kid. Adam, I think."

I could feel my entire body go rigid. I suddenly had an urge to leave, to not let her go on. I felt exposed even though I knew she had no clue that Adam was my brother. Probably even if she remembered his full name, she still wouldn't connect the dots. Harris was a common name. "Made life hard for him how?"

"He used to put him in that solitary confinement you were mentioning—in that awful shed—for hours. And one night, he got two of the other counselors to go with him: a guy named Elan and another named Ron. I only know this because one of them, Elan, felt so guilty about it, that he told me a few weeks later. That's when I broke it off with Mark. I couldn't date a guy like that. Someone who could do that."

"Do what?" I said coolly.

"Just, you know, such weird, mean things."

I sat patiently, not saying a word until she offered more. A soft breeze rustled the leaves of a willow tree near her back fence and I could have sworn it was trying to tell me something, murmuring some warning to me in the soft sway of its long, drooping whips.

She blew out a loud, frustrated stream of air. "Elan said because Mark was the leader, they felt they had to go along with what he said and yada yada." She rolled her eyes. "All that crap—the power of suggestion and that high-testosterone mentality, I guess."

"What exactly did Elan say they had done?"

"Are you going to use this information for anything particular? I mean, I've already talked to attorneys years back when that whole Miranda thing was going on, but they settled, so thankfully, I didn't need to go sit on the witness stand. I really don't want to dredge up—"

"No." I held up my hand to stop her. "There's nothing to dredge up here. Again, I'm just trying to figure out what happened to Mark, and sometimes a person's history can tell us a lot about the paths he ends up down later in life. That's all," I said calmly and reassuringly, trying my best to look professional and convince her that the things she might tell me didn't count, as if I was only working a case gone cold and not the real, blood-pumping police investigation I was actually on. And, behind all that, as excited as I was to be working the case, a part of my conscience niggled that perhaps the things she told me didn't matter in the scheme of my actual inquiries. So what if Mark Phillips wasn't the most stellar young man around in his younger years? And so what if he worked at the same place my brother attended years ago? Did it really have any bearing on his life now, before the fall? Was I wasting my time? Was I here talking to this pretty woman who'd written an innocent poem years ago to the victim, only because Adam went to Glacier Academy? *You owe me.*

But I knew that when things were messy and confusing, the only path forward was to search for more information to bring context, and from context comes direction. Plus I had dealt with a contemptible victim in my last case with Victor Lance, an animal-torturing meth addict, reconciling how just because a guy might have a lot of enemies and maybe wasn't even worth the dollars investigating, we still needed to do it. I sat up tall, feeling the wrought-iron curlicue flower designs on the back of the chair dig into my spine as I waited for her to go on.

"Apparently Mark got them to take the poor guy out of his bunk in the middle of the night, tied his hands up, and I guess they just got caught up in the frenzy of it all. Thought it would teach him a lesson." She looked across the lawn at the squirrel jumping higher and I watched her eyes absently trace its movements as it hopped from a lower branch to a higher one near the top of the tree, chip-chipping and squawking.

I could feel my mouth go dry and I when I swallowed, it felt hard and sharp. "What happened?" I asked again.

"They pretty much sexually assaulted him." She looked toward the fish pond, the sound of its aeration bubbly, playful and calming, incongruent with the things we were discussing. The squirrel suddenly quieted; the tabby had jumped back into his own yard. The bushes along the fence cast blunt shadows that mocked summer's fleeting nature. I felt an achiness—maybe just from the booze the night before, but it settled somewhere deep in my bones—to the marrow. *You owe me.*

"He and the other two made him go out into the woods near the creek. They shoved him to the ground, held him there, even choked him, and the worst was that they, well, Elan said they pulled his pants down and . . ." She raked her fingers through her hair and shook her head as if she could shake the image away. "It's horrible to imagine, but they had all put some kind of heat rub, like IcyHot on their gloved fists and well, they . . ." She bit her lower lip, clamping down on it, so I could see the pink flesh go white.

I waited a moment before I said: "And you said this boy's name was . . . ?"

"Adam," she said, then checked her watch for the time. She would need to leave for work. "I'm pretty sure it was Adam. I don't remember the last name. He was an angry boy, but he didn't deserve that. No one does, especially when they're in a treatment center that is supposed to be safe."

I stared down at my notebook for a second. My notes blurred before me like chicken scratch. I looked back at her and she looked at me innocently, a strand of dark hair falling along her pale cheekbone. "And did you report it?"

"Well . . . " She sighed and looked away guiltily, pushing the loose strand behind her ear, as if she could delicately tuck away the memories in the same way. "It was complicated. Things at that place got twisted around. Things that seemed obviously deviant and amoral suddenly came across as necessary acts of discipline because everybody played off everybody. The kids were manipulative as hell and the counselors, wrong as we might have been, felt like all was fair game to rein in the manipulation and the lies and the bad behavior.

"There was this mentality that we had to break them down to make progress. Break them down before building them back up. And before Elan told me anything, I had to swear to him that I wouldn't tell anyone. All I could do was break up with Mark and soon after that, quit. I know it sounds weird, but at the time, that felt like I was doing enough. And back then, you know, there just wasn't the same awareness about that kind of thing. Bullying wasn't even a thing yet—a campaign—in schools. I wasn't savvy, and come on, you remember what it was like to be that young," she pleaded. "Kids could be so cruel without considering the outcome. Without considering the consequences."

She looked at me, wide-eyed, for a moment, waiting for my response—for my acknowledgment that, yeah, kids were capable of truly nutty behavior—then nervously glanced at her watch again. I knew I wasn't going to be able to keep her going much longer regardless of her having to go to work. The conversation was starting to make her uncomfortable when she considered how alternate paths could have been taken. We all have them—things we could have done differently. Nathan flashed in my mind—a cockeyed smile, the smattering of freckles on his face, and his long, straight hair falling across his eyes.

"But," she continued when I didn't answer, "I hear a lot came out anyway when the Miranda incident happened, so ultimately, I believe most things got disclosed. It was smart on Global Schools' part to settle. There's no way they were going to win in court."

"Okay," I said. "Just one more thing." I took the poem out of the plastic bag and turned it over so she could see Mark's drawing of a woman standing over him, practically choking him. "Any idea what this drawing might mean?"

She studied the picture, her brow creased, then lifted her head, a disgusted look on her face and pointed to the picture. "See." She flicked her fingers at it as if it were a fly, her anger clearly rising. "He's twisted. I don't know. I really don't know other than what he thought, that I was controlling, suffocating. Classic, you know. When I tried to tell him that some of the things he was doing were wrong, his response was to tell me that I was the one with the problem—you know, *I'm* the controlling one."

Her use of the present tense betrayed that he had deeply scarred her somehow and that her resentment would always spark whenever she thought through the short-lived relationship she had with Phillips in an environment where all professional lines were blurred. I thought of the park and how it was even possible that some abuses of power may have occurred in intricate, strange ways if there was an ounce of truth to what the veterinarian, Tom Pritchard, had said about Rick Phrimmer halting the wolverine studies based on his wife's old and long-lasting crush on Wolfie. "He never tried to contact you after it ended?"

"He called every now and again, but I never called back. Eventually, he quit. I've run into him now and again over the years: the grocery store, one time at a music festival downtown, that kind of thing. I usually just stayed pleasant and distant. He was nice too and just acted like we'd never had a thing, ever. He did say something about my marriage about a year after my wedding when I ran into him. Asked me if I was happy and I said I was, but he had that condescending smirk on his face as if he knew better, as if he knew I really wasn't happy. But," she said, chuckling, "I am. He was wrong. I *am* happily married—and to a nice guy to boot."

The pitch of her voice suddenly escalated to an almost too-perky octave, as if she was trying to convince herself of something. The squirrel piped up again, picking up where she left off. I thanked her and left, its high-pitched squawks tortuously ringing in my ears.

. . .

I went out to my car, got in, and set my head down on the steering wheel until my heartbeat slowed down. I took a long breath in and let it out slowly, counting to five as I did so—something my aunt Terry, my dad's sister, taught me to do when I was young and got nervous before acting in a school play. Adam's time at Glacier Academy was much worse than I'd ever imagined.

By the time I got to headquarters, I was surprised to see Joe at work on the Fourth. He was tidying up his office and said he had been waiting for me. He'd heard through the grapevine that I'd had to ask for a ride home and wanted me to take a seat across from him at his desk. The sun slashed through his office window, beating into the old, scraped leather chair and exposing all its imperfections.

I sat down and felt sweat gathering underneath my shirt within seconds. My mouth tasted acidic from the alcohol the night before and too much coffee all morning. What Diane had told me was still sifting through me, slow and thick like molasses, but toxic and dangerous as poison.

"I just wanted to check in on how things were going," Joe said. He still looked tired. I was trying hard not to show my annoyance at Ken, who must have told someone about my call.

"They're going fine," I said and proceeded to give him a rundown of the investigation, playing down Glacier Academy and playing up the South Fork trappers, especially Martin Dorian, who, I told him, was still sitting in jail waiting to be transported to Missoula. I had planned on spending the rest of the day tracking down more information on him, and I wanted to speak to him again before he left, to see if anything else could be shaken out of him as the time ticked by. I also wanted to catch Cathy Sedgewick again to find out if she knew anything at all about the South Fork trapping situation.

Joe studied me without saying anything, his head tilted to the side and his fingers steepled on his desk before him. "But do you have anything at all to suggest that these two incidents are related?"

"No," I admitted. I didn't. "But, Chief, I really feel that they are." I wanted to tell him that I had a strong notion that Phillips was pushed and that Wolfie was simply collateral damage after the perpetrator learned that there was a wildlife camera in the area, but I knew it was just a long shot of a theory and I had zero evidence to back it up.

"I've got Ford on me. You know that, right?"

"What's new?"

"He wants a press release by tomorrow verifying that these two incidents are unfortunate, but unrelated accidents. Same ol' story—no foul play within Glacier, as if the place has walls, like an ivory tower he's been called to protect." He sighed. "Cathy Sedgewick has also come to me. Wants to know why this is taking so long and why her husband's death isn't getting figured out."

"I expected that," I said calmly. "She's come to me as well. I know she's frustrated, and we spoke this morning. I plan to visit with her again today."

"Ford thinks she would be calmed down by declaring this an accident. She gets her insurance money. Life goes on."

"She wouldn't be happy with that. She's the first to tell you that Wolfie wouldn't just fall by accident."

"She's been reconsidering. Trust me." Joe looked at his hands, his lids shading his eyes.

"Reconsidering? She was completely adamant that he hadn't done that."

"When you have a lot of time and grief on your hands, your mind goes through all possibilities. Who are we to say that Wolfie didn't stumble?" Joe looked up, his eyes hooded by grief.

"Chief," I said solemnly, changing the tone of the conversation. "How's it going for you?" I couldn't tell if he was in the mood to talk or not, but I didn't want to discuss Ford. It would bring no good for my investigation. Besides raising tourist numbers, Ford's goal was to minimize drama, unless it was the good kind that brought Sunday special-interest stories.

Joe looked at his hands again. Headquarters was quiet with many workers off for the holiday in spite of the increased tourists over the weekend, but I could hear the buzz of a lawn mower in the distance through the half-open window. The tang of fresh-cut grass seeped in, and I caught a butterfly sail by the corner of the window. "Everyone in my family's a wreck."

"Understandable," I offered and figured that was why he was in the office and not at home. Another family in crisis, I thought.

"The trial starts tomorrow. Systead will be coming in to testify. He'll be kind; he'll be truthful."

"Yeah, he will." I nodded, feeling horrible for Joe and guiltier by the second that I was adding to his stress, making him question my judgment. It was the last thing I wanted.

"So I'll be out for the week, and I need to know, Monty, I need to know that you've got this."

"I've got it, sir. No worries." I ignored the little voice in my head that said that if I didn't break this case, didn't prove I could handle the investigation, my chances of staying in a lead investigative role for Park Police were slim or none.

"I'm worried about you. Look at you." He lifted his chin to my face. "You get a black eye the first week on the job."

"Well, not entirely on the job, sir." It was a half lie anyway. I wasn't in uniform that night. "It was a freak occurrence—Dorian coming at me like that. There was a band playing, I was there, and so was he. It was a stupid deal, something I can't fathom ever happening again."

"And needing a ride?" He lifted one brow.

"Just something stupid. Personal matter with Lara." I knew Joe was well aware of our separation. "She had a family reunion that I should have never been swayed to attend. It had nothing to do with this case. I just didn't want to drive when I had a few too many."

Joe inspected me for a moment, then shifted his eyes and I could see he wasn't going to push it. "Basically," he continued, "if we can't call them accidents, but find nothing to connect the two incidents soon, we'll have to bring in either the FBI or Series 1811 from the department."

He was referring to the Department of the Interior and the four guys they have that are Series 1811, more highly trained and experienced than me in investigative services. Systead was one of them, but he wouldn't be assigned Glacier Park again, not after the way he handled the Bear Bait case. He solved it all right, but not without a lot of drama. He had struggled with Glacier Park, practically thought *it* was his enemy. Me—anything but. Again, Glacier Park was my haven. It made me feel clean and whole, wiped away my past, and made my twisted home life seem distant and smeared away like thin, wispy clouds stretching into blue oblivion behind the mountains. I'd hide out here forever as long as I could work investigations, whether they were accidents, missing hikers, or murders.

"We can't have two unsolved deaths just go cold like this," Joe said.

At the risk of being selfish, I wanted this one to myself, and I didn't have any desire for Series 1811 to come in and take over the lead. "I'll find something to suggest either way, sir, but I don't think they were accidents. For one, there's no breaks or dirt under either victim's nails suggesting neither one grabbed for purchase. It's not conclusive, but Wilson says that their skulls most likely hit first. Both cases." I left out the information Gretchen gave me about alcohol being in Phillips's system. The BAC wasn't high enough to suggest that he was drunk enough to go tumbling over the edge, and deep down, I didn't believe he had. The two had to be related. I had to stick to my guns.

"*Most likely* isn't going to cut it, Monty."

"I know. I'll have more solid evidence soon. It's just taking some time. You know there were no witnesses that we know of, so that leaves the victims' lives and that takes time. Lives can be complicated."

"Do you need more help? More hands-on research?"

I thought of Ken and how I'd been relying more on Gretchen than him lately anyway. And now, I felt completely let down by him for mentioning that I'd called him the previous night. On the Bear Bait case, Systead and I had our glitches, but we worked through them and I trusted him. With Ken, I'd thought I could count on him not to say anything, and I was chastising myself for not having better intuition, for letting my guard down. As if I'd never learned anything from my days of getting the shit beaten out of me by my brother. As if my forever-scraped fists and bruised self-esteem from my younger years hadn't taught me a thing. Trust no one. After Nathan disappeared, I never brought any friends to my home again.

Lara was the first girlfriend I had over and that was much later after we'd met in Choteau after college. And she was the first and only woman I figured I truly loved. When we'd gone on our first date, we drove down some dirt road and parked to watch the dipping sun bleed over the dramatic eastern front. We sat talking and giggling on the hood of my truck drinking some beer, and when I tucked her hair behind her ear and looked into her chestnut eyes, something relaxed in me—something whispered to me that I was finally safe as I set my lips on hers.

Now, I couldn't even trust her. Our relationship felt broken, and I pictured shards of glass scattered across that country road we parked on. Trust no one. Period. Something coiled tightly inside me. I thought of Gretchen's help—how she'd come to my rescue twice—and how unprofessional I was behaving by getting her involved. I would put a swift end to that. "No," I said sharply. "I got this, Joe. I got this. Ken's fine. I'll let you know if I need any more help."

The sunlight coming through the window bared down on me, stinging my chest and thighs. A sharp glint caught Joe's left cheekbone—sharp, bony, and pinkish from high-altitude exposure—the skin slightly lax with age and stress. "I'll tell Ford the situation's under control, that we need some more time. But I'm telling you, I won't get much from him."

"Does it matter? Even if he releases that the case is closed to the press, you'll let me still work it, right?"

"Ultimately, Monty, you know he has the final say. Last thing he'll want is to call them accidents and have you discover something down the road and make his organization look foolish. And that's exactly what I'm going to tell him to buy you more time. But you better hurry; the clocks definitely ticking."

I stood, relieved to step out of the critical sun and into the cool shade of the room just two feet off to the side. "I'll hurry, sir. It'll happen. Go be there for your family."

Joe stared at me silent and motionless for a moment, then dipped his head and closed his eyes. Then he opened them and looked back to me with deeply grooved lines between his brows, he said, "I'm counting on you with this."

35

Sometimes, when i'm driving in Glacier, the peaks surrounding me like a cocoon and Lake McDonald spreading before me with its ultrablue water, the sunlight filters through tall pine branches and flickers upon my windshield, spiking the light and offering it up like spun dreams. Something about the softly dancing light will make a memory, some incidental event from my past enter my mind whether I want it to or not. If there's nothing pressing going on, I'll let the memory trickle in, no harm in that, even if my past isn't completely torn from a Brady Bunch script. If there *is* something pressing going on, like my job, I push those thoughts away. But lately, I was having a hard time accomplishing that with all the crap with Adam and Glacier Academy hitting me straight on and out of nowhere.

One event in particular kept poking at me as I drove around McDonald Lake on my way back from an incident that Ken and I had been called to right after my meeting with Joe. We had to leave the investigation alone for a few hours to direct traffic on the Going-to-the-Sun Road near McDonald Creek because a young boy—around nine—had fallen in and nearly drowned. Thankfully, a firefighter had been visiting the park and had jumped in to rescue the boy and helped resuscitate him. He saved the boy's life. I had helped direct traffic until the ambulance came and left, then headed back toward Lake McDonald Lodge to meet Cathy Sedgewick, where we had agreed to meet because she was meeting a friend who worked there. The memory coming to me on my way to the lodge to meet her was of a cool, late fall day, not long after I had started third grade. Adam, Nathan, and I had been walking home from school. I was jumping over all the cracks in the sidewalk, trying not to hit any of them. *Step on a crack, break your mother's back*, when we reached our driveway. The house stood quiet, all the curtains drawn, and a stray, plastic bag flitted around the dead lawn.

"Better pick that up," Adam had said, "or Dad's gonna get mad that there's trash in our yard."

I went and picked it up and when I came back, my mom came out frantically, shooing Nathan off, telling him to go home quickly. She ushered us in, whispering loudly, "Get in here. Get in here or they'll see you."

"Who'll see us?" I asked.

She looked at us frantically, her hair a rumpled mess and her sweater on inside out. A film of sweat lined the skin above her upper lip. "The CIA. Come on. Get in."

Once we were in, she parted the curtains slightly and peeked through several times, checking to make sure we were safe. After we set our backpacks down, she came over to me and put her arms around me and hugged me. She smelled of sandalwood and something imperceptible, the bite of something sharp—perhaps fear. "You stick with your brother, okay, Monty?" She whispered into my ear. "He'll take good care of you."

"And you, Adam," she said, still crouched by my side and looking at him. He refused to look at her, just stood with his arms crossed and his upper lip stiff, staring at the ceiling, the anger coming off him in waves. "You protect your younger brother, okay? He trusts you, Adam."

Adam didn't answer and Mom kept saying, "Okay, Adam, okay? Will you do that for me?" But Adam wouldn't give her anything but a seething silence, until finally, I yelled at him. "Adam, answer Mom. Just answer her."

Adam glared at me, then walked away into the kitchen.

"He will," my mom said. "He'll have to. There are a lot of bad people out there, Monty. Do you understand?" I nodded that I did. I squirmed away from her grip, urgent and strong, and went upstairs. *He trusts you, Adam.* I looked back as I climbed the stairs to see Mom go back to her spot by the window.

Now, with the light flicking across my face like the reflection from spokes of a cycling wheel, I tried to remember, tried to feel whether or not there was a time when I really did trust Adam.

. . .

"You were adamant that this was not suicide," I said to Cathy Sedge-wick after we had walked down toward the lake, past a rock wall and found a bench to sit on below the front of the old lodge built in 1914. "What's changed your mind?"

"Nothing's changed my mind. I still don't think he was suicidal, but I don't know, I lay there in bed at night looking into the dark and doubt starts to creep in. What if I didn't know my husband as well as I thought I did?"

I tapped down the irrational voice inside my head that said, *What if he didn't know his wife and partner as well as he thought he did?* I waited for her to continue, taking in the peaceful scene around us: the flowerpots with bright-red geraniums, the tourists canoeing out in the still, deep lake, the birch tree to our side providing shade in the perfect eighty-five degree weather. I could smell the scent of dried pine soaking in the generous sun from the surrounding forest as well as the still damp leaves on the forest floor, vital with regeneration. Patience, you know. It works.

Cathy still looked grief-stricken, her face pale with dark rings under each eye. I felt guilty for thinking of there being a possibility of her and Ward having an affair and on some level, knew my suspicions were only borne from my own dysfunctional sense that it was beginning to feel impossible to have a healthy, happy home life. I stared at her. She contrasted sharply with the happy tourists mulling about, and I thought of the traumatized face of the mother whose boy just nearly died in the frigid, swift, and powerful water roaring down McDonald Creek. So much beauty in Glacier, so many happy families mulling around in the summer, but how many of them had deep, angry cracks running right through the center of their happy existences?

"And, so," she continued. "I started to search everything of his: his shorts and jeans pockets, all his drawers—I mean, I know you guys already did that, but I live there, and I was climbing the walls, so I just searched everything for whatever I could. Then I looked through all the jackets in the closet hallway, and well . . ." She held out her hand with a small slip of paper. "I found this in one of his fleece jacket pockets." She held it in front of me.

I took it from her fingers and unfolded it. It was a bank deposit slip. "The back," she said.

The number 7-63512A was written on it. "This is a license plate number," I said.

She nodded. "Yeah, I thought so too, but I have no idea whose or why Paul would have written it down, but it's definitely his handwriting."

I looked at it and thought about the reasons someone would write down a license number: if they'd had a fender-bender, if someone was frightening or bugging you somehow—someone you'd gotten into an argument with, if someone were following you. . . .

"Cathy," I said. "Can you think of anything at all that Paul might have mentioned to you about his work or his trapping that bothered him or had him worried?"

"No." She shook her head. She sounded like she was going to cry, her voice sad and resigned. "I keep going over and over it in my head, but there was nothing unusual. If you've found anything, it's news to me. We were plugging along as usual."

I looked out across the lake to Howe Ridge, scarred from wildfires, then peered toward the towering mountains beyond the lake's headwaters, their reflection making shadowy, kaleidoscopic designs. I could feel a private little satisfaction looking at that view, that even with some of the trauma, this was not a bad way to make a living. Finally, I said: "I don't know how to say this without upsetting you, but was your husband angry at you or distrustful of you in some way?"

She put her hand to her chest and sat up straight, scooting away from the back of the wood bench. "Me? Distrustful? Of course not. Why would you ask that?"

"I'm just checking all possibilities."

"No, you're not. You're thinking something. You found something to make you think that . . ."

I help up my hand to calm her. Her eyes were wide and scared. "I just know that there are a few things, mostly about his research, that Paul was not sharing with Sam. And, well, now there's something else here. Not sure what it means, but"—I shrugged—"I'm going to find out."

"Look—" Cathy turned to face me, her knees bony and pointing at my legs—"if you're implying something here, you need to say it."

Again, I held up both palms. "I'm not implying much. I'm curious though, as to why your husband, who seemed to tell you and his closest buddy everything, suddenly quits doing that."

She cocked her head sideways, her mouth angry, her nostrils flaring, and stood up and faced me. "I can see where you're going with this, and you're dead wrong. You think Sam and I have something going on, that's what this is about, am I right?"

"I didn't say that."

"You don't need to. Look, Sam and I have *nothing* going on. He's like a godfather to our kids, he's been a close friend to both of us, and he's been coming over a lot to check on us. That's all. If you want to make more out of it than that, then you're wasting your time and barking up the wrong tree. And frankly, if that's all you've got so far, then I'm more than a little worried about your handling of this investigation."

"Cathy. Sit. It's not all I've got by any means, but I'm being careful. If I didn't ask why Paul was keeping some things to himself, then I wouldn't be fully doing my job now, would I?"

She stared at me for a moment until the anger in her face eventually eased and she sat back down. I slowly relaxed again as well, relieved to hear her defend herself and restore my initial impression of the Sedgewick family's seemingly sacred bond.

"Now," I said, holding up the slip of paper. "When did Paul last wear the fleece you found this in?"

36

THE LICENSE NUMBER turned out to be Dorian's, so the following day, I tucked away my irritation at Ken and pulled him off his task of looking through all the surveillance tapes for signs of Phillips, Dorian, Adam Harris, or anyone else looking suspicious. After all, I knew he meant no harm, and I wanted him to assist me in questioning Dorian again.

We drove to the Columbia Falls police station where Dorian would be held for one more day before being transported to Missoula to appear before the judge. He had been assigned a regional defender named Carson Halloway from the Public Defender's Office with the state of Montana. I didn't expect to get much from Dorian, even without an attorney present. With an attorney, I knew it was an even slimmer proposition.

In the interview room, Dorian looked blank as cardboard. He stared at his hands like he had nothing better to do. His attorney, Mr. Halloway, was young, thin and gangly as a teenager in a navy suit that made him look like he was about to go to a high school debate meet any minute.

"Mr. Halloway." I offered my hand. "Nice to meet you."

"Same." He shook my hand.

I introduced him to Ken, then turned to Dorian in his orange prison wear. "Nice to see you again, Mr. Dorian." He gave me a bored glance, then looked away. "Well." I hooked my foot around a chair, pulled it out and took a seat. Ken followed. "Let's get down to business then. I'm sure you're a busy man." I smiled to Halloway. I was seated on his left, so my bad eye—with its now purple-and-yellow rainbow of bruises spreading across the socket—faced him. I had made sure to wear my contacts so the frames of my glasses wouldn't hide the bruising created by his client.

"Yes, let's do. As I'm sure you're used to, Mr. Harris, my client, Mr. Dorian here, has been instructed, of course, to let me do most of the talking. But if there's nothing off-kilter or accusatory in your questions, then I will be more than happy to instruct Mr. Dorian here to answer them."

I nodded and pulled out my notebook. "I have very few," I said. "Just several important ones."

"Such as?" Halloway asked.

"My partner and I would like to know how much contact Mr. Dorian had with Paul Sedgewick before June twenty-second?"

"My client claims that he has had no contact with Mr. Paul Sedgewick."

"That's interesting, because we have witnesses claiming that he and Paul Sedgewick got into an altercation at a bar called the Outlaw's Nest in Hungry Horse the week before we found him at the bottom of the Loop in Glacier Park."

"If you have witnesses, we'd sure like to see a list of their names, because of course, as you know, word of mouth can often be simply hearsay in small towns such as Hungry Horse."

"I'm aware of this, but we also have evidence that the victim, Paul Sedgewick, wrote down Mr. Dorian's car license number. So . . ." I turned to Dorian, holding up a plastic bag with the slip of paper with the number on it facing him. "Why would Sedgewick have done that?"

Dorian didn't answer, just scratched the side of his chin, where fresh reddish-pink stubble bordered his Fu Manchu.

"Officer Harris, you're asking my client to speculate. Clearly he has no idea what you're talking about," Halloway said.

"Most people," I continued, "jot a license number down for a fender bender or if someone does something they don't like, maybe even something illegal. Some people write 'em down if they get into an altercation with someone or perhaps think they are being followed."

"Officer Harris," Halloway said louder. "You know this is all just speculation. How in the world would my client know why a man wrote his license number down? How should my client know what's on the mind of another person?"

"Yeah." Dorian finally piped up, his voice more gravelly than before, as if he hadn't used it for a while. "For all I know, he saw my truck and wanted to buy it or something."

"And why would he want to buy your truck?" I asked.

"It'd fit all those log traps of his nicely."

Halloway held up his hand for Dorian to say no more. Dorian's lip curled because clearly he didn't like taking instruction, even from someone trying to help him out. "I'll answer if I damn well please," he grumbled.

"Mr. Dorian—" Halloway tried to speak calmly to him, but Dorian swatted his hand in the air and looked at me.

"And how would you know he had log traps if you had no interaction with him?" I asked quickly to egg him on further. This was my only hope, getting Dorian to spout off without caring what his attorney's advice was because his ego would make it leak out in spite of himself.

"I told you. I knew of him. Doesn't mean I talked to the guy."

"Several witnesses, including your girlfriend, Melissa Tafford, said you did. Not to mention that your ex-attorney friend, Rowdy, said you were asking some questions about what kind of trouble you'd get into for messing with federal traps. Now, I wonder, why would you do that?"

"You don't have to answer that," Halloway shot out his palm again.

Dorian glared at me. "I told you. She's not my girlfriend and good thing, because she'll pay—"

"Mr. Dorian, please—" Halloway said louder.

"That a threat to Ms. Tafford?" I glared back at Dorian. "I'll be sure the magistrate in Missoula understands the consequences—that people may be in danger if you're let loose on the streets."

I could hear Dorian's breathing through flared nostrils. He wanted to rip my head off as well as his attorney's. Halloway swallowed hard, then put his long, thin hand up again, this time slowly and tentatively. "Look, no need for that," Halloway said. "Mr. Harris, your guy Sedgewick's been all over the paper. That's how my client knew that he used log traps for his wolverines."

I resisted the urge to say, *Good for your client, glad to know he knows how to read.* Dorian smiled at me and asked: "You talk to your brother yet? Maybe people are getting confused. Maybe he's the one who had an altercation with your guy."

"Our witnesses have it correct," I said.

We continued to go round and round like this for a few more minutes, with me trying to get Dorian to explode in a fit of rage and let something slip that he didn't mean to. But he was clamming up further with every question and wore a shit-eating grin now that he'd brought Adam back into the picture.

Finally, I had no choice but to wrap it up. Bottom line, the guy was lying, and I knew I wouldn't get squat from him. I stood up abruptly, making Ken and Halloway flinch. Dorian stayed as still as a mountain, his arms folded and propped on his oversize chest. "Thank you for your time, Mr. Halloway." I tipped my head, then turned to Dorian. "Hope you make it safely for your arraignment. I wouldn't want you to miss that," I said to him as I exited the room.

The last I heard was Dorian mumbling something to Ken about me being a little faggot and wondering how could he stand to kiss my ass.

37

I WAS FINALLY READY to go see Adam. I had called him and arranged a meeting at his place by telling him that I was willing to listen to him about the money he wanted if we could meet and talk. He laughed because he knew it wasn't true, but said come on over anyway, as if we'd been on great terms our entire lives. If it weren't for the bitter undercut of his laugh, you'd never have known better. *Just come on over, bro!*

I clenched and unclenched my fists the entire drive to his house—a run-down cabin built years ago. I had no idea whom he'd bought it from or how he saved enough to get it, but it was his all right. I looked the title up with Public Records and found that he'd purchased it seven years before and was current with his payments.

I'd been putting off asking Adam about the fight for some obvious as well as some vague notions. Clearly, we made no music together and had chosen different paths in our lives, and blood or no blood, I'd just as soon avoid the guy altogether. But there was something extra cautioning me, something vibrating in my head akin to the high-pitched, maniacal fervor of beating wasp wings buzzing at me to stay away.

It didn't matter. Not in this line of work. I would need to question him if the Adam in Diane Hanson's story was indeed my brother. If it was, Adam had a possible, although distant, motive. On the other hand, I was well aware that it was old history and wondered why someone would take action all these years later.

Still, Adam had been in a fistfight with Phillips—and now Dorian, as unreliable as he might be, was somehow suggesting that Adam was involved in a poaching ring that was clearly unhappy about Wolfie researching wolverines in the South Fork. My brother just happened to be the only person I had found with a link to both victims.

Adam's cabin hunched at the end of a dirt road among a spread of lodge pole pines. When I pulled up, I saw one of the curtains flutter. I stepped out and walked toward the front of the house, passing Adam's Jeep on the way. Sunlight fanned through the tall canopy of pines and lit up portions of the driveway and the hood of the army-green Jeep. Off to the side of the house, in the shadowy forest, deciduous bushes and smaller trees glowed lime green and gold in the sun's rays.

Adam opened the door before I knocked and stood looking at me. He bowed his head and gestured for me to enter, saying, "That took a while. Losing your punctuality as you get older?"

I didn't reply. The cabin was clean and bare—tidy, like my dorm. It took me by surprise because I was expecting something slovenly with pizza boxes and empty beer cans strewn about. There wasn't much, but what there was—a blanket over the back of a small couch, a remote control on top of the TV, a candle on a shelf—seemed to have its place. The floorboards were worn and faded, and pale-yellow curtains hung on the windows. There were no pictures on the log walls and the place smelled of old wool-woven rugs, pinewood and fireplace ash even though it was summer, and he'd probably not used the fireplace for weeks. Adam watched me step in with no expression, his face completely blank, and I wondered if he'd practiced that look, honed it over the years. "What really brings you here?" he asked, not asking me to take a seat.

"Several things, but let me ask you, the money, why do you need it?"

He eyed me suspiciously, probably trying to surmise if I might be game for giving it to him after all.

Not a chance in hell, I reminded myself.

I walked to his small wooden table near the kitchen and swung a chair out from under, placed it near the fireplace tool set—ornate with curlicue designs—and took a seat. I didn't need my brother picking up anything long, sharp and made of iron in a possible fit of rage. "Nice little cabin you've got here."

"Thanks." Adam pulled out his own chair across from me, clearly out of reach as well, as if I was contagious. He sat down casually but his shoulders were braced. "I'd offer you a drink, but I take it you're on the job."

"Sort of," I said. "But if you'd like something, help yourself," I motioned to his kitchen, figuring he was talking about a beer or maybe whiskey.

"Nah, I'm good."

"So, about that money . . . what's it for?"

"Gotten behind on my mortgage."

"No, you haven't. I checked."

Adam laughed, a harsh, hollow sound. "Of course. Of course you have."

"So, the money?"

"What's it matter to you? It's not like you were going to give it to me anyway."

"Then why'd you bother asking?"

"Couldn't hurt to try and you never know. Maybe you'd surprise me."

I didn't reply.

"Anyway," he said. "I didn't think it was Park Police's job to find out why I need a few extra dollars in my life. Why does anyone need a few extra dollars? People get behind, especially these days."

"Okay then." I grabbed my notebook and my pen out of my pocket and opened it up to the page with notes on my interrogation of Dorian. When I looked up, Adam's blank stare had turned to a smug look, and he had folded his arms in front of his chest. I resisted the urge to ask: Do all you guys sit and stand in the same cocky way—like kings of your own universes? "I guess it's personal."

"I guess it is. So tell me why you're really here."

"Fair enough. I won't waste your time. Might as well get to the point—just as you said at the reunion the other day."

A smile crept to Adam's face. "Oh yeah, the reunion. How was it after I left? Guess I missed the big storm. Those tents hold up?"

I ignored his question. He couldn't have cared less, and I had no intention of admitting that I didn't know—that I left and haven't returned any of Lara's calls. That, basically, he had that kind of power over us. Just thinking it made my anger twist tighter inside me. I shifted in my seat and pulled my thoughts back to my notes. "I guess you've probably heard by now that we went in after you left the Outlaw's and arrested your friend, Dorian."

"Yeah, I heard. Not really something to make me weep."

"He mentioned you during the interrogation."

Adam shrugged.

"Don't you want to know what he said?"

"Whatever he said was probably a lie."

"Tell me about the poaching ring."

Adam laughed again, good and hard. "So that's what he said. And you believe anything *that* guy says?"

"He certainly listens to you. Did in the bar the other night."

Adam tilted back on his chair, balancing precariously on its back legs. "He knows I can kick the shit out of him."

"That's right. Tough Adam," I said. "I almost forgot. How could I?" I knew I shouldn't be going there, getting him pissed, but something inside me was waiting to pounce like a cat. I could feel my muscles grip and twitch. The more I tried to tamp my irritation down, the more it wanted to come out in small, electric ways. I gripped my pen tightly. "Dorian's in a lot of trouble," I said. "Could do some serious jail time." I eyed him. His face was well worn and hardened, but clinging to handsome, like some Marlboro Man. His hair was razed to a stubble, his chin set wide, strong, and angled. "I'm guessing you will too if Fish and Game finds that true."

"They're not going to find anything."

"Why is he saying they will?"

"'Cause. He's a damn liar, that's why. Look." He placed the front legs of his chair back down and leaned forward, his elbows resting on his knees and his biceps flexing, a bluish-purple vein bulging down the side of each one. He was wearing a plain, short-sleeved white T-shirt and worn, beige Carhartts. I kept my space, leaning stiffly against the back of the wooden chair. "I met some guy from Pennsylvania last fall in one of the bars in Columbia Falls. He was in town hunting, striking out. We got to talking, and he wanted to know if I knew the area and I said I did, like the back of my hand." He smiled slightly—crookedly, and I could tell he was proud that he knew the surrounding wilderness like he did. "He ended up offering me some decent money to take him to the spots I knew we could get into some elk, so I did. It was legit—right smack dab in the middle of hunting season. Anyway, I took him to a spot and he shot one. I had Dorian drive up with his truck to help us get the meat out. I paid him for helping."

"That it?"

"Then, several months later, I heard a rumor that he and that guy from Pennsylvania had some gig going. Guess he'd developed his own relationship with the guy. That he was coming out with friends and even some business associates for hunts, and word had it, not necessarily during the legal season."

"And he didn't include you in on it?"

"He called me a few times, but I declined."

"Thought you two were closer than that, good buddies and all. Why would he get something going without you—and you all able to beat the shit out of him as you said?"

"We're not that close and there's a reason he knows I can beat the shit out of him. We haven't always seen eye to eye on things, which is why he pointed to me in your interrogation. He'd like nothing better than to throw the scent off himself and onto me."

And you'd like nothing better than to throw it back onto him, I thought. "You got this guy's name. The one from Pennsylvania?"

"Look, Monty. I'm no rat. I ain't going there."

"*Ain't* going there?" I mimicked him and he shot me a frigid look. "You may just have no choice."

Adam shrugged as if he didn't care. "I start ratting people out in these parts, I'm in a lot of danger. Anyway, since when did you rejoin with Fish and Game?"

"I haven't, but you know what I'm investigating and that's the main reason I'm here. So far, you're the only suspect with personal connections to both victims—a Paul Sedgewick and a Mark Phillips."

"Wow, wow." Adam held up a hand and sat back up straight. "I have zero personal connection to your wolverine guy."

"That's not what your friend, Dorian, claims."

"I told you. He's not a friend. He can claim whatever the hell he pleases. It's not true. I didn't know Sedgewick—never met him."

I narrowed my eyes at Adam, studied him. It had been so long since I'd spent any significant amount of time with him. I couldn't remember what he looked like when he lied, but what did come crashing back to me was how cunning and lethal his presence felt. His eyes danced with excitement but looked sharp as daggers. Our conversation was controlled, and he was being completely pleasant, but underneath it all, I sensed secrets and devices I would never understand even though we came from the same bloodline. It made me edgy. It made my heartbeat pick up, and I wanted to shift in my seat again, but resisted and tried not to show it. Our dad always claimed that very cunning people were like the devil; they mixed lies with truth. "You may have never met him, but you knew who he was."

"Yeah, I knew who the guy was. He was the talk for a bit. You know, the guy who was single-handedly gonna screw up all our land-use rights because he wanted more wilderness for his wolverines."

"And you've seen him before? Even if you've not spoken to him."

Adam nodded. "Yeah, I've seen him."

"Where?"

"At the Outlaw's. He came asking around for Dorian. Asked Melissa. Wanted to talk to him about his traps."

"Why?"

"You know why. Said he just wanted a civil conversation, was sure he could shed some light on what he was doing and that once they understood, everything would be fine." Adam shook his head and looked down at the wood floor. Two rectangles of light angled and lengthened across it, picking up dust, as if exposing the flaws and hopelessness inherent in the idea of a levelheaded, educated guy like Wolfie trying to reason with a man on Whitesquad. I sensed that same burden of sadness that I had picked up on at the reunion with no clue why it would show up on him, with his messed-up, perfidious ways. It was only a flash across his face—resentment laced with a guarded frailty—and it receded quickly back into the hardness of his expression.

"What was happening that he wanted to work out?"

"You know what."

"Tell me."

"Apparently, his traps were being messed with. I don't know how or why he came to figure Dorian for it."

"Was it Dorian?"

Adam sat back in a sprawl again, tilting even farther back on his chair and shrugged. "Couldn't tell you."

I waited for him to say more. A brief image flashed in my mind of being very small and seeing who could make the other one laugh first. I wondered if he was thinking the same ridiculous thing—if he was even capable of having that kind of memory.

"What about Phillips?" I finally said when it was clear he was going to offer nothing more.

"What about that prick?"

"Why did you fight with him last year?"

"Because we ran into each other in some bar. Because I never liked the guy and he never liked me. Because there were a lot of assholes at that place you convinced Dad to send me to for"—he held up his fingers to create quotation marks—"you know—therapy."

"Don't tell me we gotta go down altered-history lane here. I didn't even know about the place. I was all of what? Thirteen?"

"Just the same. You ratted me out for smoking pot and drinking. Like who the hell didn't do that as a teen in our school?"

"You just keep telling yourself that lovely little story, Adam. Your twisted version against mine."

"You forgot to say *twisted* before yours too."

"You can tell yourself whatever you want, but I clearly remember Dad getting the shock of his life when he checked out the tracks on your arms. Yeah, so tell me again it was just pot and drinking."

"Dad, shocked? Dad, the concerned father? Shit," he said, disdain saturating his voice. "Dad wanted nothin' more than an excuse to get me out of the house once you were old enough to look after yourself. Before that time, I took care of you."

My blood pressure was starting to go way up and I let loose a sharp laugh. "Are you kidding me? As if I wasn't taking care of myself from way before thirteen. Way before you ever left the house."

"And you just keep telling yourself that nice, little lie."

I glared at him. Suddenly I was angry at myself for not bringing Ken along to keep us in check. Neither one of us would be going down this ridiculous black hole, spouting off about long-past family drama, if someone else were along. I held up my palm to halt things. "Look, when was the last time you saw Mark Phillips?"

Adam's right hand had instantly balled into a hard fist, the whites of each knuckle showing, and before he answered, he massaged it out with the other hand, let his fingers go long again. I thought of my own pumping fists on the drive over. "The last time we fought," he finally answered. "A year ago."

"And where were you on the evening of June twenty-second?" I didn't have Phillips's exact time of death, just the surveillance tape showing the day he entered with his truck, which he'd clearly driven home safely to his garage. But Wolfie's would do for now. "That would have been a Wednesday."

He thought about it. I could see him counting back in his head, still massaging his hand in the palm of the other while trying to figure out where he was. "I think I was here. Nothing going on those nights."

"Was anyone with you to vouch for that?"

"No. I was here alone. I live alone—nothing I can do about that. As you can see—I don't have any neighbors. You're more than welcome to go out and question some of the deer 'round here."

I didn't bother with a reply. I wrote the information down and stood up. Suddenly, I wanted to get out. The late afternoon shadows were pooling in the cabin's corners and strange emotions I didn't want were rallying in the edges of my mind. Lara's words, "people grow up," pinged in my mind along with a good dose of annoyance. I wasn't done with Adam by a long shot, but for now, for now, it would have to do.

"That it? All done with your questions?" He seemed surprised.

"Yeah, for now."

He looked unsatisfied, but didn't push it further. He stood up, walked to the front door, brusquely opened it, and held it for me. "Thanks for stopping by," he said. "*Always* good to catch up with family."

"Thanks for your help," I said as sincerely as I could muster in the face of his sarcasm. "I'll probably need to talk to you again before long."

"Can't wait." He smiled and shut the door behind me.

38

BEFORE STOPPING AT a convenience store to pick up a chemically processed ham-and-cheese sandwich, I had gone to the office and checked on Ken to see if he'd picked up anything suspicious off the surveillance tapes. He said he hadn't, but that he'd finally gotten some of the files rounded up from the Leefeldts, which was like pulling teeth since youth records are sealed and with little regulation of these schools, there was no pressure to keep good and accurate records around anyway. It required Ken calling numerous times to get *Mrs.* instead of *Mr.* Leefeldt on the line, who clearly wanted nothing to do with us. The missus ended up being easier to work with, and Ken pulled out a little cowboy charm, getting her to agree to send some files and a list of as many students as she could who attended during the period that Mark Phillips worked at the academy.

I thanked him and took the files home with me. I was feeling tired and agitated simultaneously. The aftermath of talking to Dorian and Adam was settling in my bones. I sat on my couch trying not to think about my brother, his lonely bare cabin, the white knuckles on his clenched right hand, and the hatred and guilt crawling up my spine while visiting him that I'd thought I'd put behind me long ago. I could hear the echo of silence in my own bare dorm, so I got up and opened the fridge and grabbed a cold beer, and went back over to the files. They were incomplete, and we only obtained them for the period of 1994 to 1996, during which the Miranda incident occurred, but Mrs. Leefeldt had also made a list of other clients whom she no longer had files for.

I felt spared that I didn't have to look at a file on Adam, although he was a person of interest. Mainly, I wanted to see all the students who'd had contact with Phillips as a counselor. I looked for anything strange that might point in the direction of a revenge situation, but I knew it was all a humongous long shot, even though the majority of the kids had mental health issues that were nothing to shrug about.

I went through the boys' files first: Jonathon Fieldland from Seattle, Washington; Zachary Gentry from Missoula, Montana; Paul Monroe from Syracuse, New York; Eric Olmsfield from Scottsdale, Arizona; Jayson Prince from Walnut Creek, California; Patrick Stoddard from Tallahassee, Florida; Lawrence Schieble from Whitefish, Montana; Bradley Talbert from Kalispell, Montana; Terrance Wicker from Stamford, Connecticut—the list went on. They all had varying degrees of clinical depression, alcohol and drug abuse, anger management problems, self-harming tendencies, obsessive-compulsive disorder, borderline personality disorder, oppositional-defiance disorder, reactive-attachment disorder. . . .

I took my glasses off and rubbed my eyes and noticed that my banged-up eye was feeling better. The girls' files were similar with more self-harming tendencies, including cutting, head-banging, anorexia, bulimia, exercise bulimia. . . . I looked at Rebecca Olson from Portland, Oregon; Katherine Fliegle from Memphis, Tennessee; Gina Bates from Whitefish, Montana; Grace Winston from Bellingham, Washington; Abigail Farrington from Long Beach, California; Britta McIntire from Bozeman, Montana. . . . The notion that parents were paying for their clinically disturbed children to be among the beauty and wild of Montana to heal, while unqualified, arrogant counselors like Phillips worked with them was incomprehensible.

When I thought of Adam in that situation, in spite of my anger at him, a weariness descended upon me. I shook it off. If there's one thing to understand in this line of work, it's that life isn't always fair. Tragedies occurred, one after the other, and all there was left to do was instill some order to the mix of it all.

My phone buzzed, and I took it out of my pocket and looked at it. It was a text from Shane Albertson saying he wanted to meet the next day and that he had some information for me, but couldn't talk at the moment because he was at some function with his wife. I texted him with a time for first thing in the morning.

I stared at the screen of my phone and thought of calling Lara. She had quit trying to call me. I recognized that we had both retreated into our own hardened spaces, wondering who would try to break through the other's shell first. Our marriage was feeling more and more like a shipwreck. I had always thought that once I broke away from my family, that I had the power—the control—to set my own course. That I could take that ship across any kind of water as long as I was careful and steered clear of its dangers—avoiding the rocks, the icebergs, the hurricanes, the white squalls . . . It didn't have to be littered with hazards like my own parents' lives were.

With Lara, I had communicated well—told her how my mother had been diagnosed with schizoaffective disorder (an umbrella disorder that covered depression and schizophrenia) in the nineties because—the doctor told my dad—she demonstrated baseline psychotic symptoms, like hearing voices in her head and extreme bouts of paranoia, but also fell easily into slumps of despair. Lara was understanding and sympathetic.

And my father, I explained to her, suffered from alcoholism. I made it abundantly clear, so I thought, that it made no sense to take the huge risk of bringing a child into this world from a family tree ragged with psychological ill health, and when she agreed, I figured we had the future covered. We had each other's backs. From our marriage on, all we needed to do was be careful, respectful—set the safe course, steer clear of obstacles, avoid the genetic iceberg protruding straight up from the chilled waters like a bright-white warning beacon.

Now, here I was as the lead on one of my first real investigative cases as a park officer being dragged straight into my family's past by some heavy anchor I thought I'd cut loose long ago.

But still, Lara and I loved each other. That had been undeniable for the majority of our relationship. I was crazy about her and she me. But I could feel that slip away as the shells formed around each of us, neither one of us wanting to approach one another for fear of getting completely shattered. And now, I wondered if it was too late—if the end result was not worth the effort and perhaps some storms should be avoided entirely instead of trying to navigate through them.

This case, which had dragged me to my own brother's den, was taking me in directions I'd never considered. An image of the ferocious wolverine that I'd read about in Wolfie's notes—wild and fierce in its cage after capture, still lashing out at any hand or object coming close—slid into my mind. Maybe I'd been fighting for things to work out between Lara and me for too long.

Shit, I thought, like at the reunion. I'd been a nice guy, maybe too nice. I'd compromised, gone to help her with her family as ridiculous as I knew the whole thing was. The motion-picture image of my leaving with the storm kicking up got me pressing the heels of my hands into my forehead, massaging my brow until I shook off the weary lack of hope settling in.

Eventually, I grabbed my laptop to switch gears and googled the kids from the files, looking for alarming or suspicious incidents, and tried to track their parents as well to see if there was anything that stood out. Again, it was a long shot. Many could not be found and among all the Facebook, Linked-In, and Twitter presences and other professional odds and ends that popped up for the ones that I could locate, I found sweet-all nothing of interest except for legal documents on the Miranda lawsuit against Global Schools.

I paid particular close attention to the students from Montana on the chance if they still were around, something interesting might pop up: Zachary Gentry, Bradley Talbert, Lawrence Schieble, Gina Bates, and Britta McIntire. Zachary and Lawrence now lived out of state, one in Seattle; one in Santa Cruz. I found nothing on Bradley Talbert, Gina Bates, or Britta McIntire.

Around midnight, my eyes were burning, so I stepped outside to get some fresh air and look at the night sky. A meteor shower was scheduled to occur, and there was no better place to watch stars than Glacier Park, away from any city where the lights hazed the night sky. The infinite stars twinkled and danced above the black mountaintops as if I was in an immense basin created by the spires of the Divide. And the Milky Way, a deluge of constellations, splashed through like its namesake suggests, like milk splayed straight across the heavens.

The truth about Glacier, the thing it did for me—since it was far more commanding and breathtaking than what anyone could describe—was take me out of myself. I was just simply another life form making my way in the unflawed, ever-fluctuating eloquence of things. I thought of the wolverine again, about its unfettered, endless movement and travels through the Divide. Glacier held magic all right—the power to take me away from my problems. So right under the deepening night and blinking and shooting stars, feeling the park's exquisite cool, summer breeze like a soothing caress, Adam and Lara began to recede to the far back corners of my mind. I watched the sky for a long time, meteors jagging across the sky and the torrent of the Milky Way so bright it ached. I watched until my neck stiffened, and when I went back in, I was able to get some sound sleep.

. . .

In the morning, I drove back to headquarters where Albertson was waiting for me. When I walked in, I could smell fresh coffee. Karen had made it and offered me a cup. I thanked her, took it with me and went to find Ken, who was already back at work on the surveillance tapes.

"This is my third time through," he said when I walked in, leaning back and letting out a long, audible exhale through pursed lips. "I'm not seeing anything at all except the first footage we've got on Phillips driving in on the morning of June eighteenth and of Wolfie on June twenty-second, consistent with the time his wife mentioned. The camera isn't wide enough to get good footage of the vehicles leaving, so I've been trying to magnify the exiting vehicles, but our equipment just isn't good enough."

I nodded. "Maybe Gretchen can help us with that." I made a mental note to call her.

When Shane arrived, it was good to see him and he gave me a big squeeze on the shoulder and a pat on my back. I introduced him to Ken, then showed him to our makeshift incident room and offered him some coffee.

"Nah, man." He gave us his signature wide grin and patted his belly under his light-beige standard game warden uniform shirt. "I just ate."

"Did you get anything more out of Dorian?" Shane asked me.

"No, nothing much. So what have you found on your end?"

"So it didn't occur to me until you told me what Dorian's girlfriend's name was—Tammy—when you called me after you arrested him. At first I didn't think anything of it, just that I didn't know or care who the hell the guy dated. Then, even though it's a common name, something about it started to nag at me," Shane said. "So I did some looking around through some of our files, and bingo, I found who I think is the same Tammy linked to an incident that took place about five months ago on the east side. Not my jurisdiction, which is why I didn't think of it earlier, but get this: in February, a woman walks into the Browning post office and tries to mail a box to Canada—to Calgary, to a post office address and bogus business named Dante's Cargo. Anyway, the attendant at the post office noticed that there was blood leaking at the box's seams, so she took her sweet time with it, went into the back room for a moment and called the police before going back to the counter and taking her payment. Police stopped her on her way out, checked the box, and bingo. Turns out it was a pelt from a freshly killed wolverine that she was sending to Canada. And the lady sending the package—a Tamara DeWitt."

"Tammy," Ken said. "Dorian's partial alibi."

"Her brother, Darryl DeWitt, is one of the guys who hangs out with Dorian," I said. I thought of the rundown, boarded-up Winnebago on her property and could only imagine what it contained.

"But that's interesting. Canada, huh?" Ken added. "I would think they had plenty of their own wolverines around."

"Doesn't matter, there's a demand for wolf and wolverine pelts in many countries. Canada's no different," I told Ken, then looked back to Shane. "And?"

"We fingerprinted the box to see if there were other prints because we figured she wasn't working alone, but only hers came up. She had put a false name for a return address—a Patty Brown, but her ID in her purse said Tamara DeWitt. And, while questioning her, they were able to get her to admit that her brother was in on it. Your Darryl DeWitt at the bar, but no one else. At the time, we had no idea there was a connection between her and Dorian or a connection between Dorian and wolverines. We've only been watching him because of possible elk poaching, but we hadn't caught him doing that yet and haven't enough reason to search his place for signs of poaching. And, of course, we've had our eyes open over his love of weapons, but can't do anything about that. Until now, that is. Thanks to you." He bowed his head toward me and removed his light beige matching uniform cap. "By the way, how's that eye of yours?"

"Better. And worth it," I said. "We'll see what the judge slaps on him in Missoula, but I'm pretty certain he'll end up with a federal crime since he assaulted a federal officer. One very unlucky punch for him, but he knew I worked for the park. Anyway, doesn't matter how much jail time he gets as long as you now have a reason to confiscate his weapons. That alone is justice. This Darryl DeWitt—" I steered the conversation back to the wolverine pelt. "Interesting that Tammy would rat on her brother, but not Dorian. I'm willing to bet she was seeing Dorian then too, and obviously still is even though he's two-timed her with Melissa." I took a sip of my coffee. "They were pretty cozy at the Outlaw's Nest the other evening."

"She's probably good and afraid of the asshole," Ken added. "He likes his threats."

I thought of Melissa, had a hard time feeling sorry for her, but a part of me wanted to. Lara used to say I was a sucker for too many people's problems—a bleeding heart. I knew that wasn't true, I just wanted to impose order where I could, help out where I was needed, and it seemed to me that Melissa was so close to getting her shit together, yet so far. Bad habits were working against her. "What were they charged with?"

"Well, since the wolverine is not federally protected, she was only charged with some small-time fines—around twelve hundred, and her brother about eight."

"I'm going to call the county," I said. "I want all of Sedgewick's box traps fingerprinted. I'm sure we'll find all the standard prints: Ward, Pritchard, Kaufland, Bowman, after we run elimination prints. But now that we've got Dorian's, if he comes up as a match, it's one more piece to pin on him. And—" I turned to Ken. "I'll see if Gretchen can get this footage in for a closer look. It would be good to know what time Phillips left on the day of June eighteenth, drove home and safely put his car back in his garage."

In the back of my mind, when I thought about running prints on the traps, was whether an unknown set of prints might turn out to be my brother's. Which meant I had an errand to run before I called Gretchen. And it involved going to Lara's.

39

GOING TO LARA'S, I heard myself think. Not—*going to our house*—anymore. My new reality was happening all on its own.

I pulled up, figuring Lara was at work, halfway hoping she wasn't and partly hoping she was so I could see her and check to see how she was doing. I pulled up and noticed her car was gone. I still had a key, so I parked in the driveway and let myself in. I knew exactly where I was going, to the basement to grab an old box of memorabilia I had tucked away years ago, but I paused in the front door and took in the view.

The living room was much more disheveled than when we lived together, and I wondered if getting rid of me with my itch for order had been a relief, if it had worn on her more than I realized. She had always sworn up and down that she loved a clean, neat place, and at times, I thought she was worse than I about always needing to pick things up instead of sitting down and relaxing, letting it wait. But in our typically tidy living room, a sweater lay lazily across the lounging chair, the silky throws—usually folded neatly over the sofa—were bunched and tangled, one in a ball in the corner of the couch, and the other on the opposite side across the sofa's arm. Throw pillows usually stacked upright uniformly against the sofa corners were thrown wherever and lying flat. A mess of catalogues, papers, and magazines lay strewn across the coffee table with no rhyme or reason.

Good for her, I thought, to relax into herself. A dose of regret and a little shame washed through me to see her real, unmasked tendencies. I also felt guilty for being in the house without letting her know, without giving her a heads-up, but it was still my place too, and I really didn't need permission.

Our wedding photo as well as other pictures of us on various vacations—Kauai, Banff, and Napa Valley—were still on the fireplace mantel. Ellis came sauntering down the hall, meowing at me and rubbing against my leg. When I went to scoop him up, he stretched, then pushed his head toward me so I could scratch it. I scooped him up, and I felt a slight ache sink into my chest as he began to purr when I rubbed my thumb behind his ears. "Yeah, yeah, I know, you miss me, buddy boy. I miss you too, but I'm in a hurry," I said, and put him back down and headed for the kitchen where the door to the basement was located. I resisted the urge to go upstairs and check our bedroom, part of me expecting to find some strange man's clothes draped over the chair in the bedroom's corner.

When I went into the kitchen, I smelled the candles Lara liked to light for dinner, a blend of sandalwood and lavender, and I felt that melancholy ache grow bigger, tugging at me, but then I saw two empty wineglasses beside the sink. I checked the recycling bin and an empty bottle of pinot noir from the Willamette Valley lay on top. That stung. Lara and I had spent our fifth anniversary visiting Oregon's wine country. I pictured her with some guy, no—actually, if I was to be honest— I conjured an image of her with not just *some* guy, but *a* particular man—Adam. She and Adam sitting on the couch in the living room, giggling and enjoying a bottle of wine from Oregon's wine country. I shook my head, practically laughing out loud. "Dude, you've got issues," I whispered to myself as I headed down the creaking wooden steps to the basement. "And you're getting an overactive imagination to boot."

Downstairs, beside the litter box against the right wall was a stack of shelves holding old boxes full of things we no longer needed, but felt we should keep anyway: old pictures, spare camping gear, college books, the first set of dishes we'd bought, but replaced several years later . . . I found the box I was looking for on the far edge under a plastic bin full of pictures from Lara's childhood. I pulled it out, set it on the gray concrete floor and looked inside. Ellis had come down to join me and rubbed against the side of my right hip as I squatted beside the box.

It was emptier than I thought it would be, containing my high school yearbooks, which weren't very large anyway, my diplomas and graduation tassels, and an ivory elephant paperweight Aunt Terry had given me when I graduated from high school. A picture of my mom, Dad, Adam, and me when I was a little over a year and Adam, five, lay on top of the yearbooks. We were in front of our old fireplace. I had no idea who took the photo, probably Aunt Terry.

My mom looked beautiful, semifaded and delicate with her fine cheekbones and large, haunted eyes. Her hair looked lustrous and full though, not the way I remembered her in her last years before she died, her auburn hair always scraggly and ratty behind her ears.

She was only fifty-four when the accident occurred. It had always been a struggle to get her to take her meds, and she got increasingly worse about it in her early fifties. I was twenty-eight and still living in Choteau with Lara when we got the news. She'd been convinced that her medicine was poison and had been flushing it down the toilet. My dad thought she had skipped a few doses, but claimed to have no idea she'd been avoiding them altogether.

One November evening while he was late at work, she began to think that someone was breaking into the house and called him. He told her to stay put, that he'd be right home. He called the couple next door that sometimes helped in a pinch, to see if they'd go sit with her, but they weren't home. When he arrived, she was gone and so was her car.

He figured she searched the house until she found the keys that he usually kept hidden in a jar in the kitchen when he sensed she wasn't quite right, and drove off in a panic. She was last seen heading east out of Columbia Falls, up the treacherous Marias Pass in icy conditions, her car spinning out of control and shooting headfirst over the edge, tumbling some two hundred and fifty feet down to the Middle Fork

River. The people who saw her go over tried to help, but she was too far below. They reported the vehicle had completely submerged and that all they could see were the headlights continuing to eerily glow under the river water while they made calls and waved others down for help.

I've quit trying to wonder what she might have been thinking as she headed east, whether she had any idea where she was going, and whether she meant to go over the edge. But I can still picture those headlights. I see them as if I was there. They shine just under the surface into the frigid, crystal-clear water as if to communicate more than the tragedy of the accident, shining past the whole of her sad adulthood to some other dimension, some place where she's content and looks like she does in the photo.

Afterward, amid the grief, a modicum of relief eventually rose in me that she was finally released from the burdens of her own misfiring brain. In the photo, there still seemed to be a small glint of hope and happiness in her blue eyes. I had a hard time recalling that spark as the years piled up, her depression crushing her—each year comprised of one weighted day stacking upon the next.

Below the picture, I found what I was looking for: an old dog collar, black with white paw prints traveling down the length of it. It had a plastic clasping mechanism, just as I remembered. I pulled it out carefully and inspected it. I put it to my nose and took a whiff, half expecting to smell the dried weed and horse-hide scent of dog fur, but it only smelled like the cardboard it had been kept in all these years.

I could still picture him—a scruffy tan-and-white pathetic thing with droopy ears that wanted to stand up like a German shepherd's, but folded and fell sideways part of the way up. Adam and I had been walking home from school and stopped at the local park on the way and played for a while. It was winter, so the playground was deserted, and out of nowhere, the dog appeared, skinny and unkempt. Adam went to it, saying he was lost and that we should catch him, so we tried. We called him, but he was jumpy, and ran when we got close.

"I have an idea," Adam said. "I've got some money that I was supposed to give to the office for a field trip, but I didn't. Let's go to the hardware store." He pointed south, where we knew one was several blocks down. "We can get a collar and a leash, and I know they have dog treats there, because I've seen 'em on the counter."

Adam took off running without even waiting for my reply and I followed, my small legs pumping faster and faster to try to catch him and my lungs sucking in the frigid air. When we came out of the store, the dog wasn't far away. He had followed us. We held the treats out for him, grabbed him, and slipped the collar on him.

I don't know why I kept the collar when I packed my things to move away for college. It wasn't anything special really. We didn't even get to keep the dog. We had brought him home, walking him and stopping to pat the top of his head and tell him that he was a good boy. Adam had already picked out a name by the time we got to our driveway. Reggie—that's what he said he wanted to call him. And when I said, *You know dad won't let us keep him*, Adam had frowned and gotten angry. *Yes he will; he'll have to. The poor thing needs a home.*

But Dad came marching right out before we even got to the front door, stumbling slightly with half a bag already on him. He wagged his finger back and forth at us, "Oh no, you don't. Whatever you boys are thinking, you can forget it."

"But, please, Dad," Adam had whined. "He's really good, and Monty and I will take care of him."

"Yeah, right you will." He'd laughed. "A dog, no goddamned way." The swearing came out more when he had had a few.

"But, please, Dad. Please." Adam elbowed me hard in the ribs to chime in, so I did.

"Please, please, Dad. We'll take care of him. We will, really."

"Yeah, right. You'll buy him dog food, walk him, and clean his shit out of the yard?"

"We already bought him a collar and leash," Adam said.

"With what? You use the money I gave you this morning for that?"

Adam looked down.

"Christ," he mumbled. "Can't trust you with anything."

"Can't we please keep him, Dad? We really will take care of him."

"What are you? Crazy? Can't you see it's way too much? Shit, your mom, she can't even take care of the two of you." He gestured meanly at us. "Can't even take care of herself, can't even take the medicine the doctors give her," he said loudly. "How's she supposed to handle a damn dog, for Christ's sake."

Both Adam and I said nothing, just stared at him.

He shook his head when he realized what he'd said, maybe had seen the expressions on our faces, and looked at the ground as if he recognized that he'd shared too much, even if what he was saying wasn't anything we didn't already know. *Can't even take care of herself.* But to hear it from him—that was a different matter. We were six and ten years old.

"Tell you what, we'll keep him tonight." He looked back at us. "But tomorrow he goes to the shelter. Understand?"

Adam wouldn't reply, but I said, "Yes, sir," and Adam glared at me for doing so.

That night, Adam and I doted on the dog. We called him Reggie anyway and walked him around the block several times out in the cold after Dad made some mac and cheese. I took him in to show Mom—thought petting him might make her smile—but she was stone-asleep and wouldn't wake. Reggie slept on Adam's bed at his feet and the next morning we got up early on that Saturday and took him out and fed him part of our ham and eggs. Mom had gotten up and made us breakfast and she *did* smile at the dog, thought he was cute, she had said. But Dad wouldn't listen to Adam's pleas when he stated that, *See, even Mom likes him.* Eventually, with Dad and Adam arguing, we put a quivering Reggie in the car and took him to the animal shelter. Adam wouldn't speak to Dad for days.

Still kneeling over the box, I pulled a plastic bag out of my pocket and dropped the collar in it. I knew why I had kept it; it was the last time I remembered my brother being human. "Game on, Adam," I whispered into the dim basement, then let out a big, drawn-out sigh. I petted Ellis one more time, stood up and left Lara's house.

When I got to my car, I called Gretchen and asked her to run fingerprints for me on all the box traps that Wolfie had used in the South Fork area. Sam Ward had gathered them for me and Ken would deliver them.

"Not you?" she asked when I told her that Ken would swing by with them later in the afternoon.

"No, as much as I'd like to see your gorgeous smile, I'm a little too busy," I said, but I felt relieved that she'd asked.

"How many elimination prints do you think we'll have to run?"

"Well, there's Sedgewick, Pritchard, Ward, Kaufland, and Bowman. Those are the only researchers who have handled them."

"Okay," Gretchen said. "I'll see if I can get my latent print examiner to put a rush on it."

"I'd greatly appreciate it. And one more thing."

"What's that?"

"I've got another item I want you to run prints on. I'll send it with Ken. The item's over twenty years old, but it's been well kept. It should have two sets on it. One will be an elimination set: mine."

40

IT WAS TWO weeks into the investigation, and Ken and I finally met Rick Phrimmer, assistant superintendent of Glacier National Park, for lunch at the West Glacier Café. Personally I had the feeling it was a waste of our time. We went because Dr. Pritchard had thrown out our own assistant super's name, Rick Phrimmer, as someone potentially unhappy with Wolfie because his wife and Wolfie dated years ago. Apparently, Phrimmer felt he came in as second choice. I wasn't considering him a real suspect, but if I wanted to be thorough, I needed to follow up on the information.

I thought about sending Ken by himself, but I knew that was a cop-out, unfair to Ken, and totally not my style. I was getting better at delegating and not feeling the need to do everything myself, but if I needed to question one of our own higher-ups, I had to do the dirty work.

Phrimmer had been in DC arguing against cutbacks of federal funds for the national parks and had just returned the day before and agreed to meet. He had a beak of a nose and a full mane of reddish-brown hair, giving him the appearance of more the artistic type than rugged outdoorsman, but both Ken and I knew that Phrimmer probably spent more time at a desk and in council meetings than out in the field anyway.

We ordered from Carol, who was happy to see me, telling me that I hadn't been in enough lately. I told her I'd been busy, but planned to get back to my more regular eating schedule soon. When she sashayed back to the kitchen, I turned to Rick. His eyes were yellowed and bloodshot, and he looked tired.

"Long trip?" I asked.

"Oh yeah, always a pain in the ass to hit DC. It's all about the economy and jobs right now. No one wants to hear about our precious wild lands, about the air we breathe, about the complexities of our planet. It's all about cuts, cuts, cuts. So yeah, I'm a little jet-lagged and grumpy. But what's this about? What do you need from me for your investigation?"

"Just some general stuff. Did you know Sedgewick?"

"Yeah, yeah, of course I did. All of us knew Wolfie around here."

"Were you involved in any way with his research?"

"Me?" Phrimmer rubbed his eyes as he considered the question. "Sorry," he said. "Not much sleep the past few days," he reiterated, then added, "Me involved?"

"In terms of press, administrative funding, or anything?"

"A little. I mean, I discuss all of our projects at length with a lot of people when I'm in DC and elsewhere, but especially in DC. The wolverine project is an important keystone study to present to politicians. Makes them get how crucial Glacier is that it's one of the few places left where you can find such a special animal that so readily exemplifies how the loss of our snowfields affects animals, and in general, upsets entire ecosystems. Plus I've had discussions with NRDC to help coordinate efforts for the park studies. But mostly, no, I don't have a lot to do with the actual program. Wolfie and Sam and all their other helpers did a pretty good job of keeping a tight ship."

"So you were actually interested in keeping the studies going?"

"It's complicated. There's only so much money to go around. We're forced to prioritize what we fund. But in general, yes, I'd say the wolverine studies have been a priority."

"It was my understanding that you weren't interested in continuing the studies."

"Whoever you heard that from, it's not true." He stared at me blankly.

"Did you like him? Get along?"

"Me and Wolfie? What does it matter?"

"I don't know. I heard that your wife used to date him at some point."

"Some point is right." He looked at me incredulously. "Some point long ago."

"I figured. Just asking. It can be a very small world around these parts."

"Yeah, it can. And quite frankly, I don't have time for this nonsense. I'm shocked that you would even bring something so trivial up." He pulled his chin in.

"Just covering all territory." I cleared my throat. "Did you know Mark Phillips?" I plowed ahead, changing the subject at the risk of irritating him further.

He laughed with disbelief. "I knew that the park had contracted Phillips to do some mapping projects, but I didn't know him well. Maybe met him once or twice around at some function or other." He scratched his scalp and looked up. "Maybe it was the spring for a Glacier fundraiser at McDonald Lodge. That's where I think I was first introduced to him. And, no, my wife did not date anyone that Phillips was involved with. At least, not to my knowledge. Now, if you'll excuse me." He stood up and threw some cash on the table. "I have a lot of paperwork to do."

I looked at Ken, who had a closed-lip smile on his face. "Nice try," he said.

I nodded. "A waste of time maybe, but necessary."

· · ·

Since I seemed to be chasing lost causes, I went to see my dad even though he's not easy to talk to, complains a lot, and sees no reason to take any advice, even if it might help him or make him feel better. But it's my nature to not let things just sit and plague my conscience, and Adam had mentioned that Dad had thrown his back out. Basically, I'd end up guilty as hell no matter what I told myself if I didn't eventually check on him.

My dad lived in the far eastern part of the valley in the foothills in a small timber-framed house he'd built after my mom died with the remains of the money he made from selling his construction company, Harris Construction. Eventually, he struck up a relationship with a woman named Tracy whom he met online and she moved in with the rest of her family—her thirtysomething pot-smoking, on-disability son, his wife, and their two children, a boy diagnosed with ADHD on Ritalin, and a younger girl named Gracie. My father never could say no to a woman, and when Tracy said her kids and grandkids needed a place to stay for just a month or two, he opened his arms and his house. Later, when a month or two extended to a year, he couldn't broach the subject of kicking them out without thoroughly pissing Tracy off. And I couldn't broach the subject of how things would be better if he didn't enable them and made them go make their own way in the world without pissing *him* off thoroughly. But my father was chronically unhappy and that gave him an excuse to continue drinking.

Tracy, who perpetually smelled like cigarette smoke, handed me a beer to take over to my dad who was propped up in a La-Z-Boy recliner with an extra pillow or two behind his back. She offered me one too, calling me honey and setting her hand on the small of my back. It made me cringe. She was always hugging me a little too long, and when she kissed my cheek hello or good-bye, her lips would always aim for the corner of my mouth even as I tried to turn my head. It made me feel ridiculous and like a little boy squirming away.

It was going on eight p.m., and they had just finished dinner. I had timed it this way on purpose: any earlier, my dad would be too cranky; any later, he'd be too drunk. Tracy had gone back to cleaning dishes in the kitchen. I was relieved that Tracy's son and daughter-in-law and kids were out on a camping trip with some friends. Tracy's son, Seth, drove me crazy. He was always acting like he was on top of everything, ready to fix anything that had broken down, or had been working hard all day. In reality, he rarely lifted a finger to help anybody with anything. If he mowed the narrow patch of lawn they had beside the patio, you'd hear about it for days. I have no idea how my father put up with it: he may have been a drunk the majority of my life, but he never tolerated laziness from Adam or me, ever.

I sat on the couch kitty-corner to him. He was watching ESPN, and it was like pulling teeth trying to get him to engage in small talk, but eventually he wanted to know how long it had been since I'd stopped in and told me where exactly his back hurt and how the pain had now migrated to his hips and neck. He explained that Tracy's car broke down the other day, but it hurt too much to lean under a hood so they had to take it to a mechanic and that cost a shitload of money that he wasn't expecting to dish out.

"Why didn't you have Seth take a look?" I said, unable to resist and against my better judgment. "He claims to know a thing or two about cars."

"He does," Tracy yelled from the kitchen. "He knows a lot, but he's been busy."

"Busy with what?" I said. "He get a job?"

"No, honey, he can't 'cause of his elbow, but he's a trooper and has been working on the lawn. Made it beautiful out there." She motioned outside the kitchen window.

"The lawn." I nodded, observing my dad who seemed oblivious to how ridiculous it was that a grown man like Seth with a wife and two kids, who had no job, was *busy* working a lawn about the size of a basketball court. He simply stared at the TV, belched once, and blew it out in front of him, then took another swig of beer.

"Come on, Dad," I said, selfishly wanting to get outside away from the stench of nicotine. "Let's go see your lawn. You should get some circulation going. Be good for your back."

After several minutes of him protesting and me grabbing him another beer, I finally got him out of his chair to show me the new and improved yard and to get some fresh air. We had walked over to a rock wall near the edge and Dad pointed out how Seth had hauled in some rocks to make it.

"That's nice," I said. "So what's he get disability for again?"

My dad rolled his eyes and reminded me that Seth had been hurt while at work for the timber company, messing up the nerves in his forearm while working some heavy equipment. "His forearm looks fine to me, though," he said. My dad's attitude about Seth was the typical familial stance of *I can bitch all I want about him because I live with him, but you can't.* So I was careful not to say anything else about how I thought Tracy and her family were taking advantage of an old, drunk guy who just happened to have a little money and a decent place to live, thanks to the construction boom in Northwest Montana. No one could ever accuse my dad of not being generous. If he had money, he shared it, even if he liked to bitch about it.

"He's lazier than a cow. Eats like one too," he snarled as we started to walk back to the patio. "So do the kids. I can't dish out enough for groceries these days."

Even though I started it, I decided I wasn't going to keep going there, so as we took a seat in some patio chairs on the porch, Dad holding his side with one hand and the other curled around his can of beer, I said, "Glacier Academy." My dad finally let go of his back and opened his beer can, the pop and fizz of it abrasive against the evening scuffling of chipmunks and birds scurrying around the bushes and trees beyond his small and still unimpressive lawn. No matter how much *work* Seth had claimed to do, there were weeds and loads of unsightly, thick, and dark green patches of grass that didn't match the rest of it. Tracy had poked her head out and told us she was going to catch some reality TV show that she just couldn't miss.

"Glacier Academy," I said again. "The place Adam went to as a teen?"

"Yeah, what about it?" He winced at his beer can at the same time he cupped his hand around his lower back. "Damn, these chairs are uncomfortable."

"You think it was worth it? You think that place did any good?"

"Shit if I know. Why do you care about it now?"

"I don't know. Just found out a little more about the place since I've been working on a case."

"Ahh." Dad nodded, like he now understood everything. "And you want to what? Blame me for sending him there. You find something that says it wasn't good enough?"

"I didn't say that, but, yeah, you hear about that girl hanging herself in 1995?"

"Oh no, you don't, Monty." He tucked his chin toward his shoulder as if to shield himself or to contain his anger. "We are *not* having this conversation."

"Why not?"

"Jesus. What do you want to imply here?"

"Nothing. I just want to know if you've kept any tabs on the place, is all. I know it must've cost a load of money to send him there."

"It sure as shit did. You know, that was pretty much his college money. But I did what I needed to do back then. You remember. Your brother was getting into all sorts of trouble. He needed to go somewhere to straighten up. Your mother certainly wasn't going to help in that department. That was some of the first big money I ever made in my life. First I spent it on him, then we were finally able to afford some real, in-patient treatment for your mother, then shit, it was your turn and you got to go to college."

"I was lucky," I said.

"Damn right, you were. You think it was easy spending that kind of cash to straighten Adam out? I'd have certainly preferred he went to college like you. Shit, I never got to do that."

"No, I don't think it was easy." He had been generous with helping me through college, but I didn't want to remind him that I also qualified for a number of state scholarships and took on some pretty good-size student loans. "I know you needed help with him. I was just curious if you'd heard about the place since then. You know, like over the years?"

He glared at me. "Like I said, Monty. What are you going there for?"

I ran a hand through my hair and sighed. "A few of the guys that worked there were pretty big bullies. Used a lot of, shall we say, old-fashioned disciplinary measures."

Dad frowned at me and took another large swig of his beer. This was his fourth one. I tried to not count when I was with him, but old habits die hard. I'd be long gone by the time he started to get belligerent, then passed out on the couch. Tracy could deal with him then. Whether they were using him or not, I considered, they still had to put up with his irascible ways when he started to go sideways. "Jesus, Monty. I told you: we are not having this conversation. Why are you putting this on me now? As if taking care of your mother my entire adult life wasn't enough of a hell, now you gotta dump this on me? What are you here for?"

"I'm not dumping anything on you. I just wondered if you'd ever heard anything after the fact. I know you believed in the place. You did what you had to; Adam was a mess. I'm not saying anything is anybody's fault."

"So you come all the way out here after not visiting for months pretending to be concerned about my back and all you want is more information on your damn case?"

"No, nothing like that. Just curious."

"What does your case have to do with that place anyway?" He asked more calmly, and I was surprised to see the small shift—the ability to brake for a change, to keep the conversation from escalating.

"One of the men that died. He used to be a counselor there."

"So?"

"So nothing." It never ceased to amaze me how I could sit sober before my dad while he drank beer after beer, and I still reverted back to childhood arguing techniques as if I was twelve again. I wondered if that's the way he still saw me—young and incapable. I wondered if he thought of his sons as nothing more than two additional burdens on his life—one because he drank and did drugs, the other a prisoner of his youth and small stature. And now, as irony would have it, he housed—burdened himself with—a man about my age *and* his entire family. My father—the very odd mix of caretaker and drunk, with more success on the drunk side.

"So you're bugging me about Glacier Academy because you're thinking Adam has something to do with your case?"

"No, I didn't say that."

"But that's what you're thinking."

"Why would you think that?" I asked.

"Why else would you bring it up?" he said. "You could give a rat's ass about what I think otherwise, so it has to have something to do with Adam, me, or your mother."

"That's not true."

"What isn't true?" he asked.

"That I don't give a rat's ass about what you think."

He looked at me, his bottom lip pouty. I couldn't tell if he really thought I didn't care about what he had to say or not, but I could tell he cared. He looked hurt for a moment—the same frailty I'd noticed in Adam—then shook it off and took another sip.

"Maybe I'm just curious," I added.

He continued to stare at me, dark, puffy bags under his eyes. He had gained more weight, his beer belly sticking out farther. His skin looked somewhat peaked for sunny July. I wanted to tell him that if he lost a few pounds, it would help his back, but there was no point. I wondered how his liver was holding up.

"Oh, just curious, huh?" A smile played at the corner of his mouth like he was preparing to humor me.

"Yeah, so after the Nathan Faraway incident—"

"Holy shit," he said. "You gonna go there too?"

"Well, it was after that that Adam started to quit going to school and get into all the drugs and stuff."

"So a lot of stuff happened in those years. I was at work a lot. I don't remember them being connected in any way."

I didn't respond.

Dad pointed his beer can at me. "I don't know what you're getting at here, but what? You implying that there was more to Nathan's disappearance than something unfortunate with a mountain lion or a grizzly or something?"

"That all the cops told you?"

"Of course that's all. Are you implying something about your brother?"

"No, I'm not. Again, I'm just –"

"What? After all these years, you gonna solve something the cops couldn't solve at the time it happened?"

He was putting me in my place with the usual hint of condescension, as if I thought I was bigger and better than I actually was, and that I should remember that I wasn't. "I'm not trying to solve anything from back then, just what I'm working on now."

"And you have evidence linking Adam to what you're working on now?"

I shook my head and lied. "No, Dad, I don't. I'm only trying to piece some things back together in my mind from the past. You never do that? Nothing from your past ever follow you around?" I could see it sting.

He looked at his beer can, then beyond the rock wall toward the trees. Two deer were feeding in the woods, their long, tan necks gracefully curving to the ground. He crushed his can with one hand, the tin crunch of it cutting through the still, soft stretch of the summer evening, and stood stiffly. "I need another," he grumbled as he headed for the sliding screen door.

$\cdot \quad \cdot \quad \cdot$

Tracy followed me out to my car.

"You know," she said. "Your father, well, he, he . . ."

"Drinks too much?" I finished for her.

"Well, yeah, I mean. He kind of passes out every night in front of the TV, then he's really cranky the next morning."

I wanted to be honest with her, lay it out crystal clear that my father has been that way for longer than I could remember. That one of my first memories was tiptoeing down the hall on Christmas Eve because I thought I heard Santa, to find my father in front of the fridge guzzling from a tall, clear bottle. I wanted to tell her that there wasn't a damn thing she or I or anyone in the world could do to change it if he wasn't interested in changing it himself, so if she didn't like it, she best pack her and her kids and her grandkids up and move on out. But the pleading concern in her eyes made me pause. I sighed instead, ignoring the reek of her nicotine breath fanning toward me. "Look, Tracy, I really don't know what you can do to make him cut back, but have you simply asked him to?"

"Yes, and it's a big fight every time."

"I can tell you that it's better, if that helps."

"Better?" She squinted at me in disbelief.

"Uh huh." I nodded. "Age has slowed him down some. Can't keep up the pace he had when I was a boy forever."

A deep frown set across her face. I looked away, toward the house, its beautiful honey-colored timber framing set against the dark forest. There was some pride welling up in me. He had built it. He had skills that transcended the disease. I couldn't see her grown son's lawn from the drive, but a deep green and lush cedar tree with its full and elegant dangling plumes stood off to the side of the house as if it were offering some kind of grace, some kind of protection. Maybe I had gotten it wrong. Maybe Tracy and her family weren't using my father. Maybe they were helping him, protecting him, giving him the gift of company in the latter part of his life. "Thank you, Tracy," I said.

"For what?"

"For being here for him."

"Yeah, well, he's good to us in a lot of ways. I just wish he wouldn't drink so much."

"Yeah, me too," I said. "Welcome to the family." I opened my car door, hopped in, and waved good-bye.

41

RIGHT AROUND MIDMORNING the following day, Ford asked to see Ken and me in his office. Outside, the day was hot, going on ninety-six degrees, which is sweltering for Glacier. We had the windows open, but there was no breeze and you could almost feel the glaciers dwindling with each inhale of the hot, dry air.

Ken was at the big table in the center of the room on his computer, scribbling down notes and I was running more of the Glacier Academy students through searches. We had given Karen some money to make a sandwich run for us, and she had just returned and was handing them out. I was in the process of making a fresh pot of coffee. The room had a lazy, late afternoon feel to it even though it wasn't noon yet. Ford stuck his head through the door and said, "Sorry to interrupt your snack break, but Harris and Greeley, I need you in my office in five."

Karen gave a rise of one eyebrow, and Ken looked at me. I had been expecting it, and actually couldn't believe he had left us to our investigative tasks as long as he had. "Have a quick few bites," I said to Ken, knowing he was always better with food on board, "and we'll head in." I carefully tucked my pen in my pocket and tidied up the file I had open beside my laptop.

Ken gobbled down several bites of a roast beef and Swiss sandwich, took a swig of some coffee Karen put in front of him, and sighed. "Okay," he said. "Let's do this."

"Good luck." Karen waved by flapping her four fingers forward over her palm as we left the room.

"So," Ford said as soon as Ken and I took a seat in front of his desk. "Since Joe's away this week, I figure I better check in with you guys. How's your investigation into the two *accidents* going?" He said accidents with increased stress and clarity, indicating to us that he didn't think for a second that there was any foul play involved and that we were wasting our time and precious Park Police resources.

I gave him a complete rundown of what we were doing to investigate the two incidents, boring him with most of the details except for the arrest I made of Martin Dorian, which grabbed his attention.

"So, this Martin Dorian? He's your prime suspect?"

"Not anymore. He has an alibi for one of the victims that checks out. Determining the TOD of Phillips has been more difficult because of the state of the body and the exposure to the elements."

"And Phrimmer? What evidence do you have on him?"

"Sir?"

"I said, what kind of evidence could you possibly have on Phrimmer for you to actually accuse him of having something to do with the death of Sedgewick?"

I shot forward on my seat and looked Ford in the eye. "We did not accuse Phrimmer of anything, sir. We simply asked him some questions because in the course of our investigation, his name was brought up as someone who didn't like Sedgewick or his work in the park. It's our duty to follow up on all leads, just as it's our duty to check out all calls on the tip line, whether they're hearsay, seem ridiculous, or not. You wouldn't want us to not be thorough, would you?"

"But Phrimmer?" Ford leaned back in his chair and spread both hands to his side, outraged. His chair squawked in agreement. "Are you two out of your minds? Are you that desperate?"

Neither one of us answered.

"Look." He leaned forward and interlaced his fingers over his desk. "It seems to me that if you've got no leads, no suspects yet, you're just shooting in the dark. That says to me that time's up, boys. Time to call these accidents."

"But, sir. We do have leads we're following. Dorian's in jail, but there's more than just him involved in this. And there was definitely some ill intent directed at Paul Sedgewick. Additionally, there are many plausible reasons for why someone would take revenge on Mark Phillips."

"But do you have any evidence to suggest that these two incidents are related and not separate accidents?"

Even though I had been waiting for this question from him, it still made me break into a sweat. The heat in the room felt thick and motionless, dry in my lungs like dust. I had nothing to give him except one Adam Harris, who happened to be the only person I'd discovered who had identifiable motives and a link to both victims, and he happened to be my very own brother. This was not something I could tell Ford. I could see him making a huge deal of it, laughing about the fact that I'm investigating a family member, urging Joe to take me off the case, and ordering up a psych evaluation. "We do have one suspect who has a connection to both people," I finally offered, leaning back in my chair.

"And who's that?"

I ignored his question. "Right now, I'm trying to see how strong that connection is—if it holds water."

"So no hard evidence yet?"

"Not yet, sir, but I've got latent prints being processed as we speak."

"Which will tell you what exactly?"

"Whoever was tampering with Sedgewick's traps."

"Still nothing conclusive there." He rubbed the back of his neck and sighed. "And when will you get this information?"

The fingerprint scanning, identification, and comparison process was actually not a quick one, like on TV with its shiny, omniscient computer databases. It took time and effort to lift the latent prints, trying to get a full, unsmeared set. And the more of them on the traps, the more layered and confusing they would get. "Tomorrow," I said, because I knew Ford was at the end of his patience. "I'll get them by tomorrow.

Ford stood up and looked out his window, then turned to both of us. "The rest of this week." He looked us both in the eyes. "Then the two of you go back to the field."

"I think," I said, "it would be a mistake to drop this investigation and simply peg these as accidents just because it's the park and that's what we're used to around here."

"I'm not saying we should drop anything, and I'm definitely not saying we shouldn't investigate all avenues."

"And that takes time and resources, sir."

"And if you feel that strongly, then maybe we need to get the DOI guys in here. Have them go at it more thoroughly."

I knew he didn't want that. He had hated every minute of it when the DOI sent Agent Systead in for the Bear Bait case. He acted as if aliens had come from outer space and taken over his park. He was just bluffing me. I knew he'd like nothing more than to call these accidental falls and move on with the happy, bucolic summer life of Glacier. "It would take Ken and me *more* than the rest of a week to get those guys up to speed," I told him. I felt fortunate that I had spent quite a bit of time around him in the past, working on research efforts for the park inholdings. He trusted me and respected me to some degree, even if he was irritated to lose me to investigative services.

"Harris, look, you know these cases go on for years sometimes. Remember that missing hiker from 2006?"

I knew exactly whom he was talking about; we all did. A young man of twenty-four who was an experienced outdoorsman had trekked into the backcountry and never came out. We searched extensively for over a month, and the family came from different parts of the United States and holed up in local hotels to wait for us to find him. They held out hope that he would come out of the woods one day, but after months of no sign, no body, we encouraged them to go back to their lives.

Then one day, years later, Charlie Olson, the same guy who called us about Sedgewick from the Loop, had a hiker approach him one afternoon and say that he'd come across a small scrap of yellow clothing and two, very small bone fragments: the phalanges from the top of a foot and part of a clavicle. Charlie brought the pieces to us and sure enough, in our reports, we found that the young man was wearing a yellow windbreaker. We sent the fragments to the National Missing and Unidentified Persons Center in Texas for identification and a match was made.

"But with all due respect, sir, there was no body with that case. It was a missing persons. With these, there are two bodies." I held up my fingers. "In the exact same area within a week of each other. It would be foolish to not investigate this fully."

"I told you." He slapped his palm on his desk. "I'm not saying no further investigation. Of course it stays open as all the inconclusive ones do until proven otherwise. All I'm saying is that this may drag out for years, just as many others have. Bit by bit, you may be able to work through this, just not on full-time duty every day in the middle of tourist season when we need officers in the field. People need to feel like they're safe out here and that there's not some killer interested in shoving them off a cliff. I tell ya, the media would like nothing more than if that were the case—give 'em something to report and stir into more of a frenzy than they already have. So the rest of the week, Harris. Then I put out a statement. We good?"

Ford watched me with a sharp glare. Eventually, I nodded reluctantly.

"Good then." He hit his desk again as Ken and I stood to leave. I would speak to Joe next week if I needed to, but I had no intention of discontinuing this investigation even if it required taking no days off and working every scrap of available time when not out in the field.

But in spite of my stubborn persistence, I couldn't help feeling a sinking sense that this case was lost just like that twenty-four-year-old hiker, and I was never going to make heads or tails of all its inconclusive pieces. I pictured the officers working Nathan Faraway's case, how at one point their supervisors probably called them in and said it was time to not only finish cutting bait, but to quit the fishing altogether, leaving a case unsolved for life—and leaving shocked families with no answers in their wake.

• • •

I didn't say a word to Ken on the way back to the incident room. As soon as we got inside, I shut the door to block out interruptions and called Gretchen to see how close she was. She said Wendy, the latent print examiner, was doing overtime trying to lift all the prints off all the traps.

"I've been helping her," Gretchen said. "But this stuff takes time, and it's about as fun as it sounds—trying to find prints that are suitable for comparison and matching the knowns to the unknowns. Trish and I will be in tomorrow morning to get all the ten-prints from everyone who's handled the traps. I've called everyone on your list for them to stop in and get scanned."

"And after you get those?"

"We'll need several more hours to make the comparisons. With any luck, I'll have some answers for you by afternoon."

I hung up and found Ken looking at me. He leaned against the counter with one leg crossed before the other, his head tilted to the side, his lower lip tucked under his front teeth pensively and his arms folded in front of him.

"What?" I asked.

He let his lip slowly pop out from his top teeth and pulled a piece of gum from his pocket and unwrapped it. "I've been working this with you. Diligently doing everything you've asked."

"So? Is that a problem? You in a rush to get back to your routine, like he wants?" I motioned toward Ford's office down the hall.

"No. No, it's not that." Ken began chewing his gum and tossed the tiny piece of crumbled foil into a bin by the counter.

"Then what is it?"

"It's just that if I'm going to help you"—he lifted his hand toward me—"I should know more. You know, be more involved."

I eyed him, slightly perturbed that he was giving me grief not two minutes after getting it from Ford.

"You weren't the only one at the bottom of the ravine that day," Ken said, still by the counter, but now he had his feet planted firmly apart and his broad shoulders squared. I could see he meant what he was saying.

I looked out the window and tugged at my shirt to loosen my collar. Guilt shot through me suddenly at his reference to the Loop, how he'd been there all three times, either rappelling down with me, or holding my lines. I knew I'd been unfair to him lately—keeping information to myself and treating him like little more than my errand boy. He was a gregarious type, all right, but he also didn't seem to mind staying busy as long as he got to go home on time to his family and ate lunch before getting too hungry. Perhaps I had misjudged him. "In what way?"

"For starters, who were you talking about in there?" It was his turn to throw his hand in Ford's direction. "Who exactly has a connection to both victims? Or was that bullshit to buy some time. Keep the boss away?"

I thought about it. I didn't want Ken to know about Adam's connection to Phillips, and I was still angry that he'd told who-the-hell-knows about me calling him for a ride home from the bar after Lara's party.

"Was it a load of crap? Or do you really have someone connected to both victims?"

"I do," I finally said, low and quiet.

Ken cleared his throat. "And are you going to fill me in about this person?"

"I will," I said after thinking about it for a minute. The bottom line was that if I was going to get on top of the case, I would continue to need Ken's help. If he wanted to act more like a partner to me and less like my minion, so be it. I could respect that. I could take my hat off to that. "I haven't said anything because it's complicated."

"Yeah, so? The whole damn case is complicated. You think I'm not smart enough?"

"I don't mean that kind of complicated."

"What kind, then?" Ken waited.

"Remember what Dorian said about my brother?"

"With the poaching ring and all?"

"Well, he also knew Mark Phillips. It was years ago, at Glacier Academy, so I figured it was a long shot, but so far, my brother is the only connection we've got between Wolfie and Mark Phillips."

"But does he have motive on both ends?"

I nodded again. "I'm afraid he does." I filled him in on Adam's days at the academy—leaving out what Diane Rieger had told me—and about the fight with Phillips the year before. I told him I was waiting to see if his prints turned up on any of the box traps.

Ken stared at me with wide eyes. If it were me listening to the story from a fellow officer talking about his own brother, I would be surprised too. In fact, I'd probably let loose one of my signature whistles, so I made the statement on Ken's behalf: I whistled, long and low.

"No shit," Ken said in reference to it. "But you don't know. It's all completely circumstantial at this point."

"No, I don't. We have nothing conclusive yet."

"Still." Ken stood up and started to pace the room and chew his gum more vigorously. "Surely you know your brother. Could he? I mean, would he?"

I looked down at the floor. It seemed like a trivial question on the surface, but it hit me like lead. To say yes was to cast out my brother, almost irrevocably. Language has the power to define. To say yes meant something I had not had time to come to grips with, might never have time to come to grips with. I could wrap my head around the fact that my father was an alcoholic and my mother was a depressed, paranoid schizophrenic. Adam—he could be violent. He could be temper driven. He could steal, poach, lie, and cheat, and I wouldn't like it, but I could wrap my head around it. But as strained as Adam and I were, I could never accept that one of my own family members could kill another human being, regardless of how much mental illness lay snared and twisted in the strands of our DNA.

Ken had quit chewing his gum and the room was silent. I could hear a songbird in the distance and the low murmurs of a car motor. A lone butterfly flitted by outside the window. I had no reason to bare such information to some gum-smacking, just-along-for-the-ride newbie, but then it hit me: I was a newbie too, at least on the lead-investigative homicide front, and if I was going to succeed, I needed help. And for some reason I wanted to talk to Ken at the same time that I wanted to keep my tangled family life completely in the dark. I liked Ken, and I wanted to trust him, and I wanted to say something for my own sanity—for the order of things in my own head. "I don't know," I finally said. "What makes a person cross that line? I'm pretty certain my brother has crossed many lines in his life, and if that's what makes someone capable of murder, than yeah, yeah, I can see it, right?"

Ken stared at me, still not chewing.

"I mean, my brother has no one, no wife or kids to care for, no major responsibilities, no sense of how rules keep us all in check. He abused drugs and alcohol as a teen, was a bigger bully than you can imagine. Cross one line here, another there . . . a little temper, a little fight, a bigger fight . . . A small thought of revenge growing bigger and bigger in one's head until it becomes an obsession. . . ." I put my fore-head in my hands and when I looked up, Ken was taking a seat again.

"That doesn't mean he doesn't draw the line somewhere. Rules or no rules, most people would never go as far as killing someone unless they're completely unhinged or sociopathic."

"I'm afraid I can't tell you with any kind of certainty whether he is either one of those. I simply have not spent enough time with the guy in our adult years to even know." I thought of a time when one of Adam's classmates had announced to the rest of his class that our mom was crazy. Adam followed him and some of his friends to the movies the following weekend, found a seat behind the boy in the dark, and dumped a small can of yellow paint over his head.

"But what about a motive—just going to the school where Phillips worked is no motive."

"No, but what if Phillips strong-armed him, did things he shouldn't have and gave him reason to hate, reason to harbor a grudge?"

"You have any proof of that?"

I didn't answer, and Ken must have sensed my reluctance to say more—to dip into darker waters.

"Okay then," Ken said, not one to invite awkward moments. "We keep working." He chewed his gum vigorously now. "Get the prints and go from there. I mean, even if his prints are on the box traps, what does that prove?"

"Nothing in terms of Phillips, but it does prove that he tampered with federal traps, then we know he's lied because he told me he's never seen them, and that's enough to bring him in for questioning on two fronts: hindering a federal investigation and tampering with federal property. It might shake him up a bit."

"Like I said then, we'll cross that bridge when we come to it."

I looked at Ken, rejuvenated to hear it said so simply. Yes, keep working, cross bridges one at a time, my mottos exactly. It was refreshing to hear him take the directive for a moment. "I apologize," I said.

"For what?"

"For not treating you more like a partner."

"It's no biggie. I know you're making the decisions here, but I just want to know where the hell we're steering this thing."

"Fair enough," I said, then couldn't resist as long as we were clearing the air—"and Ken, next time I call you for a ride, don't tell a grape on the grapevine."

Ken's mouth fell open. "I—"

I held up my hand. "I don't want to know and I don't care. I probably shouldn't have called in the first place. My mistake. I just didn't think I'd have to deal with it when talking to Joe."

"Charlie." Ken shook his head in disappointment. "Can't keep his mouth shut. The only reason I told him was because—"

"Like I said," I interrupted. "I don't want to know, and I don't care about that, but this, Ken—what I just shared with you—this or anything else on this case that's confidential gets around to Charlie or anyone else, then I start caring."

"Got it, Harris," Ken said. "I got it."

42

Wʜɪʟᴇ ᴡᴏʀᴋɪɴɢ ᴏɴ my couch that night, I became suddenly exhausted and lay down on my side, thinking I would snooze for only twenty minutes or so because it was early, only nine o'clock and I had a lot I wanted to accomplish before going to bed. I lay my head on the rough-textured throw pillow and pictured Dorian's grin, Adam's flat stare, and my mother's smile. My thoughts slid to her for no logical reason, and I found myself going down a hole trying to figure out when I first realized that something was wrong with her.

Of course, I couldn't pinpoint an exact moment in time. It was a gradual dawning with no sudden epiphany, an accumulation of things, like watching other friends' moms when I'd go to their houses to play—how their mothers didn't sleep the afternoon away; stare into space with glazed, terrified looks; or go into manic sessions of full-speed, seventy-mile-per-hour stories that didn't stop and had no rhyme or reason to them, then get angry that no one understood what she was trying to communicate—that we were in grave trouble and needed to stay locked up in the house with her or else something bad would befall us.

It might also have been the whispering of my kindergarten teachers to my father when he brought us to school, complaining that we were coming late, disheveled, and in clothes that didn't fit. When we were younger, my father hadn't made any money yet in construction and sometimes we'd go without much in the way of healthy meals. They'd wonder if we had had breakfast, and my father, tense-jawed and in a hurry to get to work, constantly angry and frustrated, mumbling under his breath: "I can't do it all."

I drifted into a restless sleep of jumbled images of snickering, pointing teens and Nathan and I running away from them under a swollen moon, trying to find our way home, getting lost at every turn and going deeper and deeper into woods snarled with thick underbrush and hard, reaching roots that grabbed at our ankles and tripped our sneakers. When I finally thought I saw my house, it wasn't our home at all. It was the county jail and when I peeked in, I saw Dorian and Adam both shackled to their chairs in an interrogation room, laughing and conspiring. Dorian spotted me, pointed to the window where I looked in, and when Adam turned and saw me, they both began to laugh—mouths wide open like black holes—their heads tilted back. They laughed so hard it sounded like roaring ocean waves, the undertow dragging me backward while I tried to stay standing, tried to figure out what was going on, but couldn't make sense of it all.

Through the roaring waves of their laughter, I heard it—a low mumble, a car motor . . .the crunch of tires on pavement in my drive. I woke with a start and instantly thought, *one of Dorian's clan.* I felt my heart pound in my ribs. For a moment, I was frozen with terror because I felt helpless, as if Adam might be right, as if he really had protected me all along, and I wasn't capable of defending myself. I shook it off and eased myself up and off the couch and slowly reached for my gun from the coffee table where I had placed it while working, the waffle grip of the handle and the weight of it instantly reassuring.

I walked across my tiny living room in small steps, trying to move sleek as a cat, but my toe caught with a rip on the lounge chair's leg and I shot forward, lunging toward my front door. I caught myself before slamming into it and stood between the door and the front window. I cocked my elbow and held my gun before my chest. I craned my neck and peeked through the side of the window as I heard a car door carefully shut.

It was dark outside, one inky-black blanket spread across the entire front patch of lawn and driveway, and I fought for my eyes to see through it as I heard the shuffling sound of footsteps. I braced the pistol with both hands and made my wrists firm and held it close to my side, my heart now in my throat. When my eyes finally adjusted and I made out who it was, I heard myself make a sound—half sigh, half moan. It was Lara. As she gently knocked, I relaxed my grip, hit the porch light, and opened the door.

She looked down by my side at the gun. I walked over, turned a lamp on, and set it back on the table.

"Your gun." She motioned to it. I suddenly felt ashamed. In all the years we'd been together, she'd never seen me have it out like that. I always had it stored safely away in a drawer at home and never had felt the need, even when we'd heard strange noises outside. A gun was never a solution to any situation when I was at home and off duty, and she knew it. "Did I scare you?"

"I had dozed off. You took me by surprise."

"I called you, but you didn't answer."

I grabbed my phone off the coffee table and looked. Sure enough, she had called twice, and I noted the current time: eleven thirty. "I guess I forgot to put the ringer back on."

She stood quiet for an awkward moment, then said, "I'm sorry. I didn't mean to intrude. I know it's late. I guess I shouldn't have just come like this, but I couldn't sleep."

"No, no, it's fine. Here, have a seat." I held my palm out. "It's no problem. I was wanting to get more work done anyway. If you hadn't have come, I probably would have slept right through till morning."

"Is, is everything okay?" she asked.

"Yeah." I ran my hand through my hair. "I was just going to ask you the same. What brings you here this late? Is everyone all right?"

"Oh, everyone's fine. Most of my family has left by now. I just wanted to see you."

I offered her some tea, water, or wine and she said, "No, thanks," then added, "Are you angry I came?"

"No, no, of course not. Look, I know I shouldn't have left you like that, but . . ." I sank into my armchair, my legs still shaking slightly from the instant push of adrenaline, then relief that it was only Lara, then fear that it *was* Lara and that something serious had happened to bring her by so late. I was going to continue speaking, but then realized I didn't really have anything to say. I wasn't interested in apologizing to her, not for what happened at her family reunion. If anything, I was still on the angry side, but I pushed it down and asked, "How've you been?"

"I've been okay."

"And your family? How'd they take the news?"

"I . . ." She looked down at her hands. "I didn't really fully explain the situation."

"Seriously? How'd you explain to your mom that I left, headed home?"

"Told her that you were really busy on a case that required you to stay up in Glacier for a few days."

"And she bought that?" I squinted at her.

"Kind of, I mean, your black eye sort of demonstrated that you were in something serious. Maybe she and my sisters didn't buy it completely, but they didn't push it. I don't think they really want to know either. I think they probably suspect something, but no one wanted to deal with it while we were all together for a reunion."

Here I had been thinking that I'd left Lara with a major drama on her hands, dealing with her humongous family and her critical parents who would be disapproving and outraged at first, pumping her for the truth and endlessly encouraging her to get back together with me, just as she'd been claiming they would if I didn't help out and put on false pretenses that we were fine. A part of me had felt sorry for her to have to handle it all, and now I realized, she'd just sidestepped it, avoided the conflict altogether. And they were happy to do the same. The thought of it made whatever warmth I was feeling to see Lara so unexpectedly, quickly vanish. "I see," I said. "So why are you here?"

The repetition of my question made her fidget and she looked irritated that I'd asked it again. "I told you, I wanted to see you."

"Why?"

"I don't know exactly why, Monty. Do I need a reason?"

I didn't answer. I knew I wasn't making this easy on her, but I didn't care. She certainly hadn't made the past year a walk in the park.

"I just, I don't know, wanted to check on you. See how you're doing. I felt bad about the way things were left."

"I did too, Lara. I did too."

"And Adam?"

"What about him?"

"Have you talked to him?"

"Why do you ask?"

"Because"—she bit a cuticle on her thumb—"because, I don't know, because of the way things ended that day. It was so crazy and you were so angry, and . . ." She dropped her hands and plopped them heavily into her lap.

"I was angry for a reason, Lara. You had lied to me. Did you forget?"

"I just didn't tell you everything because I know how you feel about him and I knew you'd overreact. It was just a fib. You're making it into a huge deal."

"If you'd been talking to my brother, you should have told me."

"I had no idea he'd show up there. I was just as surprised as you."

"You didn't seem all that surprised."

"What's that supposed to mean? Jesus, what's going on with you?"

"Nothing's going on with me."

"You look, I don't know, tired and stressed, and for goodness sake, getting your gun out?"

In that moment, I almost told her to go to hell and to leave. My resentment surprised me, how easily it ballooned, making my head spin and say things I knew I'd regret. As hurt as I was when I moved out, I'd never felt this rush of fury before. How dare she walk into my small haven in Glacier Park where I came to lick my wounds, to grieve the fraying of our marriage, and have her tell me I looked stressed? "Look," I said when I was sure I'd reined it back in, "I don't want to fight. I'm just, I guess I'm just really frustrated right now. I told you that when your reunion was done, I wanted to get this solved. Are you ready to do this thing?"

Lara looked down at her hands. She was holding her keys in her left hand. She had quit wearing her wedding ring months ago, and then I had followed her lead. That had stung too. "Do what thing exactly?"

"You know, move forward with things . . ." It was difficult to say the word. She looked up at me, her eyes drooping and sad. She looked like a child. "With the divorce."

"Is that what you want?"

I stared back at her. I wanted her to leave, but I also wanted her to stay because I wanted answers, and I was so tired of living in limbo, of feeling like no matter what I did, there was my wrecked marriage sticking to me like it was steel and I was a magnet. It seemed as if she could go on and on living this way, and that thought alone made me lose respect for her. Problems needed to be solved, not just splayed all over the place for you to trip over every minute of your life. "I don't know exactly what I want, but I know I don't want this anymore"—I waved my hand between the two of us—"and I'm sensing we can't go back, so that leaves one last option."

"So you just want to give up, just like that?"

My bubble of patience was shrinking. "Lara, what the fuck do you want from me?"

She looked at me horrified, her eyes widening—two large pools of blue. I never swore at her.

"To just to sit on the sidelines forever?" I continued. "To wait here for you whenever you need me? In the meantime you can do whatever you please, including getting a relationship going with my estranged brother?"

"You know that's not at all what I've done. You're being totally ridiculous."

"Am I?"

"Yes, Monty. Yes, you are. Why do you have such a problem with your brother?"

"You know why. Why are you sitting here acting like you don't know me?"

"I don't know everything about you. I don't know why you'd pull a gun out when the Monty I know would never have done that. I don't know why you'd hate your own brother so much after all these years and wouldn't let bygones be bygones. Just because he did some bullying and made some bad choices as a teenager doesn't mean he's some evil villain trying to ruin your life now."

"I never said he was. But I'm also adult enough to decide who I want to have in my life at this point. Who's toxic and who's not, and quite frankly, I think my brother is pretty damn toxic."

"Well, maybe you're wrong. Maybe you don't know everything and have every little thing figured out—squared away all perfectly like you think you do." Lara held her chin high and proud.

"Okay, okay." I rubbed the back of my neck and took a long, deep breath to try and find logic. "Maybe I am, so here's the deal, forget about my brother. This isn't about him. Clean and simple: you changed your mind about having children and when you couldn't persuade me to come to your side of things, you wanted to split. So here we are, and I, well, I still haven't changed my mind."

"Because you won't even consider it, Monty. You made up your mind when you were young and because you are who you are—"

"What's that supposed to mean?"

"I mean, like I was saying, because you like everything neat and squared away, all the answers in place, you think that the whole baby issue is simple—a readable case of genetics—and you've put that aside, nice and neat and squared away in your mind and you won't even consider it. But there are two of us and marriage requires compromise and sacrifice."

"Sacrifice if it's coming from my end, not yours."

Lara's back arched off the couch, rigid and ready to fight, and her mouth twisted in disgust at what I'd just said, but she didn't have a retort.

"How do you know what I've considered and what I haven't?" I said, trying to make myself sound calm and together, before she racked her brain for some lame example of sacrifice on her end. "I've spent months alone, Lara. You think this has been fun? I've had plenty of time to think through all our issues, just as you wanted, and guess what? No matter how I thought it through, it just didn't work for me. I still feel the same way, and, well, you know that. You've known it all along, so the ball's in your court. It's simple, stay with me as we planned when we got married or move on. But either way, I'm not doing this anymore."

"So my indecision is going to become your decision?"

"Yes, yes." My head was bobbing up and down ridiculously fast. I hadn't been this direct with her since we split up, with this kind of impatience and anger fueling me. I'd always been straightforward, but the patient and understanding one no matter how clean I tried to be. And I certainly hadn't planned on saying any of these things to her this evening. Now, I felt like I was flying a jet and about to release a bomb right onto our marriage for good. It made me feel strange and scared— almost dangerous and slightly off-kilter, like my mind was shifting, floating with hypoxia, and I was just going to go with wherever it went whether I had planned to or not.

Lara held her brow in an angry pinch, her eyes narrowed and on fire. "Fine." She stood up and gripped her keys. "Fine, Monty." She went to the door.

I stood up and watched her open it. Moths danced in the cone of light on the porch behind her and for a second I felt dizzy, watching wings of papery white flit behind her head like a halo. "You don't think it," she said. "But I've sacrificed plenty."

"Oh, what?" I heard myself throw out a quick and knifelike sarcastic laugh. "That you held off on going out and getting yourself pregnant? Is that your sacrifice?" I knew I was being a total asshole, and

I couldn't help it. The months of waiting for her to decide had piled up on me and created something with teeth, and I wanted her to feel the bite of pain I'd been feeling all along—that she seemed to so easily sidestep all the time, just like Adam always did when we were younger.

Lara glared at me one last time, slammed the door, and ran to her car. I watched her through the window as she backed out and drove away, her taillights like angry eyes in the night.

43

I GOT UP EARLY with the chorus of noisy birds, showered, shaved, and made some instant oatmeal and coffee. I didn't ring or text Lara, even though I thought about it. I felt horrible about the way I had treated her after she took the time to drive all the way out to see me, but a part of me felt justified and the iron fist of stubbornness still had me in its grip. I surprised myself that I had pushed the divorce issue as I had, knowing that there were things couples couldn't ever recover from once you went down certain paths. It made me feel shaky, but when I shaved, my hand was steady and sure.

Ken was ready and waiting for me when I got there, sipping coffee that Karen had made and staring at his computer. He smiled as I came in and set my carrier case on the table. "Gretchen just sent this to me." He flicked his computer monitor with a fingernail.

"What's that?" I had had enough coffee at my dorm, but I grabbed a cup from the cabinet and filled it anyway out of habit.

"She was able to enlarge the footage so we can see the exiting vehicles."

"Yeah? Find anything?" I walked over and peered over his shoulder at his screen at a magnified view of the back of a Toyota. The license plate was blurry and grainy, but the numbers could be made out. "The numbers match. So it looks like our boy Phillips did leave on the evening of June eighteenth."

"Yeah, at least his truck did. I guess there's no way to tell if that's him or not in the driver's seat."

"No, Gretchen said there's just not a clear enough shot, so it's just a shadowy blob—the back of his head. If that's him, he most likely hiked a full day on June eighteenth, a Saturday, drove to the Loop, took the shuttle to the top as our driver indicated, then hiked the Highline Trail back to Granite Park Chalet and back down to the Loop to his car and drove out. Unless, that is, that's not him in the vehicle and someone else."

"If it's someone else, shouldn't we be able to find some fibers in the car?"

"We should, but it would be a long shot. It could be fibers from anyone—a mechanic or friend or girlfriend who might've driven it. But you're right. It's worth a look. I'll have Gretchen get someone on it right away."

"Is it possible he went over the cliff on a later date?"

"Wilson said entomology shows five to seven days, so he could have come up a day later, this time with someone else, but I'm betting that's unlikely. Everyone we've spoken to that knew Phillips claims he usually hiked on Saturdays. He was expected at work on Monday, so I'm thinking he wasn't planning, at any rate, to go hiking the next day as well. So someone else must have driven him back up that same night or the next day, and if that's what happened, that person could be our killer."

"Unless that person drove him, dropped him off, then he simply fell."

"Makes no sense." I was pressing my lips into my knuckles, thinking. "This has been all over the news. If someone innocent gave him a ride or brought him up, they would have come forward by now. And why would he go back to the same hike unless he lost something and was going back for it. And if that were the case, wouldn't he drive there in his own vehicle, look around for it, then get back to work? Not leave it sitting in his garage?"

"Yeah, you're right. Makes no sense."

"No, someone most likely drove him up, and it's possible they went in the North Fork entrance where there are no cameras."

Ken nodded that he agreed.

"Good work," I told Ken. "And just to make sure, I'd like for you to double-check the footage from the time he drives out of the park for the next two days for any other suspicious cars or signs that he's with someone else. It's a long shot, but it's worth continuing to go over even though it's tough to discriminate the passengers in the vehicles."

"I'm on it." Ken turned back to his screen, looking pleased with himself for the work he'd accomplished. I went over to the sink, dumped my coffee, and watched the black liquid splash against the porcelain sink, staining it a brownish black, the color of dried blood.

• • •

I left Ken at headquarters to scour the videos again for any sign of suspicious vehicles and headed to the county offices in Kalispell to see what Gretchen had found. I parked in the large courthouse parking lot and stepped out onto the hot pavement. I had picked up some tuna salad sandwiches at a deli to bring to Gretchen and Wendy, her print examiner, and went in to their offices, signed in at the front desk with a receptionist behind glass, and waited for her to get ahold of Gretchen so she could come out and fetch me. She handed me a visitor's badge to show I was official. I clipped it onto my shirt pocket, took in the cool air-conditioning of the county building, and waited.

When Gretchen walked up, I felt the same frisson of excitement I'd felt around her when she touched my arm in the restaurant the other day. Her smile and bright eyes lit up the room. I could feel my stress abate, my shoulders melting back down into a comfortable position.

"What do you have there?" She gestured to the bag I brought.

"Tuna salad sandwiches." I held it up. "That work for you?"

"Absolutely." She smiled. "Come on back."

Gretchen was dressed in her white lab coat. I followed her through a secure door, down a long hall, and into a room with computers, monitors, and large rectangular machines with piping connected to them for chemical analysis. I'd been to the lab once before, but they didn't have as much equipment then. "You're almost catching up with the Crime Lab in Missoula," I said, motioning to the new equipment.

"Nah, we just got a little extra funding for a few new pieces to help us out in a pinch. We still send the majority of our samples to Missoula. Wendy," Gretchen called over to a brunette behind a computer screen, and she stood up, came over and Gretchen introduced us. "Wendy does all our latent print work," Gretchen said.

I shook Wendy's hand while Gretchen told me that she'd worked on the fibers out of Phillips's Toyota all morning while Wendy worked on the prints. Then, she said to Wendy, "Monty brought us tuna salad. Eat first or after?"

"If we could just go through what you've got," I said, "then I'll get out of your hair and get back to work and you two can eat whenever you please."

"Aren't you going to join us?" Gretchen asked.

"No, I already ate while I was waiting for you to finish these."

"Fair enough." Gretchen walked me over to her desk. "Have a seat." She waved to a chair beside it. Wendy thanked me for bringing lunch and went back to her workstation, saying, "Holler if you have any questions."

"We've pulled a total of eleven good prints from the traps," Gretchen said while opening her file. "There may be more, but we can't get a decent read of a few of them. Of the eleven, three of them belong to your biologists: Kurtis Bowman, Sam Ward, and Paul Sedgewick; and two of them to your veterinarians: Dr. Kaufland and Dr. Pritchard. And all of their prints are on all of the traps."

"And the other six?"

"Well, I know you can guess one of those."

"Dorian?"

Gretchen gave me a pronounced nod. "That's right. So"—she looked down at her paper again—"we've got Dorian on three of the six traps."

"What about the others?" I could feel the tension creep back into my shoulders, my neck muscles stiffening, and my breath begin to quicken as I did the math. There were five sets left. The bright lights of the fluorescent strip lighting above stung my eyes and reminded me of how little sleep I'd gotten after Lara left.

"Well, there are four unknowns, not a match to the elimination prints and not in the system. Sam Ward informed me when he came in for his that there were other people who had helped on the project since the traps had been constructed, including the guy who built the traps, so I'm guessing they belong to those individuals."

There was one identified set left and the look on Gretchen's face said it all. She looked up from her paperwork, her eyes wide, her expression tentative, her chin slightly tucked down, as if she didn't look fully up at me, it would lessen the blow.

"The last one?"

"It matches one of the prints from the collar you gave me."

I felt something thick and murky rise up in me, but I forced myself to sit still. I realized my mouth was hanging open, so I shut it to make a clean and neat line, not pressing my lips too tightly together, and I know that sounds easy, but it wasn't. It took effort and control because my pulse was quickening, my jaw tightening, and I felt various small muscles I couldn't even pinpoint twitch in my body as I sat rigidly and motionless before her.

She put out a large exhale on my behalf and ran her fingers through her hair. "You going to be all right?"

"Yeah, why?" I asked stupidly.

"I'm guessing I know whose prints those are?"

"You'd be right about that. But, yeah, I'm fine. Really. In a way, it's a relief to have some verification. To not think I'm crazy here and imagining he's involved in stuff just because I have a few bad childhood memories."

"That's true," Gretchen said.

I thanked her and stood. "I'm going to need to get on this. Any way you can rush the prints on Phillips's Toyota?"

"I already lifted some this morning and gave them to Wendy. I'll call as soon as anything is verified."

"Enjoy your lunch." I pointed to the paper bag.

"You sure you don't want to join us?"

"No, I'm good. But thanks."

"Okay, but let me know if I can help in any way."

I didn't look at her, just began to head toward the door.

"Hey," she said, and I turned. "Did you hear me?"

"I did. I'm sorry."

"No, sorry," she held up her hand. "I just wanted to make sure it sunk in. I'm here if you need anything, okay? Even if it's just an ear."

"Thank you, Gretchen. I appreciate it."

In a way, it was a relief; one with a sharp edge, but still a consolation. At least I was right not only in my argument with Lara about him still being toxic and bad news, but in the information I'd shared with Ken. It was a small, bitter solace, but it helped nonetheless because at least I had confirmation that I wasn't just seeing only what I wanted to see with this case. Any good detective takes that into consideration, and even Mack in DC covered it in his class: *Don't ever let your personal shit cloud the facts before you.*

It wasn't as strong a link as you'd hope for, but with two victims and no certainty of anything, this was the strongest connection I was probably going to get. I had someone with ties to both men, and evidence that he'd had his hands on the federal box traps used by Wolfie.

When I stepped out into the late afternoon, I felt the heat rise up from the sidewalk. A diesel truck stood by the side of the building, its hot, strong-muscled fumes strangling the air. I strode to my car, got in and felt the air from the inside engulf me. My car felt confining and savagely hot, but comforting in its own strange way. I turned the ignition, rolled the windows down, and considered what to do next while waiting for it to cool off.

44

I WENT BACK TO headquarters and filled Ken in on how I wanted to handle Adam. With his prints on Wolfie's federal traps, I had enough to demand some cooperation and to detain him temporarily for questioning under reasonable suspicion, but not enough to bring him in under probable cause.

Ken and I waited until dusk before going to Adam's. It was already getting dark a little earlier every evening since the solstice had passed. I wanted the cover of late evening shadows so that I could approach him on my own. I knew I was taking chances by leaving Ken in the car, but still, I was clinging to the notion that I could handle Adam alone—keep it civil and under wraps. After all, I was dealing with my family, and although I had no plans to show him any mercy, I still felt that there was no need to spread my family problems all over the place in front of Ken or any other officer. The lid might be off the dysfunction jar all right, but that didn't mean I needed to shake it, turn it upside down, and dump it all over the place. If I could keep it semicontained, I'd be happier.

We left the Park Police Explorer at headquarters since it was after work hours and took my Ford Taurus. We parked in the shadows beyond the reach of his porch light, so that if Adam were looking through his window—which I knew he would when he heard the motor—he would not be able to tell that I had someone with me. I wanted to keep him guessing and didn't want him to feel I'd come with assistance right off the bat in case he felt threatened.

Adam opened his front door and stepped out under his porch light as I got out. It was already going on ten, the crickets had begun their clamor, and a dim light infused the night sky. A Little Brown, the most common bat in Glacier—a species highly susceptible to the White-Nose Syndrome, zigzagged above me—catching mosquitos and other insects.

My feet felt light on the gravel, like I was walking on air. I had my phone on in my pocket with an open call to Ken. It would probably be too muffled to hear our conversation, but he'd at least hear if anything major seemed to go wrong. As I headed closer to the cabin, an owl sailed by like a portent not two seconds after seeing the bat—all stealth and poise, hunting small creatures on the ground. I was beginning to wonder if I was the hunted or the hunter when it came to my brother.

Adam stood still in his porch light, his head high, arms rigid by his sides, fists pumping and ready as if he were a lone survivor in an apocalypse. I caught my fast breathing and stilled it, even forced a small chuckle to myself at the ridiculousness of it all—as if Adam were movie-star material, all muscle and renegade. Bugs flew above his head in the light and he lengthened his neck to get a better view of the car, but I was pretty certain he couldn't see in even though a touch of deep indigo still hung in the western sky. I didn't look back to check, just kept walking to the porch in the darkening twilight, anxiety pumping through me.

When I got to Adam, I could see he'd been drinking. His pupils looked dilated in the flare of the porch light and red streaks webbed out from them. "Don't see you for years and now I can't keep you away."

"That's right. Lucky us."

"It's late."

"Past your bedtime?"

He didn't answer. "Why are you here?"

"I've got some new information that says you've had more of a connection to Sedgewick than you admitted. I'd like for you to come into the station with me, so that we can have a proper chat."

"Fuck you." He laughed. "I told you. I had nothing to do with that guy."

"Like I said, we've got evidence that shows you did, and it's enough for reasonable suspicion." I knew the lingo would mean nothing to him, but I was throwing it out anyway just to get under his skin.

"Reasonable suspicion?" he glared at me. "Whatever that means in your little world doesn't carry a lot of weight in mine. You should know that."

"And you should know that this is serious. Being stubborn isn't going to help you here. It's just going to make it worse. But cooperation," I said level and flat, with all seriousness, "cooperation will be less costly for you."

"I have no idea what you're even talking about, and I really could give a shit about your evidence because whatever it is, it isn't going to mean jack shit."

I took another step closer and caught a faint smell of whiskey. Right then and there, I should have waved Ken to come on over, but stubborn is how I was feeling—I wanted to deal with my brother on my terms. Of course, I was ignoring the lecture I'd just dished out to him—that stubbornness is far more costly than cooperation. "We don't need to go to the station; we can talk here."

"I haven't seen you in years and you come in here all ready and eager to solve your case on my back. Mr. Thorough coming out of the blue and making accusations about me. You've got to be kidding me."

"Sensitive are you? That we haven't spent more brotherly time together?"

"You can take yourself and all your little knickknacks"—he was referring to the weapons I had on the belt of my jeans: just my handgun in its holster, my Taser, and my cuffs in their pouch on the side—"and get the hell out of here."

"Look," I said firmly. "You're not under arrest. I just want to ask you some more questions. I'd prefer the station for the sake of accuracy— yeah, call me Mr. Thorough if you'd like—but here is fine too."

"That why you got your partner over there in the car?"

I shrugged. "What partner?"

"You think I'm stupid? As if I can't figure out why you wouldn't pull all the way up?"

"Maybe *you* should be a detective."

"I'd rather slit my wrists. You and your friend." He peered down the drive, and this time I did look. The car was definitely fully concealed by the dark and I couldn't see Ken. Adam had just assumed, and I planned to give him nothing—keep him wondering. "You and your partner can just leave because I'm not going to any police station." Adam turned, walked back into his cabin, and began to shut the door in my face, but I lunged forward and stopped the door with my palm and followed him in. Adam went straight to the fireplace and stood wide-legged and barefooted next to the iron tools. A reading lamp stood by a lounge chair, and a mass-market paperback and a glass of whiskey on a side table. "Spending a cozy evening reading, are you?"

"What do you care?"

"I guess I don't. Just didn't picture you as the reading type." I tried to see the title, but couldn't make it out.

"How the hell would you know what type I am in the first place?"

I glared at him for a second, and something bitter settled in the space and shadows between us. I didn't need to answer that, and he knew as well that I didn't.

"Why are you here?"

"I told you, I need to ask you some questions."

"'Bout what? Your wife? Got your undies all in a bunch because she spent a little time with me—that what this is all about? You pestering me nonstop because you think I fucked your wife?"

I tried to ignore the rage shooting through me like electricity, tried to tell myself that he was just like my dad—not particularly agreeable when drinking, but the mention of Lara in his dim cabin with sinister shadows fingering across the floor and the tangy, strong smell of whiskey made my head shift and muscles twitch. "You can leave her out of this."

Adam shook his head and began to laugh, a chuckle lined with resentment. "Just because your tidy, little life is unraveling on you doesn't mean you need to come and push your muck in my direction. Now, get out of here before I make you."

"I'm not going to say this again," I said. "I need you to cooperate with me. Let's just have a seat here." I motioned to the table we'd sat at before. I considered pulling out my notepad and pen as a show of good faith, but the hair on the back of my neck was prickling and I didn't trust Adam enough to tie my hands up long enough to grab it out of my pocket. It was his stance. He stood like a wild animal in his den, ready to protect, ready to pounce.

"And did you not hear me? I'm not interested in talking anymore."

"Why not? You got something to hide?" I saw his hand slide back within closer reach of the iron tools. My breathing became shallow.

"I don't have anything to hide. I just don't like this. You coming in here accusing me of murder because that's what you're trying to do. I can plead the Fifth any goddamn time I'd like."

"Of course you can, but that doesn't stop you from getting charged if you're too stupid to cooperate."

"You calling me stupid?"

"You and Dorian both. Go ahead, stay here in your cabin in your canyon thinking you're all safe outside the law. You're just not very smart because, guess what, I'll be back." I knew I was provoking him, but that's what I wanted. I could see the anger sizzling on him like grease on a hot pan. "Actually downright idiotic," I added and watched his hand slide back behind his hip and reach for one of the iron tools. I instantly put my hand to my belt, grabbing for my Taser but feeling my gun instead.

In the split second that I hesitated and went to switch to my Taser, Adam lunged for me, barreling into me so that we both crashed into the wall by the front door and tumbled onto our sides. The wind exploded from my lungs when I hit the floor with a hard thud. I tried to get my breath back in the same instant I struggled to position myself on top.

Adam had gotten a hold around my neck and was trying to flip me over at the same time.

A second later, through the sound of my own gasping, I jabbed the butt of my hand into his nose hard and flat and shoved him back. Rage flooded Adam's eyes, and he plunged back on top of me. Somehow, he had lost the fire iron in the spill of us toward the wall, so he wound his fist up instead, raising it above me like a cobra getting ready to strike.

He was stronger and bigger than me, but—even in the jumbled mess of us each wrapping tight and jabbing for spots that would wound—I saw it, as if time had slowed to an eternity of seconds. I saw, in this particular moment anyway, that his furiousness had receded some, that it was much less than what it was as a teen, and mine had somehow suddenly been born and grown larger and more inflated. I could feel it surging through me, permeating my body, each cell vibrating with wrath.

I used it to my advantage, and with all my ire, I forced my arm up between us, pressed into the sensitive apple of his throat with the hard side bone of my forearm and broke his armlock, flipped him off me and crashed my fist into his jaw. As I reached for my Taser, he scrambled back on top of me and had somehow managed to grab the iron. He held it up with one arm, his face a dark shadow of anger, the smell of animal rage, my own deodorant, and sour whiskey filling my nostrils.

I tried to get my knee up and under him to smash it into his nuts, but he had me, hovering above me. The bright white of his T-shirt against his tan skin that glistened with sweat somehow seemed feral, daunting, and anything but a surrender. The sheer panic of feeling his weight crush me and seeing him hold the iron poised above flooded over me. My mind skidded across images of him pushing pillows over my face until I flailed like crazy, halfway suffocating me and laughing after letting up; of him wrapping me in bedsheets as I screamed and squirmed from claustrophobia; of him locking me in dark closets and down in cold basements. . . .

I could feel a sheen of sweat prickle every inch of my skin. I wanted to spit in his face. But still, I could see him hesitate, the gears turning and him stopping himself from swinging. Again, I felt that something had shifted, that something seemed different. Adam was considering things, and I could see the glimmer of anger recede from his eyes as he did so. He was resisting the urge to just act from a base of pure rage.

I reached for my Taser and lifted it toward him, and he said. "Don't do it, Monty. Don't make me do this."

I glared at him. I wanted to shove the Taser right into his sweaty neckline, watch him writhe and twist in pain in the temporary paralysis on the cabin floorboards, but at the same moment, I was deeply curious why he hadn't bashed that iron right into me—put an end to my visit. Was he actually thinking through it all, that there was no escape? That if he hurt me, he'd spend many years behind bars for that alone, regardless of what role he played in Wolfie's or Phillips's demise?

I could feel his panting and could hear steps fly quickly up the porch, the door crash open, and Ken's voice, "Drop it now, and stand away."

Adam didn't even turn and glance at Ken. He kept his eyes on me, dropped the iron, the crash of it to the wood floor ringing loudly through the dim, still cabin. He continued to look into my eyes, then slowly stood up and backed away. Ken had his gun out, and he turned Adam around and pushed him against the wall.

"I was wondering what was taking you so long," Adam mumbled to Ken.

Ken looked surprised that Adam was talking to him. I stood up and picked up my Taser and put it away. "You okay?" Ken asked.

"I'm good," I said, still winded.

Ken said something about the assault of an officer and began to read Adam his rights.

"The plan stays the same," I said. "Let's get him to the station for questioning for much bigger stuff." I pulled my cuffs out, walked over, turned him around and pulled his wrists in front of him, and snapped the cuffs on. "Let's get some shoes on him and get him to the car."

Ken grabbed Adam's boots by the door, and Adam sat at the table and awkwardly shoved them on his feet one at a time. When he was done, Ken nudged him toward the door, and as he walked by me, he craned his neck to look at me, his stare telling me that he was far from compliant no matter where I took him or whom I got help from. His glare locked me in—seemed to spread over me and go straight to the marrow of my bones. It seemed to fill the whole cabin as if to say: *This is between you and me, brother. This is between you and me.*

45

K<small>EN AND I</small> led Adam down the drive to the car with our hands wrapped through his elbows, just in case he got any weird ideas of trying to run away from us. You never could tell with him. Just like in the cabin, a part of me thought he was too smart to do exactly as Dorian had done—get taken to the station for assaulting an officer when he hated the law and wanted no part of any police station. But he couldn't control himself, and deep down, I expected nothing less. A part of me felt smug about it, but another part pictured Adam—first with his fist up, then with the iron—holding back, the thinking playing across his eyes as he considered things, the glimmer of anger receding as he did so.

But I was being foolish. I knew better and figured I needed to push away any notion that he'd somehow changed—grown up as Lara had said—and erase those moments where I'd sensed that something was different. Letting any flicker of hope that my brother could be a reasonable man at this point was not something I could afford to let cloud my judgment or trip my determination to find out how Wolfie and Phillips died.

Adam was silent, and Ken and I didn't say a word as we drove down his drive, the headlights illuminating the gravel road ahead of us and the bushes encroaching from each side. I thought I saw a pair of eyes flickering off in the bushes, but they were gone before I could tell for sure. Finally, we made it to the smooth concrete of the highway, drove through Hungry Horse and the canyon, until the land opened up to the valley with bright-yellow canola fields like neon in the night. Pastures rolled out and created enough space for me to finally take in a long and controlled breath.

We took him to the police station in Columbia Falls since we weren't working with the county on this one and it was much closer. The station was quieter than the one in Kalispell when we'd brought Dorian in, and we took Adam to an interrogation room that had recently been built with the addition of a two-way. A young, dark-haired female officer I'd never met was manning the entrance station behind the bulletproof glass, and Officer Pontiff waited for us in back. He assisted us as we led Adam into the room.

Ken reminded Adam that he'd already been told his rights, but repeated them in an off-the-cuff way, as if such procedures had little influence over what was really at stake and about to take place.

Adam didn't say a word. We left his cuffs on and headed back to the observation room and eyed him through the glass. He looked older in the harsh fluorescents with his sharp cheekbones and jutting chin covered with a few days' worth of stubble. I lifted my hand and felt my own face, relieved to find it shaved and smooth and to think we looked nothing alike. We wouldn't even pass for brothers, I reassured myself. His short-cropped brown hair exposed his wide forehead and I could see a thick vein running down his temple. He was wearing only his faded jeans and white T-shirt, and the boots Ken had him shove on his bare feet before we walked him to the car.

I realized while I watched him that it felt good to see him stuck in that room, unable to walk out or wield his power over me or anyone else. It felt even better than when we had Dorian. I looked at Ken. "Thank you," I said. "For coming in when you did."

"You think he would have struck you with it?"

"I don't know. He was considering his options. I'm just glad you were there in time to take the option away."

"If he did kill one or both of those guys, you really think he's stupid enough to risk being brought in, just like Dorian?"

"I think all the stupidity that applied to Dorian, applies to him too."

I looked at Adam. He sat rigidly leaning over the table, his hands cuffed before him, and his fists still curled tightly. He stared blankly at the side wall, refusing to look at the two-way, his jaw set and braced—stubborn. "But he's also manipulative, so we can't let him fool us."

"He's managed to stay out of the system so far. You think you can get a confession out of him? I mean, he's your brother and all. Maybe we should call someone else in on this. It's pretty close to home."

I held up my hand. "I'm aware of that. And, yes, he's my brother, but we're not close by any means, and I haven't talked to him before this case popped up in years. To me, he's like any other thug. But you're right. I should play it safe, so that's why I'm going to let you go in first."

"Me?"

"Yeah, just to break the ice. See if you can't get that stubbornness to subside a bit. Just a little."

"How?"

"Just be your gregarious, innocuous self. Make small talk with him. There's no perfect way to do this; we just want him to settle a bit. Calm the stubbornness down a notch, so that a conversation is possible."

"But I'm the one that arrested him."

"Exactly, so start with that. Go on. You'll be fine. I'll be in as soon as his jaw unclenches."

. . .

I watched Ken go in with a glass of water and set it in front of Adam. Adam didn't bother thanking him. Ken pulled out the chair opposite and said, "Would you rather have coffee instead?"

Adam shook his head.

"Okay, well, look, man, sorry to bring you in like that, under arrest and all, but you put me in a bad spot. Holding a fire iron over Officer Harris like that. You could have killed him."

"I'm aware of that." Adam's voice was scratchy and he realized it too, reached for the water, and took a gulp. "I wouldn't have hit him with it. It's complicated."

"Complicated? How so?"

Adam shrugged. "Just is."

I bit the inside of my lip hard after hearing Adam's voice, raspy, but controlled. He had already settled down if he was going to say that he had no intention of using the iron on me. The question for me wasn't whether he meant it or not; it was his level of involvement with Wolfie.

"Because he's your brother?"

"Yeah, I wasn't fighting a cop; I was fighting . . ." His voice drifted off and he stared at the wall, whatever he was going to say dissolving in midair. Adam lifted both his cuffed hands to wipe a palm down his jaw. "He coming in here?"

"Do you want him to?"

"Hell no," he said, pulling his head back. "I've got nothing to say to him."

That was my cue. He had no choice in the matter, and I wanted him to know that. I shot straight out of the observation room and into the interrogation room with a loud jarring of the door, enough to startle them both. I know I told Ken I wanted him relaxed, but I also wanted him to know that I was in charge and this was not his turf. I pulled out the third chair, swung it around, and took a seat, my notebook in hand. "So, Adam."

"Did you not hear what I just said?"

"What's that?"

"That I could do without your company."

"Doesn't seem to me that you have a choice." I looked around the cold, cement-blocked room, then at his cuffed wrists. "Does it look that way to you?"

Adam clammed up, his gaze drifting upward to the ceiling.

"Look, I'm sure you'd like to get out of here just as quickly as Officer Greeley and I would, so why don't you answer our questions so we can move on and all get some sleep tonight. That's all we wanted to accomplish in the first place. And by the way, you don't have an option about whether to talk to me or not, but you're in luck because you do have other options to consider and I'm really hoping that you're at least smarter than your pal, Dorian."

That got his attention and he shifted his gaze to me. "If I cooperate"—he looked at me—"you drop the assault charge?"

"I'd say that would be a good bet." I tapped my pen on my pad. "Because, as you are well aware, Officer Greeley and I are actually interested in other things. Not that assaulting an officer isn't serious stuff. Just ask Dorian. It's just that if you can clear the air for us on a few other matters, it could help considerably."

"Such as?" Adam looked at me under heavy lids.

"Such as tampering with federal traps belonging to Paul Sedgewick."

I could see Adam's shoulders stiffen and he sat back in his chair, not saying anything, his hands neatly in his lap.

"We found your fingerprints on Paul Sedgewick's wolverine box traps that were being used in the South Fork drainage. You care to tell us how they got there?"

"I was in the woods. Saw the traps. Took a peek inside, that's all."

"That's all? Hmm, I guess"—I turned to Ken—"we may unfortunately have to pursue the assault charge after all. Dang it. I was hoping we could avoid that." I tapped my notebook on the table and put it away in my pocket, as if I were done. "Looks like it's going to be a short night after all. Ken, you want to get that paperwork completed?"

Adam glared at me and I could see the hate filtering back into his eyes. "Dorian called me," he mumbled.

"What's that?" I slid my notebook back out of my pocket.

"You heard me. Dorian called me. Wanted me to go into the backcountry with him to check on some traps he'd put out."

"And?"

"I told you. This was many months ago. I told you about that guy from Pennsylvania. I had called Dorian and sometimes he called me to go out hunting or trapping or whatever. Mostly hunting. I don't care much for trapping."

"But this time?"

"Yeah, I was bored, so I said I'd join him. When we were up there, we were hiking down and saw your biologist guy. We hid behind some trees and watched him check his trap, take his notes, make sure his transmission signal was working and stuff. And, well, then he left, and we went and looked at the trap. Talked about what it would take to build one like it and stuff."

"And you touched the trap then?"

Adam shrugged. "Yeah, sure. Just to inspect it."

"That's it?"

"That's it."

"So why am I having a hard time believing you?"

"I don't really give a shit what you believe."

He was stiffening again, and I could see I wasn't getting the full story. I turned to Ken. "So essentially, we could make an arrest on two counts: assault of an officer and tampering with federal traps."

"Whoa." Adam's brow furrowed. "You said if I cooperated . . ."

"You call this cooperation." I held out a palm. "Give me a break, Adam. Really, you want to go to jail to protect Dorian, who is already in jail? You want to join him? Is your whole clan that stupid? Please tell me you're not because I really don't want to think my own blood is that back-ass crazy."

Adam swallowed hard and shot me a look of pure disdain. "I'm not lying," he mumbled. "That's what happened."

"But there's more?"

"Yeah." He looked at his hands, then back up at me. "After Sedgewick set his bait up and left, Dorian went off on some political rant about how the biologist was going to use his studies to restrict our land use. On and on about wildlife corridors and just another government plan to take over land. Dorian said he'd been following your biologist, said he'd had no luck with his own traps because the wolverines were too smart, but that the biologist's traps weren't threatening and he wanted to see if he could get his own in the same vicinity."

"So then what?"

"So then Dorian came up with an idea. Said he could kill two birds with one stone: sabotage the biologist's efforts and trap some wolverines so he could make money off the pelts. Said he wanted to rig the trap with his own steel jaw, said it would fit nicely inside."

"So you rigged it?"

"No, I didn't. Quite the opposite."

I sat motionless, waiting for more.

"I told him not to, that it was a bad idea—messing with a government trap that way, but he did it anyway, not five minutes after the guy left. And, well, I actually got pissed and we started to argue about it. I told him it wasn't going to happen under my watch, so I leaned down, and started to dismantle it, take it back out, but he got even angrier. He pulled his Glock on me. The asshole has all sorts of weaponry. But I'm sure you know that. Anyway, he pointed it straight at my head and told me to back away from the trap."

Again, I said nothing. I was trying to decide whether he was telling the truth or not. He was serious, his eyes straight on me, his pupils back to normal, no fidgeting.

"What did you do then?"

"I stood up slowly, then I jabbed his arm up and away from me, and we began to fight. Eventually, I pinned him and took his gun away. At first he was pissed, but then he started laughing, told me to look to see if the safety was still on, so I did."

"Was it?" Ken asked.

"It was. He kept laughing, thinking it was funny, saying he had no intention of hurting me, just wanted to scare me. So I started to laugh too. Called him an asshole and then we walked out, him with his trap and me watching my back. From that day on though, I always knew that I needed to watch my back around him."

"That's not the way it looked at the Outlaw's last week."

"Since I pinned him," Adam said. "Since I basically could have kicked his ass, a certain anger and respect was borne for me. That's why I was able to get him to back off of you. He wasn't going to risk a fight with me in front of a bar crowd."

I studied him, still trying to decide if I was getting it straight or not, and I could tell that he could see it—could see the dilemma playing out in my head—believe my brother sitting in jail before me now or let all the years of stacked up dysfunction make me discount every word he said. Images of the intimidating, lie-spewing teen ran like a film before my eyes while I considered the alternative—the semi level-headed-sounding adult before me now who might only be in our custody because of his old ways, because he couldn't control his anger and because he liked a fight.

"You don't believe me, do you?"

I didn't answer. Out of the corner of my eye, Ken sat motionless, waiting for me to say something.

Adam shrugged heavily. There was that same frail vulnerability flashing briefly across his eyes, then the bitter hate replacing it. "I don't really fucking care," he said with venom. "It's not like I need you to believe me. If you want to put me in jail, so be it. Maybe it was worth it, knocking you on your ass one last time."

I stared at him, my muscles going rigid too. I knew he was only reverting to tough guy, but I couldn't control the physiological response to it. I was tired of holding it back, but still, I said nothing. Years of keeping my cool had paid off for me before; it would have to pay off for me now.

"You don't really care about those traps and my relationship with Dorian anyway."

"That so?" I said when I was certain my voice was calm and cool.

"Nah. There's only one reason you've got me here and we both know what that is." Adam stole a quick glance at Ken, then turned his glare back to me. "To solve the case that never got solved." He dropped his voice to a cool whisper. "Isn't that why you're in law enforcement anyway? Can't be the pay."

"It's none of your business why or what my career choices are." I knew I'd made my first mistake—giving in, saying anything back at all, taking his bait.

He looked at me smugly. "But that's it, right? That cool night," he whispered, like he was auditioning for a horror movie, his voice steely and hushed, nearly monotonous, but slicing the air in the bare room. "Full moon," he continued. "Clouds fraying across it. Wind in the trees. Dead leaves drifting to the ground."

"What? You working on a short story or something?"

"Leaves crackling beneath each step. The sound of coyotes in the distance. The fog from the river . . . You'd like nothing more than to know what happened. Right, Monty, you'd like nothing more than to know what happened after we went to the 7-Eleven that night. You'd like nothing more than to know that we went back, found your Nathan . . ." He stopped talking, and the room was dead quiet. I couldn't hear Ken's or my own breathing. An electric charge filled either my head or the room, I couldn't tell which.

"Far as I'm concerned, served him right." Adam's voice went back to normal.

For a moment, I thought he meant Nathan. "Served who right?"

"Phillips."

"Phillips?" I tried to resist sitting taller in my chair, tried not to move a muscle as I wondered if it could really be this easy. If Adam was going there after all. I considered that maybe he was tired of it all, maybe his guilt was finally brimming over and he wanted to simply be put in a small cell where tax dollars could care for him.

"You think I killed him?" His face showed no expression now. "You think I'm capable of murder? Well, you know what, I might just be." He chuckled. "But I didn't do it. If you think I had anything to do with that, then Jesus, Monty, you really suck at your job."

"You're the only suspect with ties to both victims," I said evenly.

"Can't help you with that. Maybe you haven't looked hard enough."

"You and Phillips were picked up a year ago for fighting."

"As you can see, I like to fight. Especially pricks who take advantage of their power." I couldn't tell if his comment was directed at me or Phillips, probably both.

I changed directions. "That what Sedgewick was doing? Taking advantage of his power through his brains, through his research and the likes of you and Dorian didn't like that?"

"No, I had no problem with your man, Sedgewick. He looked like he cared about the wilderness, which in my book isn't such a bad thing. It's more than I can say for Dorian. He pretended to be someone who cared about the land, but he didn't. He'd slaughter anything that moved, given the chance, and trust me, he had plenty. I had no bone to pick with your man Sedgewick."

"But you did with Phillips?

"Did." He nodded. "And that ended when we fought."

My look must have sent waves of incredulity his way because he started shaking his head in small little moves, narrowed his eyes, and pointed at me. "You sit there all smug with your notebook and your partner here." He gestured to Ken with a toss of his head and for a moment, I had forgotten that Ken was even in the room. "Not believing me—thinking I killed not only your friend, Nathan, but two other men. You're out of your mind. You're completely clueless, Monty. I was your shield, that's what I was. Get it?"

I closed my eyes in disbelief that he was going there again.

"Before you were born, want to know how it was with Dad?"

"You need a tissue or something?"

"No, you listen." Adam angled toward me. "Before you came along, he used to take me to the bars in the middle of winter. Thirty degrees out and he'd leave me in the truck for hours getting drunk and would forget to come out and turn the heat on for me until I'd have to go in and get him or freeze to death. And do you know how old I was, Monty? Four. *Four* years old."

I threw a quick embarrassed glance Ken's way, then turned back to Adam. "Like I said, if you need a tissue, sorry, we don't have one. This is a police station, not a therapy suite."

"I don't care what it is. You need to hear this."

"Maybe I do, but not now, and Officer Greeley and I, we have—"

"He couldn't leave me with Mom," he interrupted, loud and direct, his voice slicing the room. "Because she was too pregnant with you and couldn't be stressed out with me around bothering her. And I was old enough, he used to say, to hang out for just a little while in the car by myself. As if it was safe out in some bar parking lot about to freeze to death, watching him drive home drunk, hitting reflectors on the side of the road, then crossing the center line back and forth. Basically fearing my life, and eventually yours whenever Dad went all cross-eyed. When you came along, Mom got worse—call it postpartum depression on top of everything else she had. But they at least had a built-in babysitter, and I was relieved to not have to go with him until I found out it wasn't any good at home with Mom either. As bad as any bar parking lot, just different. Scared all the time that she wasn't going to wake up after taking all her pills or when she did wake up, that she'd think I was put there to spy on her."

I thought about the prospect of Adam being able to remember these things at the age of four, then realized I recalled some of the more dramatic events that involved my mother and father at that age as well. "Poor you, lots of people in this world are dealt a not-so-stellar family hand, doesn't mean it's an excuse to screw up your life." I knew I shouldn't be entertaining the discussion.

Ken was sitting there, eyes wide open, his mouth slightly ajar. I was glad he wasn't chewing his usual gum.

"Besides, you think it was nice and pleasant for me. You think I loved getting the crap beaten out of me by my *babysitter*—as you call yourself."

"Better than freezing outside in some shithole bar. Dealing with Dad's fits of anger and getting the shit beat out of me."

"Oh, and dealing with your fits of anger was any better? Huh? Living in terror that my big brother might fly off the rails and beat the shit out of me for having my hair combed in the wrong direction or think it's just thigh-slappin' fun to lock me in a basement closet for hours?"

"Hours?" He shook his head. "You don't get it. You never will. Yeah, I was a little hotheaded, still am. I admit it. I was angry. Angry that I had to be your shield. I sure as shit didn't have one. It pissed me off— the unfairness of it all and Mom wanting me to protect you from the CIA or aliens from space or anything else that popped into her head. Yeah, I was angry, all right."

"And that's supposed to invoke all sorts of sympathy? Huh, Ken." I lifted my chin to him. "You feeling all sorts of sympathy for this guy, here?"

Ken looked at me funny, cleared his throat, and said, "I think we should get back on the subject of—"

"I'm not getting back on any subject about Sedgewick or Phillips," Adam said loudly. "I didn't kill either one of those guys. I've been angry for a long time, yeah, but that doesn't make me a criminal. You can do what you want with me, but it won't be for the murder of Sedgewick or Phillips."

"And Nathan?" It came out expectantly. I blurted it out before I even considered what I was saying, and immediately I was horrified that I had. Everything seemed to go silent except for a faint roar, like the ocean in my ears. I stared at Adam like an idiot, my mouth partially open, and my grip on my pen so tight I almost snapped it in half.

A small, faint smile crept to Adam's lips that he'd gotten to me— that his little whisper act had resonated, then he slowly said: "Fuck you, Monty. I'm done here." He gave a sloppy-handed wave toward the door. "Go do your paperwork or whatever it is you do." The electricity had completely vanished from his voice. He sounded spent and exhausted, his eyes even more bloodshot in the harsh light than they appeared on his porch. "Go do what you need to do."

Suddenly I felt chilled surrounded by the cement blocks capped with the garish-green ceiling. In reality, if I were to be honest with myself, I had been thinking of my brother as a killer for longer than you'd expect, way before this case. I knew that there were things in the world—certain truths—that you could decide to look at face-on or peer to the side of, live with a little ignorance for the sake of getting by. You don't grow up in a family like mine and not learn a certain dose of denial; a certain amount of self-preservation comes from not staring directly at the blinding light for too long.

The river he had mentioned kept pinging in my mind. I remembered steam rising from water, but I didn't remember being by water that night. He was right: I wanted more, like a coyote sniffing out a weakened deer, I wanted more on Nathan Faraway than I wanted to confess. I'd never admitted it to myself. I kept it pushed down like a nightmare, like some subterranean animal that wasn't supposed to show itself in the light of day, but here it was under these bright fluorescents, peaking its ugly head out of its hole, and I was finding it difficult to turn away.

But as much as I wanted it, now was not the time. I stood up and carefully slid my chair back under the table, looked at Ken, and motioned to the door. We walked out, not saying a word, and before I closed the door behind me, I saw Adam drop his head.

. . .

"What are we going to do?" Ken said when we returned to the observation room.

"I don't know. What do you think?"

"I don't know, but I don't think he's our man."

"Why? You fell for all that family bullshit?"

"No, it just looks like he's telling the truth. Look, the reason most cops don't interrogate their own family members is because they're likely to not go as hard on them, somehow convince themselves that their relative didn't do anything, didn't commit any crime. With you, man, it seems like the opposite. Are you sure you don't have him already tried and convicted of these murders just because he is your brother?"

I thought about it, ran my fingers through my hair, and rubbed my eyes. "Yeah, I see what you're saying. I'm sorry you had to sit through that."

"I had a feeling it might go to other matters."

"That's a nice way of putting it."

"So who's Nathan?"

"Old stuff," I said. "A friend from years back that went missing and was never found. I'll fill you more in later. It's not pertinent now. I shouldn't have gone there."

"You want to press charges for the assault?"

"No." I shook my head. "Let him go. If he's guilty of murder, something else will pop up and we can get him then."

"What if he runs?"

"Then we know he's guilty. Charging him now would only ensure he kept his mouth shut, just like Dorian did. If he's out there free, he might lead us to something else."

Ken sighed, pulled out a piece of gum from his pocket, and popped it in his mouth. I was relieved to see something habitual that I had gotten used to because the world looked different all of a sudden, like I had shifted a kaleidoscope slightly to the side for a different arrangement, a different pattern that still made no sense. "Will do, Officer," Ken said to me and walked out.

I stayed put staring at Adam. He had receded back into himself, his stare toward the wall, but a million miles away on absolutely nothing. His face was slightly turned to the side, and in that particular angle, I realized his profile—the high, sharp cheekbone, the shape of the chin—resembled mine and our dad's. We were definitely related. I turned away, began to get ready to leave, wondering who the hell my brother was and who the hell he'd become—some odd mixture of brawn, anger, and his own brand of ethics. The question of whether or not he was trying to make his way in the world in a less than lethal way than I'd originally thought was plaguing my mind as I slipped out of the station into a soft pattering of rain that had moved into the valley.

46

I COULDN'T GO RIGHT home. My mind buzzed with thoughts of Adam and I felt completely revved up. First, I sat silently in my car, the droplets of rain collecting softly on the windshield and the street lights shining in the dampness of the pavement.

Columbia Falls was quiet and ghostly with only a few stray cars passing on the main drag. I wanted someplace busier, someplace with energy and laughter to shift my mind from the degree of self-loathing I was feeling for getting into it with Adam over family nightmares in front of Ken. Deep down, I was frustrated that I couldn't pinpoint whether my brother was a sociopathic lying murderer or a person who'd changed, adjusted, and grown up enough to get by in the world— someone who could still throw a good punch or hold a good headlock, but in general had moved beyond the disturbing acts of hurting others to prop himself up to higher self-importance.

I felt like an amateur because I couldn't tell. I'm sure any psychologist would tell me that the ambivalence about a sociopath is part of the process, that it's exactly what sociopathic individuals work to achieve— the illusion that they're good deep down and capable of change. They play on your own gullibility, your own belief and optimism that people you care about deserve a chance. They prey on your refusal to understand that people like my brother might just be made that way, and all the help in the world wouldn't make a difference in the long run.

I told myself I knew better than to be fooled. Sure, we were letting him go for now, but if he'd done it, I was more determined than ever to find out. I started my car and drove to Whitefish where I knew more people would be out and about the touristy town. It was going on one a.m., and I figured I had enough time just for my usual two drinks—enough to settle my nerves so I didn't have to go stare at the blank walls of my dorm, unable to find sleep and thinking of Adam, my dad, my mother, Lara, and all the things this case had brought up out of nowhere.

It was as if this case was a prism, through which collections of translucent images from my past were being filtered, tossed about, and doled out to me. It made my head spin and weakened my reasoning. I refused to let that happen. I had worked too hard to get to this point. It was important that I remained calm, relaxed even, but even more precise in my moves from here on out. I didn't want to go to a bar because I was interested in drinking: this would be no repeat of my stint following the reunion. I simply had no desire to be in my dorm alone. I craved normalcy, some smiling people—not so much to engage with them, just to be around them so that I could relax and, hopefully, think clearly.

The Snow Ghost Bar and Grill was busier than I expected and, with its golden evening lighting, looked more inviting than it did when I met the veterinarian, Dr. Pritchard, for lunch in the middle of the afternoon with only the sunlight from the front windows streaming in to illuminate the lounge. About half the tables were occupied and the bar was still lined with people, just as I had hoped. Will was working, serving drinks to the patrons lined before him. I found a seat at an empty table not far from the bar and ordered a beer from the cocktail waitress. I thought of Gretchen, halfway wished she was with me to go over the case. I wanted to ask her about the trace elements in the car, but would have to wait until morning. She didn't need to be woken up in the middle of the night with questions from me.

I was sitting near a young couple that were crooning and melting into one another. Beside them sat a wiry and white-haired man hunched over a glass of whiskey, definitely looking like he shouldn't drive. I hoped he was within walking distance to wherever he was headed after closing. Two red-faced men farther down the bar were arguing over politics with big gestures and loud voices. A round table was full of garrulous middle-aged women and some low, throbbing music droned in the background. I sat back in my chair and watched everyone, trying to shed the evening's events.

When the cocktail waitress brought me my draft, I thanked her and started up some small talk, asking her about her summer, where she was from, and whatnot. It felt good to act like everything was normal, like I was just some visiting tourist and that I hadn't just interrogated my own brother in a jail room. She said her name was Lindsay, and she wore a tank top, her shoulders sunburned as if she'd been out playing on the lake or up in the mountains all day.

"You've been busy tonight?" I asked her.

"Yeah, always this time of the year. It'll slow down for just a few weeks in the shoulder season, but even that's getting smaller and smaller these days."

The drunk from the bar stood up and staggered toward us. "I'd like another," he slurred to Lindsay. "Will won't serve me."

"Mr. Talbert, you're going to have to stop now. It's close to last call."

He looked at her with the confused face of a drunk—one I'd recognize anywhere—for a moment, shrugged, then stumbled off to the bathroom.

"Poor guy. He lives nearby." She shook her head sadly. "He's lonely. Gets drunk a lot. His son's a bartender here, so he comes in quite a bit even though it drives him crazy."

"His son works here?" I asked.

"Yeah, Will." She motioned to the bar.

"Yeah, I know Will. I thought his last name was DeMarcus?"

"Yeah, it is." She shrugged. "Not sure how that works. You better drink that one quickly if you want to get another in before last call."

"Thank you," I said. "That probably won't be a problem." I watched her saunter off to the next table, a tingling sensation starting in my arms and spreading to my fingers. I've read that some creative people, like painters, musicians, or writers, claim that halfway into their paintings, songs, or stories, it is almost no longer their piece, and that some greater energy or muse takes over—that the painting almost paints itself, and the song or story nearly writes itself.

Now, I'm not pretending that solving a case is some creative process; quite the opposite. It involves fact-finding and plenty of objective thinking, but when a case begins to come together, begins to make sense, there is a similarity to other creative endeavors. I experienced it as a game warden, as Park Police, and on the Lance case while working with Systead. At some point, all the cogs begin to rotate as one. Information that feels like it's free-floating suddenly finds gravity and pulls together into something that makes sense. Clues fall seemingly out of nowhere right into your lap and eventually, order emerges.

It feels like sheer coincidence, but perhaps it's just the power of the brain—subconscious parts leading you to a particular clue or spot that your mind has been dwelling on and steering you toward anyway, so that when the hint pops up right in front of you, it feels like luck . . . like the detective angels are out there looking out for you, when, really, your own mind has been setting you up for a break all along.

I sat and took a long gulp and as I set my beer down, I went through the files I'd researched earlier in my head. Names flashed through my mind: Jonathon Fieldland from Seattle, Zachary Gentry from Missoula, Paul something or other from Syracuse . . . a Bradley Talbert from Kalispell, Montana. I left my drink on the table and went to the men's room. Mr. Talbert, apparently Will's father, stumbled out of the bathroom stall and went to the sink and clumsily turned on the water. He looked in the mirror at himself, squinting, trying to make sense of his own sagging face.

He reached for the soap, but couldn't figure out where the push lever to dispense it was located, so I reached over. "Here, let me help you there."

He looked at me, that same baffled look, his eyes trying to catch some purchase, then muttered, "Uh thanks."

"Are you Mr. Talbert?"

"Yeah, that's me."

"Are you Will's father?"

He squinted at me, one eye completely closing, then began to laugh, his head swaying on his shoulders.

"You'd have t' ash him," he said, then stumbled out of the bathroom. "He'd say no."

I pushed the lever on the soap dispenser and watched the pink liquid trickle down onto my palm. I figured it had been purchased in bulk, which, in and of itself, meant practically nothing since—I was also certain—a hundred other restrooms open to the public used the same type. But I couldn't help think about what Gretchen had told me—that a residue of a commercial-grade soap was found under Phillips's nails. I wiped it off my hand, grabbed my phone, and dialed Gretchen's number, waking her up after all. She answered with a groggy voice, "Monty?"

"Yeah, hi. Sorry to wake you, but I need a favor. Can you look online to see if a Brad and Will DeMarcus underwent any name changes and call me back with what you find? I wouldn't call you this late if it weren't important."

I went back out and sat down with my half-empty glass of beer, and eyed it suspiciously. I got out my smartphone again and pulled up the Internet. Sometime last year, I recalled that there'd been a few incidents in the town of Whitefish where several women had claimed they'd been slipped Rohypnol, the date-rape drug, while out at some of the local bars. If I remembered correctly, the date-rape drugs, specifically Rohypnol and GHB, were difficult to detect in a normal autopsy, much less a body that had been decomposing outside and fed upon. And even the full-panel toxicity test Wilson had sent to the lab, which took four to six weeks to get back, might not show the drug. For Phillips, Gretchen had said there had been no sign of struggle, a low level of alcohol, and residue from a type of commercial soap. I searched until I found the article, but it didn't mention the name of the bars suspected.

I took my beer with me to the end of the bar farthest from the men still talking too loudly and leaned into it with one elbow, motioning to Will. He looked around, then came over. "Hey, Will," I said.

"Hi," he said. "You need a drink?"

"Nah." I held up my beer, the amber liquid rich in the light of the bar. "I'm still good."

Will picked up an empty to the side of me and put it in a tray full of other dirties.

"I wanted to ask you," I said. "Did your last name used to be Talbert?"

He looked at me and blinked several times, one of the obnoxious men laughing boisterously and saying something to Will. "They're calling me," he said. "Just a minute."

"Will," I said, catching him before he slid off. "I'm just wondering—the man over there." I pointed to Mr. Talbert now studying something in his empty glass, his head bent over it like a broken-stemmed bud. "He says you're related."

Will shook his head. "He's a crazy ol' man," he mumbled as he scooted off down the bar.

I waited for him to serve each of the men down the bar another beer, then called him over again, but he either legitimately couldn't hear me or was acting like he couldn't, so I moved closer and leaned in further. "Will," I said.

The expression on his face said he was annoyed to be bothered.

"Your brother, Brad," I said firmly. "Did he go to Glacier Academy?"

Will frowned, deeply furrowing his brow. "What?"

"Did Brad go to Glacier Academy?"

"Why?"

"I was just wondering if—"

Lindsay, the cocktail waitress, walked up and called out for two glasses of the Trouchard and a vodka martini with extra olives for the cackling table of ladies.

"'Scuse me," Will said. "I'm busy here." He hustled to the other end of the bar before I got out another word.

I walked back to my seat and studied him. After Will filled the wine and made the martini, he said something to Lindsay as she stood holding the tray of drinks. They were nearly arguing, then Will walked into the back room and she looked confused and a little angry. I put a ten on the table and went up to her. "Excuse me, Lindsay." I waved her over.

She came and I said, "Is everything okay with Will?"

"Yeah sure." She shrugged. "I mean. I guess so. He doesn't usually leave before closing, but whatever. Can I get you another beer?"

"No, I'm good. I left some money on the table. Any idea where he went?"

She shook her head, "Just said he needed to leave. Wants me to close up."

My radar shot up. I walked out the front, the only exit available to the patrons, and went around the block to where the back employee entrance was. It was dark and empty. I scanned the parking lot directly behind it for anyone getting into their car or leaving, but saw no one, just a couple giggling as they walked down the sidewalk. Will had either headed home on foot or had already pulled away.

I went to my car and got my gun out of the trunk, where I'd locked it before going in, and drove the few blocks to Will's apartment complex toward the railroad district. The windows of his apartment were dimly lit. Either Will had left a light on or he'd already arrived. I sat and watched for a moment, trying to see movement in the apartment, and also kept one eye on the street for anyone walking up on foot until my phone buzzed.

I picked it up. "What did you find?"

"That Willem's and Bradley's birth certificates show that they were born twins on April eleventh in Kalispell to an Ericka and Ray Talbert. At twenty-two, both Willem and Bradley Talbert changed their names to Willem and Bradley DeMarcus, the same as their mother and stepfather. Ericka married John DeMarcus in 1990 when the boys were nine."

I thanked Gretchen and told her I had a strong hunch, and that I was going to question Will DeMarcus again and would call her back as soon as I knew more. The fact that Will's brother was also at Glacier Academy, and had worked for Wolfie before committing suicide was interesting. It didn't mean Will murdered anyone, but I wanted to check it out, especially since Will left the bar early after he saw me there.

I drove and parked outside the apartment complex, just as Ken and I had done before, and peered up at the windows of his unit. I waited, watching for movement to see if he was inside, but I didn't see anything. I got out, tucked my gun away, locked the car, and went up the stairs and peeked inside the window. The light was coming from the hallway, but other than that, it didn't look like Will was home.

I knocked on the door, but no one came, then checked through the window again, still not seeing any sign of him. I went back down the stairs thinking I'd have to come back in the morning to talk to him. What I had learned was suspicious and interesting, but not enough to get a warrant. I strode through the shadowed street and went back to my car. My thoughts returned to Adam, and I wondered if Adam had known Bradley DeMarcus. I tried to remember the dates that Bradley was at Glacier Academy, and thought I recalled that it was several years later than Adam's stay, but that didn't mean they didn't have a connection. I dug in my pocket for my keys as I got to my car, thoughts of Adam still plaguing me, and just as I was about to open my door, I heard the click of a gun safety unlatching by my right ear.

"Stop," he said, "and hold your hands up."

I could see a man's reflection in my car window and was sure it was Will. My heartbeat shot up and I cursed myself for not being more on guard. His voice sounded strained, slightly shaky. His 9 millimeter was pointing no more than five inches from my head.

"Hold it," I said, shaking my head and raising my hands as he instructed. "Don't pull that trigger, Will. It's Will, right?" I looked slightly to my right, and out of the corner of my eye, I could see his face. I could sense fear in him, and I felt a solid dose of intense terror shoot through myself. Fear could be good or it could be really bad; scared-shitless people made for jittery fingers. People pulled triggers because they felt power doing so, or because they were angry or scared and had snapped. Or because they felt nothing at all, as if they were simply playing a video game and pulling the trigger gave them a rush. Will, he felt things, I could tell by the sweat gathering on his temple, the strain in his eyes, and the quiver on his lip.

"Will," I said as calmly as I could muster. "You need to point that someplace else. Point it at the ground." I could hear his breathing, shallow and shaky—almost staccato.

"Don't look at me. Face the car." The voice was rising. I hoped like hell someone from one of the apartments would look out and call for help. I did what he said and looked forward, back into the reflection of the car window.

"He deserved it. He hurt my brother. He *raped* my brother."

I was going to ask who, but was afraid I'd interrupt his train of thought. "I'm sure he did a lot of things," I said, still facing the driver's door of my car. "Let's drop the weapon and talk about it." My head felt light. I knew it was the adrenaline mixed with the sharp stab of fear.

"He'd come in all smug into my bar after his hikes," Will continued. "Like he was some mountain man, at one with nature, healthy and fit as can be—his own body a temple. As if he'd never hurt a soul. Talking about his hikes and all the peaks he'd bagged like they were badges of honor, and he was some hero."

"We could have arrested him for what he did to your brother if you'd gone to the police."

"No, it was years ago." I could see in the reflection that he was moving his head in small, frantic shakes. "Didn't know about it until it was too late. Until after Bradley had killed himself. Now it's too late for you. I didn't want it to come to this, just like I didn't want—" He stopped himself.

"Didn't want what?"

"Nothing," he said.

"For Wolfie to die?"

"You need to shut up now," he said.

"If you kill me, you'll go to jail."

"Not if no one knows. Not if I take you to the woods, and they never find you."

"People know I'm here—that I've come to see you." I considered my options. I could elbow him, but the safety was off, and one quick move might make him fire. I could inform him that I was slowly going to turn toward him, so that he could see my face. It always made it harder to shoot when you looked into someone's eyes, and he was obviously wanting to talk, needed to justify his actions. Facing him would give me more options.

"You're lying. No one knows, and if they do, it's a chance I'll have to take." Will's hand was beginning to shake, but he kept the gun pointed right at my temple.

"I'm not lying. Look," I said, my hands still up. "I'm just going to slowly turn toward—" and then I felt the hard steel of the gun come crashing down on my head, felt my legs go instantly numb and weak, and my body crumble as the colors before my eyes went from pinkish red and gray to black.

. . .

My limbs still felt numb. Everything seemed smeared together in my head, which seared with pain, but I tried to get control of my thoughts—tried to remember who I'd been talking to and why, and where I was, but all the answers seemed to be swirling outside my head, just out of reach. The vision in my right eye was fuzzy. I felt rough carpet underneath me, and heard the hum of a motor. I realized I was in a trunk, and the car was moving. I felt terror rise up in me, flood into my head, which already was hurting like hell.

I inhaled thick dust and felt the vibration and bounce of a rough road below me. We were on gravel. Maybe a logging road.

The bartender. Will had hit me, I remembered. Will had put me in a trunk, and now we were heading somewhere. I tried to think through the fog, but I had no idea because everything, including my panic, was swimming away as raw streaks wormed into my vision and made everything dissolve to black again.

47

I woke up, this time clearer, and I was still cramped in the trunk. My trunk, I thought, because the shape, the carpet, and the sound of the motor all seemed familiar. Still driving, but now on smooth, paved road. The same paralyzing fear overtook me. We were heading somewhere where it was very dark. My knees were tight against my chin, and my wrists were bound before my stomach. I could feel them chafing and swelling against the tight ropes, but at least they weren't behind my back. The muscles on my neck ached, my head was still throbbing as if it had been split down the center, and a pain pulsed down my curled spine.

I tried to piece the night back together again—Adam, Ken, the police station, Adam's cabin, the bartender, the Snow Ghost. It was coming back. I had had a beer. I had noticed that Will's father had a different name than DeMarcus. I had phoned Gretchen to ask about a Mr. Talbert.

Lying in the trunk while the car rolled along, one of the panels hot against my side, I remembered telling Will that I was going to slowly turn to face him, and that's when it all had gone black. With my bound wrists and my elbows jammed into my stomach, I tried to wedge my arms to my side so my hands could pat my pocket. I couldn't feel my cell phone. I knew he'd taken my gun as well because I couldn't feel it against my waist. I ran through the time I had spent in the bar, going over what had made it obvious to Will that I was on to him—or at least suspicious, and wondered if it was when I followed his drunk father into the men's room.

371

Whatever it was, this much I knew: Will had killed Mark Phillips because Will's brother, Bradley, had been hurt by Phillips. *He raped my brother* rang in my ears. I knew this as well: Will planned to take me somewhere and dump me over a cliff, just as he had done with Phillips. Just as he might have done with Wolfie, and judging by the curve of the road and the feel of the pavement, it was going to be very close to the others, if not exactly the same—the Loop. I knew better than anybody how empty the Going-to-the-Sun Road was in the middle of the night. We had been on gravel earlier, so if I was correct that we were now on the Going-to-the-Sun highway, it meant we took the unpaved North Fork Road to the north entrance with no cameras.

It had to be three a.m. Even in the middle of tourist season in Glacier Park, it was highly unlikely anyone would be passing by. People needing to travel from east of the Divide to west of the Divide in the middle of the night were not tourists. They would be people trying to get somewhere and that meant taking Highway 2. During the day in the middle of summer, Going-to-the-Sun was no place for solitude, but in the middle of the night, it was a different story. Nobody was coming to help.

I heard no sound coming from the car besides the motor, no radio, no talking. It had to be only Will. No accomplice. I remembered thinking of Adam as I was walking to my car and felt sick to my stomach that I'd been obsessing about him. Had I not had such tunnel vision, maybe I would have taken Will more seriously, maybe I would have felt him behind me—a shift of air or a soft footstep, my flesh prickling with instinct and making me turn and pull my weapon.

I forced myself to stop it. Now was not the time for second-guessing. I took a shallow, shaky breath and played it out it my head. Will would open the trunk, force me to awkwardly climb out with my hands and feet bound, holding the gun to my head. He'd still be nervous, though. I could sense that he wasn't a killer by nature. He was scared, didn't know what else to do, like a man who accidentally killed his girlfriend in a fit of rage. Will was afraid of jail, and if I were to guess, Will didn't want to kill me. He just felt cornered and was afraid of getting caught. My only chance was to make the most of that fear.

Beneath me, the car slowed and took what felt like a 180-degree turn. I knew we had just rounded the hairpin curve of the Loop. Then we parked, and adrenaline shot through me. Suddenly, a flush of images reminded me why I wanted to stay alive: Lara, with her delicate fingers and large eyes, Gretchen, luminous and glowing, smiling; Adam, angry and sneering, perhaps human after all; my job in the Crown Jewel of the Continent. Maybe I didn't have kids to fight for, or maybe I'd found some type of false sense of order in my tidiness and diligence, as Lara implied, but at least it kept me from drifting aimlessly. In Glacier, in my job, I belonged, and not as a dead corpse at the bottom of a ravine, but as an officer and a detective. I would fight for it.

I was in a full sweat when I heard the engine cut, the jangle of the keys, and the driver's door click open. Will's footsteps, crunching on the pavement, sounded like a hundred small shuffles. He was nervous, I thought, and wanted to get this over with.

The trunk suddenly popped open, and I could feel an instant cool mountain breeze wash over me. I'd have known the smell of Glacier Park anywhere—the resin of pine, the chilled sighs from the mountains, the sound of roaring water in the distance.

I saw a thick band of dark clouds from the earlier rain captured by the tall mountains and a partial moon straight above me shining a pale, very dim light on Will. I was right, his gun was pointing down at me. "Get out," he said.

I tried to steady my shaking and did as he said—made my awkward climb out of the trunk, with my hands bound before me and my ankles tied. The car swayed when I sat up, and I saw it was my car, which made sense. It would be easier to throw me in my own trunk than drag me down the sidewalk to a different vehicle. I realized this as I accidentally knocked the crown of my head again on the inside of the hood. I reflexively tried to lift my hands, but couldn't get them very high up with the ropes around my wrists. "Will, listen to me. I wasn't lying when I said someone knows I was onto you. Look at my cell phone. Check the log. I made some calls to find out why you and your brother's names were different from your dad's."

"Don't call him my dad. He's not my dad. He's just some drunk. Get out. Now."

I swung my legs over the edge to the ground.

"Hurry."

"Sorry," I said. "Will, how many are you going to toss over the edge? You think this stops with killing a police officer? No. Then, it gets even crazier."

"They won't know you've been killed. Another accident. *If* they even find you, they'll think you were up at the scene of the crime and while investigating, you fell. Just like the others."

"No, no they won't. Three bodies—one particular area? Radar goes way up. *Way* up. When it was just Wolfie, maybe, but after we found Phillips, full-blown investigation. With the guy doing the investigation added to that count, we're talking special agents from the department."

"Quit talking and walk." He shoved me toward the cliff near the road. "I'm not going to have you go down in the same spot anyway. This will be a different spot. Better. Can't see down the ravine from the road or trail. No one's going to find you."

"But I'll be missing and they'll know you were the last person I was looking into."

"Stop, just stop talking," he yelled, his voice frantic. A bubble of hope rose in me that he would not be entirely in control. Then again, frantic people did frantic things. One quick shove and it could be over. An acidic taste formed at the back of my throat and for a moment— piggybacking on one of the crisp breezes brushing across the parking lot—I thought I smelled the scent of fear that I always linked to my mother.

Coyotes began to yip in the distance, and he pushed me again. I shimmied in very small steps toward the trail where he led me, the gun at my back. My boots scuffled on the lumpy trail while the vocal call of the coyotes ripped through the canyon. Fear clogged and pounded into my chest. If I let him lead me to the edge and he pushed me over, I would die instantly, snapping against the rocks just as Phillips and Wolfie had—my broken, lifeless body relaxing into scree or maybe some stream, disintegrating into the earth while the world continued on. I'd seen it too many times already. I couldn't let him get me to the edge, but I couldn't try to juke or shove him with my body either. He was scared but still in control. One pull of the trigger and I was dead.

"Hurry," he said again. I could hear, even feel, his heavy and fast breathing against the back of my neck.

"If you take the ropes off my ankles, I can walk normally."

"Not going to happen. Keep going," he said.

He was right. He was leading me to a different area, just off the Loop and far away from the wildlife camera, but around the bend so no one could see it from the road. "When I go missing," I began again, "they'll retrace my steps. They'll go to the bar, they'll ask Lindsay if I was in for a beer. She'll tell them you left early and that I asked about that. What? You going to shove her off the cliff too? And my car. You just going to drive it back to Whitefish, for God's sake?"

"I'll deal with it."

"But they've probably already got someone looking—"

"Stop," he yelled at me again and pushed me off the trail toward an outcropping of rock.

I was getting to him. I forced myself to keep talking. "They'll look through my files. They'll see I was investigating Glacier Academy—they'll see the names of all the boys I'd researched, including your brother."

"Don't talk about my brother anymore. Just keep moving," he said, and shoved me in the back. I went flying forward, stumbling over an exposed root, my face smashing into prickly brush and sharp stones. I could feel a searing pain on my cheekbone and dirt smeared before one of my eyes. I gulped for air and turned and looked at him. My vision had blurred on one side, but I could see he was cupping his head with his hands. "Just *stop* talking!"

I clumsily got back up on my feet into a crouch position. A wet trail of blood rolled down my cheek and I could taste the grit of dirt in my mouth.

Will continued to cup one hand over his left ear and pointed the gun at me with the other. His free hand started pulling at his wiry hair. "Just shut up, will you?"

I slowly stood up.

"I didn't want this," he yelled. "I didn't *want* that biologist to die, but he had that damn film. He and that guy Ward, they came in for a beer and were talking about the wolverines, about the camera and how the one was going to go up and get it and the other was going to replace the cartridge for him over the weekend. I don't believe in coincidences. They came to my bar to talk about that for a reason. The universe was protecting me, telling me I'd done the right thing with Phillips, and now I just needed to get the film. It took me hours to find it, but I finally did, and—" Will shook his head in quick, jerky movements. "He shouldn't have fought me over it. He was stupid. He should have left me alone when he found me at the camera."

"But it was his film. His camera. He needed it."

"I didn't *mean* for it to happen. It was unlucky, but that's how it happened. I had no choice and then you came sniffing around."

"I only wanted what's right, Will. That's all I've ever wanted." And when I said it, I knew it was true—could hear the sincerity in my own voice. It really is all I ever wanted—a sense of fairness, a sense of order.

"What's right? As if that's something people can just *have*! As if *what's right* is a car or something you can own. If we could have rightness in this world, my brother would be alive today. People like Phillips wouldn't be on this planet if we could have what's fucking *right*. Bottom line is that sometimes to do what's right, you have to do what's wrong."

"Will," I said. "My brother was sent to Glacier Academy too."

He froze for a second. "You're lying."

"No, no. I'm not. His name is Adam, and he was hurt by Phillips too. I just found out—just like you said you did—that things did not go well for him there." I had Will's attention. I could see his head tilt with curiosity in the diffuse moonlight. "You know what he said? You know what he said when he found out that Phillips was dead? He said he deserved it. Said it served him right."

Will was looking at me confused, trying to tell if I was making it up or not.

"I swear, man. I'm not lying. Phillips and his gang—they took him out to the woods, had him tied up. They did stuff to him. I can understand you wanting to hurt him. When I found out, man, if he wasn't already dead, I would have wanted the same. But this stuff, it was years ago."

The anger was falling away from Will's eyes, and they got large and sad, full of a thick, palpable despair, the kind I'd only ever seen before in my mother's. "He was my twin," he mumbled. "You have any idea what it's like to lose your twin? It's like half of you is ripped away. And Phillips, he did shit. He hurt him. I found the letters."

"What letters?"

"From his girlfriend, telling him how sorry she felt for him because of all that Phillips did. How awful it must have been. I found 'em after it was too late. In his stuff in his apartment. And after he lost his job working for those researchers, he got severe. He got"—Will shook his head—"unreachable. But it wasn't the researchers' fault. Phillips made it all worse, so much worse. If he'd gotten treatment when he was young instead of getting abused . . ." Will's eyes pleaded for me to understand as his voice trailed off.

"I can imagine," I said. "Why weren't you at the camp?"

"Me?" He looked confused for a moment to be asked such a personal question, as if it was fair game to talk about everyone but himself, but then he answered. "I was fine back then. I was normal growing up. It was my brother who was depressed and moody. He's the one who started doing drugs, talked about suicide, skipped school all the time. . . . My mom and stepdad thought it would help him. And it should have. That's the whole point." Will's voice began to rise again.

"I understand, Will. I do. My brother, he was there because he was a bully and messed up on drugs too, but he didn't deserve that either." It was important for me to diffuse the hate and the zealotry behind his eyes that would justify the shove. "He was there for treatment, but he got very little of that," I continued. "I can understand *wanting* to hurt a guy like Phillips—even kill him—get a guy like him off this planet so he doesn't hurt others."

Will gave me a solemn nod, listening, captivated by what I was saying. The coyotes still called in the far distance, their yips growing fainter. They were moving away from the park, away from wolf territory. "Wolfie," I said. "I can see that that was just collateral damage—a bad thing that wasn't supposed to happen, but bad things happen in this world, Will. Right? Bad things happen?"

"That's what I said. That's exactly what I said. But now it's too late, and another bad thing *has* to happen." What I could make out of his expression in the darkness appeared transformed into something distorted and unrecognizable. In the force of his voice, I could sense righteousness straddling on his sadness and fear. On some level, Will felt justified that he had made the world a better place by killing Mark Phillips.

"No, no, it doesn't. You can still have a normal life."

"Don't be talking to me about prison. Don't even say it." He shook his head emphatically side to side.

"Okay, okay," I said. "It would just be for a while. You'd get out. People get out; they lead normal lives again."

"No, no, no, no, no . . . ," he muttered, still shaking his head rhythmically. "In prison, they're all like Phillips. No, no, no, no, no . . . ," he kept murmuring.

"Will, you need help."

"No," he screamed at the top of his lungs, ceasing his murmurs. His voice sliced the already chilled night like a blade of ice, echoing off the mountain ridges that reared up like humongous humpbacked monsters circling us, watching us. His voice rebounded back, streaking into me. An electric pulse burst through me, but I forced myself to stand still.

"Okay, okay." I held both my tied hands up. He was losing it. I knew I needed this conversation to end—the whole scene to change. In one swift move, I jammed my forearm and elbow up into his hand. The 9 millimeter catapulted through the air and to the side. I dived across the ground to grab it but felt prickly bushes and rock instead. Panic cut through me as I frantically began patting the rocky, brushy ground with whatever speed and agility I could manage with my hands tied.

Will fell to his knees beside me as I continued to search. All bets were off if Will got to it first. He shoved me to my side, toward the cliff's edge, and I fought to get back, pushing off my elbows, then onto my hands and knees and when my hand hit the ground below me, I felt the cold metal of the barrel. I instantly pulled it up and aimed it at him. "Stop," I yelled. "It's over."

Will froze in the dark, a silhouette on all fours like an animal.

"Will. It's over. I'm going to need you to lie on the ground and place your hands behind your head."

Will slowly stood up and I repeated my command. "Will," I yelled. "Get back on the ground on your stomach and put your hands behind your head."

Will's panting seemed to surround me, loud and expanding. His dark shape began to back away from me. I yelled, "Stop right there. Get on the ground, Will."

Will took two more steps back. He was right on the edge.

"Will," I heard my own voice like it wasn't mine. It sounded shrill and separate, like something that was part of the land, a tinny, fleeting breeze moving through the mountains. "I need you to stop right there. Got it? Stop right there. Look, I'm putting the gun down." I started to bend my knees, reaching for the ground with my tied wrists. I had no intention of letting it out of my hands, but I did not want Will to go over the edge. He killed two people, and I did not want to be the third. I kept my eyes on him and I wasn't sure if I was imagining it or not, but I could almost see his pale skin and the whites of his eyes in the dark. "Okay?" I said as smoothly as I could. "I'm going to put it down."

He was shaking his head again rhythmically, and there on the edge, although I knew he wasn't, it seemed to me that he had become Adam—his frame tall and sturdy, his shoulders broad, his person a split image—someone searching, wanting, and frail; but at the same time, someone solid and tough moving away, distancing. Jumping, falling. My mother's car hurtling down a ridge, steel slamming against rock, and the vehicle crashing into the river flashed in my mind for a split second.

"It's over," he whispered.

I almost didn't hear it, but then I saw his dark shape slide back. He took another large step backward, his body slipping over the rock, sliding back and over, his scream filling the night and becoming one with the faint call of the coyotes. I shot forward, flinging myself to the rock ledge, trying to catch some part of him—anything—an arm, a leg, his hair, but my hands caught nothing but the cool, pristine air and wet skunkweed. I stared at the edge, my chest heaving into the hard-edged rocky ground below me. I pushed myself up and scurried quickly to the side to try to see him, but I couldn't make out his body in the dark below. It was too far down and too steep.

I wildly untied the ropes around my ankles with jerky movements and ran back to the car, my legs feeling suddenly free without the binds. I tripped and catapulted over exposed roots and partially protruding rocks on the trail since my hands were still bound, and I couldn't use them for balance. I took gigantic gulps of the cool air as I ran, somehow managing to stay upright and making it to the parking lot without flailing face-first into the ground again. I opened the car, the artificial light flooding my eyes, which had become one with the pale and dim blue-white of the night. I instinctively squeezed them shut for a moment, then opened them and looked around. My cell phone, my keys, and my gun lay on the passenger seat. I found my MagLite in the glove box.

I picked up the phone and held it in my shaking hands and tried to call for help, even though I knew better. There was no cell reception in the heart of Glacier, and I had left my radio at the office. I ran back out to the spot Will went over without even turning on my flashlight. My eyes had readjusted to the meager blue light of the partial moon in the night within seconds. When I got to the spot, I turned the flashlight on and moved the beam over the ridge and to the ground below. All I could see was scree, rocks, and brush swaying in the breeze, but no Will. I ran over to another spot to get a different angle and tried again, but he had been right. There was no good vantage point to see below. Nobody would spot someone without knowing they had fallen. Nobody would have spotted me.

I felt a shiver run through me. I gulped the cold mountain air and repeated to myself that it was for the best—that he was a tortured soul and couldn't have lived with what he'd done. But I couldn't stop hearing the sound of Will's scream as air had blasted through his lungs and how all had gone silent except for the scuff of body and bone against hard rock, once, twice.

Then I heard a different howl, not the high strident coyote call, but an anguished moan—much closer and slowly rising, reverberating through the mountains, pitching up and up, corralling in my ears, pouring into me and expanding. I stood still listening to the wolves, my body quivering, my vision still a little blurred, and suddenly, as the wails became more numerous and lengthened, as they stretched and grew, I felt my chest well with pain—pain for Will's brother, for Will, for Adam, for Lara, for my father, for my mother, and for myself.

It wasn't just the ancient pull of sadness that had been with me since I was a boy, a sense that tragedy was never too far away; it was a lack of hope—something new, something I never let in. For me, no matter the dysfunction, there had always been an essential order to things, like the rise of the sun, the fall of the first snow, the budding

leaves of spring, the start of another school day, another workday . . .
and in that order, there was always hope that things would work out.
But now something heavy as wet sand sifted through me and washed
away the veneer I'd always shielded myself with, made me sense that
maybe things didn't really work out after all.

My legs buckled beneath me, and there among those unflinching
mountains, with the wolves howling their haunting, mournful song,
tears came to my eyes.

48

I WALKED BACK TO the car and collected my thoughts for a moment, figuring I would need to walk the nine miles down to Lake McDonald Lodge. Then I remembered that I had recently put the spare keys I usually kept at home in my console because I wanted to keep them at the office instead of my dorm since I now lived alone. I opened it up and saw them, let out a sigh of relief and with great trepidation since my wrists were still tightly bound, drove the dark and curvy, Going-to-the-Sun Road to Lake McDonald Lodge, where I rousted the front-desk help sleeping in the back office and called for emergency services.

· · ·

Ken gave me a ride back up and we watched the Search and Rescue helicopter make its way up Lake McDonald and through the mountains, its bright beams slicing across the dark mountainsides, turning swaths of trees blue and flattening the bear grass and other wild foliage. There was a very small chance that Will was still alive and injured at the bottom of the ravine, but I didn't hold out much hope. The wolves had stopped howling, and all was still but the raspy, choppy and obnoxious roar of the helicopter.

I was ordered to sit on the hood of my car, while a medic swabbed my face and told me I'd probably need stitches, and was not allowed to help in the retrieval even though I wanted to. Four other men performed it under the bright floodlights, just as Ken and I had done for Wolfie under the piercing sun two weeks ago. Two of the county officers, Walsh's men, were sent up to debrief me, get my statements, and go through all the formalities as soon as my wounds were cleaned and dressed.

Gretchen had called my phone numerous times when I had not called her back as I said I would. She had dressed and gone to Will's apartment after looking up his address, but didn't find my car. So after calling me several more times, she called the city police in for help. They had put out an APB for Will's vehicle and encouraged the police and local sheriff to stay on the lookout for my car, far away from the quiet, enveloping solitude of Glacier. When I called her back from the lodge after calling Ken and told her where I was and that Search and Rescue was on its way, she drove up.

"Are you okay?" she said, coming over to me while the medic, a guy named Warren, finished inspecting my eye. He smiled at Gretchen, then went a few yards away to grab some supplies.

"Yeah, I'm good. You shouldn't have come all the way up here."

"I wanted to," she said.

"Why?" I asked sincerely. It was clear we were becoming friends, but this woman had no obligation to me. She'd been my guardian angel through the whole case, and I had the sudden urge to know why. I wanted honesty. I didn't care that Warren was in earshot.

She looked away, then lifted a shoulder. "Gives me one more reason to say, 'You owe me,' Harris."

"I guess I'm racking up a long list of those." I was too exhausted to push it further.

"I guess you are." She gave me a smile that said she knew that whatever went down wasn't easy to witness. A pale-blue light was spreading a soft wave of early dawn over the mountaintops. The world was continuing on—the order of things forming again around me and in my mind.

I patted her hand. "Your smile," I said.

"What about it?" She brought her hand to her mouth, embarrassed.

"It's, well, it's luminous. Just as I remembered," I said, the emotion of it thick in my chest.

49

It was time to see Adam again, which would make for a total of four times in about half a decade, all of them in the last two weeks. I had always been wary about talking to him over the phone. It helped if I could see his facial expressions. I always felt at a complete disadvantage if I couldn't. I had no intention of being at a disadvantage with my brother ever again.

Nevertheless, I picked up my cell phone and I called him to find a voicemail that said, *You've reached Adam Harris with Harris Iron. Please leave your name and number and I will get back to you as soon as possible. Business hours are Monday through Friday from nine to five. Have a nice day.* It was odd to hear Adam's voice in that singsong professional tone. I looked up Harris Iron and found the address.

His business was wedged between two other shops on Highway 2 leading into Columbia Falls. It was a white Quonset hut with a fat turquoise stripe across its center and a wood-paneled front—I presumed to make it look more inviting—where the entry stood. I had no idea how long he had been working in the fabrication and forging business, but his lethal iron fire tools with the curlicue designs popped into my mind.

I entered the shop noticing that only Adam's Jeep was parked on the side of the shop. A bell on the door jangled when I opened it and an apropos, cacophonous heavy metal hit me. There was no way Adam could hear his door jingle with the music blaring. To my side was a counter with iron odds and ends scattered across it and behind the counter stood a bookshelf lined with catalogues of various designs for patio and stair railings, fence postings, gates, and more. Along the side wall were all sorts of iron implements hanging from hooks and piled on shelves, and in the far back were large storage boxes stacked and lined up.

Adam appeared from behind one of the rows of boxes, his muscled self standing taller and lifting his chin to see who stood at the front of his shop. He strode toward me and I could see his expression change from a tilted-head curiosity to a straight dead-on stare when he realized it was me. "I didn't hear you come in," he said.

I wanted to say, *Yeah, because you've got your music too loud*, but I didn't. I shrugged instead.

"What brings you here?" He walked to his counter and leaned against it, giving me a look that said I'd better make it quick so he could get back to work.

"This your business?"

"Yes."

"How long you been in it?"

"One year. Been trying to buy the building from the guy."

"That why you need money?"

"Maybe," he said.

"Why didn't you just say that was the reason?"

"I did say it was business. Why do I need to explain myself?"

"Why do you need to tell the bank why you need a loan?" I asked rhetorically. "Why does anyone need to explain themselves in the world in order to progress?"

"Maybe I don't play it like everyone else plays it." Adam gave me his signature stance, folding both arms across his chest, armoring himself up.

I wanted to say, *Obviously you don't*, but again, kept it to myself. I wasn't here to argue. "I came to tell you that we solved the case."

His eyes widened, and he reached under his counter and instantly the music's volume went soft. "That so?"

"Yeah, last night. It'll be in the paper soon."

Adam narrowed his eyes at me and nodded slowly, then gave me a cold grin, smug that it had been proven that it wasn't him.

"I visited Dad," I said.

"And?"

"And the same. Tracy and her family are still there. Seth still completely worthless except for some half-ass lawn work he's been doing."

"I know," he said. "Dad's back any better?"

"I guess. Yeah, but you know him, just as soon as it gets better, it'll get worse again."

"Eh, right about that," he said with an expression of nonchalance and a personal knowledge of a been-there, done-that-myself addict, as if our father's back pain was one and the same as his drinking problem, and Adam was at peace with it. I'd like to say the same for myself, but not sure I could.

A part of me figured I owed him an apology for interrogating him and another part of me didn't. I was doing my job, and he tackled me. I looked around the shop, the ubiquitous pieces of iron looking suddenly menacing. "Last night," I said. "You said something about a river."

Again, he smiled coldly.

"I feel like I remember condensation from water, but I don't remember the river. The cemetery was a good mile or two from the river." I was referring to the Flathead River cutting through Columbia Falls.

"It was nothing." He waved one hand in the air. "It was a long time ago. We were young. I've probably mentioned the river before, back then." His stare was cold.

I took that in. "So did you go by the river that night?'

Adam shook his head and shrugged, saying nothing.

I decided whether to push it further. I chose my words carefully. "That night," I continued. "Did you see Nathan again, after you left us?"

Adam held my gaze for another moment, then picked up a curled piece of iron that appeared to fit on the tip of an interior staircase railing and fiddled with it in one hand. "I was just messin' with you last night. I was angry. Can you blame me?"

I lifted a shoulder. Had he controlled his anger, we could have avoided taking him to the station in cuffs.

"You should let bygones be bygones, Monty."

"You're not going to answer me?"

Adam set the piece back on the counter. "I really need to get back to work. Got about ten different builders needing jobs done. Like yesterday."

I knew he'd give me nothing now. I nodded, then turned and headed for the door.

"Thanks," Adam said as I put my hand on the handle. "For letting me know you got the guy."

"You're welcome." I turned back.

"I appreciate it," he added.

"Yeah, well, after last night, it's the least I could do."

"I really do appreciate it," he repeated.

I looked at him, then beyond him to his shop. A bronze glint of early evening sun was shining through the back windows and shedding light on the sidewall of the shop, making the iron gleam yellow. I pictured my dad's timber-framed house in the hills and Adam striving to build his business. *He had built it. He had skills.* I looked back at him. That sliver of fragility I was getting used to crossed his face like a flicker of light. Then he smiled, not in a smug way, but genuinely. It brought to mind a vision of Adam at the counter of the hardware store, holding up the new dog collar he'd just purchased, and a big grin spread across his face—real, and, actually, innocent.

"Guess I'll go then," I said tipping my head and opening the door. I stepped out into the warm evening and walked to my car.

· · ·

By the time I finished the rest of my paperwork and drove across the river and swung left to head to the cemetery, the sun still hung high in the sky.

After a span of winding road, I slowed down and noticed a dark green field of alfalfa adjacent to it that wasn't previously there. If I re-membered correctly, the field used to be wheat. The other side of the cemetery still butted up against the woods leading toward Teakettle Mountain. I parked and got out and began walking its edge toward the large maple tree and the darker forest behind. Even in the bright of day with the new addition of the alfalfa field and its expansive sprin-kler system, the cemetery—with its dried and tangled weeds and lanky leftover wheat that had migrated into it—still had a forgotten and spooky feel, as if it was miles from anywhere and severed from the nearby town and busy highway of cars heading to and from the canyon that led to the park.

The place was deserted. I stopped and just stood and watched the breeze sweep graceful waves through the golden leftover wheat. It was quiet, except for the distant sound of a train and the hum of a tractor most likely working some field a good stretch away.

I looked back to my car parked on the gravel road. That had been the road we'd driven up, the five of us: Adam, Perry, Todd, Nathan, and me. As a sixteen year-old, Adam was already well muscled and towered above my small, twelve-year-old frame, and he and his buddies would laugh loud and raucously like they owned Montana, owned the world.

We were in an old red Pontiac, a gearshift between the two front seats. Perry was driving. Adam was on the passenger side and Todd was next to me. Nathan was on my right, leaving me squeezed in the middle. Nathan and I were quiet as we listened to my brother and his friends talk boisterously, swearing and laughing, amped up with all their newfound testosterone and manliness.

They were drinking beer and Adam turned around, and said, "You want some?"

Nathan's eyes slid to me, and I looked at the floor and shook my head. We had been in this situation before, and it was always the same stupid joke—Adam or one of his buddies offering us a drink they knew we didn't want. Nathan and I had talked about it—that neither one of us had any desire to join them, that we were smarter than that and wouldn't do the stupid things they did. When we said no, the three of them usually howled with laughter, thinking Adam was the funniest guy in the world for offering alcohol to us peons.

But this time was different. Adam's voice was nice, and no one laughed.

"Aw, come on," Perry said. "It's not going to kill ya. Gotta grow up sometime." Perry's voice was on the pleasant side too.

I kept my eyes forward on the gravel road, bone-white in the head-lights fanning across them. I felt something soften inside me. Things were never that simple. In spite of how much I knew my brother was ca-pable of, I still had a strong urge ticking away inside of me, wanting to fit in, desperately wanting to feel like a part of something, like I belonged for a change. All it took for me to be drawn to the light like a moth was a little sweetness in their voices instead of the usual obnoxious teasing. "Okay, yeah," I finally said. "I'll try it." I didn't dare look at Nathan, but felt his hip next to me shift, maybe his body stiffening. I knew he'd be angry, that I was betraying us somehow—as if we'd made a pact—even though we hadn't. We'd just talked about how stupid they were.

Adam handed his can of Coors back to me, and I hesitated for a second before grabbing it. A tear in the vinyl seat pinched the side of my hip. He continued to hold it out, canting it toward me to urge me to take it. Without looking at Nathan, I reached out quickly to grab it and put it to my lips, tilting it slowly up and letting the lukewarm liquid pour into my mouth. I swallowed and scrunched up my face in distaste. It was bitter and not good—like tasting dirty socks—like something was wrong with it, but I intuitively knew that nothing had gone wrong with it because it matched the smell of the beer my father drank every night and the way his breath smelled after a few. I also instinctively knew that even though I didn't like the taste or the way it made my throat feel, if I kept drinking it, eventually I would get used to it, maybe even begin to like it. I was certain that that was what Adam, Perry, and Todd had done, and probably even my dad when he was my age.

"How is it?" Perry asked.

"Fine," I said after swallowing loudly. I handed it back to Adam, and all of three of them laughed, then Todd belched obnoxiously and the three broke into an even louder howl.

"Damn straight." Adam held his can up like he was toasting the windshield, then guzzled half of it down. "That's my brother all right."

A part of me swelled with pride. Adam had actually called me his brother. I had finally done something right. I looked at Nathan, and he looked angry, his eyes narrowed, a pink flush across his freckled cheeks. "Where are we going?" he asked flatly. "We're supposed to go get Molly."

"We told you," Perry said as he slowed down and took a turn to the right. "We're just having some Halloween fun before we pick up your sister."

"Yeah, but it's late. And we were supposed to be there by eight thirty. It's already past that."

The plan was for Nathan to come home with me after school, have something to eat, then—as far as Nathan and his parents understood—Nathan was to walk a few blocks over to meet Molly at her friend's house. Only, once Nathan was at our place, Adam and his friends told him they'd give him a ride to Molly's friend's, where Perry would then offer to give them a lift home. Then, on the way, Perry would try to talk Molly into hanging out a little longer. That was the plan, Adam had told me, simple and harmless. If Molly said no, no harm done, they'd just give her and Nathan a ride home as planned.

But now we were taking a detour, and I could see Nathan was nervous. He brushed his straight hair away from his eyes and scowled as he looked out his window. It was starting to make me nervous too, but since my brother and his friends were actually being nice for a change, I was sort of enjoying myself. After all, it was Halloween night and I didn't want to go home right away anyway.

"We'll go get her in a sec," Todd offered. "We just want to check this place out. See." He pointed out in front of him. "It's so cool. It's that old cemetery everyone talks about. You know, the one that has that big, creepy tree that everyone says they hung some lady 'cause she was a witch."

"And what better place to be on Halloween," Adam said, drawing out the *ween* in a spooky voice.

"But it's late," Nathan said. "My sister will be mad."

Perry came to a stop in the middle of the gravel road and lifted his chin to outside where his headlights were fanning out. "There it is."

We all sat silently looking at it. It was a large maple, sturdy and tall off to the right of a large field of grayish-white gravestones scattered in the tangled, slumped-over grass. "No one got hung on that," Nathan protested.

"Yes," Todd said. "Everyone knows about it. It's in the library. A true-blue witch hunt. It was years ago, like in the late 1800s or something. Even Mr. Collier, my English teacher, said it was true when we were reading some book about it."

I stared at the tree. It did look spooky in the dark, the silver moonlight casting pale light across its thick, layered branches. Its leaves were past their fall glow and were dull brown, falling to the ground and surrounding it like a shroud at its roots. Then, as if on cue, Adam and Perry both opened their car doors and stepped out. "Come on," they said. To my left, Todd followed and hopped out, the cold air funneling in, surrounding us. "Come on," Perry said again. "Let's just check it out. It'll be fun."

Nathan and I didn't budge until Adam opened Nathan's door from the outside and tugged at his arm. "Come on, you two. What? You too afraid to check out some tree in the dark?"

"No," Nathan said, but stayed put, staring at the black leather of the seat in front of him. The frigid wind from outside continued to penetrate the leftover warmth of the car, biting at our cheeks.

"Come on, guys," Perry said. "Let's just go check it out."

I slowly slid over to the open door where Todd stood, and I saw Nathan look at me. He looked resigned, shook his head slightly, then, as only a true friend would, he turned to the door and placed his Adidas-clad foot out.

Now, in the light of day, two decades later, I walked up to the maple, still standing tall and proud off to the side like it didn't belong, but as long as it was there, it was going to make the best of it and guard the cemetery, maybe offer a pathway for the dead to the big, sweet summer sky above. Its full, thick branches were bathed in yellow sunlight and reached to all sides and upward. Its roots looked strong.

I ran my hand over its thin-banded, gray bark, layered like a puzzle, and thought about Adam driving off with his buddies, hollering and laughing. I knew Perry still lived in the area. He worked for one of the local timber operations. I'd lost track of Todd, but vaguely recall someone saying he had moved to Bozeman and ran a company that sold carpets and countertops. Tragically, Mr. and Mrs. Faraway eventually divorced as most do after the loss of a child. And Molly—I heard she lived in Kalispell, had a few children, and was also divorced.

I considered Adam and the price he paid in his own way the following years. I backed up and looked up at the whole tree, green and lush, then out past it toward the forest that we'd ventured into to head toward town. A shiver went up my spine thinking how something that was supposed to be a silly joke had gone so wrong and affected so many lives so tragically. The thought occurred to me that beyond the physical, real, and catastrophic act of Nathan never making it home, sometimes people just didn't find their way even when they had a home, good, bad or otherwise. My whole family might be that set of people, and it was okay, for now. I thought of Lara. Yes, there had been loads of pain and anger, and, yes, there had been loss and most likely more on its way.

In the distance, I heard the humming motor of a helicopter and wondered if it was heading to the park. I closed my eyes and inhaled the warm, sweet air and allowed myself a moment to remember Nathan: his reddish-brown hair straight as nails falling into his eyes, his fair, freckled skin, his bubbling laugh, and his hurt, angry voice the last time I saw him.

I didn't know what to make of what Adam had said about the river, but if, I considered, *if* I found out that Adam or his friends had something more to do with Nathan's disappearance than originally thought, I would make sure they all paid, one way or another. That was the least I could do for Nathan.

50

I WAS NERVOUS TO visit Cathy and the kids, but it felt right to go. It was late afternoon, the sun bright and glorious just as it was the day the case started. When I pulled up, Max came running and barking, whipping his tail back and forth. "Hey, buddy," I said, kneeling down and petting him. Cathy followed and slowly walked toward me. She looked smaller, drawn inward, but she gave me a friendly smile. I was relieved to see she was wearing gardening gloves—that she'd resumed some of the things she must have found pleasure in.

"Working in the garden?" I asked as she took off her gloves, one at a time.

"Someone needs to do it or the weeds will take over."

"You don't enjoy it?"

She shrugged. "It's hard to enjoy much of anything these days. Come on." She motioned to the porch. "I'll get you some lemonade or tea or something?"

"Lemonade sounds perfect."

Max and I waited on the porch for her to grab the drinks and sat listening to the late afternoon quiet. I could hear a squirrel busy in the woods nearby, and Max lifted his head and stared intently in that direction.

When she returned with lemonade and took a seat, she dove right in. "Tell me, Monty. Why did Will DeMarcus kill Phillips in the first place?"

I took a sip and leveled my gaze on her, trying to decide what was the best response. Normally, Cathy wouldn't comprehend the revenge—going to such violent lengths wouldn't typically register for her. Most of us, we hope, are like that, but grief made people think things they never thought they could or would consider.

Finally, I said, "It's complicated. It sounded like Bradley DeMarcus was a bit mentally ill, and I wonder if some strands of that didn't run in Will as well. He just hid it better and for much longer." I thought of my mom. In a strange way, my decision with Lara not to have children felt fortified by the investigation. After all, this case had always been about families, and somehow I had sensed that from the beginning. With no solid logic, it was what had led me to follow a long-shot lead to Glacier Academy on not too much more than a few weak strands of evidence and a niggling intuition.

"Perhaps it took losing his twin to make him go over the edge," I continued. "His brother's suicide got to him . . . made him lose his sense of composure, his sense of stability, and he began, I'm sure, to feel extreme amounts of rage. Sometimes, the only thing that quiets such rage is to begin fantasizing about payback, hurting the person who destroyed the person he loved."

Cathy shut her eyes and nodded. "I can relate," she said in a monotone voice.

"I know you can, but I'm telling you that picturing it, dreaming about having been able to stop him before he came across your husband is not going to help."

"No." She sighed. "I know it won't. My first priority is the kids. Making sure they—we—get through this."

"And I'm confident you will."

"Why are you confident of that?"

Before I replied, I could hear someone begin softly to play the piano from inside. I tilted my head in the direction of the sound.

"It's Abbey," she said. "She's our musician."

"That's why," I said, definitively.

Cathy gave me a faint closed-mouth smile. "It's just still so hard. When does it get easier?"

"A bit at a time, but it will. You'll begin to replace the pain with all the wonderful memories, all the treasures you've shared with Paul over the years. And, Cathy," I added, "you have to understand, the things that Paul loved: you, the kids, Glacier, Max, the animals, the ecosystem, the wolverines . . . they're all still here, carrying on to the best of their abilities, and carrying on is the greatest gift you can give to Paul and your children. There's nothing to feel guilty about in continuing to live when you begin to feel less numb. And you will. In time."

"Thank you, Monty. I appreciate you sticking with it. It doesn't bring him back, but somehow it helps."

"I'd hoped it would, at least a little." We finished the lemonade while I filled her in on a few more details about how the case came together in the end. After a bit, Jeffrey came out and asked if he could go to a friend's house, then added, "And can I have something to eat before you take me? I'm starving."

I set my glass down and stood up. "Looks like you've got some things to attend."

"It certainly looks that way now, doesn't it?" Cathy peered lovingly at Jeffrey. "Thank God for hearty appetites."

"He's a growing boy," I said, thanked her for the lemonade, and left her to her children.

. . .

After attending a mandatory critical debriefing session with a therapist, I got back into the usual swing of things in Glacier right away. A sow grizzly had charged a couple at the Virginia Falls trail on the east side of the Going-to-the-Sun Road, and the husband was carrying a firearm and shot at her. He didn't think he hit her, but other hikers complained about the discharge.

I was sent to assist the rangers since a gun was involved. I calmed everyone down at the trailhead and established some order, took the

shooter's information and statement, and explained to him that fir-
ing at a federally protected bear required an investigation. And after I
explained to him how capsaicin was always—and I mean always—the
better option, not only to preserve the bear's life, but because it was
more effective in stopping a charging bear since it disables their senses
temporarily when a bullet doesn't, I headed back over the pass.

I drove over the summit and part of the way down near the Weeping Wall where I stopped and got out, just like a tourist. I wanted a moment to take in the view. Then farther down, when I neared the Loop,
I pulled over again. I walked over to the rock divider beside the treacherous road and put one foot on its well-worn surface. I looked down
below, where I could have ended up several nights before. A shiver
stretched down my spine. I shook it off and thought about my day back
at work in Glacier.

I had just driven over the Going-to-the-Sun Road cutting through
and clinging precariously to the mountainsides. The road was an engi-
neering feat at the time, finished in 1933 after workers spent years sur-
veying and constructing. Several men lost their lives. But ultimately,
their persistence made the heart of the park accessible to millions, who
otherwise would never experience the wonders within.

Sacrifice, I thought. There was plenty of that. Sacrifice of the natives
to relinquish their sacred hunting grounds. Sacrifice of the men who
built it to carve a way through unmapped, untamed territory. Sacrifice
of Wolfie to record and try to make sense of the behavior of unknown
and misunderstood wild creatures. And Will, wrongly attempting to
make things right by killing in the name of revenge, for fairness, for
justice, to somehow make amends for the wrongs dished out to his
brother. And Nathan. He had sacrificed for me, had been a friend to
me. He had come along, had gotten out of the car even though he didn't
want to because that's what friends did. And that's what husbands were
supposed to do—make compromises to keep their marriages working.

Lara. She was sacrificing our marriage to pursue her need to have a
child. It was not my place to judge it. I knew I was being selfish for not

compromising on that front, but ultimately, I too was sacrificing. Just like her, I was surrendering the marriage itself because deep down, I knew she would forever be unhappy if she did not fulfill her need. And I was certain I did not want a child plagued with the kind of despair my mother and Will's brother, and possibly Will, were troubled with.

I tilted my head up to take in the long, crashing waterfalls, frothing lines cutting straight down between the ridges like white veins, thousands of feet long. I stood and watched the tourists take pictures of the panorama surrounding them, enfolding them, struck by its finely etched peaks and razor-sharp inclines and trying to get the perfect capture in their lenses. I thought of Phillips, of the strange mix of a man brutal enough to abuse others and driven enough to map the topography and hike a place like Glacier, perhaps trying to find peace with his tormented self.

But even though mapped and remapped by the likes of Phillips and other cartographers, the sense of longitude and latitude fell shy here, leaving the tourists temporarily disconnected from the ticking of the daily clock and the call of technology. I pictured Wolfie's determined wolverines loping across the vistas and scaling the peaks before me. This was my office, and one could do worse, much worse.

The shifting light danced on the ridges. The clouds passing over created gigantic shadows moving across the emerald slopes, missing the tips and leaving the points, no longer covered in snow, bathed in a gleam of silver. Sunlight flitted off the ragged edges like new promises, and hope rose inside of me. This was more than my office. This was me finding hope, and it was never too late to have hope. So much sacrifice demanded it.

Acknowledgments

I wish to thank the amazing team of publishing professionals at Atria Books for their dedicated hard work and enthusiasm in seeing this novel through to publication: my editor, Sarah Branham, for her expertise and brilliant feedback, Kathryn Santoro for her untiring, enthusiastic help in publicity, Arielle Kane and Jin Yu for their guidance and hard work in marketing, and Albert Tang for his fabulous design work. Thank you to copyeditor Toby Yuen and production editor Isolde Sauer, and thank you to Haley Weaver for assisting. I must also express my gratitude and admiration to Judith Curr, the revered president and publisher of Atria.

I owe huge thanks to my friend and wonderful agent, Nancy Yost, for countless things, but especially for her unwavering support, keen guidance, and for always making me laugh when I need it most. Thank you also to Adrienne Rosado and Sarah Younger for being so helpful.

To my dear friend Suzanne Siegel, who—lucky for me—is a former librarian and always seems to find exactly what I'm looking for when I need assistance. My gratitude is beyond words for all her valuable research, reading of drafts, excellent feedback, wise counsel, and endless encouragement.

I have an enormous amount of gratitude to my family for providing the emotional support and inspiration as I continue to write. To my husband, Jamie, I could have never completed and found my path through the publishing world without his help and reassurance. To my children, Mathew, Caroline, and Lexie, for continually motivating me with their enthusiasm. To my parents, Robert and Jeanine Schimpff, for believing in me and providing a lifetime of support, wisdom, and love. To my brothers, Cliff and Eric, and their wives, Pam and LeAnn, for bolstering me in countless ways. To my aunts Janie Fontaine and Barbara Dulac, for always sending me deeply appreciated, caring thoughts from afar.

As a lay person, I relied on generous help from Frank Garner, former chief of police in Kalispell; Bill Dial, chief of police in Whitefish; and Gary Moses, former lead ranger in Glacier National Park. Thank you to Dan Savage, veterinarian and passionate outdoorsman, for taking the time to help me better understand some of the issues surrounding wolverine research programs in Glacier. All accounts of the wolverine research program in this work are fictional and are not meant to recount the actual esteemed five-year wolverine study concluded in 2009 in Glacier National Park by a group of amazing biologists and other volunteers.

I also took a few liberties, including the creation of a Park Police force in Glacier, and the formation of a fictional school outside the park. I also tinkered just slightly with the actual terrain close to the Loop for the sake of plot. I hope I have not offended anyone who knows the area well. The Flathead Valley has several excellent therapeutic schools, and this story is in no way meant to make a statement about the quality of any of the local boarding schools. Additionally, the fictitious creation of a Park Police force is not meant to make light of the tremendous work GNP rangers do and the valuable services and law enforcement they provide.

I owe thanks to countless folks for their generous support in helping me establish myself as an author: some fellow writers, some friends, and some readers. I couldn't possibly name them all, but here are a few who have shown me extra kindness, assistance, and encouragement along the way: Kathy Dunnehoff, Janet VanDerMeer, Mara Goligoski, Dennis Foley, Marian Ellison, Christine Finlayson, Leslie Budewitz, Patti Spence, Sarah Fajardo, Jackie Brown, Ginnie Cronk, Cheryl Behr, Sandy Anderson, Kim Corette, Pat and Missy Carloss,

Steve and Meg Lull, Tony Stais, Paisley Amaya, and Sharon Healy. I thank Glacier National Park Conservancy for their kind support, all the wonderful book clubs I've participated in, both local and afar, all the extraordinary booksellers out there, and finally you, dear reader! I have been overwhelmed countless times by the heartfelt messages and encouragement I've received. It makes me want to keep trying to get it right!

Any mention of landmarks or made-up businesses resembling actual businesses is only done to gain verisimilitude. All errors, deliberate or by mistake, are wholly mine.